THE
STONE KILLER

ISBN: 978-0-9892880-2-6
ISBN-13: 978-0-9892880-2-6

I'd like to thank Kurt Pillard, Retired Commander of the Investigations Divisions, of the Colorado Springs Police Department, and retired homicide detective, Larry Herbert, whose help was invaluable in writing this novel. Thanks to my family for their love and support, my sister for her input and amazing editing skills, and to my dear friend, Tony Perriello, who has waited patiently for this book to be finished.

PROLOGUE

Saturday, early a.m.

He breathed in great ragged gulps of dry musty air as sweat rolled down his face and back, soaking the white T-shirt all the way to the waistband of his jeans. The only sounds, his own breathing as well as the labored gasps from the woman bound to the wooden beams. The planning and anticipation over the past two weeks had him riding a high almost as intoxicating as drugs, only better. A ripple of excitement raced through his body. He shivered.

A smile of pure evil curved his lips as he tossed the stone in the air a couple of times, noting the rough, pitted surface. It weighed, he guessed, about five or six, maybe even seven ounces, close to that of a baseball, perhaps a little more. It was not the weight, but the speed that did the job. At this close range, he couldn't miss. Out of the massive pile from the bin, there were only seven that he needed, each about the same size. He was that good at hitting his target. Even after all these years, he could still throw a baseball at ninety-five miles an hour. Each stone fit his hand as if he was holding a ball.

After stripping her down to her gaudy red underwear, he'd securely tied the bitch spread eagle, with ropes run through strong steel pitons used by mountain climbers. A heavy leather strap held her head in place, so she could see, but not move. She wouldn't have been able to struggle much anyway, the drug would have made sure of that.

Two spotlights, clipped to the ceiling beams, illuminated the woman in the bright glare. Even though her eyes were almost closed, he could tell she was awake. His skin quivered as the moment drew near. The bitch deserved his punishment. Her fate had been sealed for some time, just like his wife's. They were both whores, enticing men to break their sacred vows.

He fingered the stone for a second. The woman's eyes opened. She watched him, all too aware that it was time for her execution. He could almost smell her fear. Delighted by the fact. Slowly, he drew back his arm, then threw the first stone. When it struck the targeted knee, there was a loud crack as the bone broke. Shock widened her eyes, sending a shiver up and down his body. With the next blow to the other knee, the excruciating pain rolled her eyes back into her head. His insides grew hot with excitement, causing sweat to form on his upper lip. He smiled, shook himself, and hurled another stone.

She attempted to scream when he shattered first the right, then the left elbow. The destruction of the left shoulder closed her eyes, indicating she had passed out. He threw a bucket of water in her face. Her eyes flew open as her features contorted in agony. His lust for blood intensified. The destruction of her right shoulder expanded the terror, filling her mind to bursting with the knowledge of her impending death. His excitement continued to grow as he delivered the coup de grace, the final blow to the head that smashed her eye socket, turning her brain matter to gray mush.

At that pivotal moment when the stone struck the left side of her face ending the last spark of life, a surge of overwhelming heat dropped him to his knees. The waves of ecstasy washed over him again and again. Then, it faded, leaving him hollow. The exhilaration was too short lived. Now, she hung lifeless on the close fitting wooden beams that formed a large X. The structure, attached to the end of the basement wall, was just for this purpose.

He stood, turned to stare into the deep shadows at the opposite end of the room, feeling the anticipation beginning to rise again. It surprised him that it was starting so soon. He welcomed it, knowing control was necessary. Acting too quickly would spoil all his plans. He had to let this need simmer, to come to a boil, releasing it only when it was time.

It didn't matter that it was a woman, but the act itself that sent his heart pounding, the blood roaring through his veins. He had never felt so alive. The exhilaration made him feel empowered as God over life and death. Even now, the shadows hid the form of his next subject, all drugged, bound, gagged and immobilized. His senses began to tingle, but he'd force himself to wait another day. The anticipation would heighten his pleasure even more. He took a deep breath to steady himself, then surveyed the room.

The basement was long, windowless, running the width and half the depth of the house. It was even chilly at this time of the night. The end, with the crossed beams, had concrete walls with a floor that sloped a little to a drain set in the cement, just past the midway point. At the other end, the surface was still packed dirt, where coal had been stored for the furnace. The chute's opening had been sealed long ago. The earth remained. It had been a great convenience.

So, reluctantly, he turned back to the lifeless body held upright by the ropes. All he had to do now was hose the bitch down and get rid of her.

Chapter One

Saturday

At two-fifty-nine Saturday morning, in a small Craftsman-style house in midtown Colorado Springs, Morgan Jansen woke suddenly. Lying flat on her back, with fisted hands clenching the sheet, she screamed, "Oh, God! Oh, God!"

Pain, like a hot knife, sliced through her body all the way to her heart. It was as if her very soul was being ripped from her flesh. Without warning, excruciating, debilitating pain shot through both knees. All ability to move her legs was gone. Morgan screamed again as agony exploded in her elbows. Arms limp, she lost her grip on the sheet. Within seconds, another scream was ripped from her throat, as razor-sharp daggers shot deep into her shoulders. Each breath ragged, she gagged on the bile that threatened to choke her. The final agony struck, hitting her head, tearing through her left eyeball, ripping through the left side of her face and temple. She almost passed out but remained conscious.

She tried to move. It was almost impossible to wiggle a finger. It was as if the pain was binding her to the mattress. But, move she must. She had to get to the bathroom or drown in her own vomit. Struggling, every effort an utter torment, she flopped her arm onto her stomach. Each crook of her fingers took her breath as she inched back the bedspread. Jaws clenched tight, fighting back the blackness that threatened to overtake her, she shifted onto her side, managing to slide to the floor, knocking the lamp off the nightstand in the process.

On her stomach, the chill of the wood coming through her thin pink nightshirt, a dry musty odor filled her nostrils. She tried to crawl across the hardwood toward the open door of the bathroom but again was unable to move. Her eyes were only slits against a blinding light as she turned her head, fighting the urge to vomit. Then, just as abruptly as it came, the pain vanished, leaving her joints aching, as if badly bruised.

Her vision no longer blurred, but dizzy and still sick to her stomach, she sat up, was barely able to rise to her knees, finally managed to stand before staggering into the bathroom. She hung over the commode as hard spasms tore at her muscles, making her heave up the contents of her stomach. After the vomiting stopped, she moved to the sink, rinsed her mouth, threw water on her face, then brushed her teeth to get rid of the foul taste.

Oh, God, Marilyn! Was all she could think! Black dread engulfed her as she held onto the basin. Her mind was thick with fear and questions. What had her identical twin sister gotten into that could cause this horrible agony and create an empty hole in her soul? She had no doubts that Marilyn was in trouble and severely injured. No matter how much she didn't want to believe it, the despair she felt was confirmation.

She returned to the bedroom and snatched up the phone. Hands trembling, she punched in her sister's phone number, all the while praying she was wrong, and Marilyn would answer. But, the phone kept ringing, ringing until it went to voicemail. She didn't bother to leave a message.

Tears slid down her face. She fought against the notion, but deep in her heart, she was terrified her sister had taken her last breath. They had always been connected in that way, as twins are, that special bond made each aware of the other, even though miles might separate them. Tonight that link had almost been severed. Still shaky inside, she dressed in jeans, a green T-shirt and sneakers, then sat on the bed to think.

How was she going to find Marilyn at this hour? It was now after three in the morning. Her sister's favorite hangout, Dawson's, was closed. She'd give it another thirty minutes, more than enough time for her sister to get home from the bar. Then if there were no answer at her apartment, Morgan needed to call the police. First, she called every hospital emergency room she could find listed in the phone book. No one with Marilyn's description had been seen or admitted.

Her stomach churned with apprehension. She went to the kitchen and placed the tea kettle on the electric burner. Tea was soothing; tea would settle her stomach and help pass the time. After the first sip, she gagged. Not even tea was going to stop the quivering of her insides.

Twenty minutes passed. Morgan dialed Marilyn's number again. Still no answer! She sat at the dining room table hitting the redial button on the portable house phone over and over. God, she wanted to be wrong for a change. At four o'clock, she grabbed a light jean jacket, her car keys, and purse, then headed out the door into the crisp morning air. Twelve minutes later she walked through the entrance of the police department on South Nevada Avenue.

It was a three-story red brick building that occupied a full city block. The large lobby area was bright, and clean, with light beige walls. Three rows of black connected chairs were positioned across from a desk set back and along a side wall. An officer was answering the questions of a man and woman, then directed them to one of the three windows. Two Police Service Representatives sat behind a chest-high counter with double sheets of bulletproof glass. The odor of the unwashed man, standing before one of the female clerks, reached Morgan. She put the back of her hand to her nose to block the smell, feeling sorry for the clerk, as she walked toward the farthest seat away from where he stood. She could still overhear snatches of their conversation. He was looking for a local shelter for the night. The other clerk, a man, directed questions at a woman busy entering the information into a computer. Otherwise, the lobby was empty. It appeared to be a slow night considering it was the beginning of the weekend. Morgan had thought it would be busier. She took a seat and waited, wondering whether she should really be there.

"May I help you?" The clerk motioned for her to come forward.

Morgan started toward the clerk, then said, "Never mind."

She turned in midstride and rushed out the door. What was she going to tell the woman? I can't locate my sister because I have this gut feeling she might be dead. Then there would be lots of questions. Too many questions she did not want to answer. Before she spoke with the police, she needed to first attempt to locate her sister.

Fifteen minutes later, she pulled into Dawson's parking lot as a light rain began to fall. All parking spaces were empty; Marilyn's car was nowhere to be seen. Her sister's apartment was a short distance away on North Carefree Drive. Windshield wipers swishing, she drove toward the complex.

More than once, Marilyn had locked herself out. She had hidden a spare key in a fake stone behind a pot of geraniums, for just such occasions. It was convenient that her sister lived in the first building. After parking in the reserved spot, Morgan dashed through the rain to the door, retrieved the key, and let herself in. It had been over six months since she had been inside her twin's home.

It was a spacious two-bedroom accommodation on the ground floor, with a patio off the living room. Morgan wiped at her damp hair, noting that the furniture had been upgraded from a thrift store mix and match to an expensive red leather sofa and a dark gold fabric armchair. The other chair in the room was a dark blue leather recliner. A white fur rug covered the floor beneath a glass-topped coffee table. Expensive tall brass lamps occupied a place on the same style glass and brass end tables. The sofa and chair faced a large flat screen television on a console housing an extensive DVD collection.

The rug looked like real fur. Morgan stooped to feel the softness. It was a real, beautiful alpaca. Her sister had always had expensive tastes. She wondered who had paid for it all. Somebody had. The rug's cost alone was way above Marilyn's price range. Everything in the room was orderly, nothing out of place to indicate anything was wrong.

She walked into the kitchen/dining area. The sink was empty. The dishwasher held a single dirty glass. She frowned at the sight of the bright red lipstick on the rim, put the glass back, and closed the door. Marilyn was an immaculate housekeeper but had poor taste in lipstick. The color would clash with her red hair. The hallway bathroom, adjacent to the kitchen, revealed nothing. All the towels were hung neatly and precisely matched in length.

Down the hall in the laundry room, a towel had been spread over the washer to dry. On the other side of the hallway were two bedrooms, one which had been converted into an office with a desk, computer, and chair. Morgan ignored the office. Upon entering the bedroom, she stopped just inside the doorway, caught the whiff of expensive perfume, then flipped the light switch.

She gasped in surprise. It was red. Red bulbs in the lamps on the nightstands cast a warm rosy glow throughout the room. Above the king size bed was a scalloped crown cornice with red sheers draped on either side, each held in place with crown-shaped wall brackets. Not a crease disturbed the cream bedspread. A mink color fur coverlet graced the foot, making her wonder if it was genuine fur like the rug. A rose padded Fairfax chair set next to the window. How like Marilyn to decorate her bedroom in cream and shades of red.

Morgan turned away, opened the walk-in closet door and switched on the light. Everything was neatly arranged. Nothing was out of place that she could tell. She didn't expect it to be. Numerous boxes, plus photo albums on the upper shelves, were neatly labeled, listing the contents of each, except one.

She didn't touch anything, just switched off the light and closed the door. Directly across from the bed, strategically placed on the wall, were large mirrored squares she hadn't noticed before. Now the implication made Morgan's face grow warm. She left the bedroom and entered the office.

Anyone who kept a desk that neat and orderly didn't use it often, she thought. Morgan had to admit that her work area space at home was a complete contrast. In her sister's desk drawers, all items were precisely placed. Marilyn's address book was lying near the phone. She picked it up to peruse through it, then stuffed it in her purse. She could always return it later.

Right now she needed to locate Marilyn's friends. The open desk calendar showed the current day, and red-inked stars jotted next to the name Jack at ten-thirty on Friday night. That was all she could find in the office and the apartment. Finished, she hurried to the front door, eager to get out of the place.

She glanced at her watch. It was going on six as she left, locked the door and replaced the key in the rock. The rain had cooled the air a couple of degrees. Glancing around the asphalt parking area, she looked for her sister's car but didn't spot it. The sun was rising, turning the clouds in the eastern sky a brilliant red. What was that old saying? "Red skies at night a sailor's delight, red skies in the morning, sailors take warning." Was she getting a warning that there was worse to come? How much worse could it be? Marilyn was missing. She hadn't gone home with some stranger. That wasn't her style.

It was best that she go home and wait for an hour, give people time to wake up, then call her sister's girlfriends, Alice Evans and Debbie Clark. If they didn't know anything, she would go back to the police station and file a missing person's report.

Two hours later, she sat in her kitchen drinking a cup of coffee and staring at the phone in her hand. When she'd called, Marilyn's two friends had sounded hungover, groggy and not at all happy about being awakened at eight in the morning. Each gave the same story. They had remained at Dawson's, and Marilyn had left around ten that evening saying she was going home. She never made it.

The air was damp making her hair curl as, purse in hand, she headed for the front door and her car. She parked in the side parking lot and hurried to the front entrance of the police department. This time, only one person was in the lobby. Morgan slowly walked to counter, ignoring the desk and stopped before the clerk. "I want to report a missing person."

The young, dark-haired woman looked at her. "Is this person a relative?"

"Yes, my sister, Marilyn Heddrix."

"How long has she been missing?" The clerk jotted down the name.

"Since around ten last night."

"And what is your name?"

"Morgan Jansen."

"I'm sorry to have to tell you, but someone has to be missing seventy-two hours before you can file a Missing Person's Report. Have you checked with her friends?"

"Look, my sister didn't make it home last night. And yes, I checked with her friends. They don't know where she is." Tension knotted Morgan's neck muscles, and she bit at her upper lip.

"When was the last time you spoke to her?" the clerk asked, as she glanced back at her computer screen and tapped at the keyboard, before returning her gaze to Morgan.

Morgan felt her face turn red when she had to admit, "A month ago."

The clerk could not keep her skepticism hidden "Why would you believe she's missing if you haven't talked to her in a month?"

"I just know something has happened to her! She's my sister! She just would not come home!" Morgan fought back tears. Why couldn't the woman just file the damn report?

"I'm sorry," the woman said, in an attempt to be more sympathetic. "I can file an Attempt to Locate request. If they find her, they'll have her contact you. Will that help?"

She had no choice but to agree. "That will have to do, won't it," she snapped in frustration. She shouldn't blame the clerk for following procedure.

The woman arched an eyebrow at her sharp tone

but maintained her helpful attitude. "If you'll give me some information and a description of your sister, I'll make the call."

"You're looking at her," Morgan said. "We're identical twins. The only difference is my hair is not as red. Marilyn dyes her hair a light auburn. Also, she has a blue dragonfly tattoo just below her navel." She told the clerk about Dawson's and her two friends, about going to her sister's apartment to check if she had returned, plus any other pertinent information she thought might help. There wasn't much else to tell.

The clerk picked up the phone and dialed a number, then relayed the information she had been given. "They pulled a copy of her driver's license and put an ATL out for her. That's all we can do for now. I suggest you go home. I'm sure your sister will call you soon." The woman turned her attention back to some paperwork in front of her.

Feeling dismissed, Morgan turned and left the building, hurrying to her car. She'd be spending the rest of Saturday and all of Sunday looking for Marilyn or her vehicle.

Chapter Two

Monday

Detective Lieutenant Jonas Black jerked awake. The buzzing of his cell phone, made him sit up on the side of the bed, still breathing hard. Once again the nightmare had him locked in a wild chase of a shadowy figure. He'd catch the briefest glimpse of the man who had beaten, raped and murdered his long-ago girlfriend Kelly Burton, in 1998. The man always escaped his grasp, slipping deeper into the shadows until he vanished from view.

It tormented him that to date, her murder remained unsolved, and her killer was still out there. He wore the guilt of her death like a black shroud. As a Midland, Texas police officer he should have been able to protect her. He hadn't, and she had lost her life. That fact was the cause of his nightmares. Once again he shook off residual of the dream, grabbed his cell, and listened intently. His team member, Addison Clay described the latest report of a murder.

"I'll right there," he said and ended the call. His dream always seemed to happen right before a new murder in Colorado Springs, Colorado, which was too many lately. Rising from the bed, he dressed quickly, pulled on his boots, then grabbed his Stetson before going out and locking the front door. He slid into the driver's seat of his black SUV, keyed the engine and drove west toward the Garden of the Gods.

Detective Sergeant Esperanza Ortiz and Detective

Addison Clay were already there. Jonas joined them as they trailed behind Park Ranger Raul Cruz along the dusty path from Parking Area Seven, then followed the rustic red paved Perkins Trail. The trail curved toward the towering red sandstone spires, known as the Three Graces.

Through the fabric of his white shirt, the Colorado sun, peeking through the scattered clouds, was warm as it beat down on Jonas' back, while the breeze was a cool whisper on his cheek. He glanced up noting how intensely blue the sky was, especially through his sunglasses, and how the faint scent of dry earth and brush mingled with another harsher odor. High above, cutting across the sky's blue canvas, black ravens circled around and around. Waiting. It was a great day to be alive. But, the thought ran through his mind, for some poor soul it was a hell of a way to start the day. Being dead.

The call had come into 911 that morning, then was transferred to homicide at seven-thirty. Jonas had taken a quick sip from his cup of coffee, notified the rest of his team and the CSI techs, then grabbed his hat and headed for the door. By the time they arrived on the scene, a patrol officer had cordoned off the trail with yellow crime scene tape.

"Damn it, Jonas," Raul glanced over his shoulder at the man. Next to the detective, the ranger appeared a lot shorter and heavier in his uniform than his five-foot-eleven inch height and one-hundred-seventy-five-pound frame. "I thought some dumb climber had fallen the way that body's slammed into that big crevice," he said and pointed up the trail toward the Graces.

The day would get hotter, but for right now the morning air was brisk at seventy-three degrees, thanks to the clouds. The night temperature in Colorado Springs dropped into the fifties or sixties, and the day didn't heat up until around two or three. Soon the thermostat would inch up into the low nineties. Even though the morning air was not overly hot and the humidity was low, it didn't stop Raul from perspiring. He took off his cap and mopped the sweat from his forehead with a handkerchief. His tan uniform shirt felt too hot. He wasn't used to finding a dead body in the Garden of the Gods.

"From what I can see, she's all busted up and twisted like some broken doll," he said. "At first I thought she was a climber, and then I saw how she was dressed."

"What do you mean?" Jonas glanced over at Raul. The ranger looked pretty shaken up. The closer they walked, the scent, that had been faint just moments ago grew stronger. Now the breeze carried the odor of rotting meat.

"You'll see," Raul said.

Jonas, Eppie, and Clay followed as Raul led the way along the sloping path to the front of the Three Graces. The sound of buzzing flies grew louder, and the odor was overpowering. Thankful she had worn her light-weight brown slacks, a red blouse, and sensible walking shoes, Eppie pulled a tube of mentholated balm from her leather jacket pocket and smeared it under her nose. It helped to mask the odor.

"Eppie," Raul called out, "can I use some of that?" Looking a little green, he took the offered tube and quickly covered his upper lip, then started to hand it back. She waved him off.

"Thanks," he said, pocketed the tube and swiped at a fly that buzzed around his face. The body was a feast for insects. "I was making my morning sweep through the park," Cruz said, "when I saw a large number of black-billed magpies flying around the red rock formations. I figured it was a dead animal. Instead, when I came to investigate, I found her. It was hard to see the body in that crevice. I had to use my flashlight to get a good look,"

They all stopped to face the tall red sandstone formation. Raul pointed with his flashlight beam to the mangled corpse dumped into the large shadowed opening. The deep fissure, splitting the stone, was wide enough for a good size man or woman to climb into the spire.

Supported by the rough wall, just inside the opening, was the body. The woman's head appeared to have dropped forward, her chin resting almost on her chest. A mass of wavy red hair hid part of her face. Her arms and legs were bent and twisted at odd angles. White bone protruded through the skin at each elbow, knee, and shoulder. The darkness of the dried blood in the wounds contrasted sharply with the greenish-blue discoloration of the skin. Only the tops of her feet appeared unmarred, and her wrists and ankles were marked red from restraints, the skin rubbed raw. Small dainty feet with manicured toenails, were painted blood red, as red as the lace bra and panties she wore. It had taken cautious footwork to carry her up the stone ramp and dump her in the opening.

Jonas pushed at the lock of dark brown hair that had escaped from under his Stetson. He removed the hat and settled it back on his head, capturing the wayward strand and stared at the body. God, he thought, he'd never get used to the senseless murder of women. It should be easy to walk away from a woman who drove you nuts, but some men couldn't seem to do it. Then he thought again of Kelly. Some bastard hadn't walked away from her either.

"From the smell, I'd guess she's been dead a couple of days," Jonas said, leaning forward, trying for a better view into the deep shadow. Then he straightened, pulled his cell phone from his shirt pocket, and placed a call to the Coroner's office. It would take time for the rest of the team to arrive. He turned to survey the area, not expecting to find any footprints on the sandstone surface. Yet the dusty ground in front of the monument had a swept look as if someone had brushed the base and pathway with a broom or branch. Jonas looked around for the object that had been used to dust the area.

"It's over there," Raul pointed to the broken limb of a juniper tossed by the trail. "He dusted the area after he dumped her. He must not have noticed the blood on the wood. I left it for your guys. How he managed to carry her, climb up, and dump her in the fissure as ripe as she is, is beyond me."

Jonas smeared the mentholated balm under his nose, pulled on latex gloves and climbed up the sandstone ramp to get a closer view of the body. He peered into the shadowed crevice. Without the flashlight beam, he was unable to see the victim clearly. The ramp was curved, and his cowboy boots were not the best choice for rock climbing.

"Hey Eppie, did you bring your light?" he called, over his shoulder. Raul started to offer Jonas his flashlight again but held on to it when Eppie waved her larger black one in the air.

"Don't I always?" she called out.

"Come up here and shine the beam inside the crevice so I can get a better look."

Making sure not to contaminate the scene, she edged closer and directed the brighter light into the fissure.

He grinned at her. "What would I do without you?" The grin faded as he looked back at the body. "I can't see her features. Raul's right. She's busted up pretty bad. There appears to be some sort of small tattoo below her navel. Other than the initial injuries, I can't see anything else. I'd say someone was really pissed off at her." Eppie turned off the light, and they moved cautiously out of the way.

"We're not going to get anything off that rock surface," Jonas said. He dusted off his gloves and turned as the four members of the team, Alfonso Benedict, Jose Fernandez, Caroline Jones, and Rupert Williams, arrived along with the crime scene techs. The last member, Henry Pope, was not with them.

Clay and Eppie had been on the team almost from the start. Over the years as other detectives quit, transferred or retired, the others had been promoted to the position. They were all seasoned detectives except for Caroline, the newest member of the team.

Each member had their own specialty to contribute. Jonas had been promoted to Lieutenant almost seven years ago and knew every member well, plus some of the problems in their lives. Lately, Henry seemed more troubled.

"Hey, Clay," he motioned for him to come closer. "Where's Henry?"

"I haven't heard from him. Fernandez might know. I'll check with him." Clay hurried over to Jose and stood talking with him before turning back to Jonas and shrugging his shoulders.

Jonas nodded, then addressed the group. "Glad you're all here," he called out. "This is a bad one, and the clock is ticking, so let's get going. We gotta find this bastard. Listen up. We need to cover every inch of ground." He turned to Clay who stood close by. "Have Cliff Warren get plenty of still photos, video of her and the surrounding area, all the way from the Parking Lot Six and Seven to here and along the trail."

Jonas addressed his partner, "Eppie, once we're finished, and the Coroner gets here, we can try and get fingerprints to ID the victim. Maybe we can find out who she is from a driver's license." He turned to the others, "The rest of you, spread out. See if you can find where the killer might have parked a vehicle, walked up the trail, rode a horse in or anything else you can find, look for anything out of place. Somebody brought her here from some point. We need to find out how."

Five or six hikers had started to gather along the yellow taped off area. One tall man had a camera and was trying to get a better position to snap photographs, while the others were trying to see what the police were looking at.

Jonas told Clay to have Cliff photograph the crowd. Perhaps the killer had returned to view his handiwork. Jonas motioned to one of the officers. "After Cliff gets his picture, clear the area of these people and get some help out here. I don't want some gawker contaminating the scene."

It wouldn't be long before the press got wind of the murder and would be on scene with their cameras and questions. One good thing, the television reporters, and crew would have to remain parked on the road and out of his way.

Cliff continued to video the crowd, as the officer began directing the on-lookers to leave. As soon as the area was cleared, they worked as a team, quickly and efficiently searching the ground, bushes, and rocks for anything left behind. Another CSI tech retrieved paper bags from the equipment box, along with some rubber bands, then climbed up the ramp, reached into the crevice, took one of the girl's hands, bagging each before carefully backing out.

Eppie again flashed her light into the crevice. The body's condition was not as severely decomposed in the drier air as in other more hot and humid climates. It was bad enough. The weather had dropped into the sixties last night which helped cool the body temperature and slow the decomposition. Still, the skin had that bluish-green hue, and even with the mentholated balm under her nose, the odor made her gag. Death was not a pretty sight. What had this poor woman done to deserve this type of punishment? Eppie carefully stepped off the incline and joined the rest of the team to search for evidence.

An hour later, after every inch of the area had been grid walked, from both parking areas along the trail leading back to the Graces, any out of place items bagged and notated, all photos taken by Cliff.

Jonas call to Clay, "Hey, have you heard anything from Charlie Jacks?" Charles D. Jacks was the local elected Coroner.

"You might want to give him another twenty minutes. You know with their workload, they don't speed to a crime scene." Clay said and proceeded to walk the trail again, looking for anything that might have been missed, making his way back to where Jonas stood.

It was thirty minutes almost to the second when a tall, stout, salt and pepper haired man, in his late fifties, walked up the trail to where the team had gathered. Dressed in a gray suit, he was followed by two men in white shirts and navy pants,

"Well, it's a beautiful a day to be alive, isn't it boys and girls?" Jacks didn't wait for a reply, just pulled on latex gloves, walked up to the sandstone base and moved cautiously closer to the crevice and the body. "Good God, she's a mess. How the hell?" he muttered, then, "Have the techs gotten all the photographs they need, Jonas? I'd like to get her out of there and back to the morgue."

Jonas nodded, "Okay, Doc, you can take her."

Immediately, the two assistants, wearing gloves,

proceeded to work their way carefully to the victim. It was not an easy job to lift the corpse and remove her from the crevice. They succeeded, accompanied by a few under the breath expletives as the rough stone scraped the victim's flesh. Once out, she was placed in a body bag and secured on a gurney.

Jonas stooped to study the woman. Her head was turned to the left, and her hair hid any damage. Death could not conceal the beauty of the uninjured side of her face. Her red hair was almost the exact shade of Kelly's, Jonas thought and fingered a strand. But, Kelly Burton had been a long time ago. Maybe she was more on his mind now because it was July. Perhaps that was the cause of this morning's dream. The date of her death was only two days away. As always, he'd make his yearly call on the exact day of her murder.

Jonas watched as Jacks turned the victim's head. He was shocked by the destruction on the left side of her face. The area near her eye socket was broken and bloody, almost caved in. The eyeball had popped part way out, being held in place by a slender tendon. Someone had been in a rage, and it was directed at what once was a beautiful woman.

He stood and backed out of the way as the Coroner's assistants zipped the bag, lifted the gurney and prepared to leave to transport the victim to the morgue.

Charlie started to follow, but turned to the Lieutenant, "I'll start the autopsy as I soon as I get her on the table. We have a few backed up, but I'll squeeze her in. Who are you sending down?"

Jonas glanced at his watch. It was almost ten-fifteen, and the autopsy would take two to three hours, which would carry them into the afternoon. The air was already getting hotter. He took off his hat and looked up at the sky. The few scattered clouds were not offering much relief. It was going to be another hot, dry day, which they didn't need. Henry hadn't joined the team yet he noted. He'd have a talk with him later.

"I'll send Eppie to the morgue," he said to Jacks as he walked up. Since the results wouldn't be available until later, he needed to get things moving. He watched as the body was carried toward the parking lot and the waiting coroner's truck, as the team gathered once again.

"What have we got?" Jonas looked from one to the other.

Clay was the first to speak. "Not much. There's what looks like a lot of oil spots in the parking lot. It could be from any vehicle that's been parked there over the past year." He pointed up the dirt path toward Parking Area Seven and the road. "That would be the most direct access. It's a straight shot down the hill to here. I figured he chose the closest spot and carried her down. All we have so far is that bagged branch with the blood on it, and that's it. As bad as she smelled, I don't know how he could have stood the odor. He had to have wrapped her in something, probably plastic." He shrugged. "That's it."

"Hey, Jonas, I found a tiny scrap of what looks like plastic caught on a branch," Caroline beamed. Petite, pretty, with blonde hair and big blue eyes, only joining the department six months prior, she was dedicated to being a top detective. She took extra classes at the local college on forensics, blood spatter, and crime scene analysis, anything that might help her do a better job. Jonas knew she guarded her private life.

Over the past several months, after a grueling case, he had been forced to order her home to get some rest. A clear mind was better able to focus and see things a tired brain often missed. He had to admit he was guilty of putting in too many hours on a case until his mind grew fuzzy. Even he was forced to get some sleep. Caroline was enthusiastic about her job, and he appreciated her efforts.

"Okay," Jonas said, "everyone, give it one more sweep of the area, then head back to the office. The CSI folks will finish up here. Eppie, hold up for a minute. Go with the Coroner and give me a call when the autopsy is finished."

He noted the tired expression on her face. It was worry about her mother no doubt, he surmised. Having a relative dying from cancer took a toll on the entire family, not just his partner. He wouldn't mention her exhausted appearance for now but would address the issue later.

"Will do," she said, as she brushed her dark hair away from her face, then followed after Jacks. The rest spread out once again, each in a different area, and began searching for anything they might have missed.

It was twelve-thirty that afternoon by the time Jonas and his team returned to the Violent Crimes Unit. The office was a blend of cubicles in a common area, with supervisors having the offices with windows on the exterior walls. He led the way to one of the conference rooms and set up a case board. Coffee cups in hand, the team gathered around the large table with their notepads. What little evidence they had found had been dropped off at the Metro Crime Lab along with a fingerprint card. Before returning to the office, Clay had stopped by the Coroner's office. Jacks had the card ready and waiting.

What a way to start the week, Jonas thought, and in the Garden of the Gods of all places. Today was another hot one, and everyone prayed rain was on the horizon. After the last several dry years, resulting in two horrific fires, they needed rain badly. The Springs always welcomed any form of moisture, rain or snow, especially in the Garden. The residents utilized the park almost all year.

Set closer to Pike's Peak, west of Colorado Springs, the Garden of the Gods, with the Three Graces and the neighboring Cathedral Spires, were only two of the rock formations which drew thousands of tourists and residents each year. A city park, it had started as four-hundred-eighty acres donated in 1909 by the children of Charles Perkins to the City of Colorado Springs for the residents to enjoy free of charge.

The other eight-hundred-eighty-seven acres were acquired bit by bit over the years, until in 1972 when the park was designated a National Natural Landmark by the Secretary of the Interior. The land was a wonder of sandstone monuments and natural rock formations for climbers, bicyclists, hikers, runners and dog walkers to enjoy. The park was open round the clock, so there were multiple roads for the killer to access the area.

They had been handed a cruel, senseless crime.

Not that any murder ever made sense. Jonas knew how rage could drive a person to do violence against another. He had been a lot younger then, and had been forced to do things as a Marine, during the war, he didn't like to think about. To hate a woman enough to be this savage was hard for even him to understand.

A man could fight a man but never strike a woman. His grandfather had taught him that any man who would hit a woman was a coward. His grandfather was right. Someone really hated this poor girl.

He pulled out a city map from his desk drawer, folded it to the desired section and walked out to the copy machine. Enlarging the part showing the different streets and access roads to the park, he returned to the room and taped it on the case board.

Jonas glanced over at Clay. "Give Larry over in the Strategic Information Center a call. Have him check the missing person's report. Maybe someone is looking for this woman. And Clay, if you would, set up the board with the photos of the victim as soon as you can. The rest of you, check the map I put up and drive back to the park. Talk with the residents living closest to the area. Alfonso, you take the lead on this. See if anyone noticed anything unusual going on Friday night or early Saturday morning. Check for video surveillance cameras at all locations, especially the houses next to the park's road. Maybe we'll get lucky, and someone will have something recorded."

The rest of the team copied the map and headed out. From his cell phone, Clay called STIC and gave

Larry the necessary information. Now it was just a matter of waiting for a callback. Fifteen minutes later, Clay's phone rang. He snatched it off the table to answer it. Jonas watched as he scribbled something on a piece of paper.

"That was Larry at STIC," Clay said. "There are three missing women and two men. One woman is in her late twenties or early thirties, one in her mid-forties and one, a senior citizen. None of the women match the description of the victim. Also, Larry checked the other reports and may have found her. There is an ATL on one Marilyn Heddrix filed by her sister, Morgan Jansen, on Saturday morning. She fits the description of our victim down to the tattoo on her abdomen."

"Did he give you an address?" Jonas asked. Clay handed him a copy of the driver's license with a photo and a copy of the ATL. The picture looked a lot like their victim. He checked the address on the license and saw that the victim lived off North Carefree. The sister lived closer.

"Clay, go to the Coroner's office and wait for the autopsy results." The look on Clay's face expressed his opinion of Jonas' request.

"Dammit, Jonas," The man complained, his brow furrowed and his eyes narrowed at the thought of watching another body being cut open. "You want me puking my guts out all afternoon, don't you? Leave Eppie there and take Caroline or me with you if you're going to interview the sister. You know how I hate autopsies." Clay's five-foot-ten-inch slender frame belied the wiry muscles hiding beneath his clothing.

The smile that crossed the Lieutenant's face was

one of slight amusement. "One of these days, you have to get over that, Clay."

"I know that. It's not watching the Doc cutting into the body; it's the smell I have trouble with. That God awful rotten odor. Even using mentholated balm, I can't get that odor out of my nose for weeks after I witness an autopsy. It ruins all hope of me enjoying a decent meal. Besides that, it makes me realize that someday that could be me on a table. So when I die, no autopsy. I plan on being cremated right away."

"Maybe you're in the wrong profession," the Lieutenant said, as his grin widened. He was well aware Clay hated to attend autopsies, even though he did so, when necessary.

"Nope," Clay rebutted. "I like catching the bad guys. I know I'm doing the right thing, jerking scum off the streets and putting them away."

"All right, you stay here and check with Metro, then get the necessary search warrant for the victim's residence. I'll give Eppie a call and see how much longer she'll be. Caroline can go with Alfonso back to the park and question the residents. I'll go to the morgue and wait for Eppie. Charlie usually sends someone out to notify the sister," Jonas continued, "but I think Eppie is better with notification of next of kin. From the tattoo on the victim, I believe it's her, but Charlie will confirm it. If so, then we'll give him a break and go see what we can find out from her sister. And Clay, give Pope a call. Find out why the hell he didn't show up." Jonas could see him struggling with something. "What the hell's going on with Henry? You're holding something back."

Hating to betray a confidence, Clay felt it was necessary to save the man's job. "His wife left him for another man two or three weeks ago. He's not handling it well and drinking too much. You might cut him some slack today."

The divorce rate among cops was high. Most had been married before or remained single to avoid becoming one of the statistics.

"Ah, hell," Jonas said, "I'll call him later." With that, he left the conference room and hurried out of the building to the parking garage.

Located next to the Criminal Justice Center on East Las Vegas Street, the drive from the police department to the Coroner's office took nearly fifteen minutes by the time Jonas walked toward the morgue. Not even the clouds could cool the day. The temperature had to be in the nineties. This was one of those times he was thankful for his Stetson. He pulled open the door and felt the cold blast of the air conditioning as he entered the building.

Charlie had been elected to the Coroner's position with hopes of upgrading the facility. The Coroner's office had gone from completing three-hundred autopsies in the nineties to almost a thousand in 2013, despite the antiquated and inadequate facility. At one time, the offices had been so crowded with files and other supplies, hallways had doubled as storage areas, and the garage had been used to store tissue samples, boxes, and other medical equipment.

Due to budget cuts and the economy, the much

needed specialized morgue with additional administrative, investigative, evidence and storage areas had been put on hold. Instead, the morgue had been extended to occupy the section formerly used by the Sheriff's Department, which had been moved to a building on Vermijo. Jonas walked quickly to the morgue, the only room big enough for its designated use.

As he entered the large room with its white tiled walls, stainless steel tables and cold storage drawers for the cadavers, he spotted Eppie leaning against the wall watching Charlie finish up.

Jonas walked over to the table and looked down at the poor woman being autopsied. "Doc, we may have an ID on the victim. STIC found an ATL on a Marilyn Heddrix, and her driver's license photo appears to match this woman. The ATL mentions the tattoo below the navel. What do you know so far about the cause of death?"

Charlie looked up, stopped what he was doing and pushed the face shield up. Thoughtfully, he chewed on the inside of his cheek before responding. "The blow to the head is what killed her. Technically, the cause of death will be listed as a crushed frontal skull, resulting in severe temporal hemorrhage. The injuries to her knees, elbows, and shoulders could have been repaired, but she would have had major physical problems."

He rolled back the sheet covering her legs. He had straightened the joints as much as possible, but her legs were still turned at odd angles. "If you look closer, you can see what appears to be pitting in the scrapes and bruising on the skin. I estimate some type of stone weapon was used to cause the injuries. At first, I thought a baseball bat; then I found all her injuries have minuscule particles of ground stone in them. Also, note the marks on her wrists and ankles. She was tied to something."

Jonas wasn't sure he had heard correctly. "Doc, are you saying this lady was beaten to death with a stone ax or something like it?"

"Some type of stone weapon was used. From the looks of the injuries, it was round, with a rough texture, enough so that it left a trace amount behind. I haven't finished yet. I'm waiting for the toxicology results before I fill out the report." He returned to his examination of the internal organs. "Other than the injuries caused by the killer, she was a physically fit young woman. Her lungs, heart, and liver were healthy. She did have the beginning of a kidney infection."

Jonas turned to Eppie. "I want you to go with me to talk with the next of kin." He turned back to the Coroner. "Charlie, we'll notify her sister. She's the one that filed the ATL." He thought for a second, "Just to double check, what is the tattoo below her navel? I couldn't see it clearly at the scene."

Charlie rolled the sheet lower. "It's a blue dragonfly, a beautiful design. So I'd say you're right. We have a positive ID on the victim, and her fingerprints will confirm it," he said, then added, "Also, I can tell you she was not sexually assaulted, and the body was hosed down after she was killed. There were no fibers or much of anything other than the trace of stone and the damage done by birds and insects. There was nothing under her fingernails either. From the stages of decomposition, I estimate that she died sometime between two and four Saturday morning. The park was just the dumping ground."

Eppie walked toward the door, eager to be out of the room. Jonas glanced over his shoulder as he turned to follow. "Thanks, Doc. Send over the report as soon as you can."

They made a quick exit and walked outside the building into the afternoon heat. Clouds still blocked the sun and Eppie wished the sky would clear. She needed to see the fiery light. Sunlight helped to dispel the odor and shadow of death that always hovered over their lives as part of their job. She was glad her mother would not have to be autopsied. Her cause of death was a given, so she didn't have to face that prospect. She pushed the thought of her mother's impending demise from her mind and tried to focus on what her partner was saying.

"Eppie, I have the sister's address, as well as the victim's. You can ride with me to the sister's house. Afterward, I'll bring you back to pick up your car. Then we'll meet at the woman's apartment." Jonas opened the passenger door, and she climbed into the Ford Escape.

It was a twenty-minute drive from the Coroner's building to the sister's house on the north side of town. Even with the rise in temperature, now and then, there was a breeze blowing down from the Peak. After parking at the curb, he climbed out and walked to the passenger side. Eppie was already standing beside the closed SUV door and staring at the house.

It was a midsize house with a covered porch and a wood railing across the front. The grass in the front yard had been changed to zero landscaping with large pots of red geraniums and other brightly colored flowers. During the dry spell, Colorado had experienced the last couple of years, watering a lawn with city water was too expensive.

Tall round posts supported the porch roof, and there were two light blue front doors. One side must be a rental, Jonas speculated. It was an excellent choice as an income property. The two windows were trimmed in a darker blue and stood out against the white paint applied to the rest of the structure. On one side of the porch hung a wooden swing, anchored by chains to a roof beam.

As they walked up the steps, crossed the short sidewalk leading to the porch, they heard the tinkling sound of a wind chime. Glancing to his left, Jonas stared in appreciation at the workmanship of the stained glass dragonfly hanging on a chain from a beam in the roof. The dragonfly was iridescent blue and pearl colors shimmering in the sunlight and twirling in the faint breeze. It matched the tattoo on the dead woman. As he gazed at it, Jonas knew that as much as he dreaded it, he was bringing bad news to Morgan Jansen. This was the part of the job he hated most. Taking a deep breath, he reached out and pushed the doorbell.

At the same moment, Jonas was ringing the doorbell of Morgan Jansen's house, Henry Pope rolled off his sofa and hit the floor hard on his right shoulder. He let out a yelp. Immediately pissed by the sudden jolt, Henry sat up, leaned back against the front, knees bent and rested his throbbing head in his hands and moaned.

"Fuck, fuck, fuck!" he muttered.

Three weeks ago, his wife had kicked him out of the house and filed for a divorce. It seemed she'd found herself a better man to keep her warm at night. One that didn't ignore her and refrained from drinking too much.

He didn't consider himself an unattractive man. Yeah, he was getting thin on top, had developed a slight paunch at his midsection, but he was in his late forties. What did she expect? Some women at work still found him attractive. Almost as tall as Jonas, he was heavier by a good twenty pounds. On occasions, he still worked out, but for months now, he found it easier to lift a glass of scotch than a dumbbell. Maybe, he considered, his problems were getting to him.

He'd taken the weekend off citing personal problems and was to return on Monday but hadn't. It was true. He had lots of personal issues he was trying to come to grips with. Mostly it was his wife's unfaithfulness, his failed marriage, her leaving and all the debt she had left him with. The debt he would eventually handle. What he couldn't believe was that she had betrayed him with another man, in their own home. Her vows meant nothing. The fact that she had let another man touch her, while she was still married, hurt more than the fact she had left him.

Shirley was a beautiful woman, and he'd adored her. Even he had to admit his drinking partially drove her away. But, she knew when she married him what the life of a cop was like, his working all hours, the horrors he saw. It was tough on a detective, making them unaffected by murder and insensitive to a wife's worries or needs. She claimed she couldn't take waiting to hear he had been killed anymore, not to mention his bouts of drinking. She was right in many ways. He needed to regain his control. He'd already lost her; now his job was all he had left. He couldn't get fired as well.

Here it was Monday, and he was still hung over. Plus the entire weekend, from Friday night on, was just a thick fog in his mind. He had no idea where the hell he had gone after work, or what he had done other than killing a bottle or two of scotch. Booze had never made him blank out before. That unaccounted time bothered him. Actually, scared him. Now, to add to his problems, he was late for work. There was an early morning message he'd missed to meet at the Three Graces in the Garden of the Gods. He was way past being late. Jonas was going to be pissed unless he called in.

He grabbed his cell and dialed Jose's number. When his partner answered, Fernandez told him about the body. As he was in no shape to go to work, again Henry claimed a personal problem and stated he'd be in on Tuesday.

He forced himself to stand and stagger into the kitchen of his mother's big old two-story house. Day old coffee remained in the pot on the counter. He winced as a pain shot through his right shoulder when he reached to grab a cup from inside the cupboard. He stopped and stared at the back of his right hand. His knuckles were scraped, burning and covered with dried blood.

Turning on the faucet, he washed the blood off and tried to remember what he had done to cause the injury. The blackout, injured hand, and shoulder were of grave concern. Nothing surfaced but the image of Dawson's bar and an uneasy feeling. The rest was blank. He knew Tim, the bartender, well. He'd be able to fill in some of the missing pieces. He needed to go find out what had happened to him.

Cold coffee forgotten, he headed for the shower. After stripping off his clothes, he checked his face and right shoulder. There was a faint bruising starting to show beneath the skin. That could have been caused by falling off the sofa. Quickly he showered, dressed in tan slacks, a white pullover shirt, and loafers, and then headed for his car.

Dawson's didn't open until four in the afternoon, so he decided to drive to an IHOP and have breakfast. He deliberately went to one on the south side of town so as not to be seen by any team member. If what Jose said was right, they'd be focused on the Garden of the Gods and not concerned with his whereabouts. Decision made, Henry headed south on Academy Boulevard.

Chapter Three

Monday

All day Sunday, Morgan had driven from one end of Colorado Springs to the other, hoping to find Marilyn. She had visited every place she could think of that her sister might frequent. All she had gotten was a severe headache plus exhaustion from lack of sleep and little food. Sunday night, the few hours she had spent in bed consisted mostly of tossing and turning until six, at which time, she gave up on sleep. This morning, after a quick shower, she pulled on a yellow cotton short-sleeved shirt, jeans, and sneakers. She planned on continuing her hunt for her twin.

At nine, she called her boss, Veterinarian Eric Barns, explained the situation, and that she would not be in for a few days. He wouldn't miss her, as she only worked at the clinic part-time. An understanding man, he had told her to take whatever time she needed.

She drove through McDonald's for coffee and an Egg McMuffin, then to Doctor Jack Donavan's office where Marilyn worked. She sat in a parking space consuming the food, and watching the front door. When Morgan saw other people drive up, enter, and then immediately come out and drive away, Morgan had a bad feeling. She hurried inside to the doctor's reception desk.

Alice, a short chubby blonde, was working the phones and placing one call after. Debbie, taller and more slender, had dark hair and wore it shoulder length, immediately spotted her and rushed over.

"Where's Marilyn? The doctor, nor your sister

are here. We haven't heard from them. Have you seen them?" Debbie asked.

"I was about to ask you the same question," Morgan said.

"We haven't heard from them," Debbie continued. "It's possible the Doc will be in later in the afternoon. If he does come in, I doubt he'll be seeing patients. As for Marilyn, I don't know. She may have taken the day off without telling us. We're doing paperwork, and calling patients to cancel appointments."

It was the knowing look the two women exchanged that bothered Morgan. She left with an assurance that if they heard from the doctor or her sister, they would call her home or cell phone.

After that, she continued her search for Marilyn or her car. She found neither. Now it was three-thirty Monday afternoon. She walked through her front door, dropped down onto the sofa, picked up the house phone from the end table to check for messages. Nothing.

It was driving her crazy that no one seemed to believe her sister was missing. Not her friends or the police. First thing Tuesday morning, she was going back to the police station. By that time, maybe the cops would have located her sister. What she needed now was a cup of hot tea to revive her. What she needed more, was sleep. That would have to wait for a while longer. She only hoped she could stay awake long enough to have a sandwich and the tea.

Stumbling into the gleaming white kitchen, she placed the tea kettle on the burner, slapped some peanut butter on a single slice of bread and took a bite, then leaned back against the counter to wait. In no time the kettle gave a shrill scream. She jumped, aware that she had actually started to doze off. She fixed her tea, carried it and the sandwich to the living room.

Still exhausted from lack of sleep and endless hours spent in her vehicle, she sat on the sofa, took several sips of her tea and finished her makeshift meal. Her auburn hair was pulled back in a ponytail, and her eyes were again growing heavy. She knew she should set the cup on the coffee table, but continued to hold it close to her chest as the tea cooled.

When the doorbell rang, she jumped. The contents of the cup sloshed over the front of her yellow T-shirt and jeans. Brushing at the wet fabric with her hand, she hurried down the hall to the kitchen, dumped the mug in the sink and grabbed a hand towel, as the doorbell rang again.

"I'm coming!" she yelled, wiping at the stains, hurrying toward the front door. Her headache was getting worse. Plus she was in no mood for company. She looked through the window, clutching the towel to her chest. Dread churned at her stomach as she unlocked the door and opened it.

A tall man in a white shirt, dark dress slacks and boots stood in front of the open door, gripping a white Stetson in his hand. He was handsome in a rough sort of way, square jaw, dark blue eyes, a straight nose over well-defined lips. It was the way a lock of his dark hair fell across his forehead that softened his hard image. He would have made a perfect model for a cowboy advertisement. Next to him stood a pretty dark-eyed woman in a red blouse, and brown slacks.

"Ms. Jansen?" the tall man asked.

"Yes." Her heart began to beat faster, making her a little dizzy, as she opened the door wider.

"I'm Lieutenant Jonas Black, and this is Sergeant Esperanza Ortiz. We're with the Colorado Springs Police Department. Could we come in and talk with you for a moment?" He studied the furrowed brows above blue-green eyes, showing a fearful expression.

Jonas couldn't help but stare. This was a face any man would not readily forget. She looked exactly like the photo ID of the dead woman. He was looking into the same eyes and the same features. The combination, aided by a healthy golden complexion, almost took his breath away. He realized he had actually been holding his breath, and slowly let it out.

"Have you found my sister?" All too aware of how the man kept his eyes riveted to her face, Morgan moved back out of the way and gestured them inside. She had to fight the ache that tightened her chest and knotted her stomach. She was afraid she already knew the answer. If the police had come to her door, it couldn't be good. She prayed Marilyn was only injured. "Please, have a seat," she told them.

They sat on the sofa, and she sat in a chair facing them. With her back straight and her hands clasped tightly in her lap, she asked, "Is Marilyn dead?"

"You filed an ATL Saturday?" the Lieutenant asked. He was stalling and knew it. That continued look of dread on her face was disconcerting. This was the hardest part of his job, and he'd never get used to it.

"Yes, and you wouldn't be here if you hadn't found her. Please tell me what has happened to my sister. Is she injured?" Morgan stared straight into his eyes, seeing his uneasiness. He blinked and looked at his partner.

"We think we may have found her. Can you tell me the last time you saw your sister?" Eppie asked as Jonas took a small notepad and his Slim Pen from his pocket, holding the pen upright, so the camera was directed at Morgan.

She heard the click of his ballpoint pen, and her apprehension mounted. How was she going to explain to this stranger her relationship with Marilyn? "I haven't seen my sister in over six months," and, she reluctantly admitted, "I haven't talked with her in over a month."

How many times during the last thirty days had she ignored the caller ID on her phone when Marilyn called? Too many, she had to admit now. Didn't they say that if hindsight were foresight people would do things differently? She certainly would have. The hurt and anger her sister had caused was too raw, and she had needed to work through the grief before she could talk to her again. Now it was too late.

The two detectives exchanged puzzled glances. "Would you tell us how you knew she was missing if you haven't talked to her?" Eppie asked.

"Because she's my identical twin, and I just knew she was in trouble." She shifted in her chair and turned to glance at the framed photograph sitting on the fireplace mantle. She rose, removed it and handed it to the detective. It was a shot of them taken four years ago, during happier times, on a weekend trip to Cripple Creek. "As you can see, it would be difficult to tell us apart. We've always had this bond between us. I feel what she feels, and vice versa. So I awoke early Saturday morning knowing she was in trouble."

She could see the skepticism on Lieutenant Black's face while Detective Ortiz seemed to understand a sister's bond. Morgan directed her retort to the Lieutenant. "If you don't believe me, check the Internet. There are all types of case studies listed. You might even find the study done on Marilyn and me."

Oh, God, why had she said that? Now he might actually check and dredge up all the old issues. That would not be good. Their past needed to stay in the past. She took the picture from the man and put it back in its place on the mantle, then returned to her seat. "You still haven't told me if my sister is alive." She was beginning to feel sick to her stomach.

"The body of a female, fitting your sister's description, was discovered in the Garden of the Gods early this morning. We believe it may be her." Jonas saw the blood drain from her face as she gripped the arms of the chair until her knuckles were white.

"Oh God," Morgan clutched her stomach. "Since early Saturday, I've been afraid my sister was dead." She couldn't sit any longer, so she stood behind the chair and stared at Jonas. She had to ask one more time. "Are you sure it's my sister?"

"We believe so. The body has the tattoo you listed on the ATL."

"What happened to her?"

This was the part he hated, giving the relative the terrible news. "I'm sorry to have to tell you, but the woman we found was murdered." Jonas waited for the reaction he knew was coming. The how, who, and the biggest question of all, WHY, was always what the relatives wanted to know. They never wanted to believe their sister, brother, husband or any relative could have an enemy that dangerous.

"What! How! Why would anyone want to kill Marilyn? You have to be wrong. It can't be her." She dropped back into the chair. All she seemed able to do was shake her head, and let the tears she had fought to keep under control roll down her face. Marilyn couldn't really be dead! But, the life spark that always connected them was gone. There was only this darkness covering a part of her heart and knew it was for her sister.

She wiped her cheeks with her hand, rose and walked to the bathroom to wipe her face with a damp cloth. Better composed, she returned and faced the detectives. Both stood when she asked, "How did she die?"

"We're not sure yet," he lied. "We won't know definitely until we get the autopsy report." Before she could ask, he said, "You don't have to go to the morgue. The Coroner will make a positive identification. He will formally notify you and help with any funeral arrangements if you need it."

Morgan took a deep breath "Thank you. I was dreading that." She added, "Were her knees, elbows, and shoulders injured? I felt that she also had an injury to the left side of her face as well. Am I right?"

Taken aback by her question, Jonas arched an eyebrow. "How did you know that?"

A sad smile curved Morgan's lips as she walked them to the front door. "I told you, my sister and I had this connection. It was pain that woke me up Saturday morning. Horrible, horrible pain. My sister died in agony." She looked from one to the other. "I felt it. I didn't want to believe she was dead, but in my heart, I think I knew."

Jonas could not respond to the woman's claim. He didn't believe in psychic connections or abilities but made a mental note to Google anything he could find on identical twins, especially the victim and her sister. "I only have a few more questions for you. Do you know where your sister was Friday night or any of her friends or if she had enemies? Also, where she worked?"

Morgan gave him the names of Alice and Debbie, told him about Dawson's Bar and her visit to Doctor Donavan's office. "That's all I know. When I checked, the doctor had not shown up for work either. If she had enemies, I have no idea who they'd be." Her breath catching as she fought back a sob, she" clenched her fists. "If that's all, I need to call the Coroner's office and let him know I'll make the funeral arrangements. My sister and I only had each other. Our parents are dead." The full impact of what had happened hit Morgan. There was a quiver to her voice now, as if she was fighting hard to hold back the shock. It would set in soon enough. "Now, I'm the only one left," she muttered.

"Again, I am sorry for your loss," Jonas added.

"Your sister's body should be released within forty-eight hours. Once you've selected a funeral home, call the Coroner's office and give them the name of the company. They will arrange to release her remains to them." He handed her his business card feeling like an insensitive jerk. "If you think of anything, call me or," he took a card from his partner, "Detective Ortiz. One of us will call you back." He hurried out the door with Eppie right behind him. This had been a tough one on both of them. It had been eerie looking at the sister and knowing that the same face and body was lying on a slab in the morgue.

Once outside, Jonas stopped and glanced back at the house. "What do you think, Eppie? Think she's telling us everything?"

"She's holding something back. I don't think she had anything to do with her sister's murder. She was genuinely upset, and you can't fake that kind of devastation. No, I don't know what's she's hiding, but it has nothing to do with the murder. What do you think about her story of sensing her sister was in trouble?"

"Her so-called mental bond with her dead sister? Not much. I'd say it's more of a good guess based on her knowledge of her sister's habit. We need to check her out anyway." Did he want to know more about her for himself or for the case? Jonas had to admit she took his breath away. Looks weren't everything. He had dated a couple of good-looking women. Both relationships ended. Now he was attracted to a woman that believed she was psychic. Hell, he sure could find the crazy ones.

"Find out everything you can about her," he said. "If we can, get her financials. See if she's in debt.

Maybe her sister had a large insurance policy. Also, let's check her phone records for the past two weeks. See who she's been talking to. I want to know a lot more about Morgan Jansen." Even if she was a little nuts, she certainly intrigued him, and his curiosity about a woman was not easily aroused.

Morgan watched the detectives go to their car. The tall one had stopped and stood talking to the woman. After they drove away, she sank down on the sofa and stared at the picture on the mantle. It didn't matter that they hadn't gotten along these last few years. Hell, for the past three years, really. Marilyn was her other half. Only together were they a whole person. They had been one egg in their mother's womb until it split. As the old saying goes, they had been two peas in a pod, alike in every way, except personality. How was she going to make it without her sister?

She stood and walked back to the kitchen for a drink of water, then came back to stand on the front porch staring at Pike's Peak, that giant mountain that hovered over the entire city. The late afternoon sun was still bright. Soon the heat would give way to cooler evenings. Right now, she had to think, had to make arrangements to bury Marilyn. A simple service would be best, and all she could afford.

Anderson Funeral Home would do. It was a one-story building, quiet and unpretentious, set back from the curb and surrounded by shade trees. They had handled the burial of their parents. They brought their dogs to the veterinarian where she worked, so she knew the owners.

Morgan went back inside, grabbed the phone book, located their number and placed the dreaded call. Fifteen minutes later she had an appointment for the next day. Now all she had to do was arrange the burial plot at Evergreen Cemetery.

Exhaustion made her headache worse, her body screamed for rest. All she really wanted to do was curl up in a fetal ball and cry. Grabbing an afghan from the back of the sofa, that was precisely what she did. She cried for all the times she had lost her temper with Marilyn. For all the days, hours and minutes that they had not spoken or seen each other. That time was gone, lost forever. Her sister was dead. All her regrets were too little and way too late.

Finally, sleep claimed her. She slept soundly until eight-thirty. Her eyes felt puffy and gritty when she opened them. Feeling even more tired than when she curled up on the sofa, Morgan rose and walked into the bedroom. Stripping off her clothes, she pulled the long white nightshirt over her head and then entered the bathroom to brush her teeth. She didn't take the time to wash her face as her body was giving out, and she was dead on her feet.

Marilyn dead! That thought again brought tears to her eyes. Throwing back the bedspread, she climbed in between the crisp cotton sheets and thankfully, immediately, fell into a deep sleep.

At seven-fifteen, Henry walked into Dawson's. The regulars were already lined up at the bar, so he sat on a stool at the end, well away from and out of earshot of the other patrons.

When Tim automatically placed a glass of scotch in front of him, without thinking, Henry picked it up and took a sip, then set it back on the polished wooden surface and shoved it away.

"Don't you want it?" Tim asked.

"Not tonight. But, I do need some information."

"Sure. What can I help you with, Henry?"

"Was I in here last Friday night?" Feeling embarrassed to admit he didn't remember, Pope felt his face flush and hoped, in the dim light, Tim didn't notice.

"You don't remember?" the bartender smiled. "Well, you were pretty shit faced. Yeah, you were here. I thought I was going to have to kick your ass out after you got into an argument with that red-head. She sure tore you a new one."

"What red-head?"

"You don't remember her either? My God, how could you forget a woman like that? She was one hot looking babe. I'd like to have tried that ass myself, but she wouldn't give me a tumble. You sure pissed her off though." Tim turned away to fill the glass of a man sitting midway of the bar. When he returned, he continued, "I only heard part of what you said to her, but boy was she angry."

Henry had no memory of seeing or talking to the woman Tim described. "What the hell did I say to her?"

"Oh, you were ranting and raving how women use men, and when they've drained them of everything, toss them aside like they're nothing. You directed your comments toward her. I think you knew her. This woman and a couple of her friends took offense. The two of you got into one hell of a verbal fight. I thought I was going to have to kick both of you out, then you calmed down. That was around ten that night. She got up and left her two friends here. Then you left shortly after. Her friends stayed till closing. I have to assume you went home." Tim began to wipe down the bar.

"Did I get into a physical fight with anyone?" Henry asked.

"Only arguing with that woman, nothing physical. I had to finally cut you off. One minute you were fairly sober, the next, you were drunk. You were staggering when you went out the door and almost fell. If you drove your vehicle, I'm surprised you didn't get stopped. That's all I got." He threw his hands in the air, then walked away to the other end of the bar to serve a customer. He turned back to Henry, "I just remembered something. Did that friend of yours find you?"

"What friend?"

"The guy who came in looking for you after you left. He said it was important that he find you. Did he?" Tim stood waiting for an answer.

Henry glanced at the glass of scotch and wanted desperately to down it, but didn't. "Yeah," he lied, and called out a "Thanks, Tim," and left the bar. Who was the guy looking for him? Fernandez? Probably.

Where he went after leaving Dawson's, puzzled him. He felt sure he didn't go home until much later. A detective with a DUI would be in big trouble. Maybe he sat in his vehicle until he sobered up enough to drive. If he'd done that, he would remember it. His neighbor,

Mrs. Carter probably knew. She was the neighborhood watchdog, and was up until all hours and saw everything.

Pope left Dawson's fully intending on going straight home to speak with the older woman. On the way, he stopped at a liquor store, Mrs. Carter forgotten entirely.

Chapter Four

Tuesday, early a.m.

Morgan opened her eyes. Someone was calling her name. She sat up in bed and looked around. The room was dark. She had not bothered to leave the bathroom light on as she usually did.

"Well, dummy, turn on the bedside lamp, and you can see me."

If her heart could stop from fright, Morgan was sure it was about to. She knew that voice.

"Damn you Marilyn!" she exploded. It would be just like her sister to pull a stunt like this. "Is this one of your jokes? The police came to the house this afternoon and told me you were dead."

Morgan reached across to the nightstand and turned on the lamp, then whipped around to face her sister. Her mouth dropped open. Marilyn was perched on the footboard wearing nothing, but a red Au Bade bra and matching panties. "Where in the hell are your clothes?" she demanded.

Marilyn kept her face slightly averted, avoiding her sister's stunned expression. "Morgan, get a grip. I don't know who has my clothes."

"How did you get here dressed like that?" Morgan kept staring at her sister's practically nude body. Marilyn might joke around, but she would never go out in public dressed like she was now. Morgan's heart began to pound and her brow wrinkled with worry. Her voice held a touch of fear. "Why would the police come and tell me you were dead, and then you show up dressed like that? What is going on, Sis?"

"We're not going to talk about the police coming to see you right now. You're dreaming, so stop squirming and looking all pathetic. God, I hate it when you do that. You've always been such a softy. Well, until you know when," she cast a guilty sideways glance at Morgan. "That has to change. I need you to be strong and maybe unforgiving."

"Yeah, what you did made me a lot tougher." Morgan's resentment reared its head. "What you did was almost unforgivable. I am the way I am, Marilyn. I don't want to dream of you being dead! I can't stand the thought of losing you." Tears glistened in her eyes.

Marilyn was right, she had always been too easy going. The studious twin, never making waves, never in trouble, until her sister slept with her rat of a husband, Andrew. Then everything broke inside of her. After a big fight with Marilyn and Andy, she moved out of the Village Seven house and filed for divorce. She'd been thankful her parents were dead so she wouldn't have to explain what caused the rift between her and her sister. They would have disowned Marilyn.

"You're not dreaming of me being dead, but this is a dream. And you are going to have to face it, Morgan. Yes! I am dead. I am a ghost, just not one of those see-through types." She slid off the footboard onto the mattress and wrapped her arms around her knees. "I'm cold. Do you have a shirt I can borrow?" She was actually shivering.

Marilyn looked more scared than Morgan had

ever seen her. Instinctively, she wanted to help. She got out of bed, pulled open a dresser drawer and tossed her sister a heavy gray T-shirt.

"Here, put this on." She stared at her twin. This couldn't be happening. Even in a dream, it shouldn't be happening. It was cruel. All those unanswered questions. She was compelled to ask, "What happened to you? Do you know?"

"That's just it, Sis. I don't know any of the what, why or who. I have an idea of the when. I'm not even positive about that. All I do remember is driving back to my apartment. Someone had parked in my parking spot, so I had to park at another building and walk back to mine. When I got almost to my door, everything went black. That's all I remember." Marilyn pulled the T-shirt over her head and hugged the fabric closer, rubbing her upper arms to warm herself. "I'll never again be warm enough," she said, as two tears rolled down her cheeks.

Morgan sat back on the bed extending her hand to touch her sister's arm.

"Don't touch me," Marilyn said, drawing back out of reach. She sat on the mattress and leaned against the footboard, her knees drawn up to her chest. "I don't think you're supposed to touch me. Besides, I can't handle your sympathy right now."

"I don't understand," Morgan said, and let her hand drop as she scooted to lean back against the headboard, facing Marilyn. They were in identical positions, both hugging their knees and looking distraught, as they sat and stared at each other.

"I'm not sure I do either. It has something to do with me having recently died or the way I died. I don't know which. In fact, I don't seem to know much of anything." Marilyn looked at her sister and pushed her hair back from her face. "Is my face horribly messed up?"

"No. You look like you always did. Why?"

"Because something hit me on the left side of my face, and my eye socket was caved in. I was afraid of frightening you. Besides, you know how vain I am about my looks." She gave Morgan a sad smile. "Sister, promise me that you'll have a closed casket. I don't want people seeing how horrible I look."

Morgan sat up straighter. "God, Marilyn, don't talk like that. Please," she tried not to cry. The tears rolled down her face, and she couldn't stop them. "I felt your pain," she muttered, fighting back a sob. "I know what you went through. I'll never forget it. My bones still ache. I just want to know why you were killed."

"I'm so sorry," Marilyn said, as guilt and shame crossed her face and was reflected in her eyes. "I really mean that. Please forgive me for all the pain I caused you. It's been a lot, I know. As for who might want me dead," she gave a half laugh, glancing down at her hands. Her manicure was intact. Looking back at Morgan, said, "Any number of people I have screwed over. That includes several men and their wives."

"Oh Christ, Marilyn, you've been dating married men again? Mom and Dad would have had a fit."

Marilyn arched an eyebrow, "That's funny, coming from you. Anyway, they never knew, thank God." She stood up and walked toward the kitchen.

Morgan hurried after her. "Where are you going?"

"I'm hungry and thirsty," Marilyn called, over her shoulder. "Do you have a beer or some cheese and crackers?"

"You can't be hungry. You're a ghost!" Morgan said, following her into the kitchen.

"Wellllllllllll, technically, yeah. Since this is a dream, and I'm a whole person, I can be hungry and thirsty if I want." She cocked her head to the side and gave Morgan a sweet smile, then said. "You're the cook, fix us some eggs."

This time when Morgan opened her eyes, it was to see the sun shining brightly through the blinds. The dream merely a shadow of a memory, she glanced at the clock radio on the nightstand. It was seven in the morning, and it was Tuesday. Turning over, she pulled the pillow over her head. If only she could stay in bed and not have to face all the things she dreaded having to do today. But, she needed to finalize the funeral arrangements. Giving a deep sigh, she sat up and rubbed her eyes.

First, she had to call Eric again and tell him to hire a replacement, as she didn't know when or if she'd be returning to work. Then coffee was a necessary morning staple. The coffee maker would not turn on by itself because she didn't know how to set the brewing timer. Pushing back the blanket, she got out of bed, made a quick trip to use the bathroom and brush her teeth before padding barefoot into the kitchen.

The hardwood floor felt cold on her feet. The air

in the house was still chilly from the nightly drop in temperature into the sixties. A hot shower and coffee would soon warm her up. She pushed the button on the Mr. Coffee, then stared down into the kitchen sink. Two dirty plates and two cups were soaking in soapy water. The only thing she remembered leaving in the sink the night before was her dirty teacup. She glanced around and spotted a used skillet on the stove. Then she remembered the dream about Marilyn.

It had to be impossible. She couldn't have sleepwalked and actually cooked food for her dead sister. The proof she had done just that was soaking in the water. That frightened her, frightened her more than the thought Marilyn had actually been a ghostly visitor. More details of the dream popped into her mind. The gray T-shirt! She had given it to her sister to wear. She hurried back into the bedroom and pulled open the dresser drawer. The shirt was gone.

It had been freshly laundered, so she knew it wasn't in the basement. Maybe the bathroom? It wasn't in the dirty clothes basket either, not in the closet, nor was it behind or under the bed. Morgan searched every conceivable place where the shirt might be, even putting on a robe and going out to check her vehicle. No luck. The T-shirt was not in the house. It had to be with her dead sister.

What else had Marilyn said during the dream? She'd said she had no idea of what happened to her. That much was clear. There was more. Morgan was not sure if she remembered everything clearly, other than her twin's profound sadness. Marilyn had said she had been taken outside her apartment building and admitted to dating married men.

Had an angry wife killed her? She should tell Lieutenant Black about her dream but was hesitant. His skepticism about the bond between her and her twin had been rather apparent. He could doubt all he wanted; she had lived that bond, and knew how deep their connection had been. Oh, how she had lived it! All Marilyn's escapades and wild nights, right down to the moment she knew her sister was in bed having sex with her bastard of a husband.

That betrayal had left her numb. Unable to think or feel, she had left Andy, bought the house where she now lived, determined to start a new life without either her sister or her rotten husband. Slowly over weeks and months, her wounds had begun to heal. She couldn't forgive her husband. Her sister was a different matter. Eventually, maybe she could put the bitter betrayal behind her, but not anytime soon.

First, she had found the part-time job with Doctor Barn's Veterinarian Clinic, then had taken several stained glass design classes at the Art Center downtown. Finally had ended all ties with her sister. It hadn't fully worked. No matter how much she distanced herself from Marilyn, they would always be connected. Every time Marilyn called her cell phone, she had ignored the call.

That nightmare had happened over a year ago. Morgan would forgive her sister even that betrayal if she could have her back.

What about her flippant remark for that detective to Google them? What had she done? What if he researched twins and found them? Their last names were different now. Both she and Marilyn had married. Maybe they were no longer listed under case studies. The Dorchester twins had been big news in Virginia in 1994. Together, as one mind, they had helped solve a major abduction case. The case had ended in tragedy. The boy was found dead.

His parents blamed the girls for not coming forward sooner. Their mother and father had tried to shield them. But, the story went national. Every nut case in the area was after them for Lotto numbers or talking with their dead relatives. Their parents had given up everything and moved them to Florida. When Marilyn managed to get herself in trouble, they moved west, changed their names, and cautioned the girls never to talk about what they could do together.

She was almost thirty-one now, so that had been nineteen years ago. Maybe Lieutenant Black would forget about her flippant remark. She doubted it. He was suspicious of her, so he would probably research and eventually find out who she was.

Then she remembered Marilyn's warning. When her sister had started for the front door, she had turned and said, "I wasn't the only one he took. Tell that hunky detective that there will be more. He won't believe you, Morgan. So, be careful, or he'll think you're involved." Then Marilyn had walked through, not out, the front door. She had opened her eyes to the sun streaming through the blinds, the dream only a whisper in her brain.

What was she supposed to do? If she told the

detective about Marilyn's warning, he would think she was crazy. Maybe she was. Perhaps the shock of losing her sister was too much for her mind to handle. Possibly it had all been a wishful attempt to reconnect with her twin by any means possible, even if it was only in a dream. That had to be the answer. So there was a logical explanation for the dirty dishes and the missing T-shirt. She had to have been sleepwalking.

Grasping at that thought, Morgan returned to the kitchen, picked up one of the soapy plates and began to wash off the remnants of the egg. With the few dishes washed, the frying pan scrubbed and placed in the drainer, and now satisfied that the evidence of her sleepwalking was gone, she poured a much-needed cup of coffee adding lots of powdered cream.

She noted the coffee creamer was getting low and made a mental note to add it to the grocery list. She liked it better than fresh milk. At least it didn't spoil. Three sips into her first cup, the phone rang. Morgan grabbed the receiver and glanced at the stove clock. It was eight-thirty.

"Hello," she said and waited. It was the Coroner's office.

Chapter Five

Tuesday

Jonas sat behind the wheel of his SUV in the drive-thru at McDonald's and held onto the Styrofoam cup of black coffee he had just been handed. He tossed the paper bag, containing an Egg McMuffin, on the passenger seat, placed the cup in the holder, and headed to work. Once at his desk, removed the top off the cup and slowly savored the sharp bite of the hot liquid. It had been a long evening, and he had not slept that well. He and Eppie had gone to check out the victim's apartment. The key was right where the sister had said it would be.

The place was the cleanest victim's home he'd ever seen. Nothing was out of place, not even a dirty glass. There was not much to find, condoms in the drawer of the bedside table, pointing to sexual activity, a calendar listing appointments, one in red ink and starred next to the name Jack on the night she disappeared. In the closet on an upper shelf, they found several large three-ringed binders, one holding numerous cards, love notes and a single sheet of paper with a message about meeting later and signed Lover. The woman had more clothes, shoes, and purses than she could use in a year.

A photograph of a naked man, lying on the bed, was tucked away in the back pocket of the binder. Like the unsigned note, the name of the man was not written on the back of the picture. They had bagged the ring binders, the calendar for later perusal, and an envelope filled with miscellaneous papers that appeared to be valuable. Jonas had called Clay to come and stay with the CSI unit while they processed the apartment in case they found something else. Other team members were interviewing neighbors for additional information concerning the woman's activities. Each interview would be placed in the book for his review.

Eppie had to leave to check on her mother, and he'd returned to the office. The rest of the team, coming back from the Garden of the Gods, had little to report. The few surveillance cameras had captured nothing, and not a single resident living close to the park had heard or seen a vehicle in the area during the wee hours of Monday morning. This case had little evidence to go on, and that was not good. Their chance of solving this crime was slipping away with each passing minute.

Jonas had Marilyn's calendar open on his desk. It had been dusted for fingerprints, and only those of the victim was found. Spread over the last six months was the usual doctor and dental appointments, plus hair salon visits. The only consistent entry listed, week after week, was each Friday night. Always entered in red ink at ten-thirty, was the name Jack and a red star, even on this past Friday.

All the notes and cards from the three-ringed binder had old dates scribbled on the back. Several different fingerprints had been found on all the items, with one set matching the victim. As the cards were sold commercially, it would be difficult to identify every set of prints. They all had to be checked out. The only exception was the last sheet of loose-leaf paper with the note from Lover on it. It also was dated for this past

Friday. Only one set of fingerprints was found, and they belonged to the victim.

Whoever had typed the message had been careful not to touch the paper. Jonas placed the plastic sleeve containing the note back inside the binder, stared at it for a moment, then picked up the cup downing the last of the coffee, before tossing it in the trash can. One cup was not going to do the trick.

The office coffeepot was always on and would keep him supplied with caffeine. He felt on this case, he was going to need a lot of it. The only concrete evidence they might have was the blood on the branch. In reality, the DNA results would take several months, even with the new robotic DNA processing machine. Test results were not as quickly obtained the way it was portrayed by numerous television crime shows. It all took too many hours and days. By the time they received the report, the killer could be out of state.

The envelope contents had been examined and contained Marilyn's car insurance policy, plus two life insurance policies, a business card with the name of an attorney on it and miscellaneous bills and papers. Jonas had not glanced at the insurance policies but left it in Clay's capable hands to review in detail and to contact the attorney.

Jonas picked up the case study he had printed off the Internet. Last night, it had taken him over two hours on Google, sifting through all the information on identical twins, before he found a mention of the girls. It was a brief report, including photographs of the

Dorchester twins from Virginia and their unique bond. It stated that even when they were separated, each was aware of the activity of the other and appeared to be able to communicate even though each girl was placed in a different room. That was scary if it was true. He doubted the story. It made for good headlines and for research grants. But when it came to actual proof, he'd have to conduct the experiment himself to believe it wasn't a fraud. It would be easy for the parents to manipulate. There were all types of wireless communication systems in 1994. So it wasn't impossible back then to fake psychic abilities. Phony fortune tellers did it all the time.

There was the tiniest seed of uncertainty that the woman had lied. Could it be true? Did Morgan experience her sister's death? He had to admit to experiencing something strange after Kelly's death back in Texas. In 1998, Jonas had been half out of his mind with grief and guilt wanting to believe he had seen her ghost not once, but three different times. He thought he had seen her because he wanted to believe it, not that it had actually happened. Just as Morgan Jansen wanted to believe she had experienced her sister's death.

He understood how hard it was to let go of those you loved. Especially if their death had been a violent one. He hadn't been able to let go. Kelly was always there in the back of his mind. Maybe it was guilt nagging at him for not being there when she needed him. Perhaps it was him hating himself for not solving her murder.

Joining the Midland Police Department right out of college, he'd only been on the force for two years when she was killed. Kelly had been his high school girlfriend, and they planned on getting married. They'd been so naïve to believe that you dated, got married, and had kids, in that order.

Her murder in Midland, Texas on a warm spring evening had nearly destroyed him. It had been just as violent as Marilyn Heddrix death. Kelly had been beaten, raped and then strangled. At the time of her death, he had been deemed a person of interest, then cleared by his solid alibi. He had been on duty investigating a robbery on the opposite side of town.

Obsession with finding her killer and booze had destroyed his ability to do his job. With the threat of suspension, he resigned. At his grandfather's suggestion, and to keep his sanity, he enlisted in the Marines. After basic training, when a chance came for deployment, he volunteered, serving back to back tours in Afghanistan. He wanted to act, not think.

After his military discharge, he couldn't bring himself to go back to Texas knowing everywhere he looked would invoke memories of Kelly. He opted for Colorado. With his degree and military training, he joined the Colorado Springs Police Department. Every July, on the anniversary of her death, he called Midland for an update on the investigation. Her case had gone cold long ago. Several buddies still on the Midland Police Department, kept her case active.

Kelly had been so beautiful, she almost made his heart stop. The Heddrix woman reminded him a lot of her. The same red hair, smooth skin and a mouth that made him want to kiss her forever. They even had the same color eyes, that sea blue-green. The last time he had seen Kelly, her beautiful eyes had been fixed and staring. He didn't want to think about that anymore. He had enough to deal with for the moment. Right now he needed to focus on the current case file on his desk.

Jonas flipped open the folder just as Addison Clay walked into his office, gripping a Starbuck's cup in one hand, then plopped down in the chair in front of his desk. The Lieutenant looked up. "You know you look like crap, don't you?"

A day's growth of dark beard covered Clay's jaws and chin. His brown eyes were bloodshot, and he slumped in the chair as if exhaustion rode him hard.

"For your information, I haven't been home yet," Clay said and rubbed his eyes. "I plan on going home to shower, sleep for a few hours, get up, shave, change clothes and have breakfast. Then I'll be back. By the way, the victim had to be a clean freak. We found her prints and several others, yet to be identified, in the bedroom, bathroom and living room. I did find her vehicle. It was parked in a guest space at the next building. I had it towed, and Forensics will go over it today. I didn't find a purse, cell phone or any form of her identification at the apartment."

He paused to take a breath, then continued, "We checked with all the residents, who were home at the time, and no one noticed anything. Nor did any of those I talked with have a lot to say about the victim other than she kept to herself. Considering it was a Friday night, a lot of them were out for the evening. It's a younger crowd that lives there, so they like to party on the weekend. I'll keep looking for her personal items, clothes, purse, or shoes. They have to be somewhere."

Clay glanced around. "Is there any coffee left?"

"Fresh pot," Jonas said. "Did Henry show up for work today?

"Yeah. He looks worse than I do, but Pope is here. When I showed him the picture of the victim, I thought he was going to puke. He made a run for the bathroom. It surprised me. He's seen a dead body before."

After a while, the sight of a murder victim didn't seem to bother the detectives too much; to some extent, they became immune to death. They had to, or they couldn't stay objective and do their jobs. Yet, there were always some victims that bothered them more than others. Maybe this was the case for Henry Pope.

Clay rose and sauntered to the small break room to pour more coffee in his cup, taking a sip before returning to drop back down in the chair. He needed it to keep awake on the drive home where Becca would have breakfast waiting.

"We haven't been able to locate her clothes. They're probably still at the crime scene, wherever that is. I need to get some sleep." He stood, downed the rest of his coffee and tossed his empty cup in the trash can. "I'll be back as quickly as I can. And cut Pope some slack. He's had a rough time the last few weeks. Remember, his wife left him."

"Damn! I meant to call him. I'll talk to him later." Jonas said.

"Do me a favor, don't. Pope doesn't want anyone to know. Jose told me. Now I've told you. Secrets around here are a bitch to keep." He turned to leave but stopped when Jonas added.

"Find the crime scene."

"If I can." That was the question, where had the victim been killed? They didn't have a clue.

"Before you leave, send Alfonso to Metro. Also, we'll need the victim's financial and phone records. We need to know everything we can learn about this woman's last hours. When you get back, take Caroline and get the appropriate search warrants. Also, keep trying to locate the victim's cell phone. As busy as she appeared to be, I'm sure she had one. I want to know as much about her as I would my own mother.

"The rest of the team can go back out to the victim's apartment building to talk to the manager and all the neighbors again. You know how apartment buildings are; there's usually a nosey neighbor who knows everything about everyone."

Jonas paused, as a thought hit him. "See if anyone checked the apartment dumpster. If someone found her purse, maybe they kept the money and credit cards and tossed the rest." He glanced at his watch. "As soon as Eppie gets here, we're going to see the doctor where Marilyn Heddrix worked. The sister said his name is Jack Donavan. I'm just curious as to whether he's the same Jack listed on her calendar for all those Friday nights. Also, tonight, have Fernandez check out the bar where she was last seen. See if the bartender knows anything and see if they have the security tape. A lot of bars install them now to prevent lawsuits."

"Will do. Think there was some hanky-panky activity with her boss?" Clay asked.

"Hell, she was a beautiful woman and doctors are known to cavort with their nurses," Jonas called, as Clay stopped at the door. After he left, Jonas muttered to himself. "A woman like that would be hard to resist." and picked up one of the photographs of the victim. Of course, she didn't look as beautiful now. She had been stunning, as was evident by the beauty of her twin. It was still disconcerting to view the picture of the deceased and know there was duplicate living on North Institute. A woman like that would be hard to forget. She was the type to get in a man's blood and make him jealous of anyone who looked at her. Was that the motive for her death? Jealousy? It was something to consider.

Nurses in doctor's offices made good money, not enough to afford the costly furniture in her apartment. The furnishings showed she had someone on the hook, someone with money. The fur rug had cost a mint, as well as the coverlet in the bedroom. The woman had expensive tastes, and some man satisfied her appetite. Jonas would bet money, it was the good doctor. It made him wonder about the doctor's wife, and what she might know. He'd find out shortly, as soon as Eppie came in.

He glanced at his watch, it was nearly eight-thirty in the morning. He rubbed the spot above the bridge of his nose where pressure was beginning to form. Hell, he shouldn't have a headache now. He and the team had worked close to forty hours straight with little sleep on a case just before this one, and they had managed. Maybe he needed more coffee and an Advil? He stood and headed for the conference room to see if Eppie was there.

She was usually in the office by now, unless her mother had taken a turn for the worse.

Her father had been gone for over fifteen years. Her mother, Rosa, was in Hospice. Her condition was not discussed in the office, yet everyone knew what Eppie was going through. It was only a matter of time for the poor woman.

The middle child, between two older brothers and two younger sisters, they kept her informed during her work day. Each morning from six until eight-thirty, she went to spend that time with her mother. Now, Jonas found her sitting at the long table staring at the board.

"How's your mother this morning?"

"A little worse," she said. "I can see her slipping away." She looked at him with tears in her eyes, "And, I can't do a thing to help her. The doctor keeps her medicated against the pain, but, the cancer is devouring her body. I doubt if she weighs ninety pounds. I hate that damn disease! You'd think with all the breakthroughs in medicine, they'd have found a cure or better treatment for pancreatic cancer." She snatched at her tears and straightened her shoulders.

"I'm sorry Eppie." Jonas rested a hand on her shoulder, offering what comfort he could.

She continued, her anger and frustration against an enemy she could not defeat were evident. "I guess they have to an extent. Look how long Patrick Swayze was able to fight off the disease. It got him too, and now it's going to take my mother." She clenched her jaw, flexing the muscle to keep her composure. "Sorry, Jonas, normally I have better control and can handle it. It's just today, she looks so frail, and I feel so helpless." Again, she swiped at the tears sliding down her cheeks and faced him, fighting back the overwhelming grief eating her insides. "What's happening on the case?" she asked.

"Are you sure you wouldn't rather go back to Hospice?"

She shook her head. "My sisters are there. They understand I need to work. I can't sit. I have to move. I'm only a phone call away and can be there within minutes. Now, where are we headed this morning?" She was eager to occupy her mind with anything other than the impending death of her mother.

Eppie had partnered with Jonas since her promotion to Sergeant. After high school, she had worked and gotten her associate degree at the junior college, then applied for a job with the police department and was hired. After attending the academy and being top in her class, she worked the streets. She worked her way up to detective and was assigned to his team with her promotion.

He couldn't have asked for a better partner. She always had his back and he hers. Plus, he was the only one she talked to about her mother. He knew all about her, the beatings by her father, how difficult her childhood had been, up until her junior year in high school.

One night her father, after beating on her mother, the boys and assaulting Eppie, calmly left the shack they lived in to buy more beer. He never returned. After that, their family life had improved. Her mother found a job cleaning houses for the rich people living around the

Broadmoor, plus doing alterations for a dress shop at night. Rosa had worked long hours to support her five children. The two boys had joined the military shortly after graduating high school and sent money home. Life for her mother had been good for many years.

Then eleven months ago, Rosa had been diagnosed with pancreatic cancer that had metastasized to her liver and possibly other organs. Her prognosis was nil. The time would come for Eppie to face her mother's death. Right now she needed to focus on something else, anything else.

"Have we heard from Metro?" she asked.

"Not yet," Jonas stated and stared at the sparse information on the crime board. A picture of the victim was held in place by a magnetic clip. The timeline near the bottom of the board listed only the date and approximate time the victim had gone missing. That information had been supplied by the sister.

According to the Coroner, the victim had died between two and four in the morning on Saturday. They also knew that Marilyn Heddrix had left Dawson's Bar at ten that Friday night and at least made it back to her apartment. That fact was established due to finding her car at the apartment complex.

The drive from Dawson's would have taken her not more than six to eight minutes. From ten-fifteen until her body was found left a lot of unaccounted for hours and too many questions. With luck, maybe the woman's employer would have a few answers.

"I want to drive the route from Dawson's to her apartment and see exactly how long it takes," he added. "Then we'll go talk with Marilyn's employer, Doctor

Jack Donavan. His clinic is close by." They left the conference room, Jonas grabbed his hat and with Eppie following, headed for his car.

Not a vehicle was to be seen in the parking spaces close to Dawson's Bar, behind the bowling alley. Jonas had been there before and knew that the tables circled the dance floor and stage. They served a stiff drink, and the actual bar area was along the back wall, and usually packed with customers. Right now it was closed.

He drove through the strip mall off Constitution Avenue. A Subway, a Magic Wok, a karate school and a flooring store comprised the other businesses. He wondered how long they would be operating with the economy in the financial mess it was in. Bars always seemed to thrive, and the last time he had put in an appearance, Dawson's was standing room only. They only hired the best bands and served the best food. He would hate to see it go under.

He drove slowly past the building then back out onto Circle Drive, driving east toward Academy and the victim's apartment. His guess of the drive time was close. It took ten minutes. Once leaving Dawson's, Marilyn would have been home by ten-fifteen. People should have been around, either coming home or going out. Someone had to have seen something.

He pulled out of the apartment complex and headed toward the doctor's office, which was only a short drive away on Academy. Plenty close enough for a quick nooner. Jonas wondered how often the doctor and Marilyn really met besides on Friday nights.

The Medical Arts building was a new red brick building. Other office spaces were for lease, or for sale. Tall glass windows offered a panoramic view of Pikes Peak and the Front Range, as the building sat on higher ground than the other businesses in the area.

People in the Springs, as a lot of the population called their city, could almost predict the weather by the mountain. If clouds formed over the Peak, it could mean rain or snow depending on the season. If the summit stayed clear, well, the city was known for lots of sunny days.

Jonas walked toward a pretty blonde receptionist, sitting behind a circular desk. When he asked for directions to Doctor Donavan's office, she looked up at him and smiled, then stated. "I'm so sorry. I thought his office staff had reached all his patients. The office is temporarily closed." She held the smile briefly. As the phone rang, she pushed a button and spoke into her headset. "Good morning, Medical Arts Building, would you hold please?" she pushed another button, and then returned her gaze back to the Detective.

Jonas presented his identification. "I need to speak with the building manager, if possible."

The young woman pushed another button and dialed a number. She waited a few seconds, then said, "Mr. Hodges, a policeman is here at my desk looking for Doctor Donavan. Would you come to speak to him?" She paused, listening. "Yes, I told him the offices are closed." Pause. "No, he asked for you." She disconnected the call. "He'll be right out," she said and connected to the person on hold.

A door behind the reception desk opened and a

short, thin young man with dark hair emerged. "Would you come to my office so we can speak in private?" They followed him down a short hallway to a large office with a Front Range view. "Now, how can I help you?"

"We're trying to locate Doctor Donavan," Eppie said, as they took a seat in the two chairs placed in front of the desk. A nameplate read George H. Hodges.

The man sat down and folded his hands on the desk. "As Linda explained, the doctor's office is closed until further notice."

"Can you tell us why?" Jonas asked.

"I'm sure you're aware that the doctor is missing. I understand from his wife that she has filed a Missing Person's Report." Hodges looked from one to the other.

Eppie kept her eyes focused on the man behind the desk. "No," she said softly, "we were not aware that he was missing." She removed her cell phone from her jacket pocket and turned away to place a call to Larry at STIC, speaking quietly into the phone.

Jonas leaned forward and shook the manager's hand. "Mr. Hodges, thank you for your time." He stood, and nodded to Eppie. She slowly followed him out of the building, stopping just outside the main entrance to complete the call.

She slipped into the passenger seat and turned toward him. "Well hell, don't that beat all? According to Larry, the wife did file a report late Monday afternoon. He gave me the home address. Do you want to go talk with the wife now or go back to the office?"

Jonas shook his head. "Not without asking

Hanover at Missing Persons to join us. Give him a call and see if he can find the time to go with us this morning or tomorrow. Also, let's not release the identity of the Heddrix woman until we find out what has happened to Doctor Donavan."

She nodded in agreement as Jonas drove west until he was several blocks from Morgan's street. He slowed his speed wondering if he should question the sister again about her twin's boss, then decided against the idea. He'd wait. They needed to get back to the office to catch up on paperwork and track down additional information on the case.

When Henry Pope saw the photograph of the first victim, he immediately recognized her as the woman in the bar, and as his doctor's nurse. He made a run for the bathroom and threw up his breakfast. At that moment, he was in a world of shit. The fact he couldn't remember much about Friday night now worried the hell out of him. Had he been so angry at his wife that he'd killed this woman?

The victim's death had been violent from what he'd seen in the picture. There had been times he'd wanted to smash in Shirley's face but controlled himself. Had he lost that tight reign he always maintained? God, he hoped not.

And the woman; he only knew her name as Marilyn. She was a flirt, and it was apparent something was going on between her and the doc. Henry wanted to tell what he knew but had no doubts he would become the prime suspect in the case. The only thing to do was wait and see what happened. Eventually, he would have to tell the Lieutenant, but for now, it was best to keep quiet. But, secrets never stayed hidden. If he had killed her, he'd deserve any punishment the court would dish out. That was not a bridge he could face right now.

Chapter Six

Wednesday

Morgan had never felt as alone as she did that morning at Anderson's Funeral Home. Standing in the display room viewing the selection of caskets, she strolled past the five styles, unsure which to pick. There was no one to guide her. Both parents were dead. Now Marilyn!

At least when their parents had died, she'd had her sister to share the task of burying them. Marilyn had been the one forced by circumstances to handle most of the arrangements. Morgan had been too numb, from losing them both at once, and unable to manage.

Now as then, all she wanted to do was find a dark corner and cry out all the pain tearing at her heart and knotting her insides. But, she couldn't. As much as she hated it, she had to endure the agony and arrange to bury her sister. So, she swallowed the tears, biting at her lower lip to keep back her sobs.

When she pointed to a plain deep bronze casket, Mr. Anderson gave her a sympathetic smile and then told her the price. It was too high, close to ten-thousand dollars. A stainless steel casket in tan, trimmed in a darker brown, with gold flowers embossed on each corner, was the least expensive.

It was closer to what she could afford, even though it still cost five-thousand dollars. That did not include the outer vault, in which the casket was to be placed. Her meager savings was going to be strained to cover the cost of the coffin. How was she going to afford the rest of the funeral?

At one point, when Mr. Anderson explained the other necessary services needed, and the cost of each, she had bit down so hard on her lip that it left the taste of blood on her tongue. She agreed to as much as she could afford; and as Marilyn had requested, remembered to tell the Funeral Director that the casket was to remain closed. By the time she was finished, the service was scheduled for Monday morning at ten, as Marilyn's body was not going to be released until Thursday.

She had tried to keep the expenses as low as possible; but still, she was going to have to shell out seven-thousand-nine-hundred dollars. All Morgan could do was dab the tears from her eyes and head for Evergreen Cemetery. She purchased a burial plot, a vault, and arranged for the opening and closing of the grave. The total funeral cost was staggering. Over ten-thousand dollars. How was she going to pay for it all? There were only six thousand dollars in her savings account. A loan on her house was a possible solution. Problem solved? Maybe? Unless her ex-husband would loan her the money. She'd left him a voice message that Marilyn was dead.

She had to laugh at that idea. Ask Andy to help her? No way! Whatever was necessary to bury her sister, she would do. But, she would not ask her ex-husband for help. Oh, he had called back, expressing how shattered he was about Marilyn. Of course, it was all about him. Not once did he ask how she was doing. That was Andy, selfish to the nth degree. She'd gotten off the phone as quickly as she could, without telling him when the funeral would be held. Decision made and with exhaustion riding her every move, she drove home in need of food and a cup of hot tea.

Back at the house, the tea and grilled cheese sandwich revived her somewhat, but she felt mentally fatigued, causing her eyelids to grow heavier by the second. Morgan curled up on the sofa and pulled an afghan over her. She was glad to escape from all the pain and sorrow for a time and just hoped she wouldn't dream of seeing her sister. In a matter of seconds, she was sound asleep.

Her wish was not to be granted. The sound of Marilyn's voice penetrated the fog in her brain and jerked her from sleep's sweet oblivion, ending her attempt to escape. Morgan kept her eyes closed, feigning sleep.

"My God, are you going to sleep your life away?" her twin ordered. "Open your eyes, Morgan. I know you heard me."

She felt a hard slap on her shoulder. She jumped, sat up, eyes open, and pissed off at her twin, who had parked her butt on her coffee table. Marilyn wore the gray T-shirt, and red underwear, her legs, and feet were still bare.

"Are you going to keep scaring the crap out of me?" Morgan fumed.

"Yes! As long as you try to ignore the fact that I'm here, I will." Marilyn leaned forward and stared hard at her sister. "You have to listen to me. I don't want to be here any more than you want to keep seeing me, but I don't have any control over it." She stood and paced back and forth for a moment, chewing on her thumbnail.

Letting her hand drop, she stopped and demanded. "You didn't tell the cops what I told you about Jack being taken the same night as me, did you?"

"Jack? You never said it was Jack. Besides, all you said was that someone else had been abducted; you didn't say who. How was I supposed to know who you meant?"

"That doesn't matter now. Did you tell the police?"

For a ghost, her sister looked pissed.

"No, I didn't tell them," Morgan snapped back. "They're already wondering about me from the little I've told that detective about us. And you want me to tell them your boss' body is out there. Do you even know if he's dead?" Morgan threw back the afghan and slipped on her shoes. "And can't you put some clothes on?"

"Okay! Okay! But, you have to call that cop and tell him to find Jack." Marilyn's eyes glistened. Again, she plopped back down onto the coffee table. "I'm sorry, but I can't leave him out there for the wild animals to chew on. He's in the Garden of the Gods, I think, or will be." She stopped and frowned. "The only problem is I don't know exactly where." She looked at Morgan and brightened. "Tell the cops that he won't be far from where they found me."

Seeing the skeptical look on her sister's face, "Pleasssssssse! I really loved him Morgan, and he loved me. He was going to leave his wife, and we were going to be married." There was a catch in her voice, almost a sob. "I finally find the right man for me, and it costs us both our lives."

Morgan sat up straighter and folded the afghan as she cocked her head and said. "You were killed because of Jack Donavan?"

"Not because of him, but for some reason, I think it had to do with us seeing each other." She shook her head, looking confused. "I'm not sure. It's just this feeling I get that I know the man who abducted us. There was this odor. It was odd. I know I've smelled it before, but I can't place it."

Morgan pressed her for more details. "Was it a man's cologne?"

"God, I don't know. It was only a faint whiff, and then I was out. When I came to . . . ." She stopped, her eyes widening and her hands clenched close to her chest in fear. "I can't think about it. It was horrible. I don't want to remember how I died, Sis."

"It's all right. You don't have to. I know what you went through. Put it out of your mind. Concentrate on what you remember about the person who took you." Morgan started to reach out to take her sister's hand, but stopped, remembering what her twin had said about touching her. Was that still true, considering that Marilyn had slapped her awake? She would have to find out.

"That's just it. That's all I remember. But, you have to go to the police, Morgan. Please, don't forget. Help them find Jack." Marilyn gave her twin a sad smile and said, "You can wake up now." And then she was gone.

Morgan continued waiting to wake and find the subtle trace of her sister actually visiting. Then she realized that this time Marilyn was wrong, it hadn't been a dream; she was awake and sitting upright on the sofa. Had she actually been asleep or awake and saw her sister? That was impossible; she refused to believe in ghosts. Sure, as twins they had this incredible bond, but neither of them had ever seen a ghost. Now, she had a feeling that she needed to start. Because she knew her twin would not rest until she did what she had asked. God, it was all so crazy. She glanced at the mantel where she had placed the detective's business cards.

Suddenly there was a buzzing in her ears, and she shook her head trying to dispel the low noise. The sound changed, as if someone was now close to her head, and whispering. Then, she distinctly heard the words, "Call the detective."

She rose and retrieved the cards. How was that detective going to react? No doubt very suspicious. How was she going to convince him that she wasn't some nut case? That was not going to be easy either. Tapping the business card against her thumb and then, a mimic of her sister, Morgan chewed on her fingernail as she considered what to do. Decision made, she grabbed her purse and headed out the front door.

Detective Winston Hanover was the epitome of the professional man. Dressed in a gray business suit, blue shirt, red tie, and black shoes, he parked his Nissan and waited for Eppie and Jonas. They parked behind him in the circular driveway.

As he got out of his SUV, Jonas glanced at his watch. It was ten-thirty on the nose. One glance at the house was enough to impress on anyone that the home belonged to a person of wealth. He glanced at Winston.

Tension hunched Hanover's shoulders as he closed his vehicle door. From the initial reports, the case had become high profile due to the status of the doctor. It seemed that Doctor Jackson Donavan was a well-known physician in the community. Important enough, that when the wife had called the Mayor on Monday evening, the Mayor, in turn, had phoned the Chief and on down the line to him. Now he had been put on the spot for instant results.

Lord knows, Hanover had been there before and was thankful that even the Mayor, Chief and his Commander knew it didn't work that way. An immediate phone call was placed to Mrs. Donavan to set up a time for an interview. It was odd, he thought, that she had insisted she was too distraught to see him last night and set the appointment for ten-thirty this morning. The good news was that the media was not yet aware of the doctor's missing status. The story on the TV broadcast simply stated an unidentified woman's body had been found in the Garden of the Gods and the police were investigating it as a suspicious death. Nothing was mentioned about the doctor.

Winston brushed at his suit trousers in case a speck of dust might have attached itself to the fabric, adjusted his tie and straightened his shirt, then positioned the Slim Pen in his pocket, which was already set on record. His black leather shoes were polished to a military sheen, so he braced himself as he walked toward the large stone two-story dwelling with massive front doors of wood and reinforced lead glass.

Eppie also was a little awed by the vastness of the home. She estimated that the place was over ten thousand square feet. Her mother's small house of thirteen hundred square feet would fit in a tiny corner of this massive building.

The idea of having to clean this place, like her mother had done in other homes for years, made her cringe. Of course, anyone who could afford this house had the money for a full-time staff to keep it clean. She glanced over at Jonas who returned her look with an arched eyebrow and a shake of his head. A smile curved her lips as they continued to follow Hanover toward the front door.

Winston had called ahead to make sure Mrs. Donavan knew he was on his way. She stood waiting for them in the open doorway, impeccably dressed in dark blue slacks, matching pumps and a crisp white blouse with a ruffled collar extending down the front to her waist. An attractive, petite woman, she was no more than five-foot-two inches tall, with blonde hair and large blue eyes. He expected to see a woman filled with anxiety, or at least a grave concern for her missing husband. Instead, he was surprised by the greeting they received.

"Well, have you found that son of a bitch yet?" she demanded, standing with her hands fisted on her hips, then turned and walked into the house, leading the way into a large foyer with its crystal chandelier and curved mahogany stairway to the upper floor. They followed her toward the back of the house and down two steps into a twenty-five-foot open living room.

Each glanced at the other. The room's floor was covered in a cream carpet and a twenty-foot ceiling sporting a massive stone fireplace reaching the full height of the interior wall. Mrs. Donavan motioned toward two chocolate brown overstuffed sofas which faced each other before the fireplace. They were separated by an oversize wooden coffee table.

A deer antlers circular chandelier dropped from the soaring beamed ceiling and only added to the impression of the room's height. Tall wooden floor lamps offered light for reading or just sitting down to enjoy a drink and a hot fire in the winter. A Baby Grand piano, the black lacquer finish gleaming in the morning light, stood silently at one end of the room. The floor to ceiling windows offered a panoramic view of the surrounding landscape.

The French doors, on either side of the fireplace, were open and led to a large deck overlooking the back patio, and a view of the city spread out on the eastern plain. The mid-morning breeze coming off Cheyenne Mountain made the heavy maroon drapes flutter and offered a breath of fresh air.

Hell, Winston thought, even the air, scented by lavender, smelled expensive. The three detectives took a seat on one sofa, while Phyllis Donavan sat facing across from them on the other.

"Well," she gestured, leaning slightly forward to stare at them. Suddenly, she clasped her hands together, sat back and glanced down for a moment in thought, then looked up at the individuals staring at her. "I'm sorry for my outburst at the front door, but I have been worried sick about Jack and anger is my way of coping. It's not like him to stay away for the entire weekend. That's why I filed the Missing Person's Report."

Winston introduced himself and his companions. "I'm Detective Hanover, and these are Detectives Black and Ortiz. First, let me say that the department will do everything we can to locate your husband. I apologize beforehand, but in order to find the doctor, I have to ask a lot of personal questions." He waited and could see the emotional stress had created worry lines across her forehead.

"Fine," she said, feeling a flush creep over her face. Now all their secrets would be exposed. She couldn't hide the truth any longer. Phyllis placed her hands in her lap and braced herself.

Winston started slowly with the usual question to put her at ease. "Would you tell us the last time you saw Doctor Donavan?" His tone voiced the empathy he felt for the fears of all the people he had ever interviewed. Too often their worst fears came true. This woman was a close friend of the Mayor so he would tread carefully, if possible, so as not to cause her further pain with his questions.

"At breakfast Friday morning, before he went to the clinic," she said, as her eyes glistened with tears. Hands visibly trembling, she picked at the fabric of her slacks, removing imagined lint, her calm, but angry demeanor, starting to crumble.

"Would you mind telling us how he was

dressed?" Winston asked.

"He was wearing his navy blue Huntsman suit I bought him in England last year for his birthday, a white shirt, navy socks and shoes, and, oh yes, his gold Rolex watch. He was going into the clinic until noon, then check on a few patients in the hospital." She hesitated for a moment, then added, "The office is only open until noon on Fridays."

The fact that the doctor was a fashion horse crossed Winston's mind. Huntsman suits were not cheap. He had priced them on the Internet so knew they were out of his price range. Hanover had to admit he was a bit of a clothes horse himself, taking pride in looking professional at all times. Suits and shirts that would never go out of fashion were the only types he purchased. A sideways glance at Jonas in his white shirt, tan leather jacket, slacks, and cowboy boots made him appreciate his own wardrobe. The man looked entirely out of place in the luxurious surroundings.

The Lieutenant was known for his Texas roots and cowboy ways. A hard ass in many ways, he was damn good at his job. The man was not about to change his appearance to suit any job. You either accepted Jonas Black as he was or stayed out of his path. As far as a case was concerned, everything was black or white with the man. Gray areas didn't exist when it came to murder.

Personally, Winston believed in trying to stay on everyone's good side. Favors begot favors. It made for a better working relationship as well, but if necessary, he could stand his ground.

Phyllis watched the detective. Why wasn't he taking any notes? The other man sat with a notepad resting on one knee. Maybe he was keeping track of the details. It didn't matter. She just didn't want their dirty laundry in the papers for everyone to read. She made a mental note to call the Mayor again and make sure that didn't happen.

"Did he seem upset or anything?" Winston asked.

"No. It was Friday, so he was in a good mood." Her expression held a deep sadness that radiated from within.

This was not a happy woman, Hanover thought and wondered why. He guessed her age in her mid-fifties, but she was physically fit, and well-endowed with looks. He found her attractive and was sure many men would also. But still, she might end up a suspect, so beautiful or not, he had questions which needed answers. "Was there something special about Friday?" Winston asked, his curiosity piqued.

"He usually went out on Friday nights."

"Always?" Jonas blurted. He knew the infidelity rate among physicians, but Phyllis Donavan was a beautiful woman. He found it difficult to understand leaving this woman to be with another one. But then, Marilyn Heddrix would be hard for any man to resist, especially if the good doctor was not really in love with his wife.

Eppie tried to concentrate on what was being said, but her mind kept drifting to her mother. Was she having a good day? Was her pain being controlled? Her cell phone vibrated in her pocket. She removed it and checked the caller ID. It was her sister. She quickly rose, excused herself with a quick explanation, "Sorry, I have to take this." and left the room.

Jonas nodded in understanding and watched as she hurried toward the front entrance. The call had to be vital for Eppie to leave during an interview. He only hoped it wasn't bad news. He looked at Hanover. Winston had agreed to their posing questions now and then. Since Jonas knew the detective would obtain all the pertinent information he needed, he refrained from asking his own questions. Instead, observed Phyllis Donavan's reactions.

"Was this unusual for your husband to go out alone on Friday night?" Hanover nodded at Jonas, then looked back at the doctor's wife.

Head held high, Phyllis frowned. "My husband and I have been having problems of late. I objected to his routine absence every Friday night for the past six months." She paused and looked at the two people staring at her before continuing with her explanation. "Jack is younger than I am by nine years. He has a woman he visits on Friday night, some whore who works as a nurse in his office. He usually returns home Saturday morning claiming he spent the night at the hospital. I help keep his lie alive by not letting him know I am not fooled. Only this time, he never came home."

"I hate to have to ask this, but do you know the name of the woman he's seeing? We'll interview her and see if she knows where he might be." Marilyn Heddrix's name had not been released to the press as yet, so Mrs. Donavon probably didn't know she had been murdered. If she knew her, then Phyllis Donavan would become the primary suspect in the murder case.

She was almost defiant as she admitted. "As I said, I am not a fool. Her name is Marilyn Heddrix, and she lives at North Carefree. A few months ago, I hired a private detective to follow my husband. That's how I found out about his other woman. Once the detective confirmed my suspicions, I let him go."

The two detectives exchanged a quick glance. "Have you ever met this woman?" Hanover asked. "We'd also like the name and phone number of the man you hired." He wasn't ready to reveal that the Heddrix woman was dead. Gradually, he would get around to that and find out what part the wife might have played in the crime. He already had doubts about her involvement. She didn't seem the type, but Hanover was well aware that looks could be deceiving and a rejected woman was unpredictable.

Phyllis Donavan's eyes narrowed, and she stared at the detective. "Oh yes. I saw her every time I visited the clinic. It was more than I could take, so I stopped going there." That sad smile again curved her lips. "My dear husband never asked me why I stopped coming to visit him at the office. I guess it was easier for him not to have to worry I might catch the two of them together." She looked at her hands, still clasped together, and then back at Hanover. "I'll have to find the private detective's card and call you with that information," she said.

"That would be fine," Hanover said. He was almost hesitant to ask the next question because he didn't want the woman to think she was being accused of anything. The story of Marilyn Heddrix being the murder victim could be on the news at any time. To do his job, he had to ask, "Mrs. Donavan, when was the last time you saw Marilyn Heddrix?"

If she admitted to seeing the victim recently, she would become the prime suspect. She might not be physically able to commit the murder herself, but she could have hired it done.

"Not since I found out she was sleeping with my husband. Why do you ask?" She met each of their gazes with a slight frown on her face. Phyllis' suspicion was aroused. "Why are you asking?" she insisted.

"Because, Marilyn Heddrix was found murdered yesterday morning," Winston said.

All blood appeared to drain from Phyllis' face, and her eyes widened in shock. "Oh my God!" and then she gasped, "Was Jack with her?" Dread spread across her face as she waited for an answer.

"No, Mrs. Donavan, we don't know where your husband is." The detective dreaded his next question. "I apologize, but I have to ask. Would you tell us where you were last Friday night and early Saturday morning?"

Phyllis was no dummy. "I was at the Broadmoor for a charity fundraiser for autistic children until after midnight." A touch of fear showed in her eyes, and she clenched her hands together. Then it dawned on her the implication of his question. Anger replaced the fear.

She stood up and walked around the sofa, leaned forward, and braced her hands on the back. "Where is my husband, damn it. Is he dead too? What am I supposed to think after you tell me the Heddrix woman has been murdered? And, if you had it in your head he was running off with that bitch, think again."

His manner calm and steady, so as not to agitate her further, Winston said, "Mrs. Donavan, I'm not trying to upset you. I have to ask uncomfortable questions to fully do my job. That's why I have to know why you say your husband would not leave you for this other woman? Even you admit she was beautiful, and he's been having this affair for going on six months."

With a sweep of her arm, she encompassed the grandeur of the room. "Because Jack is not about to give up all this! If you think Jack has all the money, again you are very wrong. It's all my money, not his. The lifestyle he enjoys so much, including that clinic of his, is provided by me and my money, not the other way around.

"Jack makes a decent living with his family practice," she continued, "but nothing like he enjoys with me. Otherwise, in this economy, he'd just be another struggling doctor working to keep his practice going, what with all the people out of work. That has affected insurance companies as well as hospitals. The money doctors used to make has dropped dramatically. Obamacare has helped somewhat, but not enough. He's also aware that if he leaves me, his social standing is gone. I wield power in that department, and he knows it. I would financially ruin him.

"So you see, Jack is not about to give up all he has with me for a meager living with that whore." She walked around the sofa and plopped back down. "I resent your implications. Now is that all, or would you like a list of the people at that benefit Friday night?" and with almost a sneer she added, "Or you can just ask the

Mayor. He was there and will verify the time I left." As far as she was concerned, the interview was over.

Phyllis stood and walked toward the front entrance. Hanover and Jonas immediately rose and followed. "Now, find my husband." Her anger was evident as she ushered them out.

Hanover stopped in the doorway and turned to face Phyllis. "Mrs. Donavan, I again apologize if I've caused you any more stress." Winston took out his business card and handed it to her. "Do not hesitate to call me night or day if you have questions. We will do everything in our power to locate your husband. And, again I apologize for any trouble or worry I might have caused you."

He offered his hand and was amazed when she took it. He held it for a moment longer than he should have but didn't care. She was a beautiful woman in pain, and he let his feelings show in his eyes as he looked at her. Her expression conveyed appreciation, and she smiled at him as he said, "Don't forget, you call me if you think of anything else that might help us or if you have a question."

"Thank you," she said, grateful for his offer, all her anger replaced by intense worry.

Hanover knew a betrayed woman was deadly, and Phyllis Donavan had made it clear she was unhappy with the man she had married. What woman wouldn't be with a jerk like that? He guessed the husband was stupid. He had a good woman and ignored her.

Hanover walked out into the sunlight as Phyllis Donavan closed the door behind him. He faced Jonas. "Did you find out what you wanted to know?"

"Yeah," Jonas muttered. "I doubt if she had anything to do with the Heddrix woman's death. She was too surprised by the news. I'll keep her on my list, just in case. I'll see you later, and thanks for your help." Jonas hurried to his vehicle where Eppie waited.

Winston made a note to give Phyllis Donavan a call in the morning for the name of her private detective. He was certain Jonas would want to sit in on the interview when he talked with the man. After starting the engine, Winston waved to Eppie and drove away. He would contact the Lieutenant later with any new details he could find out about the doctor.

Eppie sat looking distraught, with tears in her eyes. As soon as Jonas slipped behind the wheel, he asked. "Is your mother worse?"

"Yes. I have to get to Hospice. Drop me at my car, and I'll call you later with an update. I may not be back for a few days." She wiped at the tears as they rolled down her cheeks. "My sister said the doctors believe it's only a matter of hours now."

She clutched her cell phone in her right hand as if it was a lifeline holding her mother back from the grave. No matter how much she didn't want it to happen, it was beyond the control of anyone but God. And, the Lord knew how hard she had prayed for her mother to be spared. It was inevitable, and she was being forced to face that fact.

Jonas pulled out of the driveway and turned on his flashing light, speeding the short distance down Lake Avenue and then north on Nevada until he reached the police department. He pulled into the parking lot and dropped Eppie at her car and waited until she drove away. What words could be offered to ease the loss his partner was going to feel? He had none when he of all people should. With that thought in mind, he walked toward the entrance of the building and entered, leaving all the sunshine behind.

Chapter Seven

Wednesday

The day was heating up as Morgan parked her car at the curb. The morning had been a cool blessing after the heat of yesterday. The temperature had reached ninety by three o'clock, and it was predicted to be even hotter today. Even the air smelled hot.

Another dry summer was not what Colorado needed with the threat of more wildfires. She hoped tomorrow would bring rain and cool off the afternoon. If not, at least they were blessed with cool nights, even in the summer. It made for good sleeping. Not that she had been getting much sleep since Friday night.

As she was driving up, she had seen Lieutenant Black enter the building's main entrance. Now she sat staring out the passenger window, contemplating what she was about to do.

How did Marilyn think she could just walk into the police department and say to a detective, "Oh, by the way, there's a dead body of a man in the Garden of the Gods?" How was that for sounding nuts? Her sister was crazy to think she wouldn't be the number one suspect with a story like that. The police would want to know how she knew, and how she was involved. What was she going to say, my sister told me?

"Oh, God," she muttered, and crossed her arms on the steering wheel, then rested her forehead on the back of her hands. It was too much. Tears welled in her eyes.

She had that hard empty hole in her chest again.

A silly rhyme from their childhood flitted through her mind, "All the King's horses and All the King's men" couldn't put her sister back together again. Marilyn was broken forever. They had shared that silly saying as children when things went wrong. Right now, things were as bad as they could get.

Morgan turned her head and again looked at the entrance. She couldn't do it. No matter how much she wanted to help Marilyn, she couldn't go in that building and tell that detective to look for another body. When she began to pull away from the curb, she glanced in her rearview mirror in time to see Lieutenant Black hurry out of the building and stop at the curb to stare after her.

As soon as she arrived home, she tossed her purse on the coffee table and hurried to the kitchen to check the voicemail on the house phone. Just as she feared, there was a message from the detective. He had seen her drive away and wondered if she had anything she wanted to discuss with him. Oh yes, she had something to tell him, but she had no idea how to explain it.

She dug his card from her purse and sat on the sofa, continuing to tap the card against her hand, trying to decide what to do. She went as far as getting her cell phone but still didn't make a move to punch in his number. Then, without warning and no buzzing this time, came Marilyn's voice close to her ear, "Call him!"

Morgan jumped, dropped her cell phone, and slid off the sofa onto the floor.

"Damn it, Marilyn," she yelled, just as a knock sounded at the front door. Hurriedly, she got to her feet. Through the window, she saw the detective, hat in hand, standing on the front porch. Taking a deep breath, she steeled herself and opened the door.

"Come in, Lieutenant. I was going to call you, but you saved me that chore. Where's Detective Ortiz?"

A smile softened the hard planes of his face. "She's unavailable today, but I wanted to come by and see if you would give me some more information about your sister."

She had to admit he was not a bad looking man. His high cheekbones gave him a lean appearance, his strong jaw line, square chin, and straight nose completed his good looks. But, there was an air about him that suggested a determination in him, like a wolf on the hunt, ravenous for answers. Morgan had no doubt he would not stop searching until he had an answer for every question.

Feeling short next to his imposing six-foot-three-inches, he towered over her five-foot-six height. He was muscular as if he had known hard physical labor. Under different circumstances, she might have been attracted to him, but he frightened her a little, making her nervous about being alone with him. Even though he appeared friendly, she was sure he had suspicions about her.

"Have a seat," she said, indicating the brown leather chair facing the sofa. She sat down and waited.

He took a seat, hat in hand, glancing around as if uncomfortable being there alone. He placed his Stetson on the coffee table, out of the way. "First, I wanted to check on you and see how you're doing," He explained. "Having a relative murdered is not the same as losing someone to an illness. It takes a heavy toll on a family, all the unanswered questions. The fact your sister was your twin must be even more difficult for you. I wanted to be sure you're all right."

Morgan could see the real concern in his eyes and his voice was gentle. She looked down at her hands, where she had been picking off her nail polish. "Truthfully, Lieutenant," she said, and met his gaze, "I doubt if I will ever get over this, but thank you for asking about me. I'm not good at handling a lot of sympathy right now." She shook her head. "I'm hanging on. So, I need you to find my sister's killer. That will help me the most."

Morgan clenched her fists so tightly her fingernails dug into her palms. She slowly relaxed them and took a deep breath, fighting to control all the pain and anguish boiling inside of her.

"Okay, I can do that," he said, a little stiffly, "but having someone you love murdered, in such a brutal way, strikes you in the gut and leaves you gasping for air. You feel helpless and riddled with guilt. All that's left is a lot of unanswered questions of why that person had to die. There isn't any answer that will ever make sense to you. I know. I've been there." God, he hadn't meant to say all that, but there was more to be said, so he continued. "I'm fully committed to finding justice for your sister." His eyes narrowed, as he continued, "That's why I'm here. I want your help, need your help. But, make no mistake about it, I will find this killer and put that SOB in jail, or in the ground." He took a breath and looked straight into her eyes, "So now, I need to know everything about your sister," he explained, his smile gone, but the sympathy remained. "The more I know of her habits, the places she went, her likes and dislikes, the better chance I'll have of catching her murderer." That was the primary reason, he admitted to himself, but in the process, he would learn more about the surviving twin, Morgan. And that was not a bad thing.

He found Morgan Jansen fascinating, maybe a little bit nuts, claiming to communicate with her dead sister. She was definitely different from any woman he had ever known. He had to admit he was drawn to her, and he'd not been seriously attracted to a woman since Kelly.

Taken aback by the determination in his voice, Morgan stammered. "I'm sorry. It's just that I don't know what all I can tell you." She was close to tears, and that was not going to help the detective with his case. Abruptly, she rose and headed to the kitchen. "I could use a cup of coffee," she called over her shoulder. "I'm sure you could too. I'll be right back," and left him sitting alone. Fixing the coffeepot gave her time to regain her composure.

She leaned back against the counter and tried to think. The detective wanted to know about Marilyn. How much should she tell him? How much did she really know about her sister's life over the last few years, especially the last six months? They had grown so far apart, she doubted if she knew enough to help.

The coffee finished, she took down two white mugs from the cupboard and filled them. She placed the cups on a tray, with a bowl of sugar and a pitcher of cream, and carried it to the living room.

"Would you mind clearing the coffee table for me?" she asked and waited as Jonas removed his hat, dropped it on the floor, and pushed the books to one side, out of the way. She sat down on the sofa, poured a generous amount of cream into one of the cups, leaned back and waited for the questions she knew were coming. "So, please, tell me what you want to know."

Jonas stirred sugar in the remaining cup and took a drink. The coffee was hot and mellow, not like the brand they used at the department which had a sharp and bitter taste. No, this was a smooth blend and tasted great. He savored the flavor for a second, then said, "I looked you and your sister up on Google as you suggested. It took a while, but I finally found you, the Dorchester twins. Am I right? I also found your website for your stained glass products."

"That was us," she admitted, with a frowned. "Did you check out my Facebook page as well? All it has on it is about my stained glass designs."

He looked guilty. "I saw that, but that's part of my job to investigate everyone involved in a murder. I also read what was on the Internet about you and your sister helping to find that boy." He paused and stared at her.

She cocked her head to one side and returned his skeptical expression. "Of course you didn't believe any of it, did you?"

He didn't answer immediately figuring she'd met a lot of disbelievers in her life. "I think you believe it," he said and watched a flash of irritation cross her face. He had not meant to start off their conversation this way.

But, he had to understand if what he had read was true. Were the two girls able to do what the report claimed, or was it faked as he believed? "Make me understand about you and your sister. I really want to." Jonas sincerely meant it.

"There's not a lot I can explain," Morgan said, "because I don't know. She was older than me by two minutes. Even so, Marilyn and I were so bonded because we were identical twins. Somehow we always knew where each other was and what was happening. Sometimes, we knew other things, but not always. We couldn't turn it on and off. It was what it was, a connection because we had originally been one. She was the other part of me, as I was for her." She placed her half-empty cup on the tray and leaned forward clasping her hands together.

"You're not going to be able to understand because you're not a twin. This bond exists between fraternal twins as well, but I don't think it's as strong. So please, accept that it existed between Marilyn and me, and let it go. I have had to deal with this most of my life, and I don't want to anymore." She leaned back and stared at him, waiting for an onslaught of personal questions she knew he wanted to ask. So his reply surprised her.

"Okay, I'll try not to bring up the subject again," he said, feeling relief not having to address the issue again. Crossing his long legs, he removed his Slim Pen from his pocket with a notepad and positioned the pen so it could record all of the conversations. "Now, tell me about your sister. Did you know her friends?"

"Thank you," she said, "and I will hold you to your word. As for my sister's friends, I didn't know them. I've met Debbie Clark and Alice Evans only because they worked in the doctor's office. Any others, I wouldn't know who they were. My sister and I did not run in the same crowd. We were the opposite of each other. I like peace and quiet, and Marilyn . . ." Morgan paused.

She didn't want to give the wrong impression about her sister to the detective. But, the truth would come out, or so they claimed. So it was best, to be honest. "Marilyn liked to party and have a good time. She used to say that life was too short, and she wasn't going to miss a minute of enjoying herself. And she didn't." She pondered for a moment, then said, "I wonder if she knew she was going to die so young? If she did, I never felt it. Marilyn was stronger than I am and could block me on occasions. I was never successful in doing that to her."

He arched an eyebrow at her mention again of their connection but didn't say anything. Jonas knew there had been trouble between them. Morgan had stated she had not spoken to her sister in over a month. That had to be because they had had a fight. "What caused the rift between the two of you?"

Once more, there would be no sense in lying. If the police interviewed Andy, her ex-husband, they would find out the answer. "She pretended to be me and slept with my husband."

Ouch! Jonas thought, trying not to show his surprise at her statement. He had heard of twins switching places as a joke. But, that was carrying a joke too far. "How did that make you feel?"

"What do you think?" she glared at him. "I was mad as hell. I stopped speaking to Marilyn. What would you have done, been all forgiving? I don't think so." She studied him. "I think you would have killed the bastard!" As her anger subsided, only heartbreaking sadness remained. "I left my husband and filed for divorce. Him, I never had to see again. I couldn't cut myself off from my sister. That would have been like cutting out half of my heart. Besides, she was all I had left."

"When did Marilyn sleep with your husband?" If it was recent, then that could be a motive.

God, Morgan didn't want to dredge all of it up again. "It happened a little over a year ago." She thought for a moment, then added, "I didn't have my sister killed over sleeping with my husband if that's what you think. He wasn't worth it."

"Then why did you stop speaking to her only month ago?" Her sister's betrayal was not something to be casually dismissed. What could be worse than that to cause the silence between them?

Morgan gave a deep sigh of frustration. "We'd been fighting off and on since the day I caught her with Andy. Marilyn was like a child in some ways. She never wanted to face the consequences of her actions. She wanted me to forgive her. I couldn't. Her betrayal was too raw. I'd had enough of the fighting." Basically, what she said was true. All the defending excuses and arguments from her husband and Marilyn had been exhausting. No words could excuse what they had done. Andy knew it was Marilyn he was screwing.

She stared at her hands for a second. "I stopped answering the phone when my sister called. That is something I deeply regret."

Jonas could understand her regret. He wanted to rule out Morgan as a suspect, and her explanation for not speaking to her sister was understandable. Still, there was something she wasn't saying, and he wondered what she was hiding. "What's your ex-husband's full name? We'll want to talk to him."

Morgan scowled and shook her head. "Don't even consider him as a suspect. It would be a waste of your time."

"Why do you say that?"

"It would be ludicrous to think that Andy would ever hurt Marilyn. Because, my ex-husband considers himself a lover, not a fighter, as the saying goes. I know it's a cliché, but it's the way he is. In the few short years of our marriage, which numbered three and a half, we never had an argument. The few times I got mad, Andy just walked away refusing to confront our problems. Only after I left him did he want to discuss his actions. His, not my problems with our marriage! Andrew Jansen is a self-centered rat. He still lives in our old house in Village Seven. You check him out, and you'll understand what I mean."

"Okay, who do you think might have had a motive for killing your sister?" He stared at her and waited for her reaction. She returned his gaze.

"I think it was the wife of her lover, Jack."

"You knew about her having an affair with a

married man?" This was a surprise because the wife had said the affair had started six months ago and Morgan supposedly hadn't spoken to her sister for a month, so how did she know? He doubted if the sister would have told her. Marilyn would not have wanted Morgan to know anything about an affair after causing the breakup of her marriage. No, that was something she would have kept a secret.

Oh God, Morgan thought, now comes the tricky part. How was she going to explain this? She rubbed the sides of her face and pushed her hair back. Clasping her hands at the back of her neck, she grimaced and said, "Because my sister told me so?"

"And when was that exactly?" He could tell she was still hiding something, so he kept pushing when she hesitated. "Go ahead. Tell me."

Morgan took a deep breath and plunged in. "Here's the thing. I know you don't believe we have this bond, but we do. And I don't want to tell you this, but I have to. You're going to think I'm crazier than you do already, and should be committed, or make me your prime suspect in my sister's death. I would never harm my sister. I had a dream about Marilyn."

Damn, she thought, I'm going to be screwed with this admission, but she had promised. So she went on to explain the details of her dream, all the while watching a combination of amazement, then doubt played across the detective's features. When she got to the part about Jack being abducted, his expression changed to one of intense interest.

"And where did your sister say we could find this Jack?" If the doctor had been taken the same night, then he had been on his way to, or at Marilyn's apartment.

She hated this! Hated it! Hated it! But she answered the detective, "Marilyn said he's somewhere in the Garden of the Gods too."

An explosive "Damn it!" came from Jonas, just as his cell phone rang. He excused himself and answered it. He stared hard at her, as he listened to the voice on the other end, then abruptly ended the call, returning the phone to his pocket. He grabbed his hat from the floor and said, "I have to go. Please keep yourself available for more questions."

From the expression on his face, she knew. "They've found Jack, haven't they?"

"I can't comment. But stay available." He quickly walked out the front door, closing it behind him. She watched him through the window as he opened the driver's door and slid behind the steering wheel. The engine roared to life, and he made a rapid U-turn, then drove away fast with siren blaring, heading west.

Henry Pope rolled out of bed with a throbbing head. On his way home, he'd purchased a bottle of scotch intending on only having one drink. But, from the way his head hurt, that didn't happen, plus the pounding on his front door wasn't helping either. He pulled on his pants and stumbled downstairs to confront the intrusion. When he opened the door, he was surprised to see his partner, Jose, standing there with a McDonald's cup in either hand. Without saying a word, he entered and pushed past Henry.

"My God," Fernandez said, "You stink of booze." He handed one cup to Henry. "Drink that, and then get in the shower. Jonas called. We have another body. If the Lieutenant gets a whiff of booze on you, a hangover isn't the only trouble you'll have. I'll wait for you, so drink up and get on the move, or we'll be late."

Henry stared at Fernandez wanting to dispute the accusations, but couldn't. Coffee in hand, he hurried to shower, then shave and dress. Twenty minutes later, he descended the stairs looking much better. Aftershave helped to hide any remaining odor of liquor.

When Jose got a whiff of the cologne, he said, "At least you smell better. What is that spicy stuff?"

The night's events once again a fog in his brain, "Lagerfeld," Henry answered, and followed his partner out the door wondering what forgotten surprises were in store for him to discover. His shoulder seemed sorer this morning, and there had been a couple of rips in his shirt, but no scratches on his arms.

Chapter Eight

Wednesday

"Son of a bitch!" exploded from Jonas. He stared at the sprawled body just off the paved trail. It was partially hidden from view by the scrub brush near the steps leading to the north path away from the Three Graces. The body had not been there on Monday, of that he was sure. They would have seen it or smelled it.

Jonas smeared mentholated balm under his nose and stooped to take a closer look. The injuries were consistent with that of the first victim, both knees destroyed, also the elbows, shoulders and last, the killing blow to the head. As with Marilyn, there were restraint burns around both wrists and ankles. He had no doubt that this was Jack Donavan. Christ, he thought, how was he going to explain this to the Chief and the Mayor? They had found the doctor all right. The only problem, he was dead.

Then there was the wife, he was dreading that as well. He'd call Hanover, and they could make the notification together if he wanted. That way he could find out more about the doctor and his habits. It was vital to trace the victim's movements up until the time of his death.

Most murders were not random, and he was sure this one wasn't either. The fact that the victims knew each other was not what he needed to find out. How did the killer know Marilyn and Doctor Donavan? They would take a look at all his patients and her friends. Maybe one would stand out.

He stood up as Clay approached. Jacks and his assistants had arrived and were waiting to remove the body. CSI did the usual grid search of the area with photos and video. He was surprised when Clay found the impression of half a shoe print and a few threads from some fabric on a branch. The techs made a mold of the shoe print, but in the soft soil, the edges were fuzzy, and Jonas was not sure it would be of any help. The fibers were carefully removed from the bush and dropped in an evidence envelope. At least they had something this time. It was something, more than they had with the first victim.

The DNA on the blood from the branch was not back yet. He'd call and see if the lab could speed up the results, considering the fact the doctor was a friend of the Mayor.

After a two hour search of the site, Jonas called out, "Clay, have Caroline bag his hands and release him to Jacks. Since Eppie is still out, she can go to autopsy this time. You lucked out again." He had to smile at the relieved expression on Clay's face, and then a frown took its place. "What's wrong? You should look happy that I'm not sending you."

"Caroline isn't here. I forgot to tell you she called to say she had a dentist appointment. It seems she has a problem with Novocain and might not get in at all today." He threw up his hands and tilted his head. "That's all I know. I wasn't about to pry further into her business. You know how touchy she can get about keeping her private life private."

"Dammit," Jonas said. "What's happening with this team? First Henry with problems, now Caroline." He stopped his ranting after he spotted Henry and Jose searching the area. Pope didn't look well at all. He was pale and kept avoiding looking at the victim which Jonas found odd. The man had never had trouble dealing with a dead body before.

He turned to Clay, "No, I didn't know Caroline wouldn't be here. Besides, she's never been touchy with me," Jonas said.

Clay only shook his head. No one was touchy with the Lieutenant. As the lead detective, he expected his team to be efficient as well as professional. Jonas had his sense of humor and liked to enjoy himself as much as the others, but working homicide was not like a nine to five job, it took up a lot of personal time. So when one of the team needed to be off for an appointment, the others covered for him or her.

"So now, do I have to go to autopsy or can I send one of the other guys?" Clay lowered his hands, waiting for Jonas' response.

Jonas had to grin. He should send him just to be ornery, but he needed him back at the office. "Benedict can go this time. Finish up here, and we'll all meet later." All members of his team were present, except for Caroline.

"We have a lot to go over. Also, see if you can find out what type of car Doctor Donavan drove and locate it. It has to be somewhere. Check the apartment complex where the Heddrix woman lived. He had a date to meet her so it might be there." He paused, pondering what else needed to be done, and then said. "Check out one Andrew Jansen for me. I want to know all about him. Also, see the Judge and get the warrants. Be extra careful to follow procedure. You do know this man was a friend of the Mayor?"

"I do, and I will make sure everything is by the book. See you shortly," Clay called out, as he walked up the trail in the direction of his parked car.

By twelve-thirty, the Lieutenant was back at his office sitting at his desk, sipping a cup of rank coffee, and staring at the photo of Marilyn Heddrix. Was he seeing the victim in his mind or actually thinking of her sister? They were both endowed with looks, as well as physical attributes. Were they identical in their body as well? He believed so. He had to admit he was letting his mind wander to the surviving sister a little too much. Still, he needed to gather his thoughts and focus on the case.

He picked up his cell phone and turned back to the file. After two rings, Hanover picked up. "I wanted to let you know we found your Doctor Donavan." Jonas waited for this bit of information to be digested.

"Son of a bitch," was Winston's immediate response, then "Where?"

"The Garden of the Gods, not far from the Three Graces."

"Was he killed in the same way? If so, we might have a serial killer on the loose," Winston said.

Jonas looked at the photos of Marilyn on his desk. "Exactly the same, down to the rope burns on the wrists and ankles. I'll bet the same weapon used on the Heddrix woman, was used on the doctor. I'm waiting for a positive ID before notifying the wife. That will give the team a little more time to gather whatever evidence might be available. Do you want to contact the Mayor and let him know?" Jonas could almost hear the wheels cranking in Winston's head. The Mayor was not going to like the news.

"I'll notify him now, and after we're sure it's Donavan, notify the wife." Hanover paused, then said. "I talked to Phyllis Donavan this morning. She gave me the name of her private detective, Rudy J. Scully. His office is downtown on Tejon. She also said, she had called him and told him to give us copies of everything he has on the doctor. Do you want to go with me to see what he has? He possibly can save us some time if he has all this information. "

"When?"

"How about we try for tomorrow morning if I can arrange it? I'll call you and let you know the time. It will depend on Scully. I've heard of him but never met him. Mrs. Donavan didn't hire a sleaze bag PI. Rudy Scully is a former Navy Seal. He's good at his job, and he's expensive."

"Call me tomorrow and let me know when, and I'll try to be there. You could ask Scully to come into the office. That might be better for both of us," Jonas suggested.

"Hey, Jonas, when the doctor was found, what condition was the body in?" Winston wondered whether or not Phyllis Donavan would want to see her husband. He hoped not, especially if his face was caved in. It would be a horrific last image of a loved one to have, not for just the doctor's wife, but for anyone.

"He's all busted up. The left side of his face is caved in, just like the Heddrix woman. You don't want his wife to see him. He was in his underwear and had been dead close to the same length of time. He's overripe."

"I didn't think so either," again there was silence on the line for a few seconds. "I'm headed for the Mayor's office. I'm sure he'll want to be with Mrs. Donavan when it's time to notify her."

"Okay," Jonas said. "Keep me informed about Scully and the Mayor."

"I will," Hanover agreed and ended the call.

Jonas sat staring at his phone before sliding it back in his pocket. He hadn't told Hanover everything. The case file would have the full details, and he'd have access to all reports and photos. He continued to examine the pictures in the folder.

What was the purpose of taking their clothes, he wondered? Souvenirs? The man's gold Rolex watch, yeah, it was expensive, but his suit, shirt, socks, and shoes? And where were Marilyn's clothes? Was the killer's purpose in stripping the victims, an effort to expose them for what they had done? It made him wonder about people and their secrets.

Charlie Jacks had made an addition to Marilyn's report. She had been alive when the debilitating blows to the knees, elbows, shoulders and the final blow to the head had been delivered. Marilyn had suffered a horrific death.

What Jonas couldn't understand was why display

Marilyn, but just toss the doctor's body in plain sight? What point was the killer making? There had to be a reason. After he finished with the doctor, was he in a hurry to get out of the park? Or was it that he didn't consider the man worth the display or his time?

Even if the department brought in a hundred men, there was no possible way they could monitor all the roads and accesses to the thirteen hundred and sixty-seven acres of the park. He laced his fingers behind his head and leaned back for a moment and stared into space until Clay called to him.

He stood by the desk with a brown folder and a dark green, leather-bound, journal in his hand.

"Jonas," he said, strategically placing the thick file on top of the notebook in front of the Lieutenant. A triumphant smile crossed his face, "Alfonso got Judge Jordan to sign off on the warrants we needed for Marilyn Heddrix's phone records and financial information. We discovered she had a safety deposit box, so he got a warrant for it. Surprisingly, the woman at the bank was very cooperative and accepted the warrant and gave us the contents of the box." Pointing to the pile, he said, "That's what we found."

Clay sat down in the chair and directed the Lieutenant's attention to several folded documents wedged between the folder and the book. "By the way, other than that partial footprint and the few fibers, we didn't find anything else at the dump site for Doctor Donavan. Rupert, Fernandez, and Pope are still out there canvassing for witnesses or anyone who might have heard or seen anything, also checking the cameras. What surveillance cameras are out there, didn't catch anything worthwhile the day the woman was dumped. I doubt if they'll give us anything new. And, FYI, per DMV, the doctor drove a Mercedes sedan. I'm on my way to check out the Heddrix woman's apartment complex to look for it."

"Has Caroline called in yet?" Jonas opened the folder and began sifting through the stack of papers. He was becoming concerned about his newest team member. It was unlike her not to call back if she couldn't come in.

"Not yet." Clay said, and continued, "Marilyn Heddrix's financials are nothing out of the ordinary. If you look at her bank statements, she was not all that extravagant. Her phone records are the same. Over the past six to ten months there were numerous calls to her sister, but they only lasted for a few seconds each."

The Lieutenant examined every statement going back to when the alleged affair began. There were deposits every two weeks. Payouts were for a car payment to GMAC, rent for close to a thousand dollars, the electric bill, debits to a local grocery store, a clothing store and a significant amount to a lingerie shop. All the expensive furnishings in her apartment had to have been provided by Doctor Donavan. He looked up, and his brow furrowed when he saw the sheepish grin on Clay's face. "Now why are you looking like the proverbial cat?" He hadn't reviewed the complete file as yet.

"That," Clay pointed at one folded bunch of papers, "is a possible motive for the woman's death. That's her will. It leaves everything to her sister, which," he paused to catch a breath, "includes a million dollar life insurance policy. Get this! She had a policy on the doctor for a million bucks as well, and it was signed by the doc. On that policy, her sister is listed as the alternate beneficiary if she is deceased. Morgan Jansen is going to be a wealthy young woman." Clay had a satisfied smile on his face. "Maybe she hired someone to kill her twin."

Jonas shook his head. "I don't buy that theory. Morgan Jansen would never have her sister murdered in such a way. The woman suffered horribly before she died. And, she," he stopped before saying that she claimed to have experienced the pain of her sister's death. "The person who committed these murders wanted their victims to suffer. The Jansen woman doesn't strike me as being that sadistic." Jonas picked up the green journal. "What have we got here?"

"Oh, you're going to love that. It contains some of the sexiest love letters I have ever tried to read. I only read a few, and then had to stop; couldn't take it. She goes into great detail as to what she is going to do to her lover." Clay cleared his throat, "They're not like porn or anything. They read like a passage from a novel. I doubt if any normal man could read those and not get a hard-on. They'd make him want to rush home and jump his wife, girlfriend, or jerk off. My God, if the man was the doctor, no wonder he wanted to leave his wife. Marilyn Heddrix was one passionate and experienced woman."

Clay smiled as Jonas opened the notebook. He wondered if his boss was dating anyone. If not, he should be, especially if he was going to read that journal. "I wouldn't do that here if I were you," he said, grinning.

He ignored Clay and flipped open to the middle section and began to read one of the letters.

Thunder is bouncing off the clouds in the night sky. Purple flashes of lightning snake through the black velvet and, for a brief second, brightens the front yard. The steady staccato rhythm of the rain beating on the roof plays a soothing concert for dreamland's call. I am eager for you to come to bed, and there you are.

You bring wine with you tonight. Wonderful, delicious wine! We each savor a glass, then placed the crystal on the nightstand. How quickly we disrobe. Come, hold me close and give me one of your hot, demanding kisses that will set my soul on fire. I want your flesh pressed against mine and to feel your hands caressing my body. Oh, the sweet warmth of your mouth as we taste each other, tongues probing and dancing. I hold your face between my hands and run the tip of my tongue over your lips, then kiss and nibble my way to your neck and shoulder. Your body is hot, and I feel passion's fever swelling.

Jonas stopped reading for a second, and then read the rest of the letter.

"Holy shit! I see what you mean," he said, eyes wide and surprised at how quickly the heat and power of the words invoked images of Morgan. The letter he had read certainly would arouse any man. He closed the book, took a deep breath, cleared his throat and asked, "Do you have any idea of what time frame these letters cover?" He'd take the journal home and finish reading. It was something to be perused alone like Clay said.

"I don't know for certain," Clay eyed the Lieutenant. He knew the effect the letters had on him, so no doubt they had to affect Jonas. "The dates on the letters are for May, but no year is listed. I can't tell how old they are. They're only signed with the initial M." Clay shrugged, "The initial could stand for Marilyn? She wrote one each morning and one each night. The victim entitled the journal Love Letters to R. I didn't count how many letters there are, maybe thirty or so entries, but whoever the man was, she was crazy about him."

Jonas opened the book's cover and saw the title, "Love Letters to R" printed in bold letters. Closing it, he placed it on the desk beside the open file, to be re-examined later, and asked, "Well, the journal wasn't written to Morgan Jansen's husband, Andrew, unless his middle initial is R. Have you checked where he was Saturday morning? She was the reason his marriage broke up, maybe he wanted revenge."

"I put a call into his home and left a message that we needed to talk with him. Hopefully, he'll call back or voluntarily come in." Jonas' statement that the victim caused the break between her sister and her husband made Clay curious. "What'd he do? "

Jonas felt bad explaining the pain Morgan must have felt at her sister's betrayal. "He slept with our victim," and waited for the outburst from Clay.

"Holy shit! What an asshole. If I were Morgan Jansen, I'd want him and my sister to pay."

"She's not that type of person," Jonas defended. "She did the right thing in divorcing him. But, she has a lot of regrets about her sister. Now, all we have to do is find who murdered Marilyn." He added, "Do we have her lab results?"

It was clear Jonas was changing the subject.

"Yep," Clay said, reached over, pulled a paper from the folder and read off the report. "Her alcohol level was minimal, but there was evidence of Ketamine in her system." He looked up and handed the document to the Lieutenant. "By the way, Jacks called to say he found a puncture wound on her neck. He almost missed it due to the injuries, the decomposition and the damage done by the birds."

Jonas took the paper and glanced briefly at the report before replacing it in the file. "I'm not surprised about finding a drug in her system. Whoever abducted her would have wanted to immobilize her quickly. I don't understand why no one saw anything." He checked his watch. It was after three. The day was slipping away, and they hadn't found any new evidence. "Whoever the killer is, he's meticulous."

Clay frowned, "Yeah, but they all make a mistake sooner or later. They have to, or we'd be out of a job." He shifted in his seat and changed the subject. "Have you heard how Eppie's mother is doing?"

Clay didn't want to dwell on the negative for long. Jonas could appreciate that quality. They all had enough darkness in their lives to cope with.

"Not yet," he said, "Eppie said it was a matter of hours per the doctor. I'll go by Hospice later this evening." He tapped his pen on the desk a few times. There was still no word from Caroline. "Do me a favor. First, give Caroline a call, and if you can't reach her, go by her place. Do you know her address?"

"Yeah, she has a house out east, not too far from

the Citadel." The Citadel was a shopping center that bordered Academy Boulevard. "My wife, Becca, and she are pretty good friends. We've been there for dinner a couple of times. I'll run over later and check on her." Clay stood. "Anything else I can do before I go? By the way, did you make your call to Texas?" he asked.

Jonas nodded.

"Anything new on Kelly's case?" Clay knew all about the murder of Jonas' girlfriend. Several years prior, the Lieutenant had confided in him one July night on the anniversary of her death. After closing a particularly bad case, the entire team was out celebrating. Jonas had had more to drink than his usual two scotch and waters, otherwise, he would never have mentioned it. He never spoke of it again, but Clay always asked about the case. He waited for an answer.

"Mark Struthers says there're no new leads." Mark and Jonas had gone to high school together and later, after college, both joined the Midland Police Department at the same time. Mark was the one who kept Kelly's file on his desk and was always looking for a new lead.

It was frustrating to think of Kelly's murder as being still unsolved. She had been so full of life, sweet and innocent. They had made grand plans for their future. That all ended abruptly with her death. The Lieutenant changed the subject, not wanting to remember the last time he had seen her.

"Anyway, I want you to take Benedict with you to check on her." Jonas didn't know why he had a bad feeling, but it hadn't left him since being informed that Caroline had not checked in. Clay gave him a quick nod, left the office and walked toward the elevator.

Jonas picked up the leather binder and stared at it. He wondered if Morgan knew of its existence and if so, did she know to whom the letters were written? He was sure that the woman knew more than she was telling. His gut told him she was holding back. He placed the binder on top of the file and papers, gathered up the entire bundle and opened his desk drawer, dropped it all in and closed it.

The letters were personal to the victim and not to be left out for prying eyes. Jonas stood, grabbed his Stetson and stared at the desk drawer. Positive he was doing the right thing, he retrieved the leather journal, tucked it under his arm, and left the office. There was only one place to find the answers to his questions about the letters, the victim's sister.

The inside of the SUV was close to boiling as he slid behind the wheel, keyed the ignition and turned the AC to high. He hoped Morgan was home and ready to talk.

Morgan sat on the porch swing looking through the family photo album. The pictures had been taken in Virginia when they were younger, during happier days. Someone had snapped a shot of the family at the beach. The name of the beach had long since faded from her memory, but their mother had written it on the back of the photo, Virginia Beach.

She and Marilyn were sitting on the sand between their parents. She remembered that the sun had been hot and the breeze warm on her face. That day, the water had been so blue it almost hurt her eyes. The Pea Pods, as her mother had called them, had raced back and forth along the water's edge. They had not been allowed to go in by themselves. It had been an almost perfect day for them.

If only they had known what volunteering to help find a lost boy would cost them. Morgan closed the album, not wanting to dwell on the darkness that followed that perfect day. She placed it on the seat next to her and closed her eyes, enjoying the soft evening breeze and the tinkling of the wind chimes. Somewhere a bird was singing loud and clear, and the sweet scent of her neighbor's flowers filled the air. The quiet was soothing until it was destroyed by the sharp rap on the post of the porch. Her eyes flew open, and she frowned.

"What are you doing here?" She demanded, getting tired of the numerous questions by the Lieutenant.

Jonas had thought it best to leave the journal in his vehicle just in case she recognized the book. Removing his hat, he stepped up onto the porch and took a seat in the wicker chair near the front door. "I have a couple more questions."

"Of course you do," Morgan said, stood and took the few steps to open the front door. "Come inside," she said, to be polite. "I want a glass of iced tea. Would you like coffee?"

"That would be nice if it's not a bother," he said and followed her into the kitchen. He stood in the doorway watching while she filled a glass with ice and poured tea from a pitcher, and then prepared the coffee to brew. Her slender figure looked a lot thinner. It was none of his business, but he couldn't help asking. "You look as if you've lost weight. Are you having trouble eating?"

Morgan turned and stared at him. She was surprised he had noticed or cared enough to ask. "Having one's sister murdered does not inspire much of an appetite." She walked back into the dining room, sat down at the table and motioned for him to take a seat. "Why are you here, Detective?"

He continued to stand. "Like I said, I have a few more questions."

"Then ask them. I want to get it over with." She was so tired. He was right, she wasn't eating. And last night, all she had done was toss and turn. She was afraid that if she closed her eyes, Marilyn would appear. She was torn between wanting to connect again with her twin and being fearful of what she would have to tell her. So no, she was not doing all that well.

The coffee pot gurgled that it had finished brewing. Morgan rose and returned to the kitchen to pour the detective a cup.

"You like it black with a teaspoon of sugar, right?" she called over her shoulder as she filled a mug.

"Yes, thank you," he answered. He looked around the dining room admiring the simple décor. There was nothing fancy, just a round oak table and four chairs. A hutch sat in the corner and held a set of white china dishes. A couple of country paintings graced one wall, and that was all. He looked up as she placed the cup on a coaster in front of him.

"Okay, Lieutenant Black, let's get to your

questions," she said and sat down facing him.

Jonas took a sip and looked at her. There was a stubborn set to her jaw, and she was glaring at him. "Mrs. Jansen. . . ."

"Morgan, just Morgan. I hate being called Mrs. Jansen," she interrupted.

"Okay, Morgan," her name rolled off his tongue in a pleasant way and gave him a warm feeling. "Are you aware of your sister's financial situation?"

Morgan tilted her head and scrunched her eyebrows closer together, "My sister didn't have a financial situation," she said, making quote marks in the air, "that I know of. She, like me, worked every day. We were not financially well off. So, no, to answer your question, I would not know anything about her financial affairs. She was a private person, almost secretive in some ways. She hid a lot of her private life from our parents and me."

"So you didn't know about her life insurance policies?" He waited for a reaction and got one, but it was not what he expected from a grieving sister.

"No," she said, surprised that Marilyn would even take out a life insurance policy. "If she had one, I hope it's enough to help pay for the funeral." Morgan stopped, aware of how insensitive her words had been. "God, I don't mean to sound so callous, but Marilyn's burial is going to financially break me. An insurance policy would definitely help defray the costs."

For some reason, Jonas believed her. So how was she going to take the news about the other policy on Jack Donavan? "She not only had a policy on herself, listing you as the beneficiary but also one on Doctor Donavan."

"What! Why would she have a policy on the doctor?"

"I don't know. The doc would have to die for her to collect. Maybe she was counting on him doing just that. Well, that's happened, and you're also listed as the second beneficiary." That was a bomb to drop on her, and he expected a big reaction.

"Why?" Morgan said. "I don't understand." What had Marilyn been planning? "How much are those insurance policies worth anyway?" The Detective was staring at her as if waiting for her to jump up and confess something. "Detective, I've already told you, I didn't know anything about these insurance policies. I'm surprised that my sister would put me as the beneficiary, considering the fact we've not been speaking to each other and have been fighting for the past year. You have to be mistaken." Morgan's heart was racing. This information had to put her at the top of any suspect list the police might have.

"Well, she did, and the policies are for a substantial sum. Each one is for a million dollars." Jonas watched as Morgan's eyes opened wider. She looked as if she was going to faint.

She stammered, "Ah . . . a million dollars?"

"Each," he emphasized.

Her hand flew to her mouth. "Oh my God!" she muttered, behind her hand, then let it drop and shook her head. "This is crazy. You have to think I'm behind the murders." She stood and began to pace the floor. "I'm not. I swear I did not cause my sister's death or this doctor's." Her fear of being arrested grew, and she stopped and turned to face Jonas. "Are you going to arrest me?"

He smiled and shook his head. "No, I believe you. I don't think you had anything to do with these murders. I do have something I need you to identify. It's in my SUV. I'll be right back." He rose and walked out the front door.

Morgan sank back in the chair, feeling weak as relief flooded her entire body. She waved her hand in front of her face to dispel the wave of blackness which threatened to overtake her. Exhaustion washed over her, and Morgan fought to stay upright in the chair. Once the detective was finished and gone, she was going to bed and sleep for however many hours possible.

Jonas returned and walked toward her with a green leather book in his hand. Her heart sank. Oh crap, she thought when he placed the journal on the table. She didn't say a word.

He sat down in the chair and shoved the journal toward her. "We found this in your sister's safe deposit box. Have you ever seen it before?"

"Yes. I wondered what Marilyn had done with it." She reached out and touched the softness of the leather, then jerked her hand back as if burnt by the contents.

It was clear she recognized it. "Do you know what's written in it?" Jonas asked

"Love letters. Did you read them?" Morgan felt her face grow hot under his scrutiny.

It was his turn to be embarrassed. "A couple," he admitted, glancing away, then turned back and asked,

"Do you know who your sister might have written these letters to?" From the few he had read, whoever he was, he was lucky to have a woman love him that much, especially one that looked like Marilyn Heddrix.

Morgan thought for a moment. The truth was the best answer. "No. I have no idea who she would have written that type of letter to."

"Did Marilyn ever tell you the name of this man?"

"I told you no. Marilyn would never have told me the name of any of her men." Morgan took in a breath, aware that he continued to scrutinize her face. He was embarrassing her. "Stop staring at me. You're making me uncomfortable. Please finish with your questions and leave. I'm exhausted, and I need to get a bite of food and go to bed.

"I'm sorry for staring, but when I look at you . . . it's eerie." He stopped, realizing what he had said. "I apologize. I didn't mean to say that." God, he thought, how stupid could I be. "Anyway, this is the last question, and I'll go. Do you know when they were written?"

Morgan had to think for a moment. "Maybe about eight or nine years ago," she said. She stood, and he followed suit. Grabbing his hat and the journal, he turned toward the door.

"You're taking the journal with you?" she asked, surprised.

"Yes, it's considered evidence. It has to be kept with the case file. All your sister's personal possessions will be returned once the case is closed. Until then it all remains in police custody." He walked out and stopped.

"Thank you for your time. Please get some rest."

Morgan was looking as exhausted as she had claimed. The telltale dark circles under her eyes were proof that she was taking the loss of her sister hard. There was nothing he could do about it. Besides, she was suspicious of him and his motives.

"I'm not your enemy, Morgan," he said, then hurried down the steps to his vehicle.

She stared after him, not wanting to think about his words. If he wasn't her enemy, then what was he? He definitely was not a friend. All she was to him was just a suspect in the case he was working. She didn't want to think anymore. All she wanted to do was escape from all the pain, confusion and the overload of facts about her sister that she didn't want to know.

Closing and locking the door behind her, Morgan walked to the kitchen and placed the tea kettle on the burner. A fresh cup of hot tea, a peanut butter sandwich, then to bed was all she wanted, in that order. She didn't care that the sun was still shining and it was only four in the afternoon. She, like the detective suggested, needed to rest.

Twenty minutes later, after placing the dirty cup and plate in the sink, she closed the blinds in her bedroom and stripped off her clothes. Slipping between the fresh cotton sheets, her head had barely touched the pillow before she was sound asleep.

All too soon Morgan felt a quick slap on her shoulder. "Wake up! You can sleep later. This is important!"

Morgan opened bleary eyes and bit back the nasty retort ready to blurt from her lips. She pushed up on one elbow and said, through clenched teeth, "Do you realize how exhausted I am?" She continued to push into a sitting position and leaned back against the headboard, facing her twin sitting at the foot of the bed.

Marilyn gave her an apologetic smile. "I know, Sis, I know. And I wouldn't have bothered you except I remembered the name of that aftershave I told you I smelled on my killer."

Morgan sat up straighter, now wide awake. "My God, that's great! What was it?" she demanded. "I'll call the detective and tell him."

"I don't know how much good it's going to do. I'm not sure how popular it is today, but the scent was Lagerfeld. I bought it for Jack, and he used to wear it sometimes because I liked it. It smells real woodsy and spicy like rich pipe tobacco. I love the odor. When I would snuggle up to his neck and get a whiff of that cologne, it always made me crazy wanting him. Whoever abducted me wore the same cologne."

"Lagerfeld! Daddy used to wear that when we were growing up. I didn't know they still made it or that men wore it in this day and age. Only you would like something so out of date," Morgan said, with a scowl. "Is that all you have to tell me? I want to go back to sleep. I need it." She watched the flow of emotions play across Marilyn's face. "Are you all right, Marilyn? You look as if there's more. Just tell me what it is."

Marilyn sat staring at her sister with both hands fisted and tucked under her chin. She dropped her arms, and a pained expression crossed her face. "He's hunting and has chosen someone. There isn't much time, Morgan before he kills again. God, he is so angry. It's a white-hot rage radiating out like a beam to draw his victim in. That's all I know." She paused, tilted her head to one side, adding, "Something else, I don't know what it means or what it has to do with me or my death, but ask your detective who Kelly was." Then she was gone.

Morgan stared at the spot where her sister had sat. She started to reach for the phone, wondering if she should call the detective, but cringed at the idea. Unable to stay awake any longer, her eyes closed and she gave a soft snore as she drifted into a much needed deep sleep.

Caroline Jones woke with a headache caused by too much wine from her rendezvous with her dentist, Robert Titus. They had been having an affair for the past six months, but she was growing tired of all the secrecy.

Robert was tall, handsome with black hair and hazel eyes, and was well aware of the effect he had on his female patients. She was one of them. He had made a pass at her on her first visit to his office. He made it clear he was interested in the way he accidentally brushed her breast or touched her on the leg. It apparently did not matter to him that his assistant was present at the time. Maybe she didn't care; he was paying her salary. One thing led to another, and she began sleeping with him each Wednesday, whenever she could catch an hour or two. But that was growing tiresome.

Caroline didn't like sneaking around, meeting at this apartment he kept. How many others had there been before her, she wondered. Probably many. She didn't try to fool herself into believing she was the only one.

Robert was too practiced in the art of fucking not to have had many lovers. And oh, she had to admit, he was excellent in bed. His big cock fit her perfectly, and he knew how to use it. He did things to her and made her feel sensations that she had never felt before. She enjoyed every minute of it. But, she was risking her career as a cop, and that meant more to Caroline than a good roll in the sack. Not to mention what her mother and father would say about her affair with a married man.

Her parents, Henry and Gloria Jones, would be terribly hurt. They were deeply religious and had not approved of her becoming a police officer, wanting her to become a teacher instead. She had other aspirations besides being a teacher or a cop. Her future depended on her. Trying to live on a cop's salary was not enough for what she wanted.

Becoming a best-selling author was her goal. Novels based on true crime sold well. She had been researching a story for months, one that would make a sensational book. In her office at home, she had all the research files and notes on a board and had actually started the outline. It was based on a true story of a molestation case where the wealthy pedophile got off with nothing more than a lengthy probation sentence. Once her research was complete, she'd write the book. Caroline knew she had the talent to succeed as a writer, plus she had the necessary law enforcement credentials.

And then, there was Alfonso. Sweet, lovable, steady Alfonso. He was in love with her and, maybe in some ways, she was in love with him. But the idea of being tied down to a husband and kids didn't appeal to her, so she had ended her relationship with Al, only to end up being transferred to the same team in homicide. That had been awkward.

He had assured her that it would not be a problem working with her in the same department. He had kept his word. No one knew about their prior relationship. He treated her like any other member of the team.

Now she wanted out of this relationship with Robert. That would have to wait until her next dental appointment when he expected her to meet him at the apartment. She would end it then.

Right now she needed to get home. All that wine had rendered her unable to drive safely. After Robert left for the conference in Denver, she had stayed in bed and gone to sleep. It was after two in the morning. She had missed a full day on the job. The Lieutenant would be concerned for her welfare. He was like that, always looking out for his team. She didn't want to have to explain anything. Caroline headed for the bathroom. A quick shower and she'd be on her way home.

She was glad she had decided to end the affair. As she turned on the water, she thought of Al and how happy he would be to have her back. Maybe she was in love with him after all.

Chapter Nine

Thursday, early a.m.

The bitch had scratched him. She had surprised him. As soon as the needle had penetrated her neck, she had whirled, landing a roundhouse kick to his midsection. Her small size had fooled him into believing she would be an easy target. She was strong with wiry muscles that he hadn't counted on.

He had miscalculated the strength of the drug and administered too low a dose. The medication slowed the power of the kick, but not enough, so he was only slightly winded. She was still able to grab her phone and try to dial a number. There had been a flash, and then he had knocked it from her hand. It had skittered across the road and out of sight.

He didn't have time to look for it. The woman was still able to continue to fight the effects of the drug. When he grabbed her, she dug her long nails into his flesh. Three shallow grooves extended from his left eye and down his cheek. A fist to her chin had ended her struggle.

It had all happened too fast. It had been a stroke of luck that the street was empty, with oak trees shadowing the road where he'd parked. He knew the route from the boyfriend's apartment to the house; so he had beat her home. He parked on the street in front of the neighbor's house and had waited.

Women were such fools. They never expected an

attack from someone they knew. He had never understood why they were so surprised when it happened. Just like Caroline. The expression on her face was of complete shock. Once she was out, it was just a matter of tossing her in the van, securing her hands and feet and giving her an additional shot to make sure she wouldn't wake up.

It was when he threw her purse in the van next to her that he saw it. Some of the contents had spilled out. Grabbing up the items, he reached for a leather ID wallet which had flopped open. That's when he saw the bright shiny silver badge lying next to the plastic coated identification card. His heart began to pound faster and sweat beaded up on his forehead. He hadn't known she was a cop, only had seen her at the dentist's office.

Christ, this was bad. What was he going to do now? He couldn't let her go, she had recognized him. There was no way he could turn back now. The deed was done, and he had to follow through. But it was an inconvenient wrinkle in his plans. His heartbeat slowed, and he took a deep breath. His confidence that he could deal with any consequences returned. He closed the door to the van and drove away.

Clay turned onto Caroline's block on East Uintah, immediately stopped, put the vehicle in park and turned on his dashboard light. He and Alfonso had driven by late Wednesday afternoon to see how Caroline was feeling. But her car was not there, nor was there an answer to their knock on the front door. They had peeked in the windows, but the house was dark.

After checking with a neighbor, who said they

had seen her drive away around two-thirty in the afternoon, they left. Clay had dropped Benedict off to pick up his car and then grabbed a quick bite to eat before going back out on the streets to look for the doctor's Mercedes. Now, it was seven in the morning, and there were multiple police cars, their flashing red and blue lights seemed extra bright under the trees as they blocked off the street.

The vehicles were parked anywhere they could find a spot. One was parked a short distance in front of, and one further behind, the blue Toyota Prius with its driver's door open. Yellow crime scene tape cordoned off the entire area all the way to the house. A call had gone out of a possible abduction, but he had not considered it might be Caroline.

He glanced around expecting to see Jonas or the rest of the team. He didn't see anyone as yet. Then the call that it was a police officer missing had gone out only a short time ago. Hurrying forward, he pulled his cell phone from his pocket and dialed Jonas.

"What's up, Clay," Jonas asked.

Clay yelled above the approaching sirens as three other police vehicles arrived. "You need to get to Caroline's house ASAP. Her car is here with the door hanging open and uniforms all over the place." He paused and listened. "Okay. See you shortly," he said.

Jonas had heard the outgoing call of officer down, as well as received a call from dispatch and was already on his way. Clay slipped the phone back into his pocket and walked over to an officer, showed his badge and identified himself. "What's going on?"

"We got a call about four-thirty this morning about a possible abduction." He pointed at the house next to Caroline's. "The elderly man who lives there, with his wife, was up going to the bathroom when he glanced out the bedroom window and saw a petite blonde trying to fight off a tall man. He recognized the woman as his neighbor and called 911. But, before anyone could respond, the man threw her in a dark van and drove off."

Before Clay could ask, the officer said, "And no, the man didn't get the license plate number. His eyes are bad, and it was too dark. The only reason he recognized the woman was because he could tell by her blonde hair and the way she fought. He said she looked out for him and his wife. The responding officer didn't know she was a cop until about an hour ago when we ran the plates." The man shook his head in wonder. "Who would be stupid enough to abduct a cop?"

Clay's stomach rolled, and fear settled deep inside him. Oh God, Caroline, was all he could think. He had an awful feeling. "Someone who didn't know she's a cop, that's who." His cell phone rang; he grabbed it from his pocket.

It was Benedict. "Tell me it's not true what the Lieutenant told us."

"I'm afraid it looks like it is." Clay hated Al hearing it this way. It couldn't be helped.

Benedict was quiet for a second. "How did this happen? We were just there last night. Why didn't we check further?"

Clay knew Al was feeling just as guilty as he was that they had not continued to look for Caroline. But, they both knew how she would take their heads off if they stuck their noses in her business. He also knew about the brief fling they'd had before she joined the unit. Their affair had ended by that time, but the man was still in love with her. She had found someone new it seemed, but would never give the slightest hint as to who it might be. So, hurt by her rejection, Al had backed off and left her to her secrets.

"You know Caroline would have had a fit if she had found us coming by to check on her," Clay said.

"It doesn't matter, we should have done more." Benedict refused to let go of the guilt.

"Christ," Clay countered, "we did what we could. Where were we supposed to look? This city is so spread out, where do you suggest we should have searched? Do you even know what she did when she wasn't at work?" He carried the same guilt Al was feeling.

Even Clay had to admit that being relatively new to the section, none of them, other than Al, knew much about Caroline. They knew she was good at her job and that her family lived in the north part of town, but that was about it. It wasn't that they weren't interested, but they all had their private lives and, yes, secrets that they didn't share with each other.

"Listen," he said into the phone, "get here as soon as you can. Jonas and the rest of the team will be here shortly. I don't think she made it into her house. The primary scene is centered on her car. There was a witness, but his information is not much help. No license plate number." He listened for a second and then said.

"Okay, see you shortly." He slipped the phone back into his pocket. Within five minutes, the rest of the team arrived.

Jonas headed straight to Clay. "Okay, give me everything you have so far."

Clay summarized the events of the previous evening, adding that since a neighbor had witnessed her leaving that afternoon, he figured she was fine. He had come by to check on her that morning only to find half the police force all over the place. "I'm surprised they didn't contact you sooner," Clay said.

Jonas walked over to the blue Toyota, hands encased in gloves to protect the crime scene. "They did, just before you called me." He stooped down and peered inside the vehicle. "Have you called US West Security for an emergency intercept on her cell phone service?"

"Yes, they're checking as we speak. They'll let me know right away." Clay said.

I should have known, Jonas thought, Clay would have done everything possible. "How about Forensics, have they found anything or checked her house?"

"Not much. Caroline's prints and another unidentified set were found inside the vehicle. Her gun, purse, and cell phone are missing also, and her house is locked up tight. There's no sign anyone has been in it. Her car seems to be the primary scene." Clay glanced up in time to spot Al's car. "Benedict is here, and I need to warn you, he's beside himself. I don't know if you're aware of the prior relationship between him and Caroline. He's carrying a shit load of guilt about her being abducted. He's blaming himself for not making more of an effort to find her yesterday."

"No, I didn't know about their relationship, but this isn't his fault. I need him to be focused on helping to locate his partner, not beating himself up for being human," Jonas said, rising to glance over his shoulder to see Benedict getting out of his parked car. Worry lines were etched across the man's forehead, and his strides were long as he hurried toward the Lieutenant.

Jonas understood what he was going through. He was too aware of the feeling of helplessness. It was the same way he'd felt when Kelly was murdered. The best thing he could do to help was keep the man too busy to think. He only wished that someone had done that for him years ago.

"I'm glad you made it," Jonas said, as Benedict stopped to face him. "I need you to team up with Rupert and track Caroline's movements, starting yesterday morning up to the time she was abducted. Check with her mother first," he stopped in mid-sentence. Had the mother even been notified? He called out to the team, "Whose notifying her parents?" No one responded.

Clay shook his head, "No one yet. We were waiting to see if we could find her. When Henry arrives, I was thinking of sending him with Rupert. But, I think it would be best if I go with Benedict to notify and question the parents. Maybe they will know who Caroline has been dating."

"Henry's not here yet?" Irritation was heavy in Jonas' voice.

"He's on his way," Clay said, just as his phone rang. He listened intently for a minute before turning to glance around the area. He terminated the call and said, "That was US West Security. According to the latitude and longitude, they say that Caroline's phone is close around here somewhere.

Both men began to look around the car. If the cell had remained active since the early morning hours, the battery could be low but still have enough life left to ring. Jonas stopped his search and dialed Caroline's cell number. A faint sound of trumpets could be heard across the street. The two men hurried to the car parked across from the blue Toyota. Clay went around to the other side. Lying next to the curb, the case cracked but still intact, was the missing phone. Carefully Clay picked it up and slipped it into a plastic bag and handed it to Jonas. You want to take the phone with you?"

"No, on your way to see Caroline's parents, drop it off at the lab and have them check for fingerprints and then pull the phone records. See who she's been calling." Jonas paused, then said, "Al, I want you to stay out of the search. Once you get back from talking with her parents, you operate the phones at the office and keep me posted."

Both men nodded, and then Clay pointed behind Jonas. "Company's here, and so is Henry."

Jonas ignored Pope, who looked like hell, as he hurried to join his partner. He watched as a tall, dark-haired man dressed in a suit walked towards him. Chief Madison and the public relations officer, Lieutenant Pamela Connors. He turned back to Clay. "See if her parents know what dentist Caroline went to yesterday; where the office is located. If they know, go find out what time she was there and when she left." He glanced around at all the uniformed men and women standing around the scene. "We can put these people to work. I know they want to help, and we'll need all the personnel we can get if we want to find her alive."

Clay nodded, removed his cell phone, and hurried back to his car with Benedict behind him. Jonas waited for Chief Madison.

The Chief stopped and surveyed the area. "What do we know for certain?" he asked, taking in the scene.

Jonas gave a quick summary of the facts and his orders to the team. Too many hours had passed since Caroline had been taken. That did not bode well for her. The fact that she had put up a fight might keep her alive longer than the others, especially if she had injured her abductor. All they could do was hold onto the hope of finding her alive.

"Chief, Pam," Jonas acknowledged. "We need to keep a lid on the press. We haven't talked to her parents yet. It would be a tragedy if they heard it on TV and not from us. I have men on the way to their home, but until they get there, if you would keep the reporters from naming names it would be a great help." Jonas prayed it was not too late. He hadn't seen any TV vans or any reporters as yet. Usually, they were like bloodhounds, catching a whiff of scent and immediately on the trail of a story.

Chief Madison nodded as he listened to Jonas' report. Everything that was possible was being done to find the missing officer. "You keep the search hot, and Pam will keep the reporters and TV media off your back," he gestured back down the street beyond the perimeter of the yellow crime scene tape. A television van had pulled up and was vying for a parking space with another news vehicle. "Starting now," he said and nodded to Pam. She turned and headed in the direction of the female reporter, microphone in hand, rushing toward her.

Quickly, Jonas turned back toward the blue Toyota where Fernandez was going over the vehicle again, looking for anything that might have been missed.

Henry rose as Jonas approached. "Of the two sets of prints in the vehicle, the other could belong to a family member. I'll call Larry at STIC and have him check out the prints against the driver licenses and see if we get a match, otherwise nothing."

"Do it," he said. "I want you and Rupert to team up. Check the GPS in her car and see where she's been. Track all her movements for yesterday." Jonas studied Henry, noting the scratches along his right cheek. "What happened to you?"

"Fell into the bushes outside my house," was the hesitant reply.

Jonas nodded to Fernandez, who had a strange look on his face. "Jose, check with the DMV. I want every dark-colored van in this city located and checked out. I don't care if there're a million of them. I know that's going to be impossible, but do the best you can. If this killer is strong enough to subdue a grown man like the doctor, then he can't be too senile. Eliminate those belonging to anyone too old to be considered a suspect." That was such a big IF, he thought. "We have a serial killer on the loose and need to keep this as quiet as possible. Let's get to it. And Henry, we need to talk later," Jonas said, hurrying back toward his car as his cell phone rang.

It was the Dispatch Operator. "I have an urgent message for you from a Morgan Jansen, also one from Detective Ortiz. They both request you call them. Miss Jansen needs you to call her right away."

Jonas thanked the dispatcher and decided instead of calling, would go by Morgan's house. The idea of seeing her again was appealing, but he felt a rush of guilt. Compensating, by heading back to the office immediately after stopping by to see what she had to say was a proper choice. First, he had to call Eppie. He had no doubt that her mother had passed.

Immediately, he placed the call, and as he listened to her sobs, he felt her overwhelming loss. Right now, she needed the support of her family and friends.

"Take all the time you need," he told her. "I'll let the team know you'll be out for a while. Let us know about the funeral arrangements and if you need anything, anything at all, we'll be there for you. Okay."

"Okay," Eppie said, through her tears.

Jonas didn't mention Caroline. In the days ahead, Eppie would have enough to deal with. She didn't need any additional burden to weigh on her mind at this time. As he started the vehicle, he thought how life could be a royal bitch at times.

After the Lieutenant left, Henry Pope had to fight to keep from throwing up. It had happened again. He'd blacked out and had no memory of Wednesday evening until he came to, lying across his bed. When he tried to stand, it took a lot of effort. He felt as if he'd been kicked by a horse. To top it off, he had three long thin scratches on his right cheek and no idea how he'd acquired them. He needed to talk with his partner first, and then the Lieutenant. He had to do something about the blackouts. He attributed it to the booze. If that was the cause, that had to stop. He knew it wasn't going to be easy. Booze helped keep the edge off his anger at his wife, or so he tried to believe.

He'd call Shirley later and see if he'd gone by her place and done anything to provoke her enough to scratch him. Right now, he had a job to do, and he'd better be thorough. He spotted Fernandez watching him, but ignored his questioning gaze and continued to process the vehicle's GPS, before joining Rupert.

At four-fifty that morning, the killer dumped Caroline at the top of the basement stairs, watched her limp body roll out of the blanket and land in a heap at the bottom. Immediately he charged down after her. Grabbing a handful of her long blonde hair, he dragged her to the end of the basement and the cross beams. After stripping her down to her underwear, he hoisted her up and tied her spread-eagle, making sure that the rope cut into the fragile skin of her wrists and ankles. He wanted her to feel the pain and more. And she would.

It sent a shiver of anticipation through him that she would be in agony, but wouldn't be able to cry out due to the drug injection. He touched his face. The three scratches burned and throbbed, but they would have to wait until he dealt with the bitch. He would be scarred now. She deserved the punishment he would give her.

He stomped to the big bin of stones, chose a big one, drew back his arm and let it fly.

"Bitch!" he screamed, his vision becoming nothing more than a red haze. "Whore!" he yelled and hit her with another one. The loud crack of bones breaking bounced off the walls. It struck her left knee, shattering the joint. Rapidly, he grabbed one stone after another and threw each as hard as he could, destroying the other knee and both elbows. He swiped at the sweat dripping from his forehead into his eyes. Now he didn't care where the stones struck.

Hotter and hotter his blood boiled with rage as he hammered the small, fragile body over and over until he finally sank to his knees gasping for breath. Arms raised high over his head, he cried out as wave after delicious wave of ecstasy rippled from his loins to the top of his head and back again to his pelvis. The release came as he flooded the crotch of his coveralls with semen.

Exhausted, he stood, not sure if his legs would support him. He stared at the mangled form that had once been a breathing, beautiful woman and felt nothing except relief. Quickly, he grabbed the garden hose and went to work.

The task finished, he glanced at his watch. It was nearing six now, and it was already dawn. No problem, he'd put her in the trunk of the car and dump her like the garbage she was. The cops were looking for his dark-colored van. He'd keep it locked in the garage. Besides, it needed a good cleaning anyway.

Finished with hosing her off, he cut the ties holding her to the beams and let the mangled body drop to the concrete. Wearing two pair of latex gloves, he rolled her onto the plastic sheet spread out on the floor. As a precaution, he wrapped an old blanket around the plastic and then carried her upstairs and into the garage.

He was sure the police would be searching everywhere for one of their own, so he threw her in the trunk of the car. He knew just the place to dispose of her, right where the police would be sure to find her. He would deposit the body directly under their noses. Whistling, he hurried upstairs, showered and dropped his soiled clothes on the floor. He dressed in the dark navy slacks, high polished black shoes and a dark blue shirt he'd brought with him, before going back to the garage. He grinned as he climbed behind the wheel of the old Crown Victoria and backed out. As he drove away, he thought of her lover and how he would enjoy delivering the same punishment to him. It was going to be a good day after all.

Chapter Ten

Thursday

Focused on the floor, Morgan hugged her stomach tightly as she paced back and forth from the kitchen to the front door, waiting for the phone to ring. She had called Lieutenant Black's cell phone, and when it went straight to voice mail, she left a message. When no call back came within fifteen minutes, desperate, she'd called the police department and asked to get a message to him. Now all she could do was wait for the phone to ring. But, the phone didn't ring.

At the sudden knock on the front door, she stopped pacing and hurried to open it. Hat in hand, Lieutenant Black filled the doorway. Again she was struck by his height and imposing stature.

"Why are you here?" tumbled from her mouth before she could stop it.

"The message I received said it was urgent."

"I'm sorry. It's just that I was expecting you to call, not come by." It was good to see him, even if she didn't want to admit it. He was not what she would call a handsome man. In some ways, his features revealed a tough, rugged exterior and, from experience, knew he could be just as tough on the inside. He was not without appeal. His imposing strength, softened by the concern in his eyes, was genuine and made him more attractive than the viral cowboy image she had first encountered.

She opened the door wider, "Please come inside.

I need to talk to you." She closed the door and ushered him into the kitchen where he leaned back against the counter. All too aware of him watching her every move, she needed a cup of hot tea to brace her courage and tell him Marilyn's message. God, she thought, every time this man comes around, I'm fixing tea or coffee. Oh well, tea was fortifying.

She sat two cups on the counter. "I can make coffee if you prefer," she said, reaching for the coffee in the cupboard.

"Nothing for me, thank you. I have to get back to the office." He noted that there remained dark circles under her eyes, and today she was jumpy. "You're still not sleeping well?"

"No. I can't seem to shut off my thoughts. Questions keep racing through my head, and I don't have any answers. Why! Why!" She stopped, still gripping the handle of the teapot, hesitating. Placing it on the burner, she twisted the knob to high and turned to face him. Taking a deep breath, she jumped in, "The reason for my urgent call was," she paused again, "there's been another victim abducted."

"We know," not wanting to guess how she could know. Jonas sighed. Not that psychic shit again.

"You do? Who!"

He tilted his head and raised one eyebrow. "You tell me." Psychic crap or not, how could she know so soon when only a few hours had passed since the report came in that Caroline was missing?

Wide-eyed, she shrugged her shoulders and raised her hands, palms up and shook her head. "Why would I know who it is? All I know is that my sister said the man had taken someone else and this time he was furious."

"How could your dead sister tell you something my team and I just found out?" he demanded. She was starting it again. "I don't care what you claim, you know how guilty it all makes you look? It doesn't matter what I've read about you and your sister. I don't believe in psychic abilities. I can't accept this crazy claim that your sister told you."

Morgan's jaw dropped. "How can you say that? Didn't I tell you Jack was out there? And you found him where Marilyn said he was! This isn't some story I'm making up to hide some monstrous deed. Why can't you open your mind and believe some things have no explanation?"

"I deal in facts! Hard cold facts. And that evidence states that you know too much beforehand. How are you involved in this mess? If you tell me now, maybe I can help you." God, didn't she realize she could go to prison? There was no way he could accept her wild stories. He had continued to do research on identical twins, and he would like to believe there were some things, facts or evidence could not explain. But it was hard for him to accept. Still!

"Fact one, you admitted being estranged from your sister. Fact two, she had slept with your husband and broke up your marriage. Fact three, you don't have an alibi for the night your sister disappeared. . . ." He never got to finish.

Morgan exploded with a sharp slap to his face. "Screw you and your facts! I was here, alone and asleep until pain woke me. After that, I was up the rest of the night calling my sister's apartment over and over. Check my phone records!"

He already had. The red imprint still burned his cheek. Maybe he deserved the slap, but she still had broken the law by attacking him.

"You know I can arrest you for assaulting a police officer," he threatened and saw her pale at his words. "But, I'm not going to. I don't think you meant to do that."

Tears of anger welled in her eyes. She wouldn't lie, "I meant it," she retorted, and clenched her jaw until she could control her words. Then she spat them at him, "How could you think for one minute that I would harm my sister or anyone else? Yes, we fought, sometimes like two cats. I even ordered her out of my house one time and threatened to knock the hell out of her. And yes, she slept with my husband, but I blamed Andy more than Marilyn. That bastard knew who he was screwing, had always been able to tell us apart by our tattoos. So he didn't have an excuse for what he did.

"No matter what she did or how angry she made me, she was first and always my sister. And that meant more to me than anything she might have done." Her emotions almost crumbled. "And now she's gone, and I'm hanging on for dear life trying to keep it together. Because," she hiccupped, "I'll never see her alive again. I want to scream. But if I start screaming, I won't be able to stop, and I'll be lost."

The kettle began to screech jarring her from her tirade. She turned away, clenching her jaws and got busy fixing the cup of tea. Her hand shook so badly, the teacup rattled against the saucer.

Keeping her face averted, she let the Lieutenant take the cup from her hand and pour hot water over the tea bag. Thankful the noise had stopped; she added sugar and powdered creamer and took a sip. Only after she swiped away the angry tears, and gained control, did she face Jonas. Morgan wondered if the tears would ever stop.

"I'm sorry, but siblings do murder each other," he said, his tone more gentle. "Not all brothers or sisters feel the way you say you do." He hated to have to say those words, but it was a fact. Family members killed each other all the time for all sorts of stupid reasons.

Instead of adding to her pain, he wanted instead to pull her into his arms and comfort her. God, how he understood her struggle with those emotions, had felt them tear his insides up. And still did every time he had the dream about Kelly. "You're not a suspect in your sister's death," Jonas stated, and started to move closer, actually started to reach out to her, but she turned, cup in hand, looked at him and quickly left the kitchen. He let his arms fall to his sides.

"I'm sorry for saying that," he said, and followed her. "I only said it because I'm trying to come to grips with something I can't explain or understand. The idea of your dead sister coming back to tell you about this killer disturbs me. I want to believe it, but I don't believe in ghosts. If I did, I'd be looking over my shoulder for all the bad guys I've put away."

Morgan placed her cup on the coffee table and

plopped down on the sofa while the Detective continued to stand near the overstuffed chair. She wasn't sure but had the impression that Jonas Black had been about to pull her into his arms. Maybe she was wrong. Perhaps she wanted just that but was too afraid it might not stop at only being held. God knew she needed to be able to lean on someone for a change. But not now.

She had to explain so he would not be more offended than she had made him feel. "I can't handle people offering me comfort to help me deal with the situation. If I seem distant or cold, it's only because I need to maintain control. If I surrender to my grief, I can't do what has to be done. Do you understand?" She needed him to understand in the worst way. It would have been easy to slip into his arms and let all her pain be washed away with her tears. But she couldn't do it. She kept looking at him, waiting for a reply.

He nodded, making sure to give her room. "I just want you to know that I'm here to help in any way that I can. Now, as I said, I want to believe your story. It's hard for me. So please try and explain it to me."

Morgan thought for a moment. How did you explain something that was second nature to you; that she had lived with all her life. Something that was both a gift and a curse at the same time; something that at times she hated and yet, like Saturday, was thankful she had this strange bond with her sister.

"How can I explain it to you, when I don't know how it works? It is what it is." She frowned, remembering the other things her sister had said. It was important, so she blurted it out. "Marilyn said to tell you the killer wore the cologne, Lagerfeld. She recognized it because that's what our father always wore. It's a woodsy type of spicy cologne. Not many men wear it today. I don't know why. It has a nice aroma." Morgan remembered how good her father always smelled.

Sometimes after his death, there were times, she'd catch a whiff of Lagerfeld in the house. But all too soon it faded away leaving only the memory behind. Now the very thought that her father's favorite cologne was associated with Marilyn's death was horrifying to all the beautiful memories.

Jonas glanced at his watch. He had to get back to the office. "The killer wears some type of spicy cologne you say. I'll have the lab check the clothes from your sister's . . . ," he started but stopped.

Morgan finished his sentence. "Body. Was that what you were going to say?" From the uncomfortable expression on his face, she knew she was right.

"Sorry. I'm used to dealing with suspects. Eppie is better at dealing with relatives. It's not that I can't, it's that I want to promise I'll find whoever committed the crime, and that's not always possible. But, I promise you, I will do everything in my power to find the man who killed your sister and the doctor." He turned toward the door and was stopped in his tracks by Morgan's words.

"My sister also said to ask you who Kelly is?"

He whirled around, the color drained from his face. "What did you say?" He knew exactly what she had said, but wanted her to repeat it just to be sure.

"Kelly. Marilyn said to ask you about Kelly."

Morgan was surprised at the reaction her question had on the detective. When he whipped around to face her, he was pale and looked as if he was ready to do battle. It scared her enough that she dropped her teacup sending it crashing onto the coffee table, splashing the remaining liquid over the wood and landing on the floor in three pieces.

"I'm sorry," she said and hurried to the kitchen. "I didn't mean to upset you," she called over her shoulder. She returned with a roll of paper towels and tore off several and began mopping up the spilled tea. Jonas had gathered the broken cup and stood holding the pieces as if unsure where to put them.

"I seem to be apologizing to you a lot," he said, wondering how the hell, if possible, she knew about Kelly. "Now I owe you another one for frightening you." He paused, mulling over how much to tell her. "Why do you want to know about Kelly?"

"Not me, Marilyn? She wanted to know who Kelly is, that's all. Now can we forget that I did?" She had done as Marilyn wanted. All she needed was to just be left alone and have some peace for a few hours. The house phone began to ring, breaking the strained silence between them. Taking the cup shards from him, she rushed to the kitchen, dumped the broken ceramic in the trash and grabbed the receiver. So much for peace and quiet, she thought.

It was the funeral home. She asked them to hold and returned to the living room carrying the portable phone. "I have to talk with these people. Can you wait a minute?" When he nodded, she spoke into the receiver, then listened for a moment. "I'll be there tomorrow by ten. I'll see if I can find a dress at her apartment," she glanced at the detective to see if that was allowed. He nodded. "Yes, I'll bring everything with me." After a few moments longer, she said goodbye. Still holding the phone, she returned the questioning gaze of the Lieutenant.

"Anything I can help you with?" he asked. He had a lot more question about where she really got her information.

"Will I be able to get into my sister's apartment tomorrow?" Morgan wanted to make sure she could pick up the green dress that had been Marilyn's favorite.

"Yes," he said. "We've removed anything that might be pertinent to the case. If I have time, I'd like to accompany you?"

She was surprised that he wanted to go with her. "Come along if you want. I can meet you there."

He nodded and again glanced at his watch. He had to get back to searching for Caroline. "I'll meet you there at eight in the morning, if possible. If I'm not there, do what you need to do, and I'll call you later," he said and hurried to open the door, then turned back to look at her. She stood with her hand to her throat, her eyes filled with sadness and exhaustion. "Try to get some rest. I can promise the pain will dull over time. I won't tell you that it goes away because it doesn't." No, the loss left a hole in one's heart that couldn't be filled.

Morgan wondered at the thoughtful expression on his face. Was this Kelly the source of his haunted memories? "Make it eight-thirty," she said. "Her green dress shouldn't be hard to find." She followed the detective out the door and stood watching after him as he climbed into his SUV and quickly drove away.

The office of the Violent Crimes Unit was filled with on and off-duty detectives and police officers, eager to help by answering the phones as calls came in from officers out in the field searching for Caroline. There were only so many desks available. Those milling around, unsure of how to help, were sent out in patrol cars to search for the van. Each officer was given a designated search area of the city with specific details and photos of the victim.

Jonas checked on the progress. There was nothing so far. Damn it, he thought, that wasn't good. He assembled his remaining team members in his office, Clay, Fernandez, Rupert, and Pope at his desk. They stood staring at him with grave faces.

He began, "You all know it's only a matter of time before we're in a recovery mode instead of hoping to find Caroline alive." Each nodded their agreement. "Jose found that the vans listed at the DMV for Colorado Springs and El Paso County numbered too many, even with the help of the Sheriff's Department and all the extra people, to locate and interview each and every vehicle owner promptly.

"We have people on foot, in vehicles and on horseback searching the Garden of the Gods, as that seems to be the killer's favorite dumping ground." There was little chance of finding Caroline alive, Jonas knew. He didn't express his gut feeling, but the rest of the team was well aware of how quickly, after being abducted, the other victims had been found dead. "Caroline put up a fight which has probably pissed off the killer. If she's still alive, it won't be for long. So what we have to do is find out how this killer knew Caroline. Rupert, what did you and Henry find on her car's GPS?"

Pope spoke up, "It only showed her driving to a Lake Avenue address and back home. Everything else had been deleted."

"Did you check out the address?"

Rupert answered, "It's a large apartment complex. We're checking to see which apartment she might have visited. We don't know which one as yet."

"Well, when you find out, let me know," Jonas said, then turned to Fernandez. "Jose, you and Rupert go back to her house. Look for anything that might tell us how she knew or met her murderer. Tear the place apart if you have to. There's a link between these victims somewhere." He turned to Pope who looked even more haggard than he had at the crime scene. "Henry go talk with her parent's again. Find out everything personal, no matter how small or insignificant, about their daughter. We all know she guarded her private life. Well, now we need to know all about who she was."

Pope held back as the rest of the team immediately dispersed. "You wanted to talk to me?" he asked.

"Later. We've got too much going on right now. But yeah, we need to talk about your drinking. Even under that cologne, you're wearing, I can smell the booze. For now, just do your job and stay off the liquor.

Now, get going." Jonas took note of the injury to Pope's face, three thin scratches down the right cheek. He turned to Clay as Henry hurried to his vehicle. The sudden appearance of Winston Hanover, with another man following close behind, drew Jonas' attention.

The man was tall, in his mid-forties or fifties, still in good physical condition with brown eyes that were alert to all the commotion in the room. Under one arm, he carried a thick file folder. Jonas and Clay greeted them as they approached.

Winston was quick to make the introduction, "Jonas, Clay, meet Rudy J. Scully. Can we go talk in your office? I think you'll be interested in what he has to say."

Jonas led the way, closing the door for privacy. The two men took a seat in front of the desk, while Clay stood nearby and leaned back against the wall.

Hanover continued, "Mr. Scully is the private detective Phyllis Donavan hired. He brought everything he has on Jack Donavan."

Rudy Scully looked from one to the other. "This is not normal procedure for me. I usually leave it up to my client to divulge whatever information they choose. Since Mrs. Donavan called and instructed me to give you access to the full report, here it is." He opened the file folder and proceeded to explain each photograph and how he had obtained them.

"You already know Marilyn Heddrix, and the doctor were having an affair. They were not very discreet about it either. You may not know she wasn't the first. There were several before her. And, they were all his nurses. Their names, addresses and phone numbers, with their statements, are in the file. From what I could find out, the others left his employment when they realized he wasn't going to leave his wife. I believe if anyone could have possibly enticed the good doctor away from his wife, it might have been the Heddrix woman. But not even she could get Jack Donavan to give up all he had for love. The man enjoyed his wife's position and wealth too much. As he once told a colleague, he wasn't about to buy the cow no matter how much milk it produced." Scully pulled out a report and handed it to Jonas.

"Apparently Doctor Donavan had a standing date with your victim every Friday night at her apartment. Sometimes they'd meet at her place for lunch. I'm sure you already know this." He flipped through the folder, pulled out a couple of pictures and shoved them across the table to Jonas. They were of the doctor with another man seated at a booth. Another man sitting in the booth behind the group appeared to be leaning back, his head tilted as if listening intently.

"I followed Donavan a lot. These pictures are of him at Barrett's Steak House. He was meeting Marilyn Heddrix. But, before she arrived, I snapped this one of him with his dentist, Robert Titus. They seemed to be having an interesting conversation, as you can tell from the way the man in the other booth is acting. Anyway, that wasn't my business."

Scully pulled another shot from the folder and slid it across the table to Jonas. "Here's one of him with Marilyn seated in the same booth. My job was to gather proof he was involved with his new nurse. He was, and that's what I reported to his wife." Scully pushed the entire folder over to Jonas.

"You can keep this. It's a copy of my original file. As I'm finished with the case, and been paid, I hope it helps you find the good doctor." He stood and shook hands with both men. "If there's anything else you need, give me a call, and I'll try to help in any way I can." He glanced at his watch. "I have to go. I have another appointment."

"I'll take him back downstairs," Hanover said, following Scully out of the room.

The Private Investigator didn't know about Donavan being dead. That detail hadn't been released yet. Jonas sat staring at the thick folder. Maybe it would give a more accurate timeline of the doctor's activities up to the date of his death. Anyway, he hoped so. It could wait for the moment. The doctor was no longer missing. Now, all they had to do was locate Caroline.

He walked back into the office area and glanced around. "Where's Benedict?" he asked. He hadn't seen him in the office earlier.

"I tried to get him to go home, but he refused," Clay said. "Right after we notified Caroline's parents and checked in here, he took off for the Garden of the Gods." Clay shook his head, all too aware of the torment the man was experiencing. He felt it himself. Throwing up his hands, added, "You know how Al is. He's blaming himself for not sticking around until Caroline came home. I told him there was no way we could know she was in danger. But he won't listen to anyone."

Jonas knew Clay was right. The man wasn't

thinking clearly. Benedict was running on adrenaline and guilt, and God knows what he would do if he were the one to find Caroline.

"Come on," he said, placing the new file in his desk drawer. "We need to get out to the park and find him. If he finds her body, he'll lose it. I don't want that to happen." Jonas waited for Clay to close his laptop. Without hesitation, the two men hurried to the parking garage.

Benedict's second sweep of all the roads and side trails circling the rock formations in the Garden of the Gods had not yielded a trace of Caroline. He had passed officers on foot, on horseback, and in vehicles also searching the roads and trails. He'd slow down to check if they'd found anything. With each negative shake of their heads, he knew time had run out for Caroline. His guts were in knots. Clay was right; he should have stayed at the office. But damn it, when the woman he loved had been abducted, he couldn't sit on the sidelines and not look for her. No matter what it cost him, even if it was his job.

He drove one last time along Juniper Way Loop before heading back to the office. The Lieutenant wasn't going to be happy he had defied orders to interview the parents and return to man the phones. He glanced at the main parking lot on the left side of the Loop. The road continued north to snake around the giant rock formation known as the Tower of Babel and led back south. As he rounded the bend in the road near the ravine, he saw the rear of another vehicle ahead, driving out of sight around another curve.

He never knew what made him stop his car and park. He had checked this same ravine before with negative results. Yet this time he had an uneasy feeling and felt compelled to take one more look. He got out of his sedan and walked over to the safety barrier.

There were three barriers to protect motorists from driving off the road into the ravine. The first was a long curved metal guardrail. The second was a fence of metal pipes driven into the ground. And the third was a short stone wall. Trees and bushes blocked part of the slope from view. Benedict stood studying the area. He saw nothing at first. Then, down the hill beneath the bushes, almost hidden from view, was a patch of white.

Without hesitation, he hurried to find a way down the rocky incline. The slopes formed a sharp V with loose dirt, rocks, bushes and small trees that hampered any attempt at reaching the bottom. He climbed up the slope and worked his way along the terrain until he could get a better view. One look at the mangled body covered in red dirt and dried blood, lying next to the trunk of a small pine, he recognized the blond hair and broken form of Caroline.

It was a guttural cry of pain and anger that escaped from his throat. Without thinking, he stumbled, rolled and fell to the bottom on all fours, the trees and branches tearing at his flesh, leaving bloody cuts on his face and arms. Tears blinding him, he rose to his feet and made his way partially up the slope where the body rested. Caroline was a shattered doll, joints at odd angles with bone protruding in numerous places. He sank to his knees, his chin dropping to his chest as he ignored the sharp rocks cutting into his flesh. His grief consumed him, and he threw his head back and wailed his despair.

Only the acute pain in his knees brought him back to his senses. He didn't try to reach her, but rose to his feet and clawed his way back up to the road. From the trunk of his car, he removed the yellow crime scene tape and closed off the area, before taking out his cell phone and putting out the call, "Officer down." Finally, he called Jonas, all the while feeling sick to this stomach.

He didn't want to believe it, but his gut told him beyond a doubt, the car he had seen driving away had belonged to her killer. Why hadn't he noted the license plate? Why hadn't he raced after the vehicle? Why hadn't he done a lot of things?

He couldn't leave her by herself. Carefully he made his way back down to the bottom of the ravine and again dropped to his knees. Uncontrolled tears silently rolled down his cheeks. He fought to hold back the screams of pain ripping at his insides. It was physical, this agony of loss, and he knew this wound would never completely heal.

Soon, the wail of sirens reached him. Help was on its way. But nothing could help Caroline or him. The screech of tires stopping abruptly and the sound of voices calling to him from above drew his attention. All he could do was point to where Caroline was lying and climb back up to the road. The Rescue team would take over, along with Forensics.

Jonas was waiting for him as he climbed over the

guardrail. Benedict had expected to receive some form of reprimand, but instead, his boss showed only the pain they all felt from losing one of their own.

"Go home and stay there until I call you," the lieutenant said, with sympathy. "You know I can't let you work this case. You need to understand there was nothing you could have done. Caroline is not dead because of you, take time off and come to terms with what has happened. After a few days, and only if you're up to it, come back. I'll assign you another case, but you can't be anywhere near this one." Jonas stared at Benedict. His face was haggard and streaked with dirt from his tears. The man was a wreck.

God, Jonas thought, I understand exactly how he feels. His own guilt and pain never entirely went away. Every time he saw the bludgeoned body of a young woman, his last images of Kelly flickered through his mind. The images never faded and wouldn't until her killer was caught. Only then would he be able to put her to rest in his mind.

He had buried the loss just as Benedict would have to do, or it would destroy him. Give him time to grieve, and then he would keep the man so busy he wouldn't have time to think. That was the best he could do for him.

Work hadn't helped him forget. No amount of kindness or understanding was going to do it either. And no matter what, time did not heal all wounds. They just scarred over leaving the scab beneath, ready to be ripped open at the mention of her name or the sight of a photograph.

He wished he could ease the man's agony. No

one really could. He was going to have to work through this tragedy by himself. The entire team would be there to support him and each other if needed, but all of them were going to have to come to grips with their loss in their own way.

Jonas watched Benedict stumble to his car and sit in the driver's seat resting his forehead on the steering wheel. Then he started the engine and slowly drove away.

After sending Benedict home, the Lieutenant stood beside Charlie at the railing. Clay was already busy checking the trail, where Caroline's small form had rolled and bounced down the slope. Rupert stood watching the CSI team at the bottom of the ravine collecting bloody rocks, along with anything that looked like a piece of evidence. Fernandez watched a cast being poured on a boot print they'd found in the dirt at the top of the ravine. All the evidence would be dropped off at the Metro Lab.

Henry was down at the curve in the road hoping to find anything from the car that Al had seen. Jonas doubted there'd be tire tracks. A paved bicycle lane extended almost right up to the slope of the hill.

From where the Lieutenant stood, he could see the rescue team attempting to secure Caroline's body in a Stokes basket. It was clear from the angle of her decent that the killer had walked around the guardrail, stepped close to the stone wall and tossed her body over the edge. It would have been easy for him as Caroline didn't weigh that much.

He had done this quickly, not staying around to see where his victim landed. Jonas believed he wanted her found right away, that's why he had made the dump in broad daylight. Hopefully, they'd have more to go on this time.

He watched the rescue team place Caroline in a body bag, secure her in the basket, then pull it up the hill via attached ropes. They shoved the gurney in the back of the Coroner's truck and drove away.

From what he'd seen, Caroline had pissed off the killer enough to lose control. She may have gone down fighting when abducted and gotten in a few licks, but the killer had delivered his revenge on her.

Charlie would check every spot on her body for evidence, and he intended to be there. As the Coroner waved at him before driving off, Jonas yelled to Clay he was leaving for the morgue.

He entered the room just as the attendants were placing the body bag on the stainless steel table. This was not going to be easy to watch. Even Jacks grimaced as he unzipped the bag and opened it to reveal what had once been the face of a beautiful young woman.

"This girl's own mother would have trouble identifying her," Charlie said, peeling the plastic back to reveal the entire body. "I've seen some horrible death in my years as a coroner," he added, "but this is the worst." He shook his head. "Son of a bitch, Jonas," Charlie said. "It's a shame this had to happen. I liked this girl. Every time I saw her, she was smiling. She always had a lot of questions, eager to learn. What a waste. When you get this bastard, I hope he ends up on my table."

"I'll get him," Jonas muttered, and stepped out of

the way as the Coroner's assistants helped remove the body and place it on the table.

The Coroner let loose with, "My God!"

Even Jonas choked back a gag at the sight of all the protruding bones in her arms, knees, and torso. It appeared as if every bone in her body had been broken. If she hadn't died first from all the injuries and the pain, then the crushed in face and skull would have been the death blow. This killer was one angry man, and his hatred was escalating. That scared Jonas. Who was his next victim?

Jacks paused in his examination of the body. "Go back to the station, Jonas. You can do more good there. You can't help her anymore. It's up to me to find as much evidence as possible, and I will. Go!" Charlie insisted, pointing at the door. "As soon as I finish, I'll send you the report." He returned his attention back to Caroline.

"Okay," Jonas said, "you're right." He stopped in the doorway, taking one last look at the petite, brutalized body and said, "I will find this son of a bitch, Charlie. I will!" He hurried out to his car and drove back to his office. It was going to be a long afternoon, and he already felt the weight of the case. Too many victims and too few leads.

Back at his desk, he pulled out Scully's file and opened it. The man was thorough. Detailed daily records revealed Jack Donavan's routine. He was at his clinic by nine each morning, where he stayed until usually noon or one in the afternoon. Weekdays, after a two-hour lunch, either at Marilyn's apartment or a local restaurant, his afternoon was spent making hospital rounds.

His Fridays were different. The doctor left at noon and usually met some friends for lunch then did his rounds until later in the evening and then headed for Marilyn's apartment. Jonas had to admit the doctor was a predictable bastard. Time and dated photographs supported each document, listing each person the man came in contact with.

Also, the doctor's financial records Scully had obtained revealed a steady flow of money from his practice. He was paid a salary each month, but most of his monthly business income went for office overhead and salaries. He had managed to invest in an apartment building and other stocks and bonds, but his wealth was nothing compared to what he had with his wife. Jack Donavan had not been overly frugal with his money. His wife was right. Jonas couldn't see the doctor giving up his social status even for Marilyn.

As Scully said, there was little in the file that Jonas didn't already know. He stuffed the photos and documents back in the folder and placed it in his desk drawer.

Jonas pulled out his phone and dialed Clay. When the man picked up, he said, "Meet me at Caroline's house. Rupert and Jose weren't able to check it out before we found Caroline. We're going to search every inch of the place. There has to be a connection to Caroline's killer somewhere. I know these victims are connected, and I want to know how. We're going to strip their lives bare and expose all their secrets until we find what we're missing. See you in fifteen minutes."

Grabbing his hat, Jonas left the building for the garage, climbed into his hot SUV and headed back toward Caroline's. Her car had been towed to the lab where the techs would go over it from top to bottom. He wanted to go through the house and see what he could find. As the vehicle was the primary, CSI had no reason to check the house, since she had never made it inside.

Clay arrived within the fifteen minutes and located the hidden spare house key. He often wondered how safe it was using a fake rock as a hiding place for a key. He and Jonas were solemn as they tore the yellow tape off the doorway. It was a sobering task having to search a colleague's home, no matter what the circumstances.

The house was on a quiet street nestled in the middle of the block. It was a well maintained single story brick structure with a one car garage, plenty of shade trees, front and back. Numerous flower beds added to the well-groomed appearance. Clay unlocked the door, and he and Jonas entered the living room. The inside was spacious and orderly. From what they could see, Caroline kept a well-organized home, just as she did the outside.

The living room was decorated with a dark brown leather sofa, dark wood end tables, and tall earthenware lamps. A brown leather recliner and a couple of matching cream-colored wing backed chairs finished off the furnishings. An oversized blue flowered area rug protected the hardwood floor in front of the sofa. A large entertainment center, placed against the far wall, held a large flat screen television and multiple stacks of DVDs.

The kitchen was equipped with a set of dishes, a matching set of glasses and a few pots and pans. It didn't appear Caroline did much cooking since the refrigerator and pantry were almost bare of supplies or any type of food that required being prepared.

The dining room held a long table and six matching chairs and a china cabinet displaying a blue set of dishes. It was as if Caroline had moved in, but didn't really live there.

The bedroom was the same, just the necessary furniture. A bed, with a lavender dust ruffle, a bedspread, and matching shams, a dresser, plus nightstands with tall swing arm lamps for reading. Jonas checked the master bathroom and the closet while Clay entered the second bedroom.

The closet disclosed part of Caroline's fastidious personality. Her clothes were arranged by slacks, skirts, blouses, and dresses, all in order of color and the hangers spaced an inch apart. She liked her clothes orderly just like her life.

The top nightstand drawer held a tube of ChapStick, several romantic mystery novels, a box of tissues and a notepad with a pen. The bottom drawer was empty. The drawers of the other nightstand were also void of any items.

The dresser held only her personal underwear, several sets of lingerie, and numerous pieces of jewelry, which made Jonas wonder how Caroline could afford such expensive items on her salary.

A yell came from the other bedroom, "Hey Jonas, you need to come see this," Clay called.

Jonas stopped short when he entered the room. This was where Caroline really lived. A laptop, a printer and multiple stacks of books graced the top of a large desk. Hardbacks crowded shelves of three tall bookcases lining the wall. Behind the desk, photographs of men and women were taped to a large white display board, secured to the entire back wall. Lines connected each picture to the other. Below each print was other snapshots of several boys and girls.

Clay recognized a few of the adults in the photos, but none of the children. One man was a well-known defense attorney in the area, several other pictures of men were unfamiliar, as were the images of several women.

"Did you know about this? Were you ever in here when you and Becca came for dinner?" Jonas eyed the surprised expression on Clay's face.

"Hell no! Caroline never mentioned anything about any of this. I do remember, this door was always closed. I never thought much about it. You didn't pry into Caroline's business," Clay said. "You know how closed-mouth she was about her private life."

Clay was right. She would never have shown him this office. "What the hell was this girl up to?" Jonas muttered. "Check her laptop. See if there's anything on it." He continued to study the board and the photographs.

Immediately, Clay sat down and turned on the computer. As soon as the screen powered up, he located the file of photographs and found the same pictures which she had taped to the board. Names identified each person, but that was all. Clay didn't recognize but one or two names.

Next, he opened the documents folder. Surprised at the number of files, he quickly discounted the one marked resume, and bills, but checked out the one for labeled budget.

The file that interested him the most was one listed as Retribution. Clay opened the document and proceeded to read for a few minutes before shaking his head. His voice was filled with sadness by the loss of Caroline's budding aspirations.

"Jonas," he muttered, "our girl wasn't into any type of trouble." He pointed at the screen. "It appears that Caroline was writing a crime novel. She was taking old closed cases and creating a book. From what I've read so far, it's pretty good. She seems to have changed the story somewhat. From the beginning, the story is almost the same. Children who have been molested by a family member, but who are let off with a light sentence or probation. She has a list of cases going back years. There appears to be one, in particular, she was reviewing." Clay stood so Jonas could occupy the chair.

"Well, I'll be damn," Jonas said. "Was there anything about that case which would make her a target?"

"I don't believe so," Clay said, shaking his head. "It's an old case, and it appears she was just starting to review it. She doesn't have any notes where an interview was done. All her information was taken from the case files."

"No wonder she valued her privacy. She didn't want anyone to know. Look at the name she was using," he motioned to the byline on the first page of the manuscript, "C. J. Hawks. I wonder if she ever published anything."

"I don't think so," Clay said, picking up a college workbook positioned next to the laptop. He handed it to Jonas. "She was taking a course either online or at the local college." Clay indicated the books on her desk. "These appear to be all related to writing in some way, plotting, sentence structure, exposition or narration. Caroline was as serious about writing as she was about her job as a detective."

Jonas shut the computer down, unplugged it and picked it up, "We'll take the laptop, and all those case files with us. We'll go through them and see if there's anyone in those cases whose a possible suspect. Maybe someone found out what she was doing. Perhaps we'll find something that will tell us how she met her killer."

A further search of the last bookcase produced a family photo album with pictures of her parents over the years. Another contained shots of Alfonso and Caroline together on a hike in the mountains. The books in the bookcase were mostly by well-known crime fiction writers and appeared well read.

The calendar tacked to the corkboard on the wall above her desk, listed a doctor's appointment for June, but none for July. The majority of the dates were blank. A dental appointment was penciled in for three in the afternoon on the Wednesday before her abduction and murder. No name was listed, just the word dentist.

Clay looked for bank records in the file drawer of the desk. She only kept the current month's statement and her check register. Knowing Caroline, she would list each check, who it was to and for what. He pulled the bank register from the file and ran his finger down the column until he came to a notation listed to Robert Titus, dentist. He waved the log in the air, "I found Caroline's dentist's name. If Caroline was hiding something other than her ambition to be a writer, it's not at this house," Clay remarked. "I'll get the office address and see what I can find out."

"Do it," Jonas affirmed. "I want to know where Caroline went after she left the dentist's office. From what the neighbor has already told us, she didn't get home until late. Where was she during all that time?"

They had been at the house for over an hour and needed to get back. There was only one more room to check out. It was another bedroom being used as a guest room. It, like the master bedroom, held little furniture other than a bed, a nightstand and an empty dresser. There was nothing to find, as even the closet was empty. Even the hall bathroom held the minimal toiletries.

Their search finished and finding nothing other than the name of the dentist, and Caroline's ambition to be a writer, they gathered everything and carried it to Clay's vehicle. After relocking the house and securing the yellow tape, they drove away, wondering who was next on the killer's list.

Chapter Eleven

Friday

Morgan had promised to have Marilyn's green dress to the funeral home by ten. When Lieutenant Black had not shown up by eight-forty-five, she locked the house and drove to her sister's apartment. She just stood and stared at the door for a moment, dreading to go in. And then she heard the sharp whisper. "For God's sake, go on in. Nothing's going to bite you."

Charging into the apartment, she whirled around expecting to see her twin. There was no shadowy figure of Marilyn anywhere. But she knew she had heard her sister's voice and could even feel her presence. She stopped in the middle of the living room. "Okay Marilyn, I know you're here. What do you want?"

Again she heard her whisper in a more subdued voice. "To make sure you find my dress." There was a pause. "And to tell you they found the other victim. She was a young cop. The search for her killer will now intensify. Maybe they'll catch him soon."

Morgan was stunned. "He killed a cop this time? My God!"

"Well, he's insane." She was quiet, and then Marilyn uttered sadly. "What makes a cop any more important than me? I was just as important, wasn't I?"

Marilyn had a point. "You are just as important to me," was all the answer she could give her sister. But, she was right.

Why was it, that when a police officer was killed, the hunt for the killer did actually intensify even though there might be other victims? Was it because the victim's fellow officers could no longer distance themselves from the crime and it became too personal? It became an attack against them all? Did their emotions become too exposed, and each officer realized they could be the next one to die. Morgan believed that to be the reason.

"You are as important." Morgan reiterated. "The police want to catch this man before he murders anyone else," was all she could offer as reassurance. "Now where is your dress?" she asked, and headed for the bedroom.

The dress was hanging at the front end of the closet. Slightly out of fashion, it was a beautiful dark green top with small peach flowers and a matching handkerchief skirt. Marilyn had always looked stunning in the dress.

Grabbing the hanger, she placed it on the bed and searched the closet floor until she found the matching green linen shoes. But she wasn't sure if they even put shoes on a deceased person in a casket. If they didn't, she would request they be put on Marilyn.

Quickly she collected the burial clothes, anxious to be out of the apartment and on her way. All too soon she would have to deal with sorting through Marilyn's possessions and disposing of everything. Not that she had a lot to do today, but she couldn't face the prospect of that job right now.

She needed to work on the commission for a stained glass window. After she bought her house, she had converted the next door apartment into her studio.

The hummingbird design was in pieces on the cutting table and ready to be assembled. But, since Marilyn's murder, she hadn't even been in the studio and wasn't sure she could work cutting glass today. She was still too emotional and shaky. Going to the funeral home was going to be hard enough.

And it was hard. It was just another reminder of what she had lost. Morgan declined an evening viewing on Sunday. A short service, with a closed coffin, on Monday morning, before the burial was arranged. The funeral director would put a notice in the Gazette of the date and time for the service. Not knowing any of Marilyn's friends, she wondered how many people would attend. She hoped there would be at least a few.

After dropping off the dress and shoes, and being assured they would be put on her sister, Morgan slowly drove home, glad that part of her day was over.

In the kitchen, there was a message on the machine from Lieutenant Black. He apologized over and over for not being able to meet her. Finally stating he would be in touch. That was thoughtful of him to take the time to leave a message, she thought, especially if what Marilyn had said was true. If the third victim was really a cop, she doubted if she'd be hearing from him anytime soon.

Too bad flitted through her mind. Morgan realized she wanted to see him again. She found comfort in his presence, his strength. That surprised her. Maybe it was because he was a police officer, she decided, trying to analysis her attraction to him. She couldn't. All she knew was that he made her skin tingle all over in a way no man had ever done before. That made her wonder if she caused him any unsettling moments. Probably not she decided, just as the phone rang.

She jumped at the shrill ring and grabbed the portable receiver.

"I wanted to check on you," Jonas said. "I know you had to drop off your sister's clothes to the funeral home. I would have made a point of going with you, but other things prevented me from being there."

"I know," Morgan said. "You found your missing detective. Am I right?"

"How did you know it was a detective?" he added, suspicion rearing its ugly head. "Please don't say your sister told you." He didn't want to hear those words again, even though he was sure that was what she was going to say.

"I'm sorry, but she did. I know you don't want to believe me, but it's true. I'm not lying to you. Do you believe anyone or have faith in anything?" For a few seconds, there was silence on the other end.

He finally responded to her question. "Not too much anymore. I guess I've seen too much."

He sounded weary to Morgan as if the weight of the case rested heavily on his mind. Without thinking, she said. "If you have time, come by. I'll fix coffee or even dinner if you want." God, she thought, why did I say that? The man's going to think I'm making a pass at him. And she was. Stuttering, she added, "I said that only because you sound exhausted. You're always telling me to take care of myself, but are you doing the same?"

He couldn't believe it. Morgan had offered to cook for him. But he wanted something special for her. A night away from all the pain was what she deserved. On impulse, he said, "That sounds great," really wanting to see her as well. "But I'm swamped here at work. I'll take you up on dinner another day. We can go out. I don't want you to have to cook. Will you have dinner with me at a later date?"

What was he doing asking her out to dinner? It was against all policies for him to get involved with this woman. But, he couldn't seem to help himself. He wanted to know her better, no matter what his instincts were telling him.

Morgan didn't hesitate, "Yes, I'd love to." Her heart was going to beat right out of her chest. She took a deep breath trying to slow her racing pulse. The detective would be the first man to ask her out since her split with her husband.

"I'll call you as soon as we get a break in the case. And," Jonas paused as if making a decision, "I want to believe you. I may never understand it or be able to explain it, but I know you are somehow in touch with your sister. I'll try not to doubt you again."

She released an audible sigh. The man was trying to believe her, maybe there was hope yet. "Thank you. I needed to know that. If I find out anything more, I'll call you."

"Good," he said. "I have to go."

In the background, Morgan could hear someone calling his name. "Okay. And again, thank you," she placed the receiver back on the cradle.

Jonas hung up the phone and looked up as Benedict entered his office and came to stand in front of his desk. The man looked like hell.

"I can't just stay home and sit on my ass," he said. "Give me something to do. I need to be working." His dark eyes were rimmed with red, and the pallor of his skin made him look ill.

And the man was sick over what had happened. Jonas had been ill too after Kelly's murder. Benedict had it just as bad. He was older, and Caroline's death was just as horrific.

"You can't be working on this case. You know that." Jonas said, understanding all too well how impossible it was to do nothing. He had thrown himself into work on his grandfather's ranch until exhaustion had sent him to bed.

"If you want something to do," he added, "report to the Funeral Committee. They need all the help they can get. You can help with Caroline's funeral by going with the chaplain to make the notification that we recovered her body. Then you can stay with the parents. There will be a lot more for you to do."

Benedict nodded. "Good, that's the least I can do for her. Thanks. I need this. I'll talk to you later." The detective turned and headed out the door.

The funeral arrangement for a fallen officer was not a simple affair. This would not be the first one Jonas had attended. The release of Caroline's name to the press would not happen until after her parents had been officially notified, then and only then would her identity be released. Benedict would stay with the family through the entire process. That would keep him busy for a time.

The ceremony itself was not a simple affair either. A public funeral such as Caroline's would be conducted in full military-style and ceremonial honors. There was the notification of all appropriate personnel and the planning of the event itself. One primary job was protecting Caroline's family from all the media circus that followed the death of a police officer. Benedict would make sure the service was exactly as the family wanted.

Then the department would release the death and the official public funeral notice via teletype messages, e-mails, Web site postings, and even fax notifications all at the same time and from the same source.

Fellow officers from across the country would be coming in. Time had to be allowed for them to arrive. There would be the service itself, and the coordination and control of the traffic from the church service to the graveside. Once all arrangements were completed, the funeral held and the flag presented, the family would be escorted home to mourn their loss.

Caroline's death had hit his team hard, and they would all participate in the service. Jonas wondered about Eppie's mother and about Morgan handling her sister's funeral. Who did she have? He should have offered to help. Planning to bury your parent had to be devastating for her, being all alone. It wasn't too late to call and offer his support.

He pulled out his cell phone, and stared at it, hesitant. Being engrossed with the case was no excuse for his not calling Eppie. Quickly he dialed his partner's cell number. The call immediately went to voicemail, so he left a message. Next, he dialed Morgan's number and waited. No answer. He wondered where she could be. Just as he replaced his cell phone in his pocket, the desk phone rang. It was Winston Hanover.

"Black here," Jonas said.

"Hey, Jonas," Hanover said. "Was Scully's information helpful?"

"I don't know yet. I haven't had time to review it all. We've been busy, as you can guess, with Caroline's murder. You heard we found her this morning."

"Yeah, and I'm sorry. Also, I wanted to give you a heads up. I heard it from a friend in the Mayor's office that the big man will be calling your Chief today. He wants to know what progress you've made on the doctor's case now that it's been reassigned to Homicide."

"My God, the man's body was just found Wednesday, and we've been a little busy with Caroline's abduction and murder. What the fuck do they expect? For us to pull evidence out of our ass? The Commander and Chief know better. We can't catch a killer without leads, and we have none at this time." Jonas sat back in his chair and fumed. The Mayor should have to try and do this job.

"If you can, talk to the widow again. See if she can think of anyone who wanted her husband dead. Also, we need a list of any of his patients who might have been pissed off at him and filing a lawsuit. His clinic should have that information." He blew out a breath and added, "We need all the help we can get."

"Glad to," Hanover replied, "I can do that."

"I'd send Henry with you, but he's still out at the Garden of the Gods, with the rest of the team. I doubt if they'll find much. Just like the others, Caroline wasn't killed there. I'll send Fernandez to the clinic for a list of the doctor's male patients. Even though this is a murder case, due to the HIPPA, we need a warrant." He paused for a second. "I doubt if the wife can tell us anything else, but see what you can find out." There was silence on the line for a moment.

"You still there?" Jonas asked.

"Yeah. I was just thinking, we caught a missing person's case this morning. This attorney and a woman have been missing for a couple of weeks before the first murder. The only reason I'm mentioning it is that, like in the case of your victims, it seems these two were having an affair and supposedly ran off to Mexico together."

Curious, Jonas asked, "Who filed the missing person's report?" Were there two more bodies to be found, he wondered?

"The attorney's secretary, Rebecca Allen, knew about the affair. When he didn't show up for work, she called the police. The man had already left his wife, Sydney, and she doesn't care where he is. And the woman, Carla Winslow, had already left her husband. It seems Mrs. Winslow worked for the attorney as well. He created trust accounts for the children of rich families. According to Rebecca, Carla was definitely unhappy in her marriage. Seems her husband had sexual problems. She didn't elaborate but did say Carla wanted out of the marriage. So, she hooked up with Theodore Matthews.

And, Matthews was supposed to be back from Mexico the first of last week. I've been in touch with both of their spouses. The husband of the woman," He hesitated as if consulting his notes, "Carson Winslow, couldn't care less if she is missing."

"What do we know about him?" Jonas asked.

"He's a teacher at the college downtown," Winston continued. "In fact, both spouses said good riddance. We're looking for both of their vehicles. Hopefully, we'll find them soon. But, like your case, we don't have much to go on at this point." Hanover sighed. "Let me know if you find anything."

"I can do that. Have you checked with Charlie Jacks?" If there were any unidentified bodies, Charlie would know.

"Yeah, Jacks doesn't have them either," Winston said, pausing as if formulating another statement. "I was sorry to hear about Caroline. She was a good detective," he added.

"Thanks. I'll send Jose and Pope to the clinic as soon as they show up," Jonas said. "And, I'll keep an eye out for your missing people. Maybe they decided to remain in Mexico."

"I don't think so. The attorney had a trial date with Judge Jordan. You know an attorney would have to be crazy to be late for one of his trials." Judge Jordan had a reputation for being a stickler for punctuality and preparedness. He'd slap a contempt fine on any attorney who was two minutes late or not prepared to defend his client.

"I see what you mean. It's best we consider the possibility these two are related to our case. Let's wait until you find the vehicles. Then, we'll go from there," Jonas said.

"I'll keep you posted on what's happening on my end," Winston agreed.

"Thanks," Jonas said and replaced the receiver.

He sat back and rubbed his eyes. God, he was tired. Ever since finding the Heddrix woman, he had not been sleeping well. What he needed was a decent meal, a stiff drink, and a good night's sleep in that order.

He wondered what Morgan was planning for the evening. Maybe tonight would be a good time to take her to dinner. The more he thought about it, the better the idea sounded. He needed to find out more about her sister. With this killer, he needed all the information he could find. Again he took out his cell phone and punched in her number.

Her voice was a sweet whisper when she answered. She sounded as if she had just awakened.

"Were you sleeping?" Jonas hated the idea that he might have interrupted her nap.

"Not really. I was dozing on the sofa. I saw where you called earlier. Was there something you wanted?" Morgan stifled a yawn. Actually, she had been asleep. Before, she had heard the phone ring but was too sleepy to answer.

"I was wondering. It's getting late, and I haven't had anything to eat other than breakfast. Would you have dinner with me?" Jonas held his breath. If she said no, he'd have to accept that she might not be interested in him. But he still needed more information about her sister. He was surprised when she accepted.

"I'll have to meet you. There are a couple of things I still have to do. What time and where?" Morgan was trembling with anticipation, hoping her voice didn't betray her excitement.

"How about seven at Barrett's Steak House on Tejon?"

Morgan glanced at her watch. That was over two hours away. Good, she thought, enough time to buy a new dress. The Citadel Mall wasn't that far away.

"Okay," she said. "I'll meet you there."

"Good. See you there." Jonas listened to her quick goodbye and then pocketed his cell phone. There was almost a flutter in the pit of his stomach. It had been a long time since he had been interested in a woman other than a quick fling. Morgan Jansen was not a woman to stand for a quick fling. With her, it would be all or nothing. Was he ready for that kind of commitment? He wasn't getting any younger. The big four-O was only a little over a year away. If he ever wanted to share his life with a woman, he couldn't think of a better choice than Morgan. With that thought in mind, he turned his attention back to the two case files on his desk, one being the reports of Rudy Scully.

Morgan found the perfect little black dress at Dillard's, a simple fitted pattern which emphasized her figure. She bought matching shoes and hurried home to shower. At promptly six-forty-five, she walked out and locked her back door. The drive to the restaurant took only minutes. Barrett's Steak House was known for its excellent food and wine and was usually packed. The closest parking space was located on South Nevada and a short walk to the restaurant.

Jonas was standing outside the entrance and greeted her with a smile. No, he thought, this woman definitely would not be interested in a quick fling. The urge to give out a low whistle was great, but the detective knew it would embarrass her. Instead, he issued the only compliment which popped into his head.

"Wow! You look fantastic!" Her face still turned pink. Taking her arm, he led her down the few steps and through the entrance. The hostess ushered them to a booth in the back.

Located in the basement of the old Alamo building, the interior utilized the ambiance of the old stone walls with subdued lighting. It was elegant without being stuffy, Morgan thought, as she slid into the booth. All types of attire were present from white shirts, jeans, and boots to business suits, and women in stylish dresses.

Their waitress was paired with another girl to make sure the service was attentive and efficient. The menu was extensive, and Morgan settled on the Chicken Marsala while he ordered the salmon. They each took a sip of their drinks, a glass of wine for her, and Jonas studied her over his glass of scotch.

"This is nice," she said, anything to break the silence. A quick glance around the interior and her eyes locked on a stranger. Across the room, sitting alone in a booth, a man was staring at her. For a brief instant, their eyes met. Morgan was positive recognition appeared in his, though she had never seen him before. Conscious of his stares, she turned back to listen to what Jonas was saying.

"I wanted to take you somewhere special. This is a nice restaurant, and they have great food as well." He took another sip of his drink as if contemplating what to say next. Morgan saved him the trouble.

"Why did you ask me to dinner?" she asked. "I appreciate it, but I have to wonder why." Could he have a motive other than a mutual attraction?

"Actually, I wanted to get to know you better and," he admitted reluctantly, "I want to understand your relationship with your sister."

Morgan stared at him. So he did have an ulterior motive. "Well, at least you're honest about it." She took in a breath and added, "What do you want to know?" and gave an audible sigh. Questions! He had asked her to dinner to ask more questions about her and Marilyn. "You didn't have to buy me dinner to question me some more." Morgan tried not to let her disappointment show.

"I know that. But if I know more about you and your sister, it will help me understand this bond between you." Jonas hoped he wasn't screwing up his chance with this woman.

Morgan smiled. It didn't have anything to do with Marilyn's death. She was relieved. For a brief time, she didn't want to have to think about her sister's murder. She desperately needed a break from the tragedy in her life.

"Okay, what do you want to know?" she said. "Ready or not, Detective, I'll tell you everything."

"All of it," he said, "from your birth to the present time." Jonas wanted to know every nuance of her life.

She was an extraordinary woman, and he wanted to understand every facet of her personality as well as what Marilyn was like. The woman had made an enemy, and it had cost her.

"We were born in Virginia and lived there until we were twelve. But you know that already." She studied his face and saw a slight flush spread across his features. Well, she thought, he can be embarrassed.

"Yes," he admitted. "But I want to know about your childhood. How well did you get along with your sister?"

A sad smile curved Morgan's lips. "We had a good childhood. Marilyn and I were inseparable until we turned twelve. We went to a public school and spent our summers at the beach with our parents. We didn't think we were different from other kids. It was all normal for us to be able to know what the other was thinking or feeling. How could we know? Then things changed." Oh Lord, how they changed. Morgan continued to explain as they ate their salads.

The memories raced through her mind. They were happy twelve-year-olds. Then came that dreadful summer when the boy went missing. It had started with a nightmare of being dragged from bed and stuffed in the trunk of a car. She and Marilyn had awakened screaming and crying. Their words had stumbled over each other as they told the same story to their worried parents. When they insisted it had not been a dream, their parents assured them it was.

But throughout the next four days, their

nightmares continued. Then their parents read about the missing boy in the newspaper. They made the mistake of going to the police to offer help. She and Marilyn had been questioned over and over. The cops did not believe them. They kept searching for the missing boy in the wrong places. Later, his body was found exactly where the girls had said he would be.

Afterward, she explained, the people blamed them. The press exploited their story. She told about the angry phone calls, the threats, and nutty people begging for them to contact their dead relatives. How the crazies insisted the girls could predict the lotto numbers and demanded that they do it. It all became a nightmare for their parents. People began to stalk them. It became so difficult for them to go out in public, their father feared for their safety.

As their dinners arrived, Morgan paused until the waitress left. She glanced over at the booth where the man had sat staring at her. He was gone. The waitress brought her another glass of wine and another scotch for Jonas. As soon as the woman was out of earshot, she continued.

She explained how her father had come home from the college and told them he had been fired, without a reason or moment's notice. The threats continued. To protect them, their parents packed up the house and moved to Florida. As she began to eat her dinner, Morgan waited for the detective's reaction. He was almost stone-faced.

"So the catalyst was your ability as twins to find the missing boy?" Jonas summarized. He tried to imagine how horrible that time had been for her. In his wildest imagination, he would never know how that tragedy affected both girls. "Is that also when you and Marilyn started to drift apart?"

Morgan was surprised by his insight. "Yes," she muttered and continued as she munched on a mushroom.

Their finding the boy had been the start of the rift. Marilyn had eaten up the attention, but not the accusations and blame. In a sense, the boy's parents had been right to blame them. Their parents had only gone to the police several days after the girls had told them where to find the boy. By that time, the child had been murdered. The Coroner had stated he died twenty-four hours prior to the discovery of his body. And their parents admitted at they had waited to contact the police to protect their daughters.

Maybe it was the guilt that made them leave everything behind and move out of state. They didn't want to be reminded of what had happened. Their lives became drastically different after that. They were kept close to home and not allowed to attend public schools. As a teacher, their father homeschooled them. They were escorted by their parents everywhere, even to movies. Other children could come to their house, but they were not allowed to attend any sleepovers away from home. No wonder they were rebellious, Morgan had to admit. All the restrictions drove Marilyn crazy.

"How did you end up in Colorado Springs?" Jonas asked, before taking another bite of salmon.

"Because of Marilyn," Morgan said. "God, she was wild and hated all the rules and restrictions. The girl would sneak out of the house and then deny it. When we turned sixteen, our parents found out she had been slipping out at night to meet a boy. I did the same thing, but I didn't go as far as Marilyn. I found out the boy she was meeting was the same one I had been sneaking out to see and had a crush on.

"The only problem was that Marilyn slept with him pretending to be me, and became pregnant. The final straw was when she stole money our mother had saved, lied about her age and had an abortion. She had acquired a phony driver's license." Morgan pushed her plate away and added, "As a result, Marilyn almost died. Our parents decided Florida was not the right place for us. So in 1998, we moved here. They believed they had successfully moved us away from bad influences. How wrong they were.

"Anyway, they put us in the public school system for our last two years of high school. Marilyn pretended to change. She never had to study hard. It all came too easy for her, the cheerleading, dating the football captain, all of it. Still, she had grown sneakier. Our parents never knew about her nightly escapades to meet her many lovers. She never became pregnant again. I believe something happened when she had the abortion to prevent her from having children." Morgan met the Lieutenant's gaze.

"What were you doing while Marilyn was having her fun? Did you ever join her when she sneaked out?" Was she as wild as her sister or was she more reserved? For some reason, he doubted she was that reserved. He'd read how the personality of twins was the direct opposite. He wondered how accurate it was in their case.

Morgan had to smile at his curiosity. What he didn't know, she was not about to tell him. "I got into my fair share of trouble," she admitted. "You have to understand. We had been under constant supervision since we were twelve. Our parents were trying to protect us. They couldn't. We protected ourselves with silence. We never again told them or anyone about what we saw. It would have been too horrific on mom and dad. As it was, it was horribly difficult for us. We're guilty of not knowing if we could have saved someone by going to the police. We were too afraid to tell what we knew. The public can be vicious, so we kept our knowledge to ourselves."

Jonas was astonished. She had stated that they had had other visions and could have possibly saved people from becoming victims. "You mean to tell me that you two knew people were in danger and did nothing about it?" He wrinkled his brow in amazement.

Morgan frowned at him. He was obviously shocked that they had done nothing about what they knew. "Yes, we did nothing!" she snapped.

She leaned a little forward, each word clipped and precise as she defended their actions. "Our visions were never clear. It was all a muddled mess of vague images. By the times the images became clear, the crime had been committed, and the victim was dead. Just like now with Marilyn trying to warn of the people being murdered. It's like struggling through a thick fog."

He leaned back in the booth. Morgan's claws were bared now. This was not a timid woman.

Her voice was filled with anger. "Do you think we wanted to know those things? Not only no, but hell no! I wish I could give these visions to you and see how you'd like living with nightmares most nights." Morgan tossed her napkin on the table and started to slide out of the booth.

He reached across and grabbed her arm. "Hey, I'm sorry. I wasn't trying to make you mad." When she gave him a piercing glare, he removed his hand, thankful that at least she remained seated. He hurried to add, "Please don't leave. I tell you I'm trying to understand, but I don't. I can't know how you survived all that's happened to you. I didn't mean to bite your head off. Again, I'm sorry. But it's a lot to take in. Please stay." It dawned on him that he really didn't want to ruin his chances with this woman.

Still glaring at him, Morgan moved back into the booth and resumed pushing around the mushrooms on her plate. "Look," she said, "I believe our gift, bond or whatever you want to call it, only works because we're identical twins. Since Marilyn's death, my nightmares have diminished. I only know things because she has been keeping me awake and telling me about them. When I do sleep, it's a lot more peaceful. I'd be happy if I never had another vision. But I doubt if I'll be that lucky."

The waitress returned. "Need a box?" she asked.

Morgan nodded, and after the waitress left, returned Jonas's intense gaze.

"I was not trying to upset you. I wanted this to be a relaxing night away from your problems. Having you relive your childhood was not a good idea, obviously," he said. She had no idea how sorry he was for asking about her family. "I do apologize again." He was almost afraid to ask but needed to know. "Tell me about your husband."

Morgan laughed, "My rat of a husband, what do you want to know?"

"Where did you meet him?"

"After I graduated college, I started creating my stained glass dragonflies, butterflies, and windows. It took a couple of years, but they began to sell. Since I was making fairly good money, I had to claim it on my taxes. Andy was the CPA I went to."

"When did you get married?"

Again Morgan gave a laugh, then said, "I'd had a bad experience with a relationship before I met Andy. So I wasn't ready to become involved with anyone for a while. But he was determined and chased me for about a year before I agreed to go out with him. My trust in men had been damaged. He was always honest with me, loving and caring. I fell in love with him, believed I could trust him. Finally, I agreed to marry him a couple of years later. I suppose that's why his betrayal hurt so much."

Jonas could understand her pain and why she'd cut all ties with her sister. "Did Marilyn ever explain why she slept with your husband?"

Morgan was silent for a moment, remembering all the excuses her sister had offered for her betrayal. "All the excuses in the world wouldn't justify what she did," she said. "When we were in Florida, she had pretended to be me, but I thought she'd grown up, and that would never do that to me again. All that nonsense was behind us. This was my sister, the other half of my soul. The only reason she did what she did, was because Marilyn knew she could. Her betrayal hurt me far worse than Andy's. I was thankful my parents were dead by then, so they never knew about Marilyn's betrayal." She leaned back in the seat and finished off her drink

"I'm sorry," Jonas said, and he was. That type of betrayal stayed with a person. You could try and even claim to forgive, but the memory never went away. "When did your parents die?"

"Just before Christmas in 2010. They were on their way to Denver and became involved in an auto accident on I-25. A truck lost control due to road conditions and caused a multiple-vehicle pileup. So you see, after losing my parents, thanks to my sister, I lost my husband as well." There was anger in her eyes as the memories emerged. "I don't want to think about it anymore. It hurts too much. And I've had enough anguish in the last few of years."

"I need to ask, do you think your ex-husband could have had anything to do with Marilyn's death?" Even as he asked the question, Jonas had doubts. Andrew Jansen might have a grudge against Marilyn, but why would he want to kill Jack Donavan? He wouldn't. Then who would? Their meal finished, he hated the idea of the evening coming to an end. He felt he owed her another night out. This was supposed to be an evening away from all her troubles. He had only added to her distress by drudging up old memories.

"I intended to give you a night away from your

problems. I didn't do that. I'd like to make it up to you. Would you have dinner with me again?" Jonas asked.

"I don't think that's a good idea. And, I'm not upset anymore."

He could see her physically relax, but sadness crept into her eyes as she continued, "I just want some peace in my life. I don't want to dream or hear my sister's voice telling me that there's another body to be found. I just want peace and quiet!"

He wished he could give it to her, but knew it was beyond his doing. "I would help, but I don't know how."

"I don't think you can help me," was all she had to say.

The waitress returned and shifted Morgan's uneaten portion to the box and placed it in a bag. The check, she presented to Jonas. He paid the bill and helped Morgan out of the booth. "Where are you parked?"

It was after eight-fifteen, and beginning to get dark. Jonas wasn't about to let her walk to the car alone. He led the way out of the restaurant and up the stairs to the street where they stood for a few moments. "I'm going to walk you to your car, so which way."

Morgan gestured to the east. "That isn't necessary, you know. I'll be fine. I'm only a block away on Nevada." When he refused to budge, she took his arm as they slowly strolled past the Great Western Bank building. At the parking garage on East Cucharras Street, Jonas noticed a vehicle at the exit. The man sat and waited for them to pass. It was too dark to see the driver's features, so he ignored the car.

When they reached her vehicle parked on the southwest corner of Nevada, he tried again, "Will you change your mind and have dinner with me some other evening?"

Morgan considered his request. "I don't think that's a good idea," she repeated.

"Maybe not, but I would like to see you again outside of my job." He wanted, needed to see her again.

She gave a deep sigh. Jonas was persistent if nothing else. She did want to see him again, but no repeat of tonight's conversation. "On one condition," she said.

"Anything," he replied, and opened the driver's door.

As she slid in behind the steering wheel, she said, "I cook, and no more questions about my history. I get to question you. Agreed?"

"Alright, but you may be disappointed." He gave her a big smile and closed the door. As she keyed the ignition, he added. "I'll call you."

"You do that," she called out and pulled away from the curb.

As Morgan drove away, the vehicle he had noticed before turned the corner and followed when she turned left on Vermijo. He was parked north of the restaurant and could not make it back to his car in time to follow the other one. He hadn't even gotten the license plate number. But, he thought, as he hurried to his SUV, I can go by her house and make sure she's all right.

Chapter Twelve

Friday

The killer had to fight to keep from staring at the bitch. Panic made him want to hurry from the restaurant, but he didn't. Forcing himself to take one bite at a time and not gulp down his food was an effort. When the woman wasn't looking, he kept sneaking peeks at her. It was like looking at a ghost. But it couldn't be the same whore. He knew that one was dead; he had killed her and dumped her body. So who was this evil duplicate?

He left the restaurant within a reasonable time. Compelling himself to remain calm, he quickly climbed the stairs to the street level, and then hurried across the street to the City Utilities building. There, he could stand in the shadows and watch the entrance. He waited. Finally, when he saw their heads emerge above the stairs, he lingered until they were standing on the sidewalk talking.

Once the woman pointed in the direction of Nevada Avenue, he turned and fast walked to his vehicle in the parking garage. No cars were behind him, so he sat at the exit, positive he had lost them. He was amazed to see the man and woman slowly stroll past. His heart almost stopped when the man glanced in his direction, but then turned away. When she slid behind the wheel of her car, he pulled into the street and stopped at the light on Nevada. As her vehicle pulled away from the curb, he turned the corner and followed.

It was a short drive to Platte Avenue and then left on North Institute where she continued north before turning into a driveway. He lost sight of her as she drove to the back of the house, then reappeared a few moments later and entered a side door. Parked at the curb, he sat watching until lights came on. When he saw headlights of another car coming up the street behind him, he quickly drove away. At least now he knew where the whore lived and would deal with her later. She was probably like the other one, a duplicate, just as evil. She would have to die as well.

As he drove back toward Cascade Avenue, he could feel the nagging tingle on his skin, as the anticipation began to build. He loved the feeling of power it created as it coursed through his veins. He still hadn't been able to locate that damn dentist. But he would find him. He'd call his office. The waiting was worth it. He'd enjoy the hunt for now. The man had no idea what fate awaited him. The killer smiled to himself. The dentist would definitely get his due punishment. He'd make sure of that. As for the woman, he'd keep a close eye on her. Her time would come.

Morgan had just dropped her purse on the sofa when there was a knock at the front door. She frowned as her stomach lurched at the unexpected noise. Peeking through the curtain, she saw the Lieutenant. Opening the door, she asked, "Is everything all right?"

"Yeah, I just wanted to make sure you got home safe." He wasn't about to tell her someone might have followed her home. Besides by the time he arrived at her house, the vehicle was driving away and turning left at the light. He couldn't be positive a car had actually followed her.

Morgan hesitated. "Do you want to come in?" she asked, knowing she was making a mistake.

He stared at her, trying to make up his mind. Decision made, he said, "I can't. I have to go by the office and check on things." He continued to gaze at her, damming himself for being a coward. "Yeah, I'd better go."

"Okay. Don't work too late," Morgan said, almost sighing with relief. He was one temptation she wasn't sure she could resist. It had been too long since she had been with a man. Before he could change his mind, she started to close the door.

"Hey," Jonas rushed to stop her. "If I can, would you like to have lunch with me tomorrow?" He was pushing his luck.

"Sure, call me." Morgan gave him a small smile, pleasantly surprised. After he turned away, she closed the door and locked it, but continued to watch him walk to his SUV.

Lunch tomorrow, she thought, as she hurried to put her leftover dinner in the refrigerator. She had to admit, she liked being around the detective. For some reason, she felt safe with him, not that she had anything to fear. But he also gave her a peaceful feeling, as if everything was going to be alright. It felt right being with him. Good grief, she chided herself. You hardly know the man. Still, she thought, it was good to have any form of peace in her life these days, considering everything that had happened.

Monday morning was her sister's service. All she could hope for was that other people would show up? How terrible it would be if she were the only mourner.

When she turned away from the refrigerator, Morgan was stunned to see her twin standing in the middle of her living room. Marilyn still wore the gray T-shirt and red underwear. "Damn it, Marilyn, you scared me half to death!" Morgan stormed. She shook her head, "And can't you find something else to wear besides that?"

Marilyn gave her a dirty glare. "For God's sake, Morgan, I died in this. Where in hell would you suppose I get other clothes? I'm dead, remember! I can't just snap my fingers and change what I wear. It's not that simple."

Exhaustion settled on Morgan's shoulders. She felt crappy for yelling at her sister, but it was such a shock to suddenly see her standing in the middle of the room. "Sorry," was all she muster.

And she was sorry. For the briefest time, thanks to the detective, she had been able to forget. Now, all the raw emotions rushed at her like a locomotive and slammed into the pit of her stomach. She dropped into the nearest chair and buried her face in her hands. No tears came, only the horrific weight bearing down on her heart.

There would be more tears to come, she knew. Right now, she wished she could have just come home, had a cup of tea and gone to bed. She sat back and asked, "Why are you here, Marilyn?" each word weighted with sadness.

Her sister's ghost flopped on the sofa next to the chair. Marilyn tilted her head and appraised Morgan. "You know, you look like hell. You have to do something about your looks. You'll never be able to jump that man's bones looking all sad and pathetic."

Morgan's mouth dropped open. "Are you out of your mind? What makes you think I'm interested in Lieutenant Black?" she yelled, her hands gesturing wildly.

"Oh, please!" Marilyn scowled, "Who are you trying to kid? Yourself? I can feel your hormones raging all through your body." She pointed at Morgan, "Remember, I'm your twin. I feel what you feel! And I must say he is quite the hunk. I wouldn't mind giving him a try myself."

Again Morgan's mouth dropped open, and a deep flush crept up her neck. "You are unbelievable! I thought you were so in love with Jack Donavan," she retorted.

"I am," Marilyn casually examined her nails. "And I may be dead, but I can still look and appreciate a gorgeous man."

"Get off the subject, Marilyn. Why are you here?" Morgan wanted to go to bed and not hear more about her raging hormones.

This time it was Marilyn who felt the weight of despair flash across her face. "I hate this," she muttered, almost too low for Morgan to hear.

"What!" Morgan demanded. "Tell me!"

Marilyn was compelled to say what she had been

sent to tell. "That's just it, I don't have specifics. It's all vague because nothing is definite. The killer is on the hunt for Caroline's lover. And yes, I know her name now."

Since she was dead, Marilyn wondered, why couldn't she just rest in peace? But she knew that she would not be granted it for some time. She was being forced to add, "He knows who and where to find him. If the cops don't find him first, he's dead. The man will take him and kill him the same way as Jack."

"Are you sure?" Morgan asked.

"Yes. And you have to be careful. That man saw you tonight. He'll be watching you." There it was done. She had delivered her message, and now she felt herself being drawn away as if her very soul was fading. "I have to go," she said, standing.

Morgan stared up at her sister. There was a deep sorrow in the drooping of her shoulders. "What is it?" she insisted. There was more, she could tell, could feel it.

"I don't know how much longer I have here," Marilyn whispered. She glanced around the room, and then back at Morgan. "I'm being pulled away."

"To where!"

"I'm dead, sister. I go wherever the dead go." And Marilyn could feel the pull growing stronger each time she visited Morgan.

"I can't lose you forever!" The very idea that she would never see her sister again, not even as a ghost, was devastating to Morgan. She felt a new batch of tears begin to well up in her eyes.

There was compassion in Marilyn's voice as she said, "I will always be with you, sister. You won't see me, but I'll be here." On a more upbeat note," she persisted. "I'll be around for a while longer. But afterward, I'll have to leave."

"Why?" Morgan didn't ever want to let her go. She'd be happy to be haunted by her sister forever. From the pained expression on her twin's face, she knew she would be left alone.

"Morgan, you know only a few things I've done to people. I've caused so much pain and sorrow that I have to make amends. Hey, we don't get a free ride in this life. You know what they say, Karma's a bitch. It's true. Whatever we do to others comes back on us. We have to pay for every wrong deed." Tears slid down Marilyn's face. "I've got a lot to make up for."

Morgan felt the faint brush of her sister's hand on her cheek and Marilyn began to disappear right before her eyes.

One of the last things she heard was Marilyn softly whisper, "I'll see you before I leave permanently." Before she completely vanished, she added, "Tell your detective that the killer is on the hunt again."

Morgan dissolved into tears. Rushing into the bedroom, she stripped off her dress and underwear, dropped the items on a chair, and then slipped between the sheets, and cried herself to sleep.

Henry Pope had been surprised to see his Lieutenant with Marilyn Heddrix's sister at Barrett's Steak House. Needing a decent meal, he'd made a reservation for a booth at the back. He was almost finished eating when they walked in. After they were seated, he thought the woman had looked right at him. He had never formally met her and knew her only from the picture on the crime board. When she didn't appear to recognize him, he'd finished his meal and immediately left.

He'd stood across the street from Barrett's and waited for them to appear. He was curious as to whether or not Jonas would go home with her. So when she pulled away from the curb on Nevada, he followed her, keeping another car between them. Once he saw where she lived with no sign of the lieutenant, and after the car ahead of him pulled over and parked, he drove on home.

He checked his mail and turned on the television. Jonas hadn't mentioned that little talk, so tonight, he wasn't going to drink. Henry wasn't going to take the chance of losing his job. Besides, he and Jose were going to meet up back at the office to go over the files the Lieutenant and Clay had brought back from Caroline's house. Perusing through them might get his boss off his back and again in his good graces.

Not that Jonas ever rode his men hard as long as they did their job. He was supportive of his team and went out of his way to help in any way he could. Henry's being in trouble at work was no one's fault but his own. He changed out of his business suit, switching to a pullover shirt, tan slacks and carried a sports jacket just in case he'd need it.

The evening was wearing away, and he needed to get to the office. He stared at the bottle of scotch sitting on the kitchen counter. One quick drink wouldn't hurt, he assured himself as he poured a shot into the glass.

That one was followed by another and then another. That was the last thing he remembered until he woke up just before dawn sitting behind the wheel of his vehicle in his driveway with no idea where he'd been. Son of a bitch was all he could think. Now the shit is really going to hit the fan.

Only Clay and Fernandez, from his team, were still at the office when Jonas arrived. Two men from the other Homicide team were working at their computers. Jonas took a seat in the chair next to Clay's desk, placed an elbow on the surface and propped his chin in his hand.

Clay looked at him. "You look tired," he said. "When was the last time you had a good night's sleep?"

Jonas sat up straighter. "That's a good question. When I'm finished here, I'm going home and straight to bed. Any news?" He doubted it but had to ask. This killer was too careful to leave much behind.

"Hanover called again about his missing people. He wants you to call him. And," Clay said, raising his eyebrows, "the Mayor called regarding Doctor Donavon's case. I explained we're waiting for the DNA on the blood from the tree branch. I told him how long it takes to get the results. He's going to call Metro Lab and," he made quote marks in the air, "run a red hot poker up their asses. Those were his words, not mine." Clay stifled a yawn. Hell, he was tired too.

The lieutenant rubbed the back of his neck. "Good. Maybe we'll have the results this weekend. "Do we have the GPS information on Caroline's car yet?"

"Yep. It doesn't show much. She was home for most of the morning, went to a dental office building on the south side and then to the Sunset Apartment complex. She was there until about thirty minutes before her abduction, which makes no sense unless she was there with someone." Clay frowned. "I left a message for the apartment manager to give me a call." He leaned forward and continued, "Caroline's dentist has an office with the Titus Dental Group. His nurse claims he left for Denver immediately after her appointment."

"Did you tell her he may be in danger?"

"No. We don't know for sure that Caroline was screwing around with him."

Jonas stood and went into his office with Clay following. "No, we don't," he said, "Tomorrow, I want you to check out Andrew Jansen, Morgan's husband. He's a CPA. See if he had an alibi for the time Marilyn was murdered. He slept with the victim while married to Morgan. I doubt it, but I want to know if he wanted Marilyn dead. Per Ms. Jansen, he still lives in their old house in Village Seven."

A bit shocked by this revelation, Clay uttered, from the doorway. "You've got to be kidding me!"

"No, that's what caused the rift between the sisters," he said, dropping into his chair behind the desk.

"I'd be pissed off too if I was her."

"She was, thus her divorce. When you finish with Jansen, check out Dr. Titus. See if he's married if so explain the situation to his wife. Maybe, she'll be able to reach him." From the bottom drawer, Jonas removed the green leather journal. He could feel Clay watching him.

"I can do that. But," Clay added, as Jonas tucked

the journal under his arm, "If you take that home, you're not going to get any sleep. You'll spend the night taking cold showers or jerking off."

"Maybe I have more self-control than you," the Lieutenant grinned.

"Like hell you do. I read two of those entries and I was so hot, I wanted to jump the first woman I saw." When Jonas ignored him and continued to walk toward the door, Clay followed, calling after him. "Don't say you weren't warned." He stopped briefly at his desk, dropped his cell phone into his pocket, all the while, muttering to himself, while words from the journal created images in his mind. "Hell, I'm going home and jump my wife," he again muttered and headed toward the elevators.

Jonas waved a good-night to Clay in the parking garage. He followed closely behind as they pulled onto the avenue. Clay lived with his wife, an Emergency Room nurse, in Old Colorado City on the west side of town. Jonas headed to his house on North Nevada. At this late hour, it was not more than ten minutes, and he was pulling into his detached garage.

The house was built in the twenties and needed to be renovated. The bones and foundation were solid even if the inside looked like shit with all the repairs he was trying to get done. In some rooms, the walls still had wallpaper. A list of upgrades he wanted was in his round-tuit jar. The only rooms he had refurbished were the living room and his bedroom. Too many long hours at work had prevented him from completing the majority of the jobs. He wasn't about to pay someone else to repair something he was capable of doing.

He gathered the mail from the mailbox and unlocked the front door. With a flick of his wrist, he tossed the mail and journal on the coffee table, removed his sidearm and placed it on the kitchen counter. He pulled a bottle of scotch from the cupboard and poured himself a short glass and returned to the living room to sort through the day's mail.

There wasn't much other than advertisements, which he immediately trashed. The only time he received a letter was when his grandfather sent a short note. Otherwise, they spoke on the phone a couple times a week. Those calls assured him that the old man, as he called him, was doing okay. Jonas Bristol Black might be eighty-four, but he could still sit a horse and herd his few remaining head of cattle. Jonas had to smile at the image. His grandfather was a tough old cowboy and the only family he had left.

He had bought his vehicle off a friend who had money problems and could no longer afford the payments. He was happy with the size and the trailer hitch on the back. It made it easier to help his grandfather haul stock back and forth to the auctions. He tried to visit as often as possible, but sometimes his job kept him away for months. The old man was getting up in age and death kept creeping closer with each passing year. Their time together was growing shorter.

He stifled a yawn and glanced at the clock on the fireplace mantle. It was almost ten. His shoulder muscles felt tight, and he needed to get a good night's sleep for a change. The case weighed too much on his mind and had kept him tossing and turning since finding the first victim. He locked up the house, glass in hand, tucked the journal under his arm, grabbed the gun and headed for the bedroom. Stripping down to his shorts, and once he was settled in bed, bunched the pillows against the headboard and placed the gun, close at hand, on the nightstand. Only then did he lean back against the pillows and open the green leather cover.

Written in a neat feminine script, he started to read:

Night has arrived, and the fairies and fireflies are spinning spider webs of magic around us. They light our way to a sorcerer's bed that captures all the minutes in all the hours we are together within the crystal walls so we can repeat our act of love over and over. We can stay forever in these moments. No distance, time or problems can separate us. We are one with the spell of the night.

Jonas smiled at the fantasy references. Whoever had written this journal had been inexperienced in love, but imaginative. She sounded like a naïve young girl getting her first taste of romance. Could Marilyn Heddrix ever have been this innocent or inexperienced? Could she have written these letters to the boy who got her pregnant? Morgan had said her twin was sixteen when she became pregnant and that the letters were written eight or nine years ago.

He knew Marilyn was born in 1982, which would make her roughly twenty-one or twenty-two. She wouldn't have written them to any boy, a man yes, but no boy. Maybe this was actually her first time being in love. That would explain the fantasy reference. Perhaps it was a real-life fantasy for her.

He flipped through the pages and found the one he had quickly read at the office. This time he read it carefully. The writing was more mature and experienced.

Thunder is bouncing off the clouds in the night sky. Purple flashes of lightning snake across the black velvet and, for a brief second, brightens the yard. The steady cadence of the rain beating on the roof plays a soothing concert for dreamland's call. I am eager for you to come to bed. You bring a bottle of wine with you tonight. The wine can wait. Come into bed and hold me close. Give me one of your hot, demanding kisses that will set my soul on fire. I want your flesh pressed against mine and to feel your hands caressing my body.

Oh, the sweet warmth of your mouth as we taste, tongues probing and dancing. I hold your face between my hands and run the tip of my tongue over your lips and kiss and nibble my way to your neck and shoulder. Your body is burning, and I can feel passion's fever swelling your shaft as it is pressed into my nest.

I want you inside me. I spread my legs, needing that hard deep invasion into the core of my being. But you only tease, pressing close and then pulling back. Over and over you torment me, driving the fire inside me higher and higher until I beg you for release.

You assault my senses even more, kissing my breasts, nipping my nipples and the electric current rushes through my belly and I grow hotter. I attack you, needing to love, to kiss my own path to your hot swollen

shaft. You gasp as I surround you with my hot mouth. Your body quivers and you are close to losing control. The torture is more than we can stand. Quickly you turn me on my back and plunge deep into me, and the frenzy begins. Our flesh slaps flesh until our skin is wet and slick. Passion's fury fills our minds, and all we know is the joy of spasm after spasm flooding our bodies in a thunderous climax. You are the heartbeat and joy of my soul because you love me. Never forget, I love you.
M

The fact this woman was crazy about this man was more than evident. It made him wonder what had happened between the two. Jonas had not noticed the initial before. Was it Marilyn? That was the question. As reserved as Morgan appeared, he doubted if she would be the one to have written the letters. He continued to read a couple more.

Clay was right; these intimate letters would affect most men. In his mind's eye, all he could envision was Morgan standing in the bedroom doorway wearing a see-through black nightgown. He shook his head to clear the image. Wearily, he rubbed his eyes, laid the journal on the nightstand and turned off the light.

After moving down in the bed and adjusting the pillows, he was asleep within seconds and dreaming of a naked Morgan slipping into bed beside him, kissing his mouth and loving him. He surrendered to the feel of her hot kisses and the demands of her body on his.

Fernandez remained at the office long after everyone else had gone home. He kept hoping Henry would show up, but he never did. The Lieutenant was going to be pissed when he found out. He would cover for him, but it was the last time. Henry either straightened his act up or else. Fernandez was not about to lose his hard-earned status as a detective because his partner couldn't handle his wife leaving him. He'd worked too long and too hard to get where he was. There, he'd made the decision; he only hoped he could stick to it.

Born and raised in California from a Spanish mother and an Irish father, Fernandez was a good looking man, tall, with blue eyes and dark brown hair. Other than his association with his partner, Jose pretty much kept to himself. Not that he didn't welcome company, he did, as long as they didn't inquire into his past. He didn't share his family history with anyone, not even Pope.

Coming to terms with his past had been almost impossible. All the years of therapy had not helped to understand or forgive what his father had done. He could not forgive his mother either. She had to have known, especially after Antonio's death. His brother had hung himself from a front porch beam and left a note for his mother telling of the molestation by his dad.

Their father had been arrested, and there had been a trial. His old man was sentenced to the maximum of fifteen years. Even as young as he was, Fernandez felt that was not enough years for the life of his brother. At age eight, he was immediately removed from the home and sent to live with relatives in Arizona. He never saw his mother again or knew what happened to her.

His aunt had changed his name so his father could never find him. Feeling that music might help soothe his tortured mind, she had taught him to play the piano and arranged for violin lessons. The music helped. But he couldn't wholly forget and suffered from nightmares and headaches until he was in his teens. Once he started studying martial arts, determined no one would ever hurt him in that way again, the nightmares began to fade, but never entirely left him.

Now he was sitting at his desk reviewing all the files taken from Caroline's house. They were all molestation cases involving the death of a child. There were quite a few. The originals were not allowed out of the department, so she must have photocopied them in her spare time. The documents were many, more than he would have thought for Colorado Springs. But it wasn't just Colorado Springs he discovered. Other states were included. California was one of those mentioned. The cases were all closed, so from one police department to another, it wouldn't have been hard for her to obtain the requested information. Especially, if it concerned a case she might be working on.

Suddenly he was holding his own file. Of course, the name on the folder was not Jose Fernandez; that was his new name. No, the name was of an innocent little boy whose trust in his father and other men had been shattered beyond repair. His faith in women also had been destroyed. They were supposed to protect their children but didn't. They sinned against their husbands, their children and themselves.

He tried to push those memories and thoughts from his mind and focus on his job. Stoning was a horrible way to die, but sometimes he thought the threat of that type of punishment might curtail people's urge to destroy a child.

He glanced at his watch. It was going on one in the morning. He'd make a run by Henry's to check on him. Tomorrow, he needed to go to Dawson's to see what the bartender knew about Marilyn Heddrix. Fernandez closed the current file he was reviewing, placed the stack in his desk drawer and turned off his computer. Another long day waited for him tomorrow. For tonight, he needed as much sleep as he could get.

Chapter Thirteen

Saturday

Morgan's body felt hot and slick when she awoke at seven. Even her muscles ached. Flashes of the erotic dream she had experienced during the night, involving the detective made her eyes widen. God, was she so horny she needed to dream of having sex with the man? Apparently, she was. Her face grew warm with the thought of facing the Lieutenant again with the images of his body in her mind. And the memory of him naked was not something she would forget, hard muscles, strong calloused but gentle hands, and a hot, demanding mouth. She licked her lips wanting to feel his kiss again, even if was only in a dream.

The vision was shattered as the thought of Marilyn chuckling to herself flashed through her mind. Was her sister responsible for the erotic fantasy? No, not even her twin could control a dream. It was all her own doing.

Since her divorce, she had refused to get involved with any man, not even as a date, until dinner with Lieutenant Black. Andy's betrayal had destroyed her trust in the male species, but the detective seemed different. Maybe? Was he a man she could trust?

Morgan hurried to the kitchen, pushed the button on the coffee maker and headed to the shower. She emerged feeling refreshed. The odor of freshly brewed coffee wafted through into the bedroom. She quickly dressed and returned to the kitchen, eager for a cup. Just as she was taking her first taste from the steaming mug, the telephone rang. She quickly took a sip, and then picked up the receiver.

Miss Johansson identified herself as the apartment manager. Since Morgan was listed as next of kin, she was inquiring as to when the apartment would be vacated. "The rent is paid through the end of the month," the manager said, "but I have a prospective tenant. Due to the circumstances, we can't issue a refund on the rent but might refund the security deposit. That would be on the condition you could have Miss Heddrix's possessions out by the end of next week." There was silence on the line.

Stunned at the callousness of the woman, Morgan was not sure what to say. Offended, she snapped, "Look, lady, I'm not even sure the police will allow me to move any of my sister's property. I'll have to call them and get back to you." Miss Johansson spieled off her phone number expecting her to jot it down.

"Fine!" Morgan yelled at the woman and slammed the phone back in the cradle. Hand on her hip and fuming, she carried her cup to the dining room and sat down at the table. After several deep breaths, she still could feel the anger over the insensitivity of the woman.

She returned to the kitchen and grabbed the receiver. Leaning back against the counter, she dialed the police department and asked for Lieutenant Black. The wall clock showed it was almost nine-thirty, so he should be in.

"Lieutenant Black here," was the quick response after the phone barely rang one time.

"Lieutenant, has my sister's apartment been

released?" Morgan demanded, and then hurriedly went into the details of her earlier phone call.

"Well, good morning to you," came the cheerful reply.

"I'm sorry," she muttered, surprised at how cheerful he sounded. "That woman made me so mad I wanted to punch her. I have to remove my sister's clothes and furniture by the end of next week. So can I do that?" Just to spite the manager, Morgan almost hoped he'd say no to her request.

"I believe your sister's apartment has been released. Hang on and let me check." He put her on hold and checked with Forensics. They were finished, as it was not the primary crime scene. He contemplated asking her to lunch, but another time would be better, especially after the dream he'd had about her last night. He had to admit Clay had been right. That damn journal had affected him and was probably responsible for the vivid dream.

He took her off hold, "Yes, you can have access to your sister's apartment. Forensics is finished with it. Do you need any help?"

"No, I don't think so. I'll be donating most of Marilyn's stuff to charity." Morgan didn't know how much of her furniture or clothes she'd want to keep. The fur piece on the bed she might bring home, also the rug and possibly the TV, and any family photos. She'd donate what she didn't want to Hospice. "When can I go to the apartment?"

"Any time," Jonas said. He looked up and met

Clay's questioning eyes. The man always seemed to appear out of the blue and at the moment, the wrong time. "I have to go," he added, not wanting to have to explain who was on the phone.

"Thank you," Morgan managed, her anger now dissipated. "If you need to get in touch with me, I'll be at the apartment. I might as well start going through her things," she said. She was dreading the job. It was such a final act, the disposing of someone's possessions.

She also wondered if her sister would appear to give her a hard time about giving away her possessions. If she did, Morgan was in the mood to throw any nasty remark right back at her. Her irritation continued as she gathered her purse and car keys.

She stopped and looked around at her living room furniture, wondering if she should keep her sister's sofa, chairs, and tables. Her own furniture was old and well worn. Marilyn's furniture would look better. At least it would add some color to the room. Decision made, she hurried to her vehicle and drove to the apartment.

When she arrived, the yellow tape was off the door. She entered and stopped just inside. The red leather sofa would definitely brighten up her house, as would the rest of the living room furniture. She'd have to call her boss at the animal clinic and see if he knew someone with a truck.

As for the bedroom, Marilyn's bed would be donated to Hospice. Morgan could not imagine sleeping one night on that mattress, no matter how well it was made. But, the rose-colored Fairfax chair would look great in her bedroom. It was a traditional style which she liked, so she added it to her mental list of things to keep.

When Morgan entered Marilyn's walk-in closet, she could smell the faint odor of her sister's cologne. She flipped on the light switch and then pulled a paisley print green jacket close to her face. Marilyn always wore L'Air du Temps perfume because it was light, not overwhelming, and the fabric smelled of her sister. She dropped the sleeve, fighting back the tears that threatened to well in her eyes and looked at the rows of clothes.

When searching for the green dress for the funeral, she had not really taken notice of all the clothes, matching purses and shoes. There were many items still with the price tags dangling from a sleeve or neckline. All Morgan could do was stand and stare in amazement. Most of the clothes had a designer label. The same applied to the purses and boxes of shoes. She doubted her sister had paid for any item in the closet.

She began pulling anything with a price tag off the rods, appreciating the luxurious texture of the material. Those she placed in a pile on the bed. Going to the kitchen, she returned with a box of plastic bags. The clothes Marilyn had worn would go in one bag for Hospice. The new clothes she'd carry out to her car. The same would apply to the shoes and purses.

Amazed how quickly she had sorted through everything, she left the top shelf of the closet for later. She wasn't ready to delve into the photo albums and already had enough to fill the back of the Chevy HHR.

Suddenly, there was a buzzing in Morgan's ears, then she heard the whisper of Marilyn's voice. "I'm glad you're keeping most of my things. I wouldn't want just anyone to have them. Besides, you and I are the same size. We even wear the same size shoes. Your house and wardrobe can use an update." Marilyn appeared and took a seat in the Fairfax chair.

Morgan ignored her remarks, instead turned to the dresser. The first drawer she opened, she uttered, "My God."

Stacked neatly in three long rows were expensive bras and matching panties. One row and half of another still had the price tags on them. Morgan could no longer keep silent. "Do you think you had enough underwear?"

"Well, I can't help it if Jack liked to buy me expensive things," came the quick response. "You might as well keep the new sets, especially if you plan on having sex with that hunky detective. Men like sexy underwear on women. Cotton panties and bras don't cut when it comes to men." Her voice almost purred as she said, "Men like lacy red or black underthings, even if you only wear it for a few minutes."

"There's nothing wrong with cotton. It may not be sexy," Morgan countered, a little too bitterly, "but it is comfortable." Marilyn could always piss her off. Indignation made her bite back. "Is that why you died in the red ones? Were you meeting your lover that night?" Morgan felt her stomach clench for the hateful remark. How could she say such a vicious thing to her murdered sister? Quickly, she added, "I'm sorry I said that. I didn't mean to sound so bitchy."

Marilyn brushed it off. "It doesn't matter. It's true. Jack and I had a standing date every Friday night. He loved my sexy lingerie." A deep sadness filled her voice, and she wiped at her eyes with the tail of the gray T-shirt. "You can tell that detective that his wife knew about us."

Morgan stopped stuffing clothes in the garbage bag and said, her voice softer, "I'm sure the detective has that information."

"He might, but does he know we only discussed our plans at the office or here? I doubt if he knows that," Marilyn stressed, and then gave Morgan a sly smile. "Maybe you should call him and tell him."

Morgan turned and faced her twin. The bitterness was still evident in her voice as she said, "I'll tell him, but I want you to know he has the journal. He found it in your safety deposit box along with your insurance policies."

Overwhelming sadness filled Marilyn's voice. "I'm so sorry, Morgan. I need your forgiveness for so many things."

Morgan took a seat on the corner of the bed. Eyebrows scrunched together and staring at the floor, she slowly raised her head and stared at Marilyn. "Why did you do it? Why did you try to destroy Robert?"

"I wasn't trying to destroy him! He deserved to suffer. I made him pay for what he did to you! He used you," Marilyn defended.

"Yeah!" Morgan exploded, "and I used him. Then you pretended to be me and blackmailed the man." She wished she had something to throw at her sister, but cooled down as she realized it wouldn't do any good. "What did you do with the money, and where did you put those damn photographs?"

"I cut a slit in the back cover of the journal and slipped them in between the leather and cardboard." Marilyn gave a slight shrug to her shoulder and clamped her teeth together in anticipation of the outburst. She ignored the question about the money.

Morgan jumped up. "You did what!" she yelled, clasping her hands on either side of her head. "Oh my God! What if the detective finds them? What is he going to think?"

"Look," Marilyn insisted, "what does it matter if he finds the pictures? We're twins, remember. Besides, he believes I wrote the journal anyway." She rose and walked to the other side of the bed. "You have nothing to worry about. The detective will never connect you to the snapshots."

Morgan didn't trust that her sister was correct. What if he did find the photos and knew they were of her. Their tattoos were different colors. And the one photograph showed her tattoo clearly. How was she going to explain her involvement with a married man? Would he believe her if she told him the truth? She hadn't known the man was married until they were deeply involved.

If the Lieutenant did learn she had written the journal, she would have to deal with it. She forced the dreadful thought out of her mind and focused her attention back on sorting all the items in the dresser drawer.

"I wouldn't be in this mess if you hadn't stolen the journal," she threw at her sister. "Why couldn't you leave it alone? The affair was over as soon as I caught him in the lie." Morgan felt like crying for all the bitter moments that existed between them.

As if reading her mind, Marilyn snapped back, "Because you were always miss goody good! This was the one time I could show Mom and Dad that you weren't Miss Perfect. They knew I was a screw-up, but you! I wanted to tear you down in their eyes." She paced the floor beside the bed and uttered a harsh laugh. "It didn't matter, they didn't believe me. They refused to believe it was you in the picture. They accused me of fabricating the whole thing. What does it matter now, we're all dead, except you."

Morgan dropped down on the bed. She had to agree, none of it mattered anymore. Still feeling miffed, she jerked open another drawer. This one held numerous boxes of jewelry, gold necklaces with matching earrings, white and black pearls, long three strands, and short ones. Several sported diamond rings. Her sister had a fortune casually stashed in a dresser drawer instead of a safety deposit box. Again, she was astounded by the money Jack Donavan had spent on her twin. She was still aware of Marilyn's presence, her eyes watching her every move.

Without commenting, Morgan dropped all the jewelry cases, one at a time, into another bag and tied a knot in the top, all the while glaring at her sister. She wasn't sure if she'd ever wear any of the gold necklaces or rings, but she did love the pearls.

Talk about excess, she thought as she gazed at the multiple plastic bags lining the floor at the foot of the bed. Marilyn had more clothes, shoes, jewelry than anyone could possibly wear or use. "Did you use the money to buy all this stuff?" she barked.

"Some of it," was all that Marilyn had to say.

"Then, I'll keep most of it. Robert owes me that much," she said, and let a smile curve her lips. "He did teach me all about sex. He wasn't a complete waste of time." She gave a low chuckle.

Still, a sliver of guilt sneaked through her since all the bags were destined to go to her house. It also forced her to reconsider whether she needed all the clothes she was taking. A resorting job had to be done but at her home.

In the kitchen, she was surprised to find only one set of dishes and only a few pots and pans. All could go to charity. Marilyn was not one to cook much, as Morgan enjoyed trying new recipes.

Her sister was still watching as she continued opening cupboards and drawers. "It's a pity," Marilyn said, "when a person's life comes down to what they possess. I didn't do much with mine, did I?"

"You were a nurse," Morgan offered. "I'm sure you helped people when they needed you most."

"Oh shit, Morgan, you know damn well I was a selfish bitch. I never thought of anyone but myself, not you, not Mom or Dad. Not even Jack. My life was filled with nothing but mistakes. And, I have to eventually pay for those," she said as if devastated. "What is that old saying? If you want to dance, you have to pay the piper or something like that. My time is coming to pay for what I've done." Tilting her head slightly as if listening to something, she looked at Morgan and abruptly said, "I have to go. You," she pointed her finger at Morgan, "be careful," she said and began to disappear. "I told you, my killer knows about you and has been watching you."

Before Morgan could protest, Marilyn was gone. Her smile vanished as a sudden chill made her shiver at the thought that a cold-blooded monster had seen her. She needed to tell the detective. Now more aware and watchful of her surroundings, she quickly carried the heavy bags to her vehicle and stowed them in the back. Once she was finished, she locked the apartment door and hurried to her car, locking herself in.

No one appeared to be watching, but the skin on the back of her neck tingled and her muscles felt tight. The few people she saw walking were a couple, a woman entering an apartment and someone in a car driving away toward the main road. Feeling a little less paranoid but still uneasy, she quickly started the engine and drove out of the complex.

Shortly, she pulled into her own driveway. It took only five minutes to unload the vehicle and carry the bags into the bedroom. After what Marilyn had said, she made sure all the doors were locked. The clothes, she'd go through again later and decide what she would actually keep. For now, she placed the bag with the jewelry out of sight at the back of her closet and hurried to the kitchen to call the detective.

The killer drove away and turned north on Academy Boulevard. He had been parked across from the entrance, waiting for her to leave. When the bitch had exited the building, she seemed wary and nervous, even looking around as if expecting to see someone watching her. Immediately, he decided to go and not give her a chance to spot him.

The intensity of his need to locate the dentist was growing with each passing day. It was a surprise to find out that Robert Titus lived not too far from his own home. He considered breaking in and waiting for him but trashed that idea after driving past the house and seeing a woman carrying bags of groceries inside. The wife? Probably. No, he'd wait and catch him alone, maybe when he came home late as he usually did. His late arrival home made the killer wonder what he was up to since he had dispensed with his girlfriend. He'd find out. But for tonight, maybe he'd check out this duplicate version of that red-headed bitch. A plan began to form in his mind, and as he drove away, he smiled. But the smile never managed to reach his eyes.

Chapter Fourteen

Saturday

Jonas was still sitting at his desk at one o'clock that afternoon. He was going over the file again for what seemed like the hundredth time. He had placed two phone calls to Henry Pope's cell phone and one to his home. No answer at either. The DNA results were in on the bloody branch. No match to any database. Also, the lab reports were mainly the same for the first two victims, Marilyn Heddrix and Doctor Jack Donavan. Both had been drugged, restrained and beaten to death with large stones.

But Caroline's report was different. She had drugs in her system as well but had managed to fight her abductor and fight hard enough to leave him marked. Charlie Jacks had taken scrapings from under her fingernails and found tissue. He was hoping they could match DNA to the blood on the branch or someone. That would prove it was the same killer. There was no doubt in his mind that all three murders had been done by the same man.

Caroline's death had gotten to Jonas more than any other. It ripped open the old scars on his emotions created to help him cope with Kelly's death. Now he felt raw, exposed and injured. Kelly was not only beautiful but kind to a fault, and he had loved the beautiful red-haired, golden tanned girl.

Unlike Caroline, Kelly's home life had been

anything but idyllic, a drunk for a father and a weak, abused mother. He had tried to remain indifferent to what was happening in her home, but couldn't. Jonas had wanted to protect her but failed, and paid the price for it. Her father had beaten him until he was black and blue.

Because of Kelly, he didn't press charges. But as a Deputy Sheriff, her father accused Jonas of trying to take advantage of her. He denied the charge, and Kelly backed him up. His Chief claimed her father was only protecting his daughter. A reprimand in his file was the most he received. And within two months, Kelly was dead. After that, Jonas withdrew into himself, present, not fully functioning. Due to his drinking too much, and at the urging of his grandfather, he resigned and joined the military. His emotional detachment and deployments overseas had served him well in the Marines and later on the job with the Colorado Springs Police Department.

And he needed that detachment from the victims to be able to clearly focus on each case. But he couldn't now. Caroline's murder had changed that. Anger was building in him and the rest of his team. He could see it in each man's eyes. Especially Benedict's. The man had loved her more than just a causal affair.

The other victims were just as important, but maybe it was because she was one of their own and had been murdered in such a vicious manner. The killer had been in a rage and bombarded her slender frame over and over until most of the bones in her body were broken before he delivered the death blow. It had taken Caroline longer to die. She also had been drugged. And the killer had stripped her as he did with the others.

Clay had been unable to locate Marilyn's clothes,

purse, shoes or cell phone. The doctor's expensive suit and cell phone had not been found either, and Caroline's purse and clothing were missing. What the killer wanted with his victim's possessions was a puzzle. Trophies, Jonas wondered? That would be an awful lot of trophies to try and hide.

They had been unsuccessful in locating where the killer had murdered his victims. The abduction sites had been nonproductive. The few potential witnesses had claimed not to have seen anything. Only the old man across from Caroline's house had offered information.

In frustration, Jonas slammed the file closed just as Clay entered the room. He dropped into the chair in front of his desk. "Well, how was your evening?" he asked as a smile curved his lips.

Trying not to snap off a remark and to lie effectively with a poker face, Jonas said, "Fine. Why?"

"Because you took that damn journal home, that's why. Don't sit there and try to tell me that those letters didn't give you a boner. If they didn't, there's something wrong with you." Clay leaned back in his chair and stared at the Lieutenant. He could tell Jonas was trying not to smile.

"How's your wife this morning," came the response.

"Just fine," Clay said, "Happy as all get out. I put a smile on her face last night. Satisfied?"

"Is she?"

"Oh yeah!" Clay said and then grinned. Turning serious, "Did you call Hanover back? He sounded as if he really needed to talk to you."

"I'll give him a call in a minute. Did you locate Andrew Jansen and Robert Titus?

"Andrew Jansen is a prick from the word go. He's good looking and a smooth talker. He has a solid alibi for the time the Heddix woman was killed. I talked to the woman he was shacked up with, an Evelyn Travis. He's her accountant. They were busy doing a little accounting of their own. They spent the evening together starting with dinner, and it progressed to his spending the night at her house. They were together all night, until seven o'clock the next morning.

"As for Robert Titus, no, I didn't locate him. But, I did speak with his wife. They live in a big expensive home on Wood Avenue. You should see the place. It's a monster of a house. Seems the dentist went out of town late Wednesday evening and isn't due back until early tomorrow morning." Clay hated to mention it but knew Jonas would want to be reminded. "What time is the viewing for Eppie's mother?"

"Six to eight this evening. Are you going?" Jonas was dreading it. Funerals and weddings were two things he didn't like to attend. Too many memories jumped out to stare him in the face. But, he would go for Eppie sake. As it was, he felt rotten for not making it by Hospice the other evening; but Eppie knew how time-consuming a case could be. Tonight, he had to be there just so she would know that he still cared in his way. Not that their relationship had progressed much beyond consensual sex between friends. Yet she needed his support at this time. His focus returned to what Clay was saying.

"Yeah, Becca and I will be there. Have you talked to her?

"No. I've left her alone. She has enough to deal with at the moment without me calling to remind her of her loss. Her sisters are with her, and I think the military brought her brothers home. I'll see her this evening, even if it's just to stop by for a second. It will help her to see us there." Jonas stopped Clay before he could say anything. "I know people from other departments are collecting money to help with the funeral expense. Would you check with our team to see who wants to donate?"

"I can do that. The Commander and the Chief will want to be included, as well as the entire department. Eppie's going to need all the help she can get. Funerals aren't cheap." It made Clay wonder if he had enough life insurance to cover his expenses if something should happen to him. He'd have to check with Human Resources. He didn't want Becca to have to worry about money.

Cripes, too many funerals in too short of time. He wasn't sure but thought the Heddrix woman's funeral was scheduled for Monday. He wondered if Jonas was planning on attending. Caroline's funeral would be later in the week to allow out-of-state fellow officers to arrive. He wasn't sure what day was scheduled for the service but would find out. Before he could say anything, the Lieutenant's phone rang. As Jonas picked up the receiver, Clay wasn't expecting the worried expression on his face or the sudden command.

"Let's go, Clay. We have to get to Morgan Jansen's house. She thinks our killer has been watching her."

When Jonas and Clay arrived on north Institute, they saw her peeking out the window watching for them. She quickly opened the door and let them in.

She wasn't expecting anyone other than Lieutenant Black. Had he told this man about her bond with her sister? She doubted it. That complicated the situation. How was she going to explain Marilyn's message? This man was shorter than the Lieutenant by about four inches. His dark brown hair almost matched his eyes, which were staring at her and making her feel as if she was a bug being examined. He had a strong jaw line and laugh lines at the corners of his eyes, which were regarding her with amazement.

Stammering, he muttered, "I'm sorry. Jonas said you were a twin, but I didn't realize how identical you were. It's like looking at a ghost."

"Yeah, I know," Morgan said. "But believe me, I'm not my sister. We were as opposite as you can get." She headed toward the kitchen calling over her shoulder. "What can I get you to drink?"

"Nothing," was the reply from both men, stopping her in midstride. She turned and took a seat on the sofa.

Leaning over the coffee table, Clay stuck out his hand and introduced himself, "Sorry again. I'm Detective Addison Clay. I'm filling in for Jonas' partner, Eppie Ortiz."

"It's nice to meet you." His handshake was firm, but Morgan sensed she was making him nervous. She doubted he was as anxious as she was, trying to explain her situation to someone new.

Jonas delivered a questioning stare at her and got right to the matter. "Why do you think the killer might be watching you?" Anything was possible, but the man, and it had to be a man, had been targeting men and women who were having affairs. He didn't think Morgan Jansen was involved with a married man; she was adamant that she was not like her sister.

Morgan almost squirmed under the detective's intense gaze. Oh great, she thought, not even a chance to come up with a plausible story. Then it hit her, "You remember last night at the restaurant?" Morgan watched surprise arch Addison Clay's eyebrows. Jonas' current partner didn't know about last night's dinner. She smiled to herself. "Anyway, when we were at the restaurant, a man kept watching me. And I felt as if someone was watching me when I was at Marilyn's apartment."

It wasn't a lie. The man could have been there. She had felt uneasy, and Marilyn had warned her to be careful. It was best that the police know the killer had seen her. So this little white lie served a useful purpose.

Jonas felt the knot begin to form in his stomach. There was more than she was saying. It was probably because Clay was there. He hadn't explained to any of his team about Morgan's claim to be in contact with her dead sister. They'd discount anything she had to say. He didn't want that to happen. She had been on target about Jack Donavan and where to find him. Jonas switched the subject. "Do you know a dentist by the name of Robert Titus?" He wasn't prepared for the blanching of the color from her face. Why did that question trouble her?

"Yes," she answered honestly. "Marilyn went to him for dental work. I knew him only briefly." God, she prayed he didn't start digging around deeper into her past. Had Robert deleted all those e-mails? Hopefully, the man had erased any connection to her or her sister, other than a professional one. "Why are you asking?"

"Because we think he is somehow connected to the case. Other than his being your sister's dentist, do you know if she was involved with him?"

Morgan could feel the other detective watching her intently. "I would have no way of knowing who Marilyn was involved with. Like I've told you before, she was a secretive person."

Jonas was hoping for more. So there was a connection between Marilyn and the dentist. He now knew, thanks to Rudy Scully's photograph, that Doctor Donavan had known the dentist as well.

In case Morgan was right, and the killer was watching her, he'd have a protection detail at the front and back of the house to make sure she was safe until either he or Clay could return for the evening. It would have to be him or another team member inside the house just in case. He needed to go to the office to call Hanover back.

Jonas made a quick call to his Commander to arrange the detail. The entire time Morgan's eyes were glued to his face. He could see she was filled with questions. He turned to Clay.

"I want you to stay here until the protection detail arrives. Don't let Morgan out of your sight. And you!" He pointed to Morgan. "Stay inside and do as Clay tells you. I'll be back within the hour." He checked his watch, grabbed his hat and hurried out the door before either could object to his orders.

Once he was back at his desk, Jonas quickly called Hanover. "Hey, you left me a message?"

"Yeah, I did. Have you checked out my two missing people?"

"Not yet. Give me their names, again." He jotted down the names of Carla Winslow and Theodore Matthews. "When did they go missing?"

"Almost four weeks ago."

"And Charlie Jacks still doesn't have them?" Jonas thought it was strange that no one had heard from the two. "Have you found their vehicles?"

"Yeah, the woman's vehicle was parked in the lot at the attorney's apartment complex. His sedan was in an airport lot."

"Did you check with the hotel in Mexico?"

"Yes. The pair never checked in, and there's no record of the two getting on a plane headed for Mexico, either in Colorado Springs or Denver." Winston sounded frustrated. His case was looking like more than a simple missing person's situation.

"That doesn't sound good." In fact, it sounded like Hanover's case was going to overlap his and be labeled a possible homicide. The only problem was, there were no bodies so far. Jonas hoped there wouldn't be either. "By the way, how'd it go with Mrs. Donavan? Was she able to supply any additional information?"

Jonas hadn't seen or spoken to Winston since he'd

delivered the bad news to the widow.

"Nothing new. The poor woman's devastated. The Mayor's not very happy either. I keep telling him we're all trying to locate the killer. I've been able to keep him off your back so far. I'm going to talk with the respective spouses of my missing people and their relatives again. Carson Winslow has a sister, Elizabeth. We're going to interview her as well. We'll see if she's heard from the wife. They were pretty good friends from what I've learned. Do you want to come along?"

"Thanks for keeping the Mayor happy. I can't go, but I'll send Clay with you. I have a slight problem in my case that I need to take care of. Will that do? I also have to stop by the funeral home and see Eppie this evening. Her mother's viewing is tonight." He needed to have a private conversation with Morgan, and then, if necessary, he'd take her with him to the viewing.

"Tell Clay I'll meet him here at the office. Thanks. Tell Eppie I'll stop by if I can get away, and that I'm sorry for her loss. Talk at you later." Hanover ended the call.

Jonas sat thinking about what Hanover had said about his missing victims. He stood and went to review the crime board. The photos of each victim stared back at him. There was the connection between Marilyn Heddrix and Jack Donavan. That was a given, they'd been having an affair. What possible connection did Caroline have to them? Was she a victim of opportunity? Was she possibly involved with someone that no one knew about? How did the dentist fit into the picture, or maybe he didn't fit into this mess in any way?

Their efforts to locate the doctor in Denver had

been a bust. All they could do was leave a message at the hotel and interview him when he returned from his trip. Jonas wanted to have a long conversation with him. He'd find out one way or the other if the man had been involved with Marilyn or her sister.

Now two more people were missing. They appeared to have been having an affair. Were they connected to his homicide case? Since Marilyn knew the dentist, as did Caroline, and both women used him for their dental care, and per Scully's report, the doctor knew the dentist, how involved were these people with one another?

What about the spouses of the missing couple? Who were they? Were they connected with the victims in some way? Jonas added the names of Carla Winslow and Theodore Matthews to the board, with the date they'd gone missing. He'd obtain a photo of each from their driver's licenses. He stepped back to study the timeline of each. No trace of them had been found other than their vehicles. So where were they? Jonas had a nagging suspicion that they were no longer alive. Morgan hadn't mentioned them in regards to her sister's death. He made a mental note to ask her about it.

Hanover had said he had spoken with the wife and husband. Jonas would like to talk to them as well and add his own questions.

He looked at his watch. He'd been gone longer than he'd planned. He needed to be back at the house. Quickly he headed to his SUV and back to North Institute. Even though he knew Eppie would understand if he didn't make it to her mother's service, on a personal note, he needed to pay his respects for his partner's sake. He'd make sure the men in the protection detail were on alert before running to the funeral home.

When he arrived, a patrol car was parked in front of the house and one stationed in back, at the end of the driveway near the alley. He took the three steps in one stride and knocked on the front door. Clay peeked out before opening the door. Once inside he glanced from Morgan to the other detective. She gave him a sideways frown and remained seated on the sofa.

Jonas explained to Clay what he needed and sent him back to the office. He was to accompany Hanover to the interviews with the spouses and the one with the sister-in-law of the Winslow woman. All these people were connected somehow, he was sure of it.

"What was the frown about?" Jonas asked after Clay left.

"Does Detective Clay know about Marilyn?" When he gave her a blank look, Morgan continued. "You know what I mean, about her ghost?

Jonas shook his head and took a seat in the chair at the end of the coffee table. "I haven't mentioned it to any of my team. I don't want them to think I'm crazy."

"Like me, you mean." She gave him a hard look and stood. Well, she decided, she wouldn't mention that Marilyn had been the one to warn her about the killer watching her. With a shake of her head, she headed to the kitchen. Her stomach started to growl, and she realized there had been no lunch. "I'm starved. I hadn't planned on cooking you a dinner tonight, but tonight's as good as any."

"It can't be tonight. I have to leave for a short time. You remember my partner, Eppie Ortiz?"

Morgan turned back to face him. "Yes, I remember Detective Ortiz. She was nice."

"Well, her mother died and there's a service this evening. I need to drop by for a short time. I was going to take you with me, but you should be fine with the two officers keeping a lookout. I'll let them know I'll be gone and to be alert. Besides, I won't be too long. I don't think you have anything to worry about while it's daylight." He retrieved his hat and started for the front door.

Morgan followed him. "I'm still going to cook. You probably will be hungry when you come back. I'll fix some hamburgers, French fries and a pitcher of iced tea. The officers in front and back can eat while you're gone. I'm sure they'd appreciate a hot meal. Tell them I'll call them in when it's ready."

Jonas gave a grin and said, "I'm sure they will. I'll tell them to wait inside. That way, I know you'll be safe while I'm gone."

"Okay, I'll also put a pot of coffee on." Morgan waited at the door until the two officers came inside and stood looking around, appearing uncomfortable. She closed and locked the door after Jonas. "Have a seat at the table, and I'll have the burgers ready in no time," she instructed.

"Thank you, ma'am," they said in unison and took a seat.

Morgan noticed that even seated the two men

remained watchful. One sat near the front door, and the other faced the back and side door. Without trying to engage them in conversation, she got busy preparing the meal and added a salad.

After the meal and clean up, the men returned to their vehicles and Morgan entered the bedroom. She surveyed the multiple bags on and beside her bed. If she wanted to sleep, she would have to put away everything she had brought from the apartment.

First, she removed most of the clothes in her closet to make room for what she planned on keeping. Quickly she realized that it would be all of her sister's designer dresses, blouses, and slacks. Her old clothing, other than her jeans and T-shirts, could be donated to charity. The boxes of shoes she lined up along the floor of the closet and placed the purses on the overhead shelf. The bag of jewelry remained hidden away at the back of the closet. The rest of the stuff at Marilyn's apartment would have to wait.

Finished for the evening, Morgan returned to the living room and curled up on the sofa to watch television and wait for Jonas to return.

When Clay arrived at the office, Hanover was sitting at his desk and stood when he walked off the elevator. Getting right to the point, he said, "I have Sydney Matthews waiting in an interview room. And, she's not happy about being here, so let's get this over with." He led the way down the hall to a room and opened the door.

Sydney Matthews stood when they walked in. A tall, willowy blonde with big blue eyes, the lips of her

Cupid's bow mouth was pressed into a frown. Fire flashed in her eyes when she saw the detectives, and she demanded, "I've been waiting here for over thirty minutes! What's taking so long?"

"I apologize," Winston said. "I was waiting for Detective Clay to arrive. We believe his case and your missing husband's case might be connected."

"I've told you, that bastard is not missing. The son of a bitch ran off with his research assistant, Carla Winslow. They're somewhere in Mexico spending part of my divorce money."

"And, Mrs. Matthews, I explained to you that your husband never made it to Mexico. Neither did Mrs. Winslow. Now his secretary told us, he had a court date this week with Judge Jordan. I know you don't know the judge, but your husband wouldn't miss that court date."

That bit of information seemed to make the woman stop and think. "I do know about that judge's reputation. Lord knows, Ted complained about him enough." She was silent for a moment, then asked, "If he's not in Mexico with that bitch, where the hell is he?" Looking from one to the other, as if the detectives should have the answer, she then muttered, "That explains why my attorney has been calling me. He wants to locate him so the bastard can be served with divorce papers. That can't happen if he's missing."

Suddenly, it was as if the reason she was sitting in a police interview room hit her. "You can't think I had anything to do with Ted's disappearance?" Again she turned from one to the other. "Well, I didn't! If he's missing, you look for someone else to blame it on. I had nothing to do with it. I've been taking care of my sick mother this past week." She sat giving the two men a stony glare. "I want to call my lawyer."

Those words put an end to the interview. "Certainly, Mrs. Matthews," Winston said. "We're not implying you had anything to do with your husband's disappearance. We do need to talk with your mother to verify your alibi. But for now, go home and call your lawyer. And, thank you for coming in on the weekend." He waited as she stood and walked to the door, standing still, waiting for him to open it. "I'll escort you downstairs," he said and glanced over at Clay, opened the door and followed the woman into the hallway.

Eppie, looking regal and as beautiful as ever, stood at the entrance to the small chapel where her mother's service was being held. Her sisters and brothers were beside her, each supporting the other in their grief. They all knew they had done all they could for their mother. Their features expressed that inner peace mixed with the sense of their loss.

As people filed in from the outside, they smiled and received the offered hugs and condolences before the individual walked away and down the aisle to the front where Rose lay at her final rest. Each filed past the casket, paused for a moment, and then took a seat in one of the numerous folding chairs set up for the occasion.

Eppie left the group of family members and hurried to greet Jonas, slipping into his arms and resting her head on his shoulder. "Thank you for coming. I needed to see you here," she whispered under his chin.

Numerous on-duty and off-duty fellow officers that they both knew were present. He nodded in greeting as she led him to a row of padded chairs placed against one wall in the reception area.

She continued to hold his hand even after they were seated. "Do you regret what we had?" she asked, a faraway look in her eyes as if she wasn't really there, but watching a past event. A slight sad smile curved her lips and just as quickly disappeared. She shook off the memory and focused on Jonas.

"No Eppie, how could I regret caring about you? I still care, but you know we never should have gotten involved." Their brief affair had ended just as quickly as it began. The baggage he carried from Kelly's death kept a barrier between them. She hadn't been able to breach it. He released her hand and shifted in the seat, so he was facing her.

"Yeah," she agreed. "You're right in that department."

"I couldn't give you what you wanted or needed, Eppie. I never was the right man for you." They had both agreed to end the relationship, each admitting that it wasn't working.

The sex between them had been fantastic, but sex alone couldn't build a lasting bond. Jonas was surprised when Eppie was the first to suggest they stop seeing each other. He immediately agreed but was sad that he couldn't give her what she had hoped for in the relationship. Jonas had held himself just out of reach from a complete attachment to any woman, fearing what had happened to Kelly could happen again. He didn't want that on his conscience. Deep in his gut, Jonas felt his love for Kelly had caused her death. That fact haunted him creating a barrier between him and any woman.

So they had gone their separate ways. Their friendship grew stronger as a result. Eppie was well aware she could count on Jonas to be there for her, as now.

"How are your sisters and brothers holding up?" he asked.

"They're handling it," she gave that sad smile again. "We have no choice but to handle it. Momma's gone, and there was nothing we could do to prevent it. That's what I wanted to talk to you about." She sat up straighter and stiffened her shoulders. "I want to come back to work Tuesday. And," she glared at him, "why didn't you tell me about Caroline sooner?" she admonished. "Dammit, Jonas, I'm not some unstable school girl going to pieces over the loss of her mother. I had months to come to terms with her death. You should have told me!"

Jonas knew she was going to be pissed off after hearing about Caroline's murder from some other source besides him. "Look, maybe I should have been the one to tell you, but my God, Eppie, you had enough to deal with at the time."

"Yeah, well, I forgive you this time." She rested her hand on his arm as if touching him gave her added strength. She turned tired eyes on him. "I'm feeling so damn guilty."

"What in the world for?" Jonas uttered in

amazement. What did she have to feel guilty about? She and her sisters had been there for their mother day and night.

How many nights had Eppie spent at the hospital sleeping on the sofa in the Hospice room or in a chair just to be close to her mother? Only after one of her sister's arrived did she rush home to shower and change clothes and then come to work. The entire time since her mother was diagnosed, the woman had functioned on little sleep, raw nerve, and caffeine.

"Why are you feeling guilty?" he asked, concerned about her mental state.

"Because I feel relieved that Momma's finally at peace." She looked up at him as tears welled in her eyes. "I shouldn't feel glad my mother is dead! I should be screaming and crying instead of relieved." A tear slid down her cheek. She wiped it away.

"Eppie, your mother was suffering. It isn't wrong to want that suffering to end. No child wants to witness their parent in pain. So, stop feeling guilty. You should be thankful your poor mother is no longer hurting. Be happy for her, but don't ever let yourself feel guilty."

"Thanks," she said. "I needed to hear that. It helps Jonas."

Jonas held her close for a moment before releasing her. Looking at her now, he realized how thin she had become over the last month. Maybe returning to work would help her. He had missed his partner. Clay was great, but he wasn't Eppie.

"Okay, you can come back to work Tuesday, but

only if you start taking care of yourself and eating more. You're too damn skinny!" he scolded. "I'm sorry I have to leave so quickly, but this damn case has the Mayor on our backs." He rose, then added, "I don't know the exact date for Caroline's funeral yet, but as soon as I do, I'll call you." He paused wondering if he should say anything else. It would be best to keep her informed about the case.

"Morgan Jansen's sister is to be buried Monday at Evergreen," he added. "I'll be there. She doesn't have anyone. Besides, the killer might show up in the crowd, if there is one. I don't think the victim had many friends." He shifted his feet and, hat in hand, said, "We'll see you on Tuesday. Call me if you need anything."

"Thanks for coming. I may try to make it to Evergreen on Monday. If not, I'll definitely be at work Tuesday," she said.

Jonas left the building, saddened to know that in a few days he would be attending another such sad occasion. Knowing how alone Morgan was, he was glad he had decided to attend the funeral of her sister.

Eppie watched after Jonas before walking down to stand gaze at her mother. Cancer had devoured Rosa's already slender frame. The woman lying in the casket was only a shadow of her vibrant self. Tears streamed down Eppie's face as she leaned over and kissed her mother's forehead, then whispered, "I'm sorry, Momma. I'm so sorry. Please forgive me. I never meant to worry you or cause you pain. Rest now, and know everything will be alright with us."

She held tightly to the side of the casket, just as

she had held onto her mother's hand all that last night. Refusing to let go even when they tried to make her rest, holding tight, trying to pull her mother away from death's grip until Rosa took her last breath. Eppie almost crumpled to the floor but forced herself to remain upright. After her composure returned, she turned, head bent, tears streaming down her face, and walked back up the aisle to join her family.

Chapter Fifteen

Saturday evening

When Jonas arrived back at Morgan's, he stopped for a report from the officer stationed in front of the house. All had been quiet. Of course, it had been daylight, and now the sun was just setting. He'd be sleeping on the sofa tonight to make sure nothing happened. He knocked softly on the front door, and when Morgan answered, she appeared as if she had just awakened from a nap.

"You're back," she mumbled. "Have you eaten yet?" she asked, as he entered and tossed his hat in a chair.

"No. If you have an extra hamburger, I'd appreciate it."

"Do you want coffee," she called over her shoulder and headed to the kitchen, to make a fresh pot just in case.

"Yes, thanks," he said, taking a seat at the dining room table. "The guys outside will need coffee to help keep them awake." He felt drained after the visit to the funeral home, so would need coffee as well. "Do you need any help," he called out, feeling like an idiot sitting down while Morgan did all the work.

"No. I'm fine," she said, coming to stand in the kitchen doorway. "How was Eppie?"

"Considering everything, she's doing okay. She's coming back to work Tuesday."

"Isn't that a little soon?" God, when her parents had died, she'd stayed off work for three weeks. The loss of both at the same time had devastated her and Marilyn. That was one of the few time she had seen Marilyn cry. She'd only returned to work at the vet's clinic because Eric had asked her to. He was shorthanded, otherwise, the answer would have been no. She had even let her commissions for stained glass slide, aware that trying to be creative at that time was impossible.

Morgan admired Eppie's strength to be able to go back to duty so soon. "She's a tough woman," she said, in admiration.

"Yes, she is. She's also one of the best partners' I've had. She's detail-oriented and focused. She doesn't miss much but can be hard as nails, yet still cares a lot about people." Jonas suddenly realized how much he relied on Eppie, and how effective they were as a team. He could always depend on her to have his back.

He smiled as a thought struck him. Eppie was as great in bed as she was a detective. There were times he missed their sexual relationship, but all it did was muck up their working partnership. What they had now was better for them both.

Morgan placed a plate in front of him loaded with French fries, a hamburger, a bowl of salad. A mug of steaming black coffee came next. He looked up at her and grinned. He was ravenous and proceeded to devour the food.

When Morgan sat down with only a cup of coffee loaded with cream, it dawned on him that she wasn't eating. "Where's yours?"

She smiled, "I ate earlier."

For some reason, he almost doubted her except he remembered that she had claimed to be starving. "Okay," he said, "as long as you've eaten."

"Oh, I did," she assured him. And she had eaten, almost a whole hamburger when the other officers ate. Lately, her appetite had been nearly nonexistent. She forced herself to eat only because she didn't want to become ill.

After he finished his food, Jonas refilled his cup and continued to sit at the table. "I need to ask you something."

"What?" Morgan rose to refill her cup and stand in the kitchen doorway.

He stared at her wishing she would return to the table. As if reading his mind, she did just that, to sit and cup her chin in her hand and return his gaze.

Jonas shifted, feeling awkward under her continual stare. "Would you stop looking at me as if I'm going to drop another bomb of horrible news on you?" He relaxed a little when she sat back in the chair, a slight smile on her face.

"I didn't mean to make you uncomfortable," she said, then sat up straighter in the chair. "What do you want to know?"

"Do the names Carla Winslow or Theodore Matthews mean anything to you?" He waited, watching a puzzled expression play across her features.

"No, I don't know them. Why?"

"Because they're missing and could be another set of victims."

Morgan carried his plate and cup to the kitchen and placed them in the sink. "Why do you think they're dead," and she knew that was what he believed.

"Because they had been having an affair. Each had left their spouses and were going to Mexico. The only problem is that no one has seen or heard from them since. It's a missing person's case right now, but Detective Hanover and I believe it is connected to mine." He rose and leaned against the doorframe while she washed the few dishes. "Has your sister mentioned them?" Had he become a believer? He guessed he had. She'd been on target so far.

She had to hide the smile that curved her lips. The detective was actually asking if she had heard from Marilyn about his missing people. "I'm sorry," she was forced to say, "Marilyn hasn't said anything to me about anyone else."

"Well, I thought I'd ask just in case." He continued to stand in the doorway.

She fixed the coffeepot for the morning, and they settled on the sofa to watch TV. As the sun sank behind Pikes Peak, Morgan brought a light blanket and a pillow and placed them on a chair. The evenings in Colorado turned chilly at the high altitude, even in the summer. Once the house cooled off, a light cover felt good.

"At the restaurant, you questioned me about mine and Marilyn's life. Tell me about you. Where did you grow up?" she asked, settling in against a pillow. "I want to know all about you, everything." She could tell he wasn't expecting her to question him.

Jonas was uncomfortable talking about himself, always had been. His life, up until Kelly's death, was idyllic. His grandfather had seen to that. "There's not a lot to tell. I was born and raised in Texas on my grandfather's ranch. My mother died when I was six. My father worked on an oil rig in the Gulf. I only saw him when he came home three to four times a year. He'd spend a few days with Gramps and me, then take off for Galveston or New Orleans. He was the best father he could be, considering."

He thought of how young his father, Jason Black, had been. Married at nineteen, widowed at twenty-five. After losing the love of his life, their father/son relationship hadn't stood much of a chance. Faced with huge hospital bills and a meager wage job, he'd jumped at the chance to work on a rig in the Gulf. He made good money and sent it home for Jonas' care.

Maybe that's why his grandfather spent so much time with him. His small cattle and quarter horse ranch was known for top-notch stock. And he and Jonas worked it together until as a boy, he became fascinated with crime shows on television. He watched all the mystery stories, true crime and even took online courses relating to criminal justice while in high school.

He related all this information as Morgan sat listening, enthralled by every word. Then she dropped the bombshell.

"Tell me about Kelly."

Jonas stopped what he had started to say and stared at her. "I'd rather not talk about that," he said.

After all the information he had insisted she tell him, he was going to refuse to discuss someone in his past. "Like hell," she said. "You made me drag up a lot of painful memories Friday night. I have a right to hear about this Kelly person. Marilyn is the one who brought her up, so I deserve to know what happened to make you the way you are. Who was Kelly?" she demanded.

Jonas was hoping a simple explanation would satisfy Morgan but doubted it. He hesitated as the images of that painful night surfaced. "Kelly Burton was my fiancé. We dated all through high school and college. We were planning on getting married. After I graduated, I joined the Midland Police Department since I had a degree in Criminal Justice." He paused to catch his breath as the images of her battered body hit him like a dagger to the heart. "She was murdered one spring night. Her killer was never caught." He stopped, feeling the gut-wrenching anger that filled him every time he thought about her unsolved case.

"Oh my God, I'm so sorry." Morgan felt terrible for making him relive that episode in his life. She could tell it still bothered him. His body was tense, and he had the look of a man who would like to hurt someone. She only hoped it wasn't her. Still, she couldn't help but ask, "What did you do after her death?"

"Stayed drunk for a time. I was a cop when the murder happened. So after I sobered up, I became obsessed with finding the killer. I couldn't focus on anything else. It cost me my job. I was given a choice, get help or get fired. I resigned and joined the Marines. So now you know it all."

He had needed the action, the hunt. Afghanistan gave him that. He was good at ferreting out terrorists in the villages. An IED changed that. He was sent to a VA hospital in the states. After a year in the hospital, due to the shrapnel wounds to his back, he was discharged and sent home.

Physically, he was okay, but at times he wasn't so sure about his mental state. He still had nightmares and a good night's sleep was a luxury he appreciated. He was grateful when Morgan interrupted his thoughts.

"How long were you in the Marines?" she insisted.

"Four years. I spent most of my time in Afghanistan. Got discharged and moved here so I could join the police department. I couldn't go back to Midland other than for a visit. The Springs was close enough so I could keep a check on my grandfather. Now I'm done talking."

True to his word, Jonas didn't offer any additional information about himself, but settled back and tried to keep his attention on the television. Morgan had no choice but to do the same. It made for a quiet evening.

Around ten, they called it a night. After Morgan went off to her bedroom, Jonas turned off the lights and stretched out, knowing he would not be getting much sleep.

Outside the sound of a vehicle passing by the house could be heard every now and then. Somewhere an owl was hooting. Off in the distance came the wail of sirens and Jonas wondered what could be the reason, fire, vehicle accident, or what. Would he be getting a call?

He closed his eyes for what he thought was only a moment. When he opened them, he thought he was dreaming at the first brush of Morgan's lips on his. It was almost entirely dark in the house. Only the outside street light broke up the blackness as he stared up to see her standing naked beside the sofa. He sat up.

"Morgan?" he muttered softly, in case she was sleepwalking. "What are you doing?"

"I want you," she whispered and offered her hand.

"This is crazy. Are you sure about this?" Jonas asked. When she didn't reply, he needed no urging. Knowing he was breaking all the rules, Jonas stood and took her into his arms, covering her mouth with his. He wanted her just as much. Immediately, her kiss deepened, and she clung to him pressing her body closer. He was instantly hard and throbbing.

Backing away, she led him to the bedroom and pushed him down on the bed, leaning over to give him another kiss. Slowly, one at a time, she unbuttoned his shirt and spread it open, all the while nibbling and caressing his lips with her tongue. Her hot hands rubbed his chest and then her fingers found his nipples. She straddled him and leaned over once more to kiss and probe his mouth as she tweaked each nipple between her fingers. She was driving him wild with her teasing.

Suddenly she sat up and slipped down onto his thighs. Quickly she unhooked his belt, unzipped his pants and tugged them down with his briefs, freeing his swollen shaft. With a sigh, she impaled herself and began to thrust her hips hard against him while reaching behind to caress him.

Jonas groaned, trying to focus on what was happening. He couldn't think straight. All he knew was that the woman he desired was straddling and riding him to an explosive climax. All control lost, and too quickly, he expelled his semen.

Still, Morgan didn't stop her attack on his senses but continued to thrust harder and harder, while tasting his mouth and twisting his nipples. She was almost savage in her assault. He grabbed her shoulders and forced her to sit up, while she continued to drive his penis into her, never ceasing until, suddenly she cried out, her body stiffened as she climaxed.

She fell forward and rested on his chest, her head facing the window. Confused by what had just happened, Jonas rubbed her back. "What the hell was that about," he muttered, close to her ear.

Suddenly she sat up, stiffened and turned to stare at the window. Without answering the question, she slid off his legs and faced the glass. One slow step at a time, she walked to the window, bent over close to the pane and stared out into the night.

The sound of pounding feet retreating down the driveway toward the back of the house brought Jonas upright and out of bed, jerking his briefs and pants up. At the same time he was uttering, "Son of a bitch, son of a bitch," over and over.

His gun was on the coffee table in the living room. He'd been caught unprepared, and in a compromising position with the woman he was supposed to be guarding. Whoever had been outside the window was long gone. He whipped around to locate Morgan. She had climbed back in bed under the blanket and was sound asleep. He rushed to grab his gun and returned.

"Damn it!" he exploded when he saw her even breathing, and charged to her side of the bed and shook her roughly. She opened her eyes and glared up at him.

"What the hell are you doing?" she yelled, and then lowered her voice. Glancing around, a look of fear crept into her eyes. "Is something wrong?"

"I'd say something's wrong. Why the hell did you walk naked to the window? Who was out there?" Jonas wanted to strangle her. Why hadn't she said something about seeing someone at the window?

Now Morgan was sitting upright in bed, all too aware that she didn't have a stitch on under the covers. She clutched the blanket to her chest and stared at Jonas. "What do you mean? What happened? Why am I naked?" All too quickly she became aware of tenderness between her legs that could only mean one thing.

"Did we have sex?" She was almost in tears. "I trusted you!" she shouted before he could respond. "How could you take advantage of me?"

Jonas could see his career sliding right down the drain when he heard her words. "My God, no! I didn't. I swear. You came onto me. Please, you have to believe me. I don't know what's happening here tonight."

"What do you mean?"

"With you." He stammered, and started to sit at the foot of the bed, but continued to stand when she scooted back against the headboard. "Look, I promise, you have nothing to fear from me. Something strange is going on. You were acting weird and then, you know" he grimaced, "after we, er, there was someone outside the house. Look, I have to go check on my men, so please stay put."

He pulled his shirt together and buttoned it and was pushing the tail down in his slacks when the pounding on the front door jarred them both. Morgan immediately jumped from the bed and ran into the bathroom.

God, what a fucking mess, Jonas thought, as he rushed to the door and opened it.

A white-faced Officer Gordon stood staring at him and in a rush of words reported, "Someone was at the side window. I chased him down the alley, but he got away." The officer paused long enough to take in a breath, "I had to call 911. Bennett is out, and his breathing is shallow. The paramedics should be here any second."

Morgan emerged from the bedroom dressed in jeans and a T-shirt and stood barefooted just in time to hear the conversation. Sirens wailed as the rescue truck roared to a stop in front of the house. Officer Gordon took off at a run and led the paramedics to the back.

Jonas spun around to face Morgan. "Please give me a chance to explain what happened."

"I'm not stupid, Jonas. I can tell we've had sex. Since I don't remember it, I want to know what happened and you'd better damn well have a good explanation!" She dropped down onto the sofa to wait as he charged out the front door.

Officer Gordon returned to stand guard while Jonas rushed to the back of the house, gun in hand.

He had watched the bitch ride the detective harder and harder. Outside the bedroom window, he'd had a perfect view. They were shadowy silhouettes in the faint light, but he could still see everything she did to the man. It was the sly flash of white teeth she cast in his direction several times during her sexual display as if she knew he was watching. It only reinforced his certainty that she had to die. He had seethed with fury as the detective gave a gasp and expelled his contaminated seed into her. Then rage filled him, even more, when she stiffened, cried out and slumped forward onto his chest.

The slut, the whore! Those words echoed off the walls of his mind over and over until; she calmly stood, turned and walked naked to where he stood on the other side of the glass, bent down and stared back at him almost nose to nose and gave him an evil grin. She scared the hell out of him.

He had choked when he saw her face. It wasn't the perfect features of the woman living in the house, it was the devil come back to terrorize him. He found himself staring into the face of a dead woman, the left side caved in and one eyeball hanging by a thread of flesh, and oozing blood.

Without thinking of caution, he turned and ran as fast as he could to his van, past the knocked out police officer. Even now, out of sight and almost home, he was still trembling from the shock of seeing that hideous face. It didn't make sense. It had to have been his imagination. She couldn't exist. He had done his job and executed her. She was dead and soon to be buried.

But that devil image wouldn't leave his mind. Once the van was well hidden in the garage, he rushed to the basement and paced the cold stone floor back and forth. He had to think about what had happened. What he needed was a stiff drink to help clear his head. He left the basement, secured the door with the double deadbolts and entered the kitchen.

Three shots of bourbon later, he felt calmer and was convinced he had imagined it all. It was the shadows and faint alley light that had played tricks on his eyes. He couldn't have seen Marilyn Heddrix. Still, the image of her grinning at him through the window made him shiver. Once again, he paced the floor. Knots made his insides ache, and the unmistakable prick of longing for release begin to build.

The cop had been too quick. The woman's attempt at fighting back had been unexpected. Her death hadn't given him the release he desperately needed. Nothing compared to that overwhelming wave after wave of pure ecstasy that made him soar, while watching the life leave their eyes. No amount of sex could give him that high, only Robert Titus would supply that type of fix.

He'd called the office Friday and discovered the dentist was out of town but would be returning early Sunday morning. A perfect time to grab him was right when he arrived home, in his driveway, before anyone was up. He could park down the street and watch the house. His plan set the killer glanced at his watch. It was long past midnight. He wouldn't be able to sleep anticipating what lay ahead. Quickly, he gathered the necessary items, rope, the gag, the drug in the syringe and a thermos of coffee to help him stay awake. Stowing the assortment in a black bag, he hurried to the van and cautiously drove the short distance to his victim's house.

Now it was just a matter of waiting.

When Jonas came back, he stopped just inside the front door, ready to face whatever was coming. Morgan was sitting on the sofa waiting for him. Oh boy, he thought, from the furious look in her eyes, how am I going to explain this mess.

"Did you see anyone?" she demanded, barely refraining from slapping his face. She had done that once. If she did it again, he might arrest her, but considering the situation, she doubted it. What she really wanted to do was kick him right in the balls, and then out of her house. But according to Marilyn, she was in danger, and he was the only one she trusted to protect her.

Quickly, before she could say anything else, he said, "He was gone by the time I got out there. They're taking the injured officer to the ER to be checked out. I called for another man to take his place. But I doubt, with all the commotion he created, whoever was out there will come back." Jonas dared to sit in the chair next to the coffee table and face Morgan.

"Now that you've done your duty chasing the bad guy, you need to explain to me, in detail, what happened to make you have sex with me." The words spewed from her mouth as if she was shooting nails at him.

Her eyes blazed, and he could see the flush in her cheeks. Morgan Jansen was close to despising him and had a good reason for it. He should have known she normally would never do something like that. "I swear to God," Jonas said, "I would never have touched you without your consent. But when you stood there all naked and beautiful, I wanted you so badly, I didn't stop to think."

She sat back looking perplexed and unsure. "What do you mean, I stood there naked?"

"Just what I said!" His voice was louder than he intended. Calmer, Jonas explained what had transpired. When he finished, she stared at him wide-eyed.

"Oh, my God!" she paused for a moment and then yelled with all her pent-up fury. "Marilyn!"

As soon as Morgan shrieked out her sister's name, Jonas couldn't help but notice the sudden drop in the room's temperature. He wasn't prepared for Morgan's stormy rise from the sofa or her twisting back and forth searching the room. Looking around, he tried to find what she was looking for. He could see nothing, but it kept getting colder and colder until he could almost see the vapor of his breath. He rose, looking from side to side.

In the far corner near the kitchen, a mist began to form taking on the faint shape of a woman. He couldn't believe what he was seeing. This was impossible, his mind kept insisting. In his world, ghosts didn't exist. Jonas stood transfixed as Morgan charged toward the mist and followed as it drifted away toward the bedroom. He hurried after her, not really wanting to confront any form of an apparition, actual or a figment, but needing to make sure Morgan was safe.

She stood facing the bed. What appeared to be a vague image of her twin sat at the foot, still dressed in the red underwear and a gray T-shirt, her mouth curved in a wide grin. When the apparition focused its attention on him, Jonas could see the faint outline of the underlying damage to the left eye socket, but nothing wrong with the joints of her arms or knees.

His mind tried to absorb what was happening. He wanted to believe he was imagining everything but knew better. Was he really seeing Marilyn Heddrix's ghost? His rational mind said he wasn't seeing things, but would bet he had to be a little crazy. His attention was jarred back to the raging woman in front of him.

"Damn you, Marilyn!" she stormed. "You did it, didn't you?" There was no doubt in her mind that somehow Marilyn had been behind her sexual encounter with the detective. If her sister had been alive, Morgan was certain she would have strangled her.

"Damned I am, sister," Marilyn conceded. "And yes, you needed a release from all the tension you've been under. You're too thin and look terrible. Besides, I needed your body to be able to protect you. The killer was watching, and I had to scare him away. But you have to admit, you feel more relaxed, don't you. I know I do." She smiled a slow, wicked grin. "Oh, you were not totally unaware of what was happening. Deep down, you knew and enjoyed every moment with him." She turned her head in Jonas's direction. "I know, I felt it," she whispered, gave a sad smile, and then was gone.

The warmth of the room returned, and Jonas continued to stand and stare at the foot of the bed. "What just happened?" his words tumbled out. "Did I see what I think I saw?" he mumbled, almost to himself, but loud enough for Morgan to hear.

"Believe it!" Morgan said, hotly. "Now you know what I'm dealing with. My sister is dead, but she isn't gone." She returned to the kitchen and stared at the wall clock. Almost forty-five minutes had passed. She was exhausted and all the events of the week were driving her down.

My God, she wondered, why is all this happening? Had her world gone completely mad? She wanted to curl up in a fetal ball and let the tears drain her body until her only solution was to go sleep and forget all that had happened. Maybe when it was time for her to wake up, all would be sane again. She doubted that would happen. So instead of going back to bed, which she needed, she placed the tea kettle on the stove and leaned back against the counter, folded her arms across her chest and stared at the floor. The tension between her and the detective needed to be resolved.

Jonas stood just inside the kitchen doorway, not really sure what to do or say. He asked the question that was troubling him the most, "Are you going to despise me for what happened?"

Morgan had to admit, that he had done what most men would do when confronted with a naked woman offering herself to him. He had followed her to bed and had sex with her.

She was aware of the sexual attraction she felt for him, and now knew he felt it also. Marilyn had been the instigator in what had happened, so she could not, in good conscience, place all the blame on him.

"No, I don't despise you," she said, looking up.

As she faced Jonas, her cheeks grew warm at the thought that he knew the most intimate parts of her body.

Jonas was sure she did despise him regardless of what she said. He had violated her trust. It may not have been entirely his fault. From what he knew about her so far, she was a quiet, reserved person. He should have known Morgan wouldn't do something that out of character. "All I can do is say I'm sorry and promise it won't happen again." He added, "Unless you want it to."

He left her standing in the kitchen. "It's been a rough night. Tomorrow, I'll have another team member stay with you, as I have paperwork to catch up at the office. I think that's best."

Morgan's shoulders dropped. "I don't want someone else here."

"It's better this way," he insisted. "If I stay here, it's going to lead to trouble and loss of sleep for me. I'm not going to tell you that I don't want you, I do. Maybe last night was a mistake to you, but it wasn't for me. I need to distance myself from you so I can catch this killer." He raked his fingers through his hair. "Man, thoughts of you fill my head, and I can't think straight." He had to get control of himself. He waved her away. "Go to bed and get what sleep you can. Dawn is only a few hours away." He stretched out on the sofa positive he had made the right decision.

He was wrong, Morgan thought, she didn't think of it as a mistake. Granted, she had been angered by what happened at first, but not for what he believed. If she had to be honest with herself, she was pissed off because she didn't remember any of it.

Yeah, she had been angry when she thought he had taken advantage of her, but after learning it was Marilyn's manipulation, she couldn't blame him, only her sister. Disgusted by her twin's actions, Morgan hurried to the bedroom and got back in bed. As tired as she was it wasn't long before her eyes closed and she fell asleep free of dreams.

Chapter Sixteen

Sunday a.m.

Robert Titus smiled to himself as he drove onto the southbound I-25 access ramp at five-forty Sunday morning. The drive back to Colorado Springs would take about an hour, depending on traffic. He'd be home in plenty of time for church services which would make his wife, Angela, happy.

Considering everything, he was pleased with himself. He'd received the Award of Excellence in Dentistry at the final banquet of the three-day conference. Afterward, he had managed to hook up with the tall, big breasted blonde from the event for an evening of fucking. They had spent a couple of hours together and then she had gone on her way.

As far as he was concerned, the award and the blonde made for a successful three days away from his spouse's constant doubts of how he spent his time. She was suspicious but had no proof. He always managed to convince her she wrong.

He was prepared for the interrogation he knew was coming once he walked through the door. Angela would never be able to face the fact that one woman could never be enough for him. She was so easily deceived.

His extracurricular affairs were exciting, always living on the edge of being caught. He loved it, but the anxiety associated with it gave him panic attacks at times.

His doctor had put him on Xanax to combat the stress of gambling on losing everything. But he couldn't stop. He was addicted to the thrill.

Caroline was his latest. She was his dental patient. That was how he met most of his women. They'd meet once or twice a week, depending on her work schedule, at the one bedroom apartment he maintained off Lake Avenue. Her petite little body was perfect and, unlike his wife, she satisfied all his sexual needs.

There was one woman he'd been involved with years ago that had cost him, cost him dearly. He didn't like to think of her, but she was always there, hovering with her threats.

It had been a two-week conference in Florida. She was a college student in her twenties. So eager to learn, they had two weeks of hot experimental, glorious sex in her little apartment on the beach. Then the nightmare began. She declared she was in love with him. He had tried to dissuade her that she was wrong.

Foolishly, he had allowed her to take a couple of photographs of them together, arm in arm on the beach, and several of him naked on the bed. How could it have hurt, she lived in Florida, he lived in Colorado. Then, there were the sexually explicit e-mails she sent him. After a month, he had told her to stop and admitted he was married. The e-mails ended.

How stupid could he have been? He was stunned when she showed up at his practice in Colorado a month after he returned. For a short time, they took up where they left off in Florida. Then suddenly, she changed.

Morgan Dorchester was no longer naïve. She

demanded money and lots of it. When she set the terms of his payments, she made it clear she could destroy him in every conceivable way possible. So he had paid and paid and then discovered there were two of them, twins. One was Morgan, and one was Marilyn. He was never sure which one was which. By then it was too late, so he kept paying and taking his Xanax to help him cope.

Then one day, Marilyn called the office. As long as he never contacted Morgan again, he was off the hook. She made it clear the threat would always be there. And she would not hesitate to use her evidence to ruin him if he ever contacted her sister. Of course, he immediately agreed. That seemed to be the end of it. But he knew she would make good on her threat, so he made sure to stay as far away from Morgan as possible.

Time passed, and Marilyn did nothing to carry out her threats. He resumed his life. Robert had his various flings. Then, he met Caroline. She was perfect for him and was not interested in a permanent relationship. She made that fact clear from the start. So their affair worked, plus he had his other flings whenever he was out of town. The last few years had been good for him. Caroline made it so.

He sighed as he turned onto the side street off Wood Avenue and pulled into the driveway, not paying any attention to the other vehicles parked on the road.

The killer had been waiting for the dentist to arrive home since before daylight. All the time, his anticipation had been growing. He could feel the excitement, his senses were on a high. The air smelled of roses and freshly turned earth. His eyes picked out a yellow butterfly flitting back and forth along the driveway. He licked his lips to relieve the dryness and smiled. This was a quiet neighborhood, but the sound of the few vehicles on the street seemed louder than usual. Even the ticking of his watch could be heard, causing him to look down. It was almost seven. Soon he would have the dentist in the van and be on his way to his basement.

His excitement rippled through his body, tightening every muscle with anticipation at the thought of Robert Titus bound and ready for execution. He needed a release from all the horrific tension and was eager to feel the flood of ecstasy race through each muscle from head to toe. A Cadillac SUV turning onto the street caught his attention.

Right on time, he thought, as the dentist's vehicle drove into the driveway. Before the man could turn off the engine, the killer eased his van up behind the SUV. He was out of the driver's side and rushing up behind the man as he exited his vehicle. With one swift motion, he grabbed Robert Titus from behind and jabbed the needle into his neck. The man dropped like a rock to the pavement and began to thrash, clutching at his throat and struggling to breathe, his body jerking until it became still.

Stunned, as the dentist suddenly stopped moving, panic set in. This was not supposed to happen. He leaned over and felt for a pulse. There was none. The man was dead. Again he was being deprived of his right to execute the guilty. Everything was going to hell too fast.

He only hesitated a second before racing to jump behind the wheel of his van and drive away, all the while beating his fist against the dash and uttering every cuss word he could remember. He slowed down. It was early. There was another man who needed to be punished just as much, if not more, than Robert Titus. He was the worst of the lot. His time had come. He would not be deprived again.

The ringing of Jonas's cell phone roused him. He had dozed off and on for the remaining hours before dawn, never really letting himself fall into a deep sleep. Now his eyes felt gritty. He rubbed them, glanced at his watch and raised up. It was seven-fifteen. Grabbing the phone from the coffee table, he growled a, "Yeah," and immediately sat up straighter.

"We've got another body. It's the dentist," Clay said, his tone exasperated. They had failed to locate the man in Denver, and now he was dead.

Jonas glanced up when Morgan came to stand in the doorway. "I'll be right there. What's the address?" Noting the street number off Wood Avenue, he ended the call.

"I have to go," he said to Morgan. "The sun is up so I believe you should be safe. I'll have one of the officers stay in the house with you. The other can keep watch out back. He didn't wait for her reply but hurried from the house to his vehicle.

From a block away, Jonas could see the flashing

lights of the police cruisers. Police cars barred the side street all the way to the end of the next block. The primary focus was centered on the body of a man lying on the concrete beside the open door of a black SUV. Charlie Jacks stood near the body, along with a couple of paramedics. It seemed that, for a change, the Coroner had beaten him to the crime scene. He wondered who had called him. It had to have been Clay.

His team had been whittled down from eight to four, Jose, Rupert, Clay, and Henry. Only Jose and Clay were present so far. Rupert came running up to the scene as Jonas walked toward Charlie. Once again, Henry Pope was a no-show. Time to have a hard talk with the man.

"What've we got?" Jonas asked, directing his question at Clay.

"We have one Robert Titus, our dentist." Clay said and pointed at the open driver's side of the vehicle. "His wife was expecting him home by seven to go to church at eight. She didn't hear him drive up because she was in the shower. When she saw his vehicle, she came out to check and found him. She immediately called 911. When the paramedics got here, he was already dead. It appears he had exited the SUV and died soon after."

"Any sign of a struggle?" Jonas looked from Clay to Charlie.

The Coroner shook his head. "I don't think he had time. There's a puncture wound in his neck, but I can't be sure what killed him until I do the autopsy." Jacks motioned for his assistants to bring the stretcher and a body bag.

Clay stood next to Jonas as the body was placed in the bag and loaded into the van. "The paramedics called dispatch when they discovered Titus was already dead, and our officer called the Coroner's office," he said, "Charlie called homicide because of the puncture wound and got me. I called you as soon as I found out who the victim was. I've already talked to the wife. She wasn't much help. All she could tell me was that he left Wednesday evening to attend a conference in Denver until late Saturday night. He was to come home in time for church." Clay stared after the Coroner's truck as it drove away. "Someone put a halt to his church plans."

"The wife couldn't offer anything else?" Jonas glanced over at the tall windows, hoping the woman wasn't watching.

Clay could understand his concern. Watching your husband being hauled away in a Coroner's truck could be almost as traumatic as finding his body.

"A female officer is with her for now, at least until the son and daughter arrive. It shouldn't be too long. They live close by. Do you want to talk to them? I doubt they can offer any additional information."

Other than the puncture wound, there was no need to alarm the family by calling the dentist's death a homicide. Even if they were reasonably sure it was.

"Not now. I want to get the autopsy first. You interview the family. I have to get back to Morgan's house and check on her. If everything's okay, I'll go to the office. You take care of things here. I'm fairly sure we know who killed this man." Jonas started to walk back to his vehicle, stopped and turned once again to Clay. "Did you meet Hanover?"

"Yes. We couldn't find the woman he was looking for. We were going to meet up today, but he's on his own finding Winslow's sister."

"Okay, I'll probably be at the Jansen house or at the office. I need to check a few things out. I'll give Winston a call and tell him you're tied up here. Maybe I'll go with him to talk to the brother and see if he knows where his sister might be." Jonas drove back to Morgan's house. He parked his car at the curb, but didn't even consider seeing her. He walked to the back to check with the two officers on guard duty parked near the alley. One was sitting in the cruiser keeping watch, while the other was on guard inside.

"How's it going?" he asked, stooping down next to the driver's side.

"All's quiet so far," the officer said.

Jonas was thankful for that. "Good," he said and caught a glimpse of Morgan looking out the back bedroom window, waved and then added, "Stay alert. I don't want anything to happen to this woman. I'll have lunch brought to you. If you want coffee, I'm sure Ms. Jansen will brew a pot. Just call your partner and have him ask her. Any problems, call me. I'll be at the office." He didn't hesitate but walked straight to his SUV. He'd call Hanover on the way.

At seven-fifteen, having prepared everything for Mass at eight, Father Paul Bortorelli knelt before the Alter at St Christopher's Church and prayed earnestly for his sins. His sins being mainly in the form of one Elizabeth Ann Winslow, who at that very moment occupied his bed in the house left to him by his late brother. He was lost and didn't know how to stop committing the same sin over and over. Elizabeth was too hard to resist, and truthfully, he didn't want to abstain from the wonders of the flesh she had shown him.

The image of her lying naked and tucked close against him, the scent of her perfume filling his nostrils, the taste of her lips, sent his mind reeling. Even now kneeling, he wanted her, needed her and felt himself grow hard. He had finally admitted that he was in love with her. And as miracles could happen, she loved him. Deserting Lizzie was out of the question; she was pregnant with his child.

He had tried hard to be a good priest but was always aware that he was missing something in his life. This morning's prayers were to ask for forgiveness because he was leaving the church. He'd already turned in his letter of resignation to the Bishop. He couldn't give up Lizzie, and therefore, did not deserve to remain a priest. They would be married and make a life together to raise their child. The house he now owned was paid for, and he had a degree in counseling children. Getting a job shouldn't be a problem.

Just as he started to rise to his feet, a sharp prick in his neck stopped him. As he slowly turned his head, the face before him was well known, and he was shocked to see the rage reflected in the man's features. That was the last thought to enter his mind as his surroundings faded into black.

Fury made him want to stomp the priest to a pulp where he had fallen. It was a fight to control his emotion, not to let loose the frenzy of his hatred toward this man. He was the worst of the worst, this blasphemous bastard who called himself a man of God. He was the vilest sinner of all. The punishment he would deliver against this man was well deserved and befitting his crime.

Effortlessly, the killer threw the priest over his shoulder and made his way out the back door to his waiting van. The fact he'd quickly have the priest tied to the crossbeams, and it wasn't even seven-thirty yet, helped to ease his fury. It was going to be a good day after all.

At that same time, Elizabeth Ann Winslow stretched her slender body, tightening each muscle, then relaxed and smiled in satisfaction. Paul had been fantastic in bed this morning. For a priest, she was surprised at what an accomplished lover he was. Maybe he'd experienced sex before he joined the priesthood. She didn't care if he did, he was hers now.

Lizzie wasn't a particularly religious person so felt no shame in having sex with a man of the cloth. When going to church one Sunday, she had seen the new assistant priest to Father Michaels and was unable to keep her eyes off him. She had never been so sexually aroused by the sight of any man. Maybe it was the temptation of him being forbidden fruit. But the priest made her feel hot all over, to the point she was sure her face was red.

After that, she was determined to meet him. She did after the service. When they came face to face, it was as if lightning shot a bolt between them. The look in his eyes showed he had felt it also. His hand was shaking when he took her slender one in his and thanked her for coming to the service. Within weeks, he was sharing her bed. Within a few months, Paul said they couldn't go on the way they were, living in sin. Marriage was the only solution as he couldn't give her up. Lizzie was thrilled. After he explained his decision to resign from the church, she told him about the baby. He was overjoyed at the news, which made her happy. So they began to make plans.

His brother had left him a house, free and clear of any mortgage, and they would live there. They began redoing the interior and created a room for the baby. That was where they would start their life together. It was heaven for a couple of months until she began to show and went to tell her brother, Carson.

After their mother's death, it had only been her and her brother for years. It was Carson who raised her, put her through high school and college. But he was a control freak, and she hated that. She wasn't allowed to date during high school, not even when she attended the local college, or he would cut off the money. At his wife's urging, she got a job and moved out of his house. But Lizzie knew, Carla Winslow didn't help anyone unless it benefited her.

Lizzie was glad to be on her own, with her own apartment and making her own money. God, she was in her thirties. Over the following years, her relationship with her brother improved somewhat. He still tried to control her, but she defied him. He seemed to accept the fact that she was now an adult, and didn't need him to take care of her anymore.

That was until four weeks ago when she told Carson about her pregnancy and Paul. He went ballistic, called her a whore and ordered her from his house, shouting at her never to return.

And so she stayed away, becoming engrossed with repainting the house and preparing to get married. It was all planned. A quiet wedding performed by a Protestant minister who didn't know Paul had been a priest.

Now she needed to get her butt in gear and go back to the apartment and pack up more boxes to bring over to the house. Lizzie was using the car that belonged to Paul's brother. It didn't matter that she didn't have a valid driver's license, it was a short trip between her apartment and the house. But, she was a cautious driver. Without another thought, she got out of bed and headed for the shower.

Jonas called Hanover on his way back to the office, only to learn that Carson Winslow was coming in to give a statement that morning. He'd have to hurry to do the interview, but he'd make it.

When Winslow arrived at the office shortly after nine, he was not what Jonas Black expected for a college professor. Dressed in a dark blue shirt with the sleeves rolled up, jeans and sockless loafers, he was tall and good looking with bright blue eyes, and holding a bottle of water in his hand. He stood at the entrance to the office looking confused unsure where to go.

Immediately, Hanover walked over to greet him and ushered him to an interview room. Jonas followed and took a seat across the table from the man, noting a slight discoloration on his left cheek.

He was soft spoken and friendly. "What can I do for you, gentlemen?"

Hanover took the lead. "I've been assigned to investigate your wife's disappearance."

"As far as I know, she's with that attorney she left me for," Carson said. The friendly attitude disappeared. There was a touch of anger in his voice, and Hanover pounced on it.

"You seem pissed off about it."

"Of course, wouldn't you be? After almost twenty years of marriage, she comes home from work one night and tells me she's leaving me for another man. I don't excite her anymore. How would you feel, other than pissed off."

Hanover arched an eyebrow. Even he had to admit the man had a point. If some woman did that to him, he wouldn't be thrilled about it either. "When was the last time you saw your wife?"

"The night she packed her bags and left me. I haven't heard from her since, nor do I want to." Carson's eyes flashed with resentment. "I know nothing about my soon to be ex-wife or her lover's whereabouts. When exactly was she supposed to have disappeared? I'd like to know in case I need an alibi." The professor sat waiting for a reply to his question, looking directly at Hanover.

"We believe it was a couple of days after the night she left you," Hanover said.

"You're not sure when she went missing, are you?" Carson stated, still holding onto his water bottle, then gave a smug smile.

There was an irritating self-satisfied tone to his voice that made Jonas want to bust him in the mouth. He glanced at Hanover and saw the muscles of his jaw clenched tight.

The detective felt the same way because the professor was right, they had no idea exactly when Theodore Matthew or Carla Winslow went missing. It could have happened any time during a three-week window. But, the pair had not been seen since the day they were to leave for Mexico. Hanover was reasonably sure they had vanished the same day but had no proof. "We have a fairly good idea, but can't be positive at this point."

The question didn't seem to bother the man. He gave a slight smile as if he knew he had a solid alibi and there was no connecting him with his wife's vanishing act. "What time do you believe she went missing?"

"She and Theodore Matthews were supposed to catch a one o'clock flight for Mexico on that Friday. The surveillance cameras show the attorney's car pulling into long-term parking and a man and woman, supposedly them, walking to the terminal. They never made it to the plane."

"Well, on Fridays, I'd have to check my calendar, but I usually have class from one until three in the afternoon."

"We'll check that out with the college."

"You do that, Detective. I have nothing to hide, and I had nothing to do with my wife's disappearance. She left me, remember. Anyway," Carson said, "until you know exactly when she went missing, I can't give you a solid alibi, can I. And, unless you have questions about something other than my wife, I'm leaving." He started to rise.

"I do," Jonas said, and the man sat back in his chair. "What do you do at the college," he asked.

"I teach a creative writing course for aspiring authors. Why?" His anger had subsided, and he again offered a polite smile.

Jonas' interest was piqued. He took a gamble with his next question. "Did you know a Caroline Jones?"

"I don't think so. Did the young woman go to the college?"

"We believe she was taking some courses there." Jonas was disappointed in the man's reply. He knew Caroline took criminal justice courses at the college at times. He also was sure she was studying creative writing there as well. The books on her desk were proof of it. "Are you the only creative writing teacher at the college?"

"No. There are a couple of others that teach at night. I also have a night class."

Maybe Caroline was taking a class with one of them. He'd call the college on Monday.

"What about a dentist, Robert Titus?" He tossed out the name, hoping for more of a reaction.

"Yes, I know him," Carson said, his manner still calm, but suspicious. "He's my dentist. Why?"

"No reason." There was no sense in revealing unnecessary information. Carson Winslow wasn't buying his reply.

"You had to have a reason for asking?" he insisted.

"Do you know where your sister is, Professor Winslow?" Hanover diverted the subject.

"My sister?" The man was genuinely surprised by the question and looked confused at the odd inquiries. "At her home I suppose. Why?" He looked from one to the other.

"We thought she might have been in touch with your wife," Hanover said.

"I doubt that." Carson appeared adamant about it. "They didn't get along that well. Elizabeth was furious when Carla left me the way she did." He paused and shook his head. "No, I doubt my sister would even talk to Carla."

Jonas didn't believe they were going to get much more out of him. The man didn't appear to be trying to hide anything, and this was only an initial interview. If Hanover had reason to suspect foul play with Carla Winslow's disappearance, he needed more evidence. Winston hadn't found a relative or a friend of the couple who spoke ill of the professor. All of his colleagues, Hanover's people had interviewed at the college, spoke highly of the man. Their few friends blamed the wife for the failed marriage. But, Jonas felt there was definitely something off about the man.

Hanover gave a brief nod to Jonas, stood and

extended his hand to Carson. "Well," he said, "thank you for coming in. If we have more questions, we'll let you know."

Jonas stopped him. "Could you wait one minute?" He left the room and returned shortly with a photograph and shoved it across the table to the professor. It was a picture of Caroline. "Are you sure you've never seen this woman before?"

The man studied the photograph, his features impassive, and shook his head, then took a long drink from the water bottle and set it on the table. "I don't believe so. I have a lot of students that don't take my class but want recommendations for books to study. She could have been one of those students. I don't know her." He stood, and again started to leave.

Jonas threw another question at him. "Would you mind giving us a DNA sample? We only have to swab the inside of your mouth."

"I'm well aware of how DNA is collected, but no. If you want my DNA, get a warrant." The friendly professor was gone. "I also know, as the husband of a missing woman, I'm the logical suspect. But as I said before, I had nothing to do with my wife's disappearance," he walked to the door, water bottle in hand.

They had no proof he'd committed a crime, so Hanover was forced to let him go and escorted him to the elevator.

When he returned, Jonas was back in his office at his desk.

Winston sat in the chair across from him.

"I followed the bastard almost to his car, hoping he'd toss that water bottle. He knew what I was after. When he slid behind the wheel, he held up the bottle as if in a salute. I do not like that man one bit," he said. "That son of a bitch is as guilty as sin, and he knows I know it. He thinks he's so much smarter than we are. Well, we'll see. I'm going to be digging into his past all the way to the day he was born," he swore.

"Mrs. Winslow and the attorney had a flight scheduled out of the Springs leaving at one in the afternoon," Winston continued. "We checked the surveillance video at the airport. It was gray, rainy day, and there was water on the camera lens, but around eleven that morning, it shows the attorney's car parking in the long-term lot, then a man and woman hurrying to the terminal. We lost them after they entered the building. I don't believe the couple ever got on that plane. The airline is going to send me a list of passengers for that flight. We're still checking other surveillance videos to see if we missed them in the terminal.

"Also, I'm going to the sister's apartment again. I still want to ask her where she was the night the attorney's vehicle was driven to the airport. She's involved in this somehow. We haven't been able to locate her so far. Hell, her brother's a smart bastard. He could have killed her to cover his tracks." He stood, and asked, "Why do all these criminals think they can get away with their crimes?"

"They all think that. Some will actually escape being caught, but we do catch the majority, thank God." Jonas said. "Do me a favor," he said, feeling guilty for what he was about to ask. It wasn't that he didn't trust Fernandez, but he was Henry's partner.

"What'd you need?"

Send one of your men to Dawson's Bar out on Constitution and Circle. Have them talk to Tim, the bartender. I need to know what happened the night Marilyn Heddrix was there. I want their security videos. I know that place has cameras everywhere. They're well concealed, but they're there. Get me whatever they have. Clay can review them." Jonas felt certain Henry would be on any surveillance the bar might have, but he wanted to know who else was there at the same time, and who left before Marilyn.

"I can do that," Hanover said. "I'll have my guy go by tomorrow night. Right now, I'm going to a late breakfast," and started toward the elevator.

"Thanks," Jonas called after him. Winston gave a quick wave as he entered and the doors closed.

Jonas sat back in his chair. He was tired of looking at files that revealed nothing new. They hadn't missed anything that he could see. The evidence just wasn't there. This killer had been meticulous. Very careful indeed. And, the DNA results were still not back, plus all the lab work on each victim so far was the same. Each had Ketamine in their system. Maybe Jacks would find something different in the dentist. He doubted it.

When the rest of the team returned, they gathered in his office for a quick meeting. "Do we have anything to help us catch this bastard?" Jonas looked from one to the other. "Clay, did you talk with the son and daughter of Doctor Titus."

"Yep," Clay replied. "You should have stayed. Rupert and I almost had a fight on our hands. Daddy's little darlin'," he said, "was more than pissed off at her mother for not kicking Daddy out a long time ago. It seems she caught him at the office kissing one of his female patients but never told her mother. Then she found out her mommy knew and put up with it because they were Catholic. The son refused to believe it, and so the big argument ensued.

"Anyway," Clay continued, "it seems he had several different women over the years. I think Marilyn Heddrix was one of them. The daughter mentioned him having to pay someone off. From what we know about Marilyn, it sounds like something she'd do. I think the wife knew about the blackmail as well."

"Find out for sure. Get a warrant and check the bank records. Go back as far as you have to," Jonas said. "I'll also ask Morgan what she knows about it."

While the team was still standing at Jonas' desk, a white-faced Hanover burst out of the elevator. Jonas was surprised when the man rushed into his office.

"We've got a missing priest!" he called out.

Jonas stood as everyone turned to face Winston. "Son of a bitch! Is it our killer?"

"Yeah, it is. An elderly woman had arrived early to have confession with Father Bortorelli. She came in the front door in time to see a man carrying the priest over his shoulder and out the back way. She was afraid to catch up with them but did carefully follow and witnessed a van pulling away. So she contacted the head priest, Father Michaels. When he couldn't locate his assistant, he called the police. When 911 transferred the call to me, I rushed over here to get you. I believe this is another abduction by our killer and it's barely ten."

"He's escalated dramatically if it's our guy. He missed out on the dentist, so he kidnaps a priest? That doesn't make any sense. How does a priest fit into this case? All his prior victims have been having affairs. Who would a priest be involved with? A Roman Catholic priest at that." Jonas said

"I don't know. Maybe priests get horny like the rest of us. Maybe he met a woman. How should I know?" Winston said, in frustration. "I do know we'd better get on it. Chief Madison attends that church and is going to be all over this case as soon as he hears. I think he's friends with Father Bortorelli. Plus, I won't be surprised to hear from the Mayor as well." As if on cue, Hanover's cell phone rang. Winston rolled his eyes and answered the phone. "The Mayor," he mouthed.

Jonas turned to his team. "Clay, you and I will go to the church with Hanover and see what we can find out about the priest. Jose put out a BOLO on the van. I'll go talk to Father Michaels. See if he knows whether the priest was involved with a woman. I know it'll be a shocker if he was, but we have to know. The man's life is at stake." He paused. "Let's go. We have a lot to do."

Jonas tapped Winston on the shoulder to let him know they were following him to the crime scene. He acknowledged with a nod while keeping a running conversation with the Mayor.

St. Christopher's Church on North Cascade was

of medium size and constructed of native stone. It had been built around 1912 to give spiritual comfort to the local residents, and still served the community in that capacity, but with fewer parishioners. Several squad cars were parked along the street, while the drivers were stationed at the front and near the back of the church.

Father Michaels, a tall, stately priest, dressed in his Sunday vestments, was waiting on the front steps, wringing his hands as they pulled up and parked. As they hurried toward him, he led the way inside the church and stopped beside an elderly white-haired woman sitting in a pew at the back.

When they reached her, the priest introduced the lady as Gladys Carroll. "Mrs. Carroll is very frightened. She's afraid the man who kidnapped Father Bortorelli will come after her."

Winston sat next to her and took her hand. "I will assure you that protection will be provided to you," he said, patting her hand. "Now, can you tell me what you saw?"

Her voice shaky, Gladys Carroll related what she had seen. "All I really saw was that man carrying Father Bortorelli out that little door back of the altar. I followed him," she was starting to shake, "to the door and peeked out. All I could see was a dark van driving away down the alley." She looked at Hanover. "Please find Father Bortorelli. He's such a good priest."

"Thank you. You've been a big help," Winston said, and again patted her hand. He motioned a female police officer over. "Please escort Mrs. Carroll home and stay with her until I call you." The officer nodded, assisted the elderly lady to her feet and followed her out of the church.

Jonas and Winston turned to Father Michaels. "Where were you when all this happened?" Hanover asked.

"I was in the rectory next door getting ready for mass. I found Mrs. Carroll pounding on the front door and calling for help. I rushed to the church, leaving her at the rectory with the housekeeper. She was too upset to come back here with me at the time. Father Bortorelli was nowhere to be found, so I called 911. That's all I know. Only when we heard the sirens would she return to the church."

There had to be more, Jonas believed. Why kidnap a priest? What had the man done to make himself a target of the killer? "Father Michaels, what can you tell us about Father Bortorelli?"

"Other than he's a good priest and our congregation likes him, not much. He maintains a room at the rectory." Jonas could tell that he was hesitant to say more.

"Did he live there or somewhere else?" Winston asked.

Again Father Michaels hesitated as if choosing his words carefully. "Father Bortorelli has not been himself lately. He has been troubled. I received a copy of a letter he sent to the Bishop. He is planning on leaving the priesthood."

This shocked the hell out of Winston and Jonas. Together they asked, "Why?"

"I can't say," was all Father Michaels added.

Jonas knew the priest wasn't going to reveal anything said to him in a confessional. And he suspected that was what had happened. The young priest had confessed his sins and told why he was leaving the church, knowing Father Michaels could say nothing.

"If you know something, you need to tell us," Jonas insisted.

"I can't reveal what was said in confession," the priest said.

Jonas could tell the Father wanted to be of more help but was bound by the laws of the church. The man was also aware his knowledge might save the younger priest's life.

"Can we see his room?" Winston asked.

"Certainly. But there's nothing there. He moved all his belongings out of the rectory a week ago." Father Michaels' eyes lit up. "That's right. That's right. I remember he said his brother had left him a house. The poor man passed away at the first of the year. I believe the Father has been renovating it in his off-duty time. You might want to check it out. Maybe you'll find some of your answers there." The priest almost beamed. He had kept his vows and still helped to find the missing priest, he hoped.

"Where is this house?" Jonas asked, motioning for Clay.

Father Michaels' face fell with disappointment. "I am so sorry. Father Bortorelli never said the location. It was in his brother's name. Maybe you can find it that way. His name was Joseph Anthony Bortorelli."

Clay jotted the name down and hurried out to his vehicle to run it with the Clerk and Recorder. Within a few minutes, he had the address on Cache la Poudre. They thanked the priest and hurried to their vehicles.

It took barely five minutes to locate the home. It was a neat little rancher with a front porch and a swing. The basement windows were visible as Hanover and Jonas hurried to knock on the front door. When no one answered, they peeked in the front window. No one appeared in the living room. Paint buckets sat on a white drop cloth. The house was definitely being refurbished.

"We'll need a warrant. In the meantime," Jonas said, "why don't you and Clay wait here? I'll call Fernandez and have him contact the judge and get a warrant. I don't think there'll be a problem and hopefully, it won't take long.": He paused to glance around the neighborhood. "I have to go check on Morgan Jansen and ask her about her sister and the dentist. I'll be back as soon as I can."

Clay shook his head and took a seat in the swing as Hanover punched in a number on his cell phone. He thanked God for the shade trees in the front yard and the cooling breeze as his boss headed for his vehicle.

Jonas made a quick stop at the office and found Fernandez waiting for him.

"What did you find out about the van?" he asked, tossing his hat on a desk.

"Nothing. I was just leaving to pick up the search warrant. Hanover had already called the Mayor. Judge Jordan has signed it." Fernandez started for the elevator but stopped. "Lieutenant, I really need to talk to you about Henry," he said.

"Okay. But it'll have to wait for now. I see Pope didn't come in when we were called out on this case."

"No, he didn't, and I haven't been able to reach him." Fernandez looked troubled and anxious. "I really need to speak with you as soon as possible."

"Let me go check on Ms. Jansen. You pick up the warrant and deliver it to Hanover. Call Clay, he'll give you the address. Then meet me back here, and we'll talk." Jonas picked up his hat and walked out with him.

Chapter Seventeen

Sunday

Morgan was getting tired of being cooped up in the house. Every time she tried to stick her head out the door, she was told no by the police officer. In desperation for some alone time, excused herself and went into the bathroom. She sat on the commode lid wondering how long she was going to be under guard. Suddenly she looked over at the bathtub and saw Marilyn sitting on the side. Her face was grim, and she looked distraught.

"He's taken a priest!" Marilyn blurted out.

"Good heavens. When did that happen?"

"Early this morning."

"Do the police know?"

"Yeah, but it won't do them any good. Jonas won't find him. He's already dead," Marilyn said, shaking her head.

"God, no!"

"That monster was in a frenzy. The man killed him shortly after the poor priest was abducted." Sounding frustrated, Marilyn continued to rant. "Why in the hell can't I see more? Why is it always after the fact that I get these images of the victim's body? I'm sure I know the killer, but I can never see him clearly. His image is always fuzzy like an out of focus picture." She hit the wall with her fist and registered surprise when a thump sounded.

"Hey, what's going on in there?" came a yell from the other side of the bathroom door.

"Awe shit, Marilyn, don't do that," Morgan whispered. "That cop heard you." It dawned on Morgan what she had done. "How did you do that?"

Marilyn looked as surprised as her twin. "I don't know," she said. "I have to go. Your detective is back," and with that, she disappeared.

Morgan could hear Jonas talking to the police officer. She hurried and left the bathroom, anxious to find out about the priest that had been taken.

He was alone in the living room when she came into the kitchen. He looked as if he was now the one not sleeping well. "You look terrible," she said.

"Thanks," he grimaced. "Nothing that a decent night's sleep won't cure." He confirmed her suspicion. "I need to talk with you about your sister and Doctor Titus," Jonas said.

Dammit, Morgan thought. To ward off his questions, she tossed out her news. "The priest is already dead."

Jonas stared at her, all thoughts of Marilyn and the dentist vanished out of his mind. "How do you know?" he demanded. "I only found out a short time ago that he was missing." From the guilty expression on her face, he knew what she was going to say. Doubts reared its head, and Jonas beat her to it. "Marilyn told you? Right?"

Morgan shrugged her shoulders. What could she say? And, she didn't care anymore. She was tired of the questions and innuendoes. She spat the words at him, "Think what you will, but Marilyn said he was killed shortly after he was taken." She plopped down on the sofa and waited for his reaction. It wasn't long in coming.

"Great! Dammit! Son of a bitch!" He threw his hat across the room, and it landed on the dining room floor. He picked it up and placed it on the table.

"When did Marilyn tell you about the priest?" he asked, before taking a seat in the chair across from her.

"Just before you arrived. I was hiding from your cop in the bathroom. I just wanted a few minutes alone. I didn't get it. Marilyn appeared and told me about the priest being taken. She's also frustrated because she can't see the killer clearly. She claims she knows him but is unable to identify him."

"That's a lot of help."

Morgan didn't miss the sarcasm in his voice. "Don't say it like that. You'd still be looking for Doctor Donavan if it wasn't for her. She'd tried to warn you, but you were too skeptical to believe in our abilities." Morgan was angered by his words and lashed out in defense of her sister.

He ducked his head and accepted the barrage of angry words aimed at him. "Guilty as charged," was all he could say, along with another apology. "Again, I'm sorry for shooting off my mouth."

"You should be sorry." Morgan was still upset. "Are you staying here this afternoon?"

"No. I just came by to check on you. I have to get back." There was still the slightest touch of cynicism in his voice when he said, "now that I know it's going to be a recovery instead of a rescue."

"Just go!" His words struck Morgan the wrong way. She stormed at him. "I'd prefer that you don't come back. I can't take this from you anymore. I'm burying my sister tomorrow, and I don't need you doubting everything I tell you when she's trying to help." She was close to tears but refused to let him see her cry.

"Christ," Jonas said. "I didn't mean to upset you. It's been a hell of a day so far. Again, I apologize. I need to go back to the office, but I'll come by around dark. I doubt if you'll have any trouble until then."

"Go and don't come back," Morgan yelled at him. She fought back a sob and added, "Take your cop friends with you. I don't want them here!"

She backed up as Jonas charged across the room and grabbed her by the shoulders. He wanted to shake her but kissed her instead. All the stress had cracked her protective shell. Softer, and gentler now, he released her, took her hand and led her to the sofa. Pushing her down onto the cushion, he sat beside her.

"I will come back at dark. You need protection. Your sister told you the killer has seen you, and I'm not going to let anything happen to you." He tried to force a smile from her. "Marilyn may be a ghost, but if I let anything happen to you, she'd murder me. I've seen her, remember. I don't have doubts about the bond between you. So please, trust me and stay put." He rose and retrieved his hat. "The police officers stay, one in the house, one outside." With that, he left to go back to the office, his question about Marilyn's dentist completely forgotten.

Fernandez, Clay, and Hanover were all waiting for him when he walked off the elevator. "Where's Rupert?" he asked. After the confrontation with Morgan, Jonas was a bit pissed off. He turned to Jose, "And where in the hell is Pope. Does the man want to lose his job?"

"That's what I've needed to talk with you about," Fernandez stated.

"Okay, we'll talk. First, any word on the priest?"

They all gave him a blank stare and gave a negative shake of their heads. At that moment, Rupert walked off the elevator and joined them. "I talked to the priest's Bishop. Father Bortorelli is leaving the priesthood to get married," he said, letting the bomb drop. He looked from one to the other.

"Well, damn!" Winston blurted out. "That explains things. Who's he marrying? Do you know?"

"Nope and neither does the Bishop. I asked." Rupert looked around the room. "Henry's not here yet?"

"That seems to be the general consensus. Do you know why?" Jonas wondered if Rupert might know more than Fernandez.

"Jose asked me to go by and check on him," Rupert admitted.

Jonas gave Fernandez a questioning gaze, wondering what else the man knew and hadn't said.

"I asked Rupert to do it because he won't talk to me. He's been drinking a lot since his marriage broke up. The man's an emotional wreck, and he's pissed off." All the team members looked guilty, even Winston.

Had they been covering for Pope? Jonas wondered. Had the man crawled that deep into the bottle? "Look, people, you can't help Henry by covering for him. Someone needs to tell me what's going on. Fernandez, my office now! The rest of you, keep looking for the priest and find out what woman he was planning to marry."

As the rest of the team headed for the elevator, Fernandez, knowing he had a lot of explaining to do, entered Jonas' office and took a seat. "I told you before I had to talk to you," he said, in his defense, "but we were all busy with the case."

"That's true. So now, I'm listening. What do you know about Henry?"

"That he's in more trouble than he realizes." How to explain his suspicions? "You remember you told me to check out Dawson's Bar, the night Marilyn Heddrix was abducted?"

"Yeah"

"Well, I finally located the bartender, Tim Daly, this morning. Went by his apartment. He wasn't happy being awakened that early. He remembered the redhead from that Friday night. It seems she got into a fight with Pope. He left the bar right after she did." He let the statement hang in the air for the Lieutenant to come to his own conclusion. "He also remembered me coming in looking for Henry. That was around eleven that night. I missed him. I went by his house; he wasn't home." Fernandez was deeply troubled by the information he had withheld.

"Do you think Henry may have had something to

do with her death?" Jonas demanded. The killer being a cop would explain why he was so careful. A cop would know how to avoid leaving evidence. It made his gut clench to think one of his own could be that vicious. There was more, he could tell by Fernandez's face. "Spill it. What else have you withheld from this investigation?"

Squirming in his chair, Fernandez blurted out the rest. "I hope not, but after every single victim, Henry has not been home at the time of the abductions, not after the Heddrix woman, Doctor Donavan and lastly, Caroline. And, he's got scratches on his face, hands, and arms. He's drinking way too much, and I believe he's been blacking out. Also, he uses Lagerfeld aftershave." Fernandez looked distraught. "I don't want to think Henry is capable of such crimes, but he has a lot of anger over his wife leaving. The anger in him is scary."

Jonas' stomach was becoming more knotted by the minute. If Pope was the killer, the press was going to have a field day. They'd be broadcasting the department as incompetent and trying to protect one of their own. That would be ridiculous. No way would the department protect a murderer, especially if he was a cop. Every police officer and their actions were constantly under scrutiny as it was. Now, Henry was possibly the prime suspect in their murder case. He'd have to be brought in for questioning.

"Do you know if he's home?" Jonas hoped it would be an easy apprehension.

"I don't know for sure."

"You take two officers and go pick him up. If he's not home, find him and bring him in for questioning, even if you have to cuff him. Understand? I want him here within the hour." Jonas fought to control his rising temper.

He'd noticed the scratches on Henry's face himself the morning of Caroline's abduction but thought nothing of it. He'd not even considered Henry when Jacks had said she had fought back and had tissue under her fingernails. Why hadn't he asked Pope about it then instead of ignoring it? He wished he could justify his actions due to being frantic to find Caroline.

Fernandez rushed out of the office leaving Jonas sitting behind his desk, looking troubled. All the murders had happened in the middle of the night. Even the bodies had been dumped before dawn except for Caroline.

The first two killings had been coldly calculated and done with only seven blows each. Caroline had not been killed in the same way. She had been viciously beaten to death. The killer had been in a rage. And per Fernandez, Henry Pope was in a rage over his wife's leaving

Jonas picked up the phone and called Rupert, issuing an order for him to meet Fernandez at Henry's house. Then he called Clay to find out how the search for the priest was progressing. Not very well. They had located the brother's house, and they were at that moment on their way there. Jonas asked for the address and said, "I'll see you in a few minutes."

When he pulled to the curb on Cache La Poudre, Clay and Winston stood waiting on the small front porch. The house was in an older section of town and in need of repairs. From the looks of things, the padre was in the process of renovating the exterior. Jonas spotted an entire wall where the paint had been scraped, and a fresh coat of white had been applied.

Still in a pissed off mood, he growled, "Do we have a warrant? I don't want any problems here."

Clay produced the paperwork authorizing entry and knocked on the door three times. He checked the front door. It was locked. When no one appeared, he started looking for a hidden key. When that failed, he gave Jonas a sheepish grin and produced a set of lock picks and proceeded to open the front door.

"I intend on asking you about that little stunt," Jonas directed at Clay.

"Just one of my hidden talents," he came back. "I have lots of talents you don't know about," he said and entered the house.

The interior was sparsely furnished, with a sofa and a TV. A floor lamp was placed next to the couch, and an old sawed-off table served as a coffee table. Work was being done on the interior as well, two cans of paint sat next to one wall. They each took a room. Winston went to the back to check both bedrooms and the bathroom. Clay and Jonas searched the rest of the house.

After a short time, Hanover came out from the back, "Well," he said, "a woman has been staying here. There are women's clothes in the closet and feminine products in the bathroom. There's nothing out of the ordinary to find back there. A few pairs of jeans, some slacks, and shirts, some underwear in the dresser. He definitely was not living here alone. Our priest really does have a lady friend, and I think she's pregnant. A bassinet is set up in the back bedroom."

Jonas and Clay stood by the dining room table looking through an assortment of advertisements and unopened mail. Clay waved one unopened letter in the air. "I think I just found out who our priest was planning on marrying. This is a letter addressed to one Elizabeth Winslow."

Jonas took the envelope from Clay and let out with a loud, "Crap! Winston and I talked to the brother this morning. We need to talk to him again. Hey, Hanover, do you remember where he said he lived?"

"I don't think he said. But we can find out." With that, he took out his cell phone and made a call. Within a couple of minutes, Winston had the address. "He lives on Wood Avenue.

Jonas and Clay looked at each other. That was too much of a coincidence. Finishing up with the front rooms and kitchen, other than the name of the woman, and the fact she was pregnant, their search was a waste. They still hadn't located the sister. Maybe they'd find her at the brother's home.

After securing the house, Clay joined Jonas in his vehicle, and they headed to the address Hanover had given them.

The two-story home was located not far from the house of Robert Titus, but definitely far enough away to be in the lower income bracket. From Del Norte north, the homes went up in value. But, just the Wood Avenue address was a perk for the owner.

They parked at the curb and made their way

toward the entrance of a large two-story Victorian home. The odor of roses filled the air as they walked up the steps and onto the wide front porch. Jonas and Clay walked to the end of the porch and looked toward the back. All along the driveway to the back garage, the fence was lined with roses of every color. Jonas would bet that the backyard was also filled with flower beds and more roses. The professor certainly loved roses.

Winston pushed the doorbell, and they waited. Through the open side windows, they could hear the chimes ringing all through the house. After two more rings of the bell, suddenly the sound of heavy profanity and pounding footsteps on the hardwood floor could be heard coming their way.

The door was jerked open and "Come in," was issued and Carson Winslow hurried down the hallway holding a bloody washcloth to his face. "Give me a minute. When I heard the bell, in my rush, I fell into a bunch of rose bushes. I need to get the thorns out of my face. Have a seat, and I'll be right there," came the call from down the hall.

They took seats in the living room and waited, looking around the ornate room. Winslow's home was decorated as if it was still in the Victorian era. Even the furniture looked like it was from the late eighteen hundreds. Everything was dust free and polished to a high gleam. Jonas wondered if the rest of the house was as ornate. He glanced over at Hanover who appeared overly calm. It made him wonder if that bloody washcloth had also caught his attention.

In no time, the professor appeared in the doorway holding a bandage to the left side of his face, to stop the bleeding. Jonas could see the start, near his eye, of several oozing grooves extending down his cheek and a couple on his hands.

Carson kept the bandage pressed to his face for a few minutes, then excused himself again. "I'll just go clean these up so I won't bleed all over the place," and returned to the bathroom. Shortly, he came back with a bandage taped to his cheek.

"What can I do for you, detectives?" He remembered the two detectives from the interview at the police department. "Have you located my sister?"

"This is Detective Addison Clay, a member of my team," Jonas said. The professor acknowledged him with a nod and returned his gaze back to the Lieutenant. "That's why we're here," Jonas continued. "We can't seem to locate her? Do you have any ideas where we might find her?" The man had been cooperative so far, and Jonas hoped he'd continue to do so.

"Did I give you her address?" Winslow asked.

"Not yet. We checked for a driver's license, but didn't find one, not even an identification card."

"I'm sorry. I don't believe Lizzie drives, anyway, not that I know of. She lives in an apartment on Alexander Road." He immediately provided her address and Jonas wrote it down.

"Thank you. Have you heard from your sister?" Winston asked.

"No, I am sad to say, I haven't." His regret seemed genuine from his expression, the furrowed brow, the look in his eyes. "We had a disagreement about her planning to marry a priest. I argued against it, but she is determined to do it anyway. She says they're in love." Carson shrugged his shoulders and said, "Who am I to stand in the way of someone's happiness. I wish her the best, after all, she is my baby sister and love is a powerful thing," he added.

They stood, and Clay suddenly said, "I saw all your roses on the way in, would you mind showing me your backyard? My wife loves them, and I want to create a flower bed of yellow roses for her. I don't know much about growing them, so maybe I could get some pointers from you."

Carson Winslow beamed, "Certainly. Come this way," and led the way through the kitchen and out the back door. The yard was mostly flower beds of every color rose that anyone could want. "First, you need good soil and the proper fertilizer." He opened an outside door that led down to a basement and motioned to a rough wooden table filled with rose food, fertilizer and an assortment of yard implements. "I started growing my roses in containers before creating my flower beds. They're beautiful, but the thorns are hazardous to my hands and arms. Now my face." He rattled on for a few minutes about proper soil and care, then handed Clay a book on container gardening.

Graciously, he accepted the book and tucked it under his arm. "I'll study this and let you know how it goes. Hopefully, I'll have some success," Clay said, and followed Winslow out of the basement to where Hanover and Jonas waited near the back porch.

Jonas shook hands with the man, "We have to leave, but thanks for your help. We'll see if your sister is at home. I'll let you know what we find out."

"I'd appreciate that. My silly sister doesn't even own a cell phone, so I can't call her. Please let me know that she's alright."

That statement made Jonas wonder why, if he was concerned about Elizabeth, he hadn't driven to her apartment to check on her. Was it because he knew exactly how she was?

Winslow followed them along the pathway to the front of the house and watched until they drove away. He hurried back inside the bathroom, pulled the bandage off his face, and, in the mirror, examined the scratches running down his cheek. He glanced down at the wastebasket. The bloody washcloth was still there, but only one of the gauze pads he'd used to clean the wound.

"Son of a bitch!" exploded from his mouth. That fucking detective! He had to have stolen the pad. Now, they'd have his DNA. His anger began to rise. Dammit, Elizabeth, he wondered, where in the hell are you?

He returned to the kitchen and glanced at the wall clock. The hour was growing late, and he still had a lot of work to do. With that thought in mind, he locked up the house and hurried to the garage. He needed to locate his sister.

"That was a clever way to get a look at his basement," Jonas said, as he and Clay drove away.

"Well, at least we know now that his basement is clean. That place is as orderly as his house," Clay said. "Don't you think with us coming by, that he'd be a little more concerned about his sister? I don't trust that man," he added, then "If you don't need me, I'll head home for an hour. Becca will have dinner waiting. I like to join her whenever possible. I'm gone so much as it is. So, if you'll drop me at my car, I'd appreciate it. "

"Sure," Jonas said, "Be back as quickly as you can," wishing he could go to Morgan's house and have a nice quiet meal. He doubted if she would even talk with him now since she told him to leave and not come back.

Jonas called Hanover. "I'm going to the office to meet Pope."

"I'll go to the girl's apartment and see if she is there. If she isn't, I'm going to stop for dinner. I'll be back as soon as I can," Hanover said.

"Okay," Jonas agreed. That way, they'd accomplish more. Besides, he wasn't looking forward to having to reprimand one of his team. But, Pope had a lot of explaining to do. From what Fernandez said, he had been withholding information. Jonas hated to believe the man was more involved in the case than they thought. He'd know soon enough. A quick call to Fernandez to see if he had located Pope confirmed they were almost at the office.

Jonas hoped there was a reasonable explanation for whatever was going on. To think Pope would be guilty of such crimes was hard to believe, he thought, as he pulled up behind Clay's vehicle and stopped.

"See you later," Clay called, and hurried to his car.

When Jonas got to his office, Fernandez and Pope

were waiting. Taking his seat, he studied the detective. The man looked worse than the last time Jonas had seen him, dark circles under his eyes, unhealthy pallor to his skin and stubble of a beard on his face. Even from where he sat, Jonas caught a whiff of booze.

"Where did you find him?" he asked Fernandez.

"Drunk on his living room floor."

"You could have cleaned him up some," Jonas said.

"This is cleaned up," Fernandez said, in his own defense. "You should have seen him before I dumped him in the shower. He smelled worse than this. He'd vomited on himself and was laying in it. God, you should see his house, empty booze bottles all over the place. I don't think he's eaten in days either."

From the expression on Fernandez's face, Jonas could tell he was disgusted with his partner. Pope could see it also.

"Don't look at me like that Jose," Henry said, scowling at Fernandez. "I remember how pissed off you were when your girlfriend dumped you. So don't act so high and mighty with me. For God's sake, get me a cup of coffee and some aspirin. My head is splitting," he begged and hung his head in his hands.

Fernandez left and returned with a cup of steaming black coffee and the requested pain pills. "Here, take these and drink the coffee. You have a lot to explain."

Jonas waited until the man had finished the first cup and was on his second one before stating, "Okay, Pope, I have given you a lot of leeway this past week because your partner told me what was going on."

Pope shot his partner a nasty glance.

"What was I supposed to do, let you lose your job?" Fernandez demanded.

Pope just shook his head and faced the Lieutenant. "I know I've screwed up, but. . . ." He never got to finish.

"Screwed up! Is that what you call it?" Jonas leaned forward, his arms on the desk. "When you're late for work, that's screwing up. Which by the way, what is your excuse for missing most of this past week when you were needed? Did you even call in?" Jonas looked at Fernandez for confirmation that his partner had notified him.

"He called me," Fernandez said, lying.

Henry straightened up in his chair. "I don't have an excuse. My wife left me, and I lost it. I've been drunk for over a week," he admitted. "And I have a serious problem. I can't remember anything when I sober up. I don't know where I've been or what I've done."

Jonas was ready to tear him a new asshole, but that was not what he needed. Pope would expect through chewing out, and the Lieutenant proceeded to give him one. "Not only have you been missing work, staying drunk, but you've also withheld vital information about this case. What the hell do you think you're doing not telling me you knew the victims?"

"God, Jonas, I wanted to tell you. But when I saw that photo of the Heddrix woman, I almost puked. In fact, I had to hurry to the bathroom before I threw up."

Jonas was fighting hard to control his temper, and

hear the man out before placing his ass behind bars as a potential suspect. If he did that and the press got wind of it, they'd have a field day. They were all over the murders as it was, always trying to wheedle information out of the detectives. He could just see the headlines on TV and in the papers, "KILLER COP CAUGHT." And the Chief and the Mayor? He didn't even want to think about the fit they'd have and the repercussions down the line, even the loss of jobs.

He settled back in his chair and said, "Alright, tell me how you know the victims?"

Henry threw his hands up, "Doctor Donavan was my doctor, and the Heddrix woman was his nurse. That's how I knew them, I swear. I never saw them outside of the office before, but I did witness their close friendship in the office. It was no secret that they were involved with each other. Last Friday night, I did run into Marilyn Heddrix at Dawson's Bar."

"Caroline was your co-worker," Jonas said. "Tell me how you know the priest."

"What priest?" Henry looked confused by the question.

"Father Bortorelli from St. Christopher's Church!

Puzzled Henry shrugged. "I've never heard of him, why?

"Because he was abducted early this morning, that's why! What do you know about it?" Jonas shouted. "I want to know what you have to do with these murders."

"Murders! God, help me? Did I do these killings?" The skin of Henry's face turned a shade paler. He looked like he was going to throw up. "Oh God, oh

God," he said, over and over, "What have I done?"

Fernandez, who had sat quietly while Henry was getting his ass chewing, chimed in. "I don't believe Henry had anything to do with killing these people. Especially, not the way the victims were murdered." He studied Jonas' face for any sign of doubt. "Lieutenant, you can't honestly believe Pope would kill Caroline like that." He drew in a breath. "If he were going to kill someone, he'd shoot him. Henry is not this sick son of a bitch killer."

"Yeah, but look at the evidence," Jonas said. "He was in a rage over his wife leaving him for another man."

Pope again glanced at Fernandez, who looked guilty for disclosing that bit of information as well.

"Every time there was an abduction during the night, Henry was off the clock," Jonas continued. "It would have been easy for him to access Marilyn Heddrix's home address and," he emphasized, "he knew she was having an affair with the doctor. I'll bet he even knows Doctor Robert Titus."

"Ah, shit!" Henry exploded. "Yeah, Doctor Titus is my damn dentist, and he was also Caroline's. I saw her at his office. Let me guess, Robert Titus is also dead?" He grew even sicker when Jonas nodded.

The Lieutenant laid it out for him. "Do you realize, you were either late getting to the crime scene or didn't show up at all for each of these murders? And, you know all the victims and who was sleeping with whom. How does that make you look?" Pope was growing paler by the second. "Guilty as all hell," Jonas finished for him.

"I swear, Lieutenant, I didn't kill these people." Henry was so distraught, he was close to tears. "I couldn't hurt Caroline. She was my friend."

"You'd better start telling me everything you know, or I'll slap your ass behind bars and to hell with the consequences," Jonas commanded

"That's just it, I don't remember any of it. I know I got in a fight with the Heddrix woman at the bar only because Tim, the bartender, told me I did. All the rest is a blank. I have no memory of anything, not leaving the bar, how or when I got home even. All I can tell you is that I woke up with a severe hangover the next day. The same thing has been happening most mornings. I get drunk the night before and wake up with nothing."

Good grief, what am I going to do with this man? Jonas wanted to believe Pope, he really did. Was the man capable of murder? Some cops were forced to shoot a suspect and kill them. If they were lucky, most never had to pull their guns. Jonas found it hard to believe that Henry could be that cold and calculating to pull off these types of murders.

No, he was guilty of only one thing, drowning his sorry ass in a bottle. Well, his drinking was going to end today, or he was finished as a cop. "Henry, I agree with Fernandez. I don't think you committed these murders, but until we can prove it, you're still under suspicion. I think you should talk to a lawyer. I'm going to suspend you. But, until you're cleared, you can't be here. I need your badge and your gun.

"Another thing, if you touch one drop of booze, you're going behind bars. You will stay home, stay sober, get your act together and report to Fernandez three times a day. I even want him to tuck you in at night." Jose nodded in agreement. "Are we clear? I'm taking a chance here. If this leaks out that you might be a suspect, the Chief will have all of our asses and our jobs. And I know how you think booze helps the pain you feel. Believe me, it won't." Jonas knew all too well that nothing eased the ache of loving the woman you love.

Jonas turned to Fernandez, "I want him to check in with you by cell phone. If it pings off any tower other than the one it's supposed to, find him and haul his ass into lockup." Henry was one shade this side of gray. "Take him home and make him eat something. Also, have him drink a lot of orange juice. That'll help with the hangover. Now get out of here, the both of you. If either of you holds information back from me again, you can kiss your jobs goodbye."

Jonas watched as the two men left his office. What a fucking mess, he thought. God, he was taking a chance. Morgan had already said the priest was dead. If so, where was the body? No doubt the killer would dump it for all to see.

He rubbed his eyes, feeling more tired than usual. The weight of the case was really wearing him down. They needed a break, any kind would do. He only wished he knew when it was coming.

He glanced at his watch and realized the afternoon had slipped by. His stomach growled. He'd pick up something and take it back to Morgan's. All he could do was hope she would let him in. A quick check in with

Hanover was necessary. Elizabeth Winslow was not at her apartment either. Winston was headed to a restaurant for dinner and would call her later.

Jonas called Morgan. Surprised by the friendly tone in her voice, the detective was almost suspicious but ignored it. When he suggested take-out, she declined and said she had already cooked dinner, chicken, and rice, salad, with herb bread and fresh coffee or wine, whichever he preferred.

As he grabbed his hat, it dawned on him suddenly, tomorrow was Monday, the day of Marilyn's funeral. He hadn't mentioned going with Morgan, but he would tonight.

It was almost five-forty-five when he knocked on her front door. She opened it and motioned him inside. The table was set, and the food was ready to be served. She dished up two plates and had Jonas take the food out to the two patrolmen on duty for the night. She didn't have much to say other than to tell him to have a seat and carried the dishes to the table. Morgan poured a glass of wine for herself and filled Jonas' cup with coffee.

After devouring a reasonable portion of the food, Jonas helped clear the table. Once the dishes were washed and the kitchen cleaned, Morgan refilled her wine glass and said, "You know I have to bury my sister tomorrow. She was my last living relative, and now she's gone." She inhaled the wine and poured another glass full, and went to sit on the sofa.

Jonas followed, a little concerned by how quickly she was drinking each glass. At the rate she was going, she'd be drunk on her butt in no time. He took the wine bottle, placed it in the refrigerator and out of sight before joining her on the sofa.

"You might want to go a little easy on the wine," he said.

"Why?"

"You don't want a wine hangover tomorrow."

"Yes, yes I do. That way maybe I'll be numb and not feel anything." Morgan muttered, almost to herself.

"I'll go with you if I can," he offered.

"Thank you, I would appreciate it." Tears started to well in her eyes but faded. "I didn't think I had any more tears left," she said.

"You will tomorrow," Jonas told her, knowing the impact would hit her hard. "Her service will be the worst part. Then, only time will help. You don't ever get over a death, you only learn to cope with it. As time goes by, the pain becomes bearable, but never completely goes away. That loss is always there in the back of your mind."

"Is that how you feel about Kelly? She's always in your mind?" Morgan leaned back and took another sip of wine.

"No, not as much as before," Jonas said, staring at her.

Morgan almost missed seeing the desire in his eyes. She sat up straighter. "I've been doing a lot of thinking about my sister," she went on slowly, turning to face him. "Maybe she had the right idea. Live for today. You don't know what's going to happen tomorrow. You may be murdered like she was.

"I've lived my life always doing the right thing. I

studied hard, went to college, and did everything my parents expected of me. What do I have to show for it? I missed out on a lot of fun. Marilyn didn't. She was a lot braver than I was." Without hesitation, she leaned over and planted a kiss on Jonas' mouth. "I don't plan on giving up anything else. I want you," she whispered against his lips.

"Hold it," he said, pushing her at arm's length. "Is this you or is Marilyn pulling a trick on us both?" He wasn't going to take a chance on being the object of Morgan's fury again. Once had been enough. Earlier she didn't want him to come back, and now she was willing to have sex with him? God in Heaven, he wondered, what is going on here?

"I wouldn't care if it was Marilyn, but it isn't. I want you and have wanted you again since the other night. You set me on fire. All I know is, if you don't make love to me soon, I'm going to rape you." The look in her eyes said she was prepared to follow through with her threat or make an attempt.

Jonas knew what he was contemplating was all wrong, but God how he wanted her. He was losing his self-control and found himself as close to falling in love with this woman as was possible without jumping off the cliff. If he made love to her now, Jonas knew he'd be a goner for sure. But if he didn't, that regret would be with him for the rest of his life. His only hope was there'd was a net to catch him at the bottom.

"Come on," he said, "we need more privacy than the living room." He led the way to the back bedroom, checked the windows to make sure the blinds were closed this time and turned to face her. He took a step back.

She was already naked and waiting. Quickly, he shed his clothes, feeling the throb as his erection grew. God, how he wanted her, wanted to taste her, kiss her and drive her wild. He didn't want this to be a quick coupling, but slow, intense lovemaking that Morgan would not forget.

She moved toward him, and he met her midway in the room. She raised her hand and caressed his face, leaning in to kiss his lips. All she could think about was the burst of heat in her pelvis and how good he tasted. Slipping her arms around his neck, she arched against him, eager to feel his flesh touching hers, and the hardness of his penis pressing against her.

His lips were demanding as he explored her mouth, tasting her, needing much more. With one swift motion, he lifted her into his arms and placed her on the bed and covered her.

She lay back wondering what excited her so much about him. Was it the hot demand of his kiss, the lingering scent of the soap he had used that morning? Perhaps the feel of the rough calluses on his palms when he caressed her skin? The gentle way he held her, the hardness of his body, all these sent her emotions racing, her heart pounding and desire for him soaring.

All she knew was that she wanted him, needed him to love her until all her heartaches and pain disappeared. Morgan had been holding on so tight she felt as if her body would break at any moment if she let go. It was a fight against the immense pain waiting to overtake her. To feel was what she needed, to relish the heat of him deep inside her, driving her to the edge of oblivion, and letting her forget for a while. So she opened for him, needing him to chase tomorrow's agony of Marilyn's funeral from of her mind.

Jonas had no intentions of satisfying her needs so quickly. Instead, he traced her jawline with his tongue, then feathered his kisses along her neck to her shoulder, then down to her breast. She appeared to be lost in the sensations. So, close to her ear, he whispered, "Don't think, Morgan, just feel, enjoy and relax."

He knew how hard she had been fighting to keep it together. Had Morgan let go and let the grieving process start? He doubted it. Knowing she wasn't sleeping well, hell neither was he, and that she was losing weight she could hardly spare, only showed she wasn't eating. Maybe making love to her would help her finally relax enough so she could rest.

Jonas cupped each breast and suckled one nipple then the other. Morgan tried to wrap her legs around him, but he pushed them further apart and eased down to open her wide. Lightly, he brushed her nub with his tongue, just enough to make her draw in a breath and arch toward his mouth. Knowing he was going to lose it at any second, he rose to his knees, pulled her to him and entered her, thrusting deep. The wave of heat that hit him destroyed any hope of his taking it slow and easy.

She matched him thrust for thrust, holding onto his shoulders and forcing him deeper and deeper. It was as if she was attacking all the demons that plagued her, in an attempt to drive them away. He felt the beginning of the contractions of her pelvic muscles tightening around him. That was his undoing. He couldn't stop his own from happening. She kept propelling her body against him until they both stiffened, crying out together as a hard climax rocked their bodies.

Jonas rolled off her and pulled Morgan close. Tears were streaming down her face, and she was sobbing. "It's going to be alright," he tried to reassure her.

"No," she uttered between sobs, "it will never be alright again, ever. She's dead, and after tomorrow, she'll be gone forever, and I'll be alone."

"You don't need to be alone," Jonas said, all too aware of the turn his feelings for this woman had taken. He couldn't let her go out of his life, even if she did see her sister's ghost. Hell, he had seen Marilyn's ghost. So he knew Morgan wasn't crazy as he'd first thought. No, she was the most caring and sane person he had ever known.

He didn't want to rationalize what he felt but found himself doing just that. Was he in love with her? Yeah, he believed so. That had to be it. Because why else would he want to kill anyone who tried to harm her. All he could hope was that she cared as much for him.

Her eyes were starting to drift shut. Jonas pulled her closer against him and placed a protective arm across hers. Listening to her steady breathing, he knew she was asleep. She needed it more than he did. Slowly, his eyes closed as well and soon his breathing matched the rhythm of hers.

Chapter Eighteen

Monday

No one ever wanted to destroy a cell phone as much as Jonas Black did the next morning. Naked, he grabbed his jacket and pulled the thing out of the pocket, punched the talk button while trying not to wake Morgan. It failed. She raised up on her elbow, gave him a sleepy "Good morning. What time is it?"

He put a finger to his lips for her to remain silent. "What!" he barked into the phone.

"You want the bad news first or the good news?" Clay barked back.

Jonas' conscience pricked at him. Clay sounded as if he hadn't been to bed. "Where are you?" he asked.

In a chipper but sarcastic voice, Clay said, "At church. And it's a glorious morning for a fucking body to be found on the steps of St. Christopher's Church." In a more somber tone, he said, "You need to get here. This is as bad as Caroline's body. The man is busted all to pieces. He doesn't even look human, he's so broken."

"Son of a bitch!" exploded from Jonas, making Morgan sit up in bed.

From the look on his face, she knew what had happened. Marilyn hadn't appeared to tell her, but she knew they had found the latest victim. Oh God was all she could think. When was it going to end? All these lives destroyed all because of what? It was hard for her to fathom anyone hating another person so much, to do what this killer had done. But it had happened, and it was Jonas' responsibility to find the man.

That scared her. What if he got hurt, shot or even killed? She couldn't stand the thought of that happening. "Please be careful," she said. "I'm afraid for you."

"I'll be fine," he said, getting dressed. "I'm not the one he's after, you are. Remember what your sister said, he was watching you. You might want to get dressed. I'll send one of the officers inside to stay with you. I have to go. Clay's already at the scene," he said, shoving the bottom of his shirt into his slacks. Looking around for his boots, he found them just under the bed.

He was all too aware that so far Morgan hadn't mentioned anything about what happened between them last night, so he didn't. He stopped long enough to sit on the bed and pull on his boots.

Suddenly, she was next to him, her arms slid around his neck, her lips were close to his ear while she pressed her naked body against him.

"Thank you for last night," she whispered and kissed his cheek. "That's the first good night's sleep I've had in months. I needed you, and you were there for me."

He kissed her lightly on the lips, "We'll talk when I get back," he said and kissed her again. "Don't go taking chances. Both officers will escort you to the funeral home, the cemetery and then back to the house. They have their orders. Do as they tell you, and they'll keep you safe. I don't want anything happening to you." He stood, looked around for his hat as Morgan scrambled off the bed and grabbed a robe. She pulled it on as she followed him from the bedroom.

He found his hat on the dining room table, turned and kissed her again and hurried out the front door. Morgan watched as he rushed to his vehicle and drove away. There was no sense in going back to bed. The service was scheduled for ten that morning. It was to be a brief affair.

She wondered who would show up. Hopefully Debbie and Alice from the office, but for some reason, she didn't think so. Jonas would try and be there for her, if at all possible. That's why she realized, she was falling for the man. She was falling in love with Jonas Black. Morgan smiled, and suddenly felt the slightest warm caress on her cheek. It had to be Marilyn. But, she wondered, why didn't she appear like before?

There was a soft whisper close to her ear. "I can't. I have to wait. Terrible things are about to happen. Be careful," was all she said, and then Marilyn was gone.

Tears started running down Morgan's face. Was this it, the final time she would ever be in contact with her twin? The full impact hit her in the gut, and Morgan crumpled on the sofa and let all the pent-up pain and sorrow wash over her. She cried until she couldn't cry anymore. Her eyes were puffy, and her nose was running. On her way through the kitchen, she pushed the button on the coffee maker and returned to the bedroom. Pulling off the robe, she tossed it on the foot of the bed. A nice long shower was what she needed. Naked, she headed for the bathroom.

When Jonas arrived, Clay was busy talking to the officer who had discovered the body. Jonas walked over and cringed as he looked down at the broken form of

Father Bortorelli. The one thought that entered his head, oddly enough, was the killer had at least left the poor man a small amount of dignity. He had been stripped of all his robes except for his boxer shorts. The CSI techs were busy searching the area for any sign of evidence and taking photographs.

The priest had not been a big man, slight of frame, his muscles still had been wiry. Now bone protruded from various areas. A significant amount of blood had pooled under the victim's head and shoulders. There was a large wound on the left side of his head, but it was not the crushing blow that had killed the other victims. Charlie Jacks was busy with his examination and glanced up at Jonas.

"I think this man died here on the steps," He said, shaking his head. "Most of the broken bones would have been agonizing, but I don't think he was dead when he was dumped. There's too much blood. It looks like he bled out right here. Dammit, all to hell. Who kills a priest?" Charlie demanded.

"A nut job, that's who," Jonas replied, "How in the hell did this killer carry the priest in his condition and dump him on the steps of this church without anyone hearing or seeing him," Jonas asked, to no one in particular.

A member of the CSI team came around from the back of the church in time to hear the question. "Wrapped in plastic and probably from the alley out back and down the sidewalk between the church and the building next door. We found blood droplets. They could be from the victim," the tech, Cliff Warren, said.

"Thanks," Jonas said, and headed to the back, being careful where he stepped. Clay followed. Both men agreed that it was doubtful there had been much traffic on the street in the wee hours of the morning. It would have been easy to pull up to the curb, dump the body and drive away. Why park behind the church.

An alley ran behind the building making accessibility easy. Jonas stood glancing up and down the dirt road. He'd have Cliff check for a tire print. Maybe they'd get lucky for a change. He had to agree, the killer must have parked out back, carried his victim to the front steps, dumped him and ran back to his vehicle. The priest didn't weigh that much for a big man to cart, and all the properties along the dirt road had six-foot-high privacy fences. It would have been easy for a man the size of Carson Winslow.

"All these houses back up on the alley. Check to see if anyone saw or heard anything," Jonas told Clay. He doubted that anyone had heard or seen anything, but it might be worth a try.

"Ah, shit," Jonas muttered, "it's going to be like the last time, nothing much to go on," as they headed back to the front of the church. He looked around for the few team members he had left. Some of Hanover's folks had joined in to help with the case, and it was appreciated. He spotted Fernandez and Rupert. Pope, being on suspension, was not allowed at the scene. Jonas needed to check with Jose to see if he had spoken with Henry that morning.

"Have Hanover's men check out the houses," he told Clay, "I need you with me. Charlie will keep us informed about the autopsy. We need to go back to the office, all of us, and review everything again, all the lab reports, DNA, whatever we have. Did we ever get the list of patients from both doctors?"

"Yeah. It took some doing due to the HIPPA law, but Judge Jordan finally gave us warrants for both doctors. We explained, we only wanted the names of the male patients, between the ages of forty to fifty-five, and not their medical information. It took the doctor's offices until yesterday to give us what we asked for. A couple of Hanover's people are making a comparison of each list as we speak. With luck, they'll have it done today by the time we get back." Clay popped a stick of gum in his mouth. "The coffee was bitter this morning. My mouth tastes like I ate something nasty, and I haven't even had breakfast." He grinned when Jonas arched an eyebrow.

"What about a list of the parishioners at the church? Do we have a list of those?"

"Do you really think this is a church-going type person?" Clay said. "Hey, let me kill the priest and then attend church later to ask forgiveness for my sin?" When Jonas only stood and looked at him, Clay shook his head and said, "I've already asked the Bishop for a list when the priest went missing. I don't think our guy is on it, but we'll check it out."

"Good, because we're missing something. I just don't know what, but my gut tells me we should have caught this bastard before this." On the way to his vehicle, Jonas stopped to speak with Fernandez. He had called Pope before coming to the crime scene. The man was awake and had just gotten out of the shower. Jonas cringed at that news. Another pinprick of doubt about Henry's innocents was stuck in his brain. He couldn't wait any longer. They needed to get a warrant to search his house. The man was going to be furious, but it had to be done. He gave the news to Fernandez and told him to get it done as soon as he was finished there.

Damn, he thought as he turned his vehicle south, I hate this case. Then he remembered the funeral. Morgan was probably getting ready. He should be with her and felt guilty. He was going to miss it, and he hated that. It couldn't be helped. Maybe he'd have time to run by and let her know he was thinking about her. He felt better with that decision.

Jonas had just gotten off the phone with the Commander. The Mayor had called the Chief, demanding to know how the press had found out about Father Bortorelli? They were not releasing his identity but had confirmed that a priest from St. Christopher's had been found on the front steps of the church, murdered.

All he could tell the Commander was that he had no idea how the news media had gotten wind of the murder, but he'd try to find out and get back to him. Commander Paulson grumbled but agreed to pacify the Chief and the Mayor.

After that, he gathered his team of Clay, Rupert, and Fernandez, along with Hanover in the conference room to review the crime board, files, and reports they had been working on. They were seated around the table with notebooks open and pens handy.

"Okay, guys, let's examine what we've got." They all had gone over the evidence, but sometimes it helped to go over a case out loud to see if anyone might have a fresh idea or a different slant on things. He nodded to Clay who rose from his chair and walked to the board.

"We have very little physical evidence," Clay said, "but thanks to the Mayor, the DNA results are back on the bloody branch and the tissue under Caroline's fingernails. The good news is, they're a match. The bad news, we haven't been able to match them to anyone in any database. That partial footprint was a bust, as well as was the piece of plastic. It was Visqueen like you would buy from Home Depot," he hesitated, "that Caroline found at the Garden of the Gods. Also, Doctor Titus' autopsy report shows he had Ketamine in his system, which was used by our killer. It turns out he had heart trouble, and his death was caused by a reaction to the drug." Clay looked disgusted. "This is the worst case for hard physical evidence," he said, his frustration evident.

"Here's what we know for sure," he continued, grouping the photographs of the women with their known lovers, "the victims were involved in illicit love affairs. Marilyn Heddrix with Doctor Donavan, Caroline," he hated to have to expose his co-worker's affair, "with Robert Titus. Our latest victim, Father Bortorelli with a young lady by the name of Elizabeth Winslow." Clay didn't have a photo of Elizabeth to put on the board.

"We are desperately trying to locate her," he went on, "in case the killer has targeted her. Sources have told us that they think the killer wears Lagerfeld men's cologne." Jonas had never said how he came by that bit of information, and Clay never asked. "So boys and girls" he looked at the men in the room, "if you wear that aftershave, you automatically become a suspect. We interviewed friends and family of each victim; some knew of the affairs, others were shocked or angered by the news.

"Anyway, Hanover's team found approximately seventy-five people on the two lists who were treated by Doctor Donavan, and also Robert Titus. A list of parishioners at St. Christopher's has been requested, and we should get it today. Each is being checked out, their phone records, financials, family members, anything that will connect them to our victims. That's happening even as we speak.

"A lot of these people have been eliminated from the list already. Also, Hanover's two missing people might be possible victims, but it has not been verified. No bodies have been found." Clay turned to Winston, "You have something to add about your missing people?"

Hanover had been leaning against the wall but straightened up when Clay directed the attention to him and faced the people in the room. All eyes were glued to him as he said, "My missing people are Carla Winslow and Theodore Matthews. Carla is the wife of Carson Winslow. Theodore is or was an attorney here in the Springs. His wife's name is Sydney. The pair went missing about three weeks before these murders started. They supposedly ran away together to Mexico. But, they never arrived at their hotel.

"Carla Winslow's vehicle was found at the attorney's apartment complex, and his car was located at the airport. I don't believe they ever left Colorado

Springs. Their related spouses are still considered persons of interest. Both have alibis, Mrs. Matthews was at work and caring for her sick mother. Mr. Winslow was supposedly teaching a class. Both don't much care if their spouses are ever found. That's about it, except, no one vanishes entirely without leaving some sort of trail.

"Matthews liked to have a good time and spend his money at fancy restaurants. There's been no credit card, or cell phone activity. Nor has he withdrawn money from his bank account. That applies to Carla Winslow as well. I personally believe they were the first victims and both are dead and buried somewhere. They were also patients of Doctor Donavan and Titus. That's one reason why checking out the people on these lists is important," Winston said. "Carson Winslow, I believe, is our killer, but we have no proof. He refused to give a DNA sample." Hanover grinned, and said, "But, he threw a bloody bandage in his bathroom trash can. I retrieved it when he took Clay out to the backyard. That sample is already being processed at the lab."

Jonas nodded to Winston, thankful the man had stepped into the bathroom on the way out to view Carson's roses. With any luck, his DNA would match the blood on the branch and from the skin under Caroline's fingernails.

"We obtained his background records. He was born and lived in California for most of his life. His father left home when the boy was six. His mother had to raise Carson and Elizabeth alone without any help from the dad. The mother, Karen, worked as a waitress to support them. The kids attended public schools and seemed to be doing well even though they were poor.

"Everything appeared fine until Carson turned fourteen," Winston continued. "That's when he seemed to undergo a personality change. He became more withdrawn into himself, but was still active in sports, especially baseball. Then, when he turned sixteen, he dropped out of all sports. Shortly after, his mother died from an asthma attack complicated by COPD. An inhaler was found on her dresser, and one in her purse, but for some reason, she didn't use it. According to the paramedic's report, they might have saved her if she'd used her inhaler. The theory was that son let his mother die. But again, there was no proof. Carson claimed to be in his room asleep and woke up to go to the bathroom. He found his mother and called 911. He went to a group home and his sister, Elizabeth, was placed in a foster home. They managed to stay in touch with each other. Carson even worked and went to college, graduated with a BA in creative writing, and a minor in criminal justice. He also claims to have been home sleeping during the times of these murders. We can't prove otherwise until we get the DNA results. A neighbor with a sleeping problem verified he was home. Claims she could hear him snoring through the open windows.

"This man is brilliant and thinks he can outsmart us. I believe he is involved in the disappearance of his wife and her lover. Unfortunately, we have nothing to connect him to these other murders. Now, with his DNA," the statement hung in the air, "that might be a different story." Hanover gave a confident smile and again leaned against the wall.

It was difficult for Jonas to utter the next words. "Until then," he admitted, "we do have another suspect, Henry Pope, who we hope to rule out."

Everyone in the room looked shocked. "I know, I know, Pope is one of our own; but we have evidence that makes him also a suspect."

Fernandez stood in defense of his partner. "I don't believe Henry is capable of these crimes," and looked around the room at the faces filled with surprise and suspicion. Every cop knew that thin line they walked. Each day they were confronted by anger or temptation to cross over to the dark side of the law.

"I don't want to believe it either, but the facts are troubling," Jonas countered. "His wife left him around the same time that Hanover's people went missing. Pope has been drinking excessively, and he uses Lagerfeld. He was absent from work the morning after each crime. Since the murders happened in the middle of the night, Henry could have committed them. He is also one of the men on both doctor's lists. I don't have a connection to the priest as yet, but there may be one. And," Jonas hated suspecting one of his own, "he knows police procedures and is capable of killing someone."

His next nail in Henry's coffin was the final link to the victims. "Jose, I asked Hanover to send a member of his team back to Dawson's Bar. I've been to Dawson's myself. They do have a digital security system with cameras hidden all over that joint. Their records confirm your report of Henry having a fight with Marilyn Heddrix, and her leaving. It also shows Henry followed her out of the bar. You were caught on those cameras later. We got nothing from the outside cameras because they were not working at the time."

Jose sat down with a sick look on his face. Everything the Lieutenant had said was true. Henry was guilty of each and every fact, but beating a person to death with a stone weapon, he'd never believe it. "Henry wouldn't do this," he insisted, then remained silent.

"Well, I hope not, but we have warrants to search Pope's house, Carson Winslow's and Sydney Matthews' homes. Other members of our homicide team are waiting to serve those warrants as we speak. We're looking for anything that will lead to this killer." When no one had a question or comment, Jonas had Fernandez and Rupert join Hanover's men to issue the warrants

Jonas stood and thanked Winston for all his help and asked him to be the one to search Pope's house. He didn't want any of his team involved in that. After he left, Clay waited for Jonas by the conference room door. "Back to the church or hunting for Elizabeth Winslow?"

"The Winslow girl," Jonas said, walking the short distance to his office to retrieve his hat. "Also, I want to run by Anderson's Funeral Home long enough to let Morgan Jansen know I didn't forget." He glanced at his watch, it was almost ten-thirty. "It's on the way back to the priest's house and not far from Elizabeth's apartment. It will only take a minute." Hat in hand, they headed for the elevator.

Morgan sat on the sofa in her black dress and shoes and hated the ticking of the clock. It was nine-thirty, and the service for Marilyn started at ten.

Anderson's Funeral Home was only ten or fifteen minutes away. Her stomach was tied in knots, and her hands were shaking. She wished that Jonas was with her, but realized he couldn't be. He had another body, the priest.

She hadn't heard anything from Marilyn since that brief whisper this morning. Had she gone to wherever a ghost goes? Was their connection now broken? Morgan didn't want to believe it, but she hadn't had a sense of her since then. If it was true, then half of her had died as well, and she would never be the same.

With that thought still weighing on her mind, she grabbed her purse and left for the house with a police car leading the way and one behind her. Her shadows she called them, glad they were there, but would be happier when they were gone.

Once at Anderson's, she parked in the back spot reserved for relatives. A limousine would take her to the cemetery with the police escort and then return her to the funeral home to pick up her car. And then it would be done. All she had to do was submit a claim with the insurance company so she could pay for Marilyn's funeral.

She had completely forgotten about the insurance until now. Only reminded of them because the director at the funeral home had called while she was in the shower and left a message to contact him about payment. She had returned his call and explained about the insurance policies. He had agreed to accept five-thousand dollars and wait for the rest. At least that was off her mind for the moment.

When Morgan arrived at Anderson's, she was surprised by the number of people at the service. It was mostly patients her sister had cared for. Everyone appeared shocked to see her and discover she was an identical twin. None had known.

Marilyn may have had her faults, but her patients seemed to care about her. All gave their condolences and offered to help if she needed it. Morgan just wanted it all to be over before she fell apart. Jonas made a brief appearance on his way back to his office. He squeezed her hand and told her to hang on. All too quickly he had to leave, and she was alone again.

She made it through the service and the brief prayers at the graveside. She stood watching as they started to lower the casket. But when it disappeared below ground, she turned and ran for the limousine, not waiting for her guards to catch up.

"Get me to my car," she told the driver, who immediately started the engine and drove away. All the deaths revolving around her sister was suffocating.

Once back at Anderson's, she ran to her vehicle and immediately drove away, making a beeline for the house, not even thinking about her police escort. Cracks were forming in the tight façade of her emotions. Soon she would shatter and become a quivering mass of tears and heartache. She had to make it home before that happened. What she needed was to let herself grieve, but she couldn't let herself fall apart in the car. Her well of tears was far from empty she realized, as one slid down her cheek.

Her garage butted up against the alley behind her

house for easy access. Pulling onto the dirt road, she pushed the garage door opener, anxious to get inside before she collapsed. Once inside, she quickly got out, locked the vehicle and closed the overhead door. Just as she exited the side door and turned toward the house, a sharp sting hit her in the neck. Before she could reach up to feel for an insect, everything around her dissolved into darkness.

Clay waited in the SUV while Jonas made a quick trip into Anderson's Funeral home. As soon as he returned, instead of going to the priest's house, they drove to the apartment on Alexander Road. They knocked on the door and when there was no answer, went to look for the manager. The man appeared to be recovering from some type of illness. His complexion was pasty, and Jonas noticed a yellow tint to his skin. Liver cancer, he wondered. God help the man if that was the case, was all he could think.

After showing the manager their IDs and badges, the man didn't even mention a warrant, he unlocked the second-floor door, and they went in. Partially filled boxes were sitting around the living room, kitchen, bedroom, and bath. Elizabeth Winslow was in the process of moving out, and Jonas suspected he knew where. He wondered who was going to help move her with the priest dead. Maybe that's where she was.

They didn't disturb anything but left after having the manager relock the door. Within minutes they were at the house Father Bortorelli had been trying to renovate.

It too was locked up, and Elizabeth was nowhere to be found.

As far as Jonas knew, no one had informed the girl that the priest was dead. He would hate to have her discover it from the news media or some other way. They needed to locate her for her own protection. She was the next logical person the killer would go after. If he didn't have her already. There was no way to really know if that had happened or not. Her brother hadn't been in touch with her and didn't seem that concerned for her welfare. Jonas wondered why and bet the brother knew precisely where his sister was.

Not sure where to look next, he ordered a patrol car to wait at each residence and keep a lookout for Elizabeth. There was nothing more he could do for the moment but head back to the station. His cell phone rang just after he turned onto Nevada Avenue. He answered it, listened for a moment and immediately pulled over to the curb.

"What the hell do you mean she's missing?" he demanded and glanced over at Clay. "I don't care what happened, find that girl before she ends up dead if she isn't already!" Jonas snapped his phone shut and tossed it on the dashboard. "Son of a bitch! Son of a bitch! Son of a bitch!" he yelled and slammed his hand against the steering wheel.

"What's happened?" Clay said.

"Morgan Jansen just got abducted. At the cemetery, she was so upset she left her guards behind and had the limousine take her to her car. She didn't wait for the escort but drove away. She made it to her garage, but not into the house." Eyes flashing with anger, Jonas hit the steering wheel again. "Why in the hell didn't they drive her there and back?"

"I'll bet she refused to ride in a cruiser."

"Hell, one of them could have driven her vehicle. I'm sure as hell going to find out why that wasn't done." Jonas pulled away from the curb and headed toward Morgan's house, changed his mind and kept driving to the station. There was nothing he could do at the house. Morgan was gone.

My God, he thought, it can't be happening again. Was he going to lose the woman he loved to murder a second time? His gut knotted with anger. No! He couldn't let that happen. Somewhere in all the information they had, the identity of the killer had to be there. All they had to do was look again and find it.

"Clay, go find out what happened exactly, then come back to the office. I'm going there now. We'll do better sifting through the information we have than running all over town looking for her. We're not going to find her that way. When you're done, come back to the office. I'll call in the rest of the team. We've missed something. That has to be the reason this happened." He turned on his siren and raced down the avenue all the while feeling a sick dread in the pit of his stomach.

Five minutes later, Clay was on his way, and Jonas was walking off the elevator and headed straight to the crime board. "Listen up," he said to the group gathered around. "Our killer has changed his MO. The mistake I made was believing he only took his victims at night. Well, that has changed. About fifteen minutes ago, he abducted Morgan Jansen from her home even though she was under guard by two of our guys." Jonas nodded as Hanover approached. "Winston, did your guys finish comparing those lists of patients?

"Yeah," Hanover said. "Of the seventy-five men my guys found, we eliminated all but ten. We're in the process of whittling that number down by double-checking their background, and everything about them. We haven't received the Bishop's list as yet, but I doubt if it will matter." They all turned when they heard Clay's voice talking to Benedict.

Clay hurried forward waving several sheets of paper in his hand. "I stopped and picked up Benedict. I know you said he can't work this case, but I figured we could use all the help we can get," he explained. "And, I called the Bishop. Here's his list. I agree with Hanover. I don't think our killer is on it." He handed the list to Winston, who immediately gave it to one of his team.

Clay looked from Winston and back at Jonas. "I was right about the guard detail. Your girl took off by herself from the funeral home. The guys were only a minute or two behind her. One of them took up his station at the front while the other drove around to the alley. By the time Taylor pull onto the dirt road, all he saw was the tail end of a Crown Victoria pulling onto the street at the other end. He thought Miss Jansen had gone into the house. It was too late by the time he realized his mistake."

Jonas's frustration showed on his face. "Dammit to hell, we got nothing. That girl could be dead by now!" When he voiced the possibility, his stomach started to churn, and he felt sick. He didn't want to have to identify

Morgan's body. "I want this son of a bitch found!"

Hanover's man came hurrying over to Winston, pointed at the piece of paper in his hand, and then rushed back to his computer. "Jonas, we may have something here. There is only one possibility left on the list, my missing woman's husband, Carson Winslow. Winslow is now the prime suspect. He has a connection to St. Christopher's. His sister goes to that church."

"Holy shit!" burst from Clay's mouth. "We've been looking for her. She was considered to be the next target. If her brother is the killer, he may have her and Morgan Jansen."

There was a flurry in the room when Jonas issued orders to Rupert to go to the priest's house and sent Benedict to the girl's apartment to find her. Hanover ordered two of his team to the professor's classroom and another to check Winslow's house. Another member, Jackson Howell, was busy searching the computer for more information about the man.

Jonas felt helpless. It was the first time in his life, he didn't know in which direction to go, instead wanted to rush out and knock down every door looking for Morgan and the sister. That wouldn't help, and he knew it. All he could do was pray that the two women were still alive.

Suddenly the desk phone rang. Hanover picked it up. It was an officer down in the lobby. Winston kept glancing over at Jonas as he listened. "Bring her upstairs, now!" he said and hung up. "Elizabeth Winslow is alive, and here at the station. The officer watching the priest's house picked her up when she returned there about twenty minutes ago."

The elevator dinged and they turned to face the doors. A police officer accompanied by an attractive, slender blonde woman got off. The officer handed Jonas a note, and then took the elevator back down.

"Right this way," Jonas said and led the way to his office, joined by Hanover and Clay. Elizabeth Winslow looked confused and worried as she followed Jonas.

"Have a seat, Miss Winslow," Jonas directed.

"Would you please tell me why I'm here?" she asked, as she sat down. I haven't done anything wrong."

"Well, you were driving a car without a license. That's not why you're here." He watched a guilty expression settle on her face. "We don't care about that." She visibly relaxed until he added, "We believe your life is in danger."

"From whom?" she asked, staring at Jonas, while fear crept into her eyes. "Who would want to kill me?"

"Possibly your brother. You do know his wife is missing, don't you?"

She looked at him in disbelief. "Carson told me she left him for another man. I know he was furious, but that had nothing to do with me. He's a bit of a control freak, but my brother would never hurt me." She looked from one to the other, their gaze centered on her. She was becoming more frightened.

Jonas was wary as he asked, "You and Father Bortorelli are involved with each other?"

A slight smile curved her lips, and her eyes were filled with the love she had for the man. "Yes, I know

he's a priest, but he's leaving that behind to marry me."
She placed her hand on her stomach. "We're going to
have a baby. Paul will be such a great father."

Oh God, Jonas thought, she didn't know and
glanced up at Clay and Hanover. "Miss Winslow, I am
sorry to have to be the one to tell you, but Father
Bortorelli is dead."

All the color blanched from her face, and she
slumped in the chair. Clay rushed from the room and
returned with a cup of water and pressed it to her lips.
She sipped from the paper cup and sat up straighter.
"What happened to him?" she asked, fighting back the
tears.

"He was murdered." Jonas said and wished Eppie
was there.

"What!" she whispered. "Why? By whom?"

"We believe it was your brother. We think he
also has murdered his wife and four others."

"Are you sure?"

"Fairly positive. We need to find your brother.
Would you happen to know where he might be at the
moment?"

"No! I haven't spoken to Carson since our fight
over Paul." Her hand flew to her mouth as the realization
hit her. It had been a nasty fight, and for the first time in
her life, she was afraid of her own brother. She gripped
the arms of the chair. "If he isn't at the college, or at
home, he may be at one of his other properties. He owns
two other houses on the north side of town. He's
renovating them." If he had murdered Paul, she hoped

they killed him. She sat shaking, unable to control her body.

"We need those addresses," Jonas said, his voice held an urgent note.

"I don't know them," Elizabeth said, stammering, feeling contrite for not knowing, but she had never been to either one.

Hanover left the room. Jonas could see him standing next to Jackson's desk. After a couple of minutes, he returned with the address of both houses.

Jonas quickly rose. Hanover ordered Jackson to keep Elizabeth Winslow in the office for her own protection. They headed for the elevator, both men on their cell phone arranging for additional backup. Clay followed Jonas to his vehicle and slid into the passenger seat. Hanover hurried to his own car and with sirens blaring, lights flashing, they headed north with four squad cars following.

Jonas drove as fast as he dared, all the while praying they'd be in time to save Morgan. The house was on Monroe Place, not too far from where Winslow's main home was located. He pulled up to the curb, and they bailed out making a beeline for the front door.

He had the whore, the slut, securely drugged and in the trunk of his Crown Victoria. Carson Winslow grinned in satisfaction. He had used the car this time because the cops would be looking for the van. They hadn't seen this coming. They expected him to wait until the middle of the night before trying to snatch her. But he'd fooled them. So, he'd taken the priest instead. Now, it was her turn, and he'd grabbed her right under their noses.

It always amazed him while in class that no one ever guessed or thought of him as being capable of committing the act of murder. They looked at him and saw, what? A tall, friendly man who wouldn't hurt a soul, so they thought. How wrong they all were. He delivered justice, justice for their evil ways. Just like he did to his mother.

Oh, how she had pleaded for him to help her. Begged him to call the paramedics as she lay choking and gasping for air. He'd watched the life slip right out of her, grinning the entire time so she could see how much he hated her. Now he had his prey, a woman just as malicious as his mother had been. She preyed on men just as his mother had done. Using them for her own sexual gratification just as his mother had done to him.

His inability to perform sexually had caused his marriage to fail. Carla wanted sex and made fun of him when he couldn't get an erection. She had insisted he take those nasty pills. Then she did things to him to get him aroused and used him over and over until he hated her as much as his mother. He wanted a pure woman, not some whore. Then, his dear wife committed the worst sin of all, she slept with another man. He had delivered their punishment with a smile.

Forcing those thoughts from his mind, he focused on getting back to his house to deliver his form of justice. Turning onto the street, he drove north, away from midtown where the cops would be swarming all over the place at any moment. He was confident he had gotten away clean. The license plate was dirty and barely visible. It would be hard for anyone to make out the numbers. Besides, he'd grabbed the bitch, dumped her in the trunk before the other cop had time to make it around to the alley.

Within fifteen minutes, he was at his haven, his private secure place where he enjoyed the fruits of his labor. The beam was waiting for his next victim, and she would soon be tied like those before her, stripped, spread eagle and waiting for him to deliver her punishment.

His stomach knotted. The image of that horrible face of his first kill that had stared at him through the window jumped into his mind. He shuttered. It had to have been his imagination. He shook the feeling of fear off as he pulled into the garage next to the house.

It didn't take him long to carry the woman from the vehicle, into the house and down to the basement. She didn't weigh much. Within minutes he had her stripped down to her gaudy black lace underwear and secured to the crossbeam.

He stood back surveying his handiwork, and then looked down at the pile of stones he had accumulated over a period of time. He'd found most along river beds and at the landscaping company. They were all the perfect size. Initially, they were to be used to build a fire pit and flower beds. But he'd found the ideal use for them instead.

Of course, he cleaned them with bleach after each execution so they'd be ready for the next sinner. And there would be more to come. All he had to do was look for them, and he'd find them. There were so many out there. But first, he'd dispense his punishment on this bitch and then go locate his sister.

He picked up the first stone but stopped. The woman's eyes were closed. He turned on the hose and sprayed her with water. Her eyes flew open. He watched in horror as the straps holding her head, arms and feet fell away, and she floated down to stand at the foot of the crossed beams. Slowly she raised her head to stare at him with that same terrifying face he had seen at the window. And then, she gave him a wide toothy, evil grin.

Carson Winslow screamed.

Jonas kicked in the front door of the house, with Clay and two other police officers right on his heels. They checked each room on the first floor. Nothing. Jonas motioned for the other officers to go upstairs as he and Clay searched for the basement door. When he heard the unholy scream coming up from below, he raced back into the kitchen. Clay pointed to a curved scratch in the tile floor. Together, they pulled the pantry away from the wall and found the door.

Jerking it open, they started down the steps. When Jonas was almost to the bottom, he stopped. Clay almost ran into him before coming to a stop behind him. Disbelieving their eyes, they stared at the scene before them. It was a whirlwind of stones surrounding the figure of Carson Winslow. The man continued to scream as he hurled stone after stone at the woman before him.

Without hesitation, two shots rang out as Jonas and Clay fired their guns. The man continued to stand upright, staring, his eyes fixed on the terror before him.

Jonas and Clay began to see the horror the man was seeing. Superimposed over the figure of Morgan was the broken image of her twin, arms raised, bones protruding, but in complete control of a rotating mass of rocks.

It didn't matter that the man had been shot and was dying. Marilyn had no mercy. The first stone hit Winslow in his right knee, the next took out his left. He crashed to the floor, landing hard, and falling backward, broken legs folded under him. Scream after scream echoed off the concrete walls, as Marilyn dished out her own justice to her killer and he breathed his last. One after another, stones slammed into his soft flesh until the cracking of bones made even Jonas fight his churning stomach. Then she picked him up, slammed him onto the crossbeams and tried to hang him by his broken arms. The protruding bones and torn flesh wouldn't hold him. He slid to the floor into a mass of torn bloody tissue and fractured limbs.

The whirlwind stopped, the massive pile of rocks dropped to the concrete on top of Winslow. Marilyn lowered Morgan to the floor. Turning to face Jonas, she smiled and nodded to him, looking normal again. Without a word, she hovered over her sister's form. Jonas would wonder later if he really heard what he thought she said.

"My time here is finished, for now, Morgan. I don't want to, but I have to leave you. Know I will always be a part of you." With that, she became a bright glow surrounding her twin. And then, she was gone.

Jonas rushed to Morgan's side. "Call the paramedics," he yelled to Clay and picked Morgan up in his arms. He carried her up the stairs and out to his vehicle to wait for Fire Rescue. Clay followed close behind, while the other officer secured the scene with yellow tape.

"Did you see what I just saw, or have I gone nuts?" Clay asked.

"I don't know what we saw, and I have no intentions of trying to explain it." There was no way anyone could explain what happened in that basement. He looked at Clay. "My advice to you is to keep what happened to yourself. As far as we know, we found Morgan drugged and Carson Winslow trying to stone her. We shot him to protect her. That's what my report will say. As far as I'm concerned, this case is solved. If you value your job and sanity, put what we saw out of your mind and never bring it up again. That's what I intend to do." Jonas hoped he'd never experienced anything like it again. Clay nodded in agreement as the sound of sirens drew closer.

They whisked Morgan away in the rescue truck, heading for the nearest emergency room. Jonas followed, leaving Clay behind to control the crime scene. Before he drove away, he gave him another warning to keep it all to himself.

"You don't have to worry. I don't know a thing about what happened in that basement other than we had to shoot Winslow." He gave Jonas a salute and headed back inside Winslow's house, just as the crime scene team arrived.

EPILOGUE

Morgan was kept overnight for observation due to the drug in her system. Jonas stayed by her side until he knew she was out of danger. Sometime in the wee hours, he left the hospital and drove home, dropping onto his bed fully clothed, not bothering even to remove his boots.

By eight the next morning he called Clay for an update. Carson Winslow's shooting was ruled as justified. He had gone over and over his statement to the Commander that the scene was precisely how they described it. Miss Jansen on the crossbeam, under the influence of some type of drug and Winslow beginning to throw stones at her. To save her life, they'd been forced to shoot the man. He'd stumbled into the bin holding all the rocks, and it collapsed on top of him. After making sure he was dead, they removed Ms. Jansen from the crossbeams. That was his story, and he was sticking to it.

The Commander and Chief were happy that the killer had been caught. After all the 't's were crossed and the 'i's dotted, the case file was boxed up and marked closed, and any questions about Winslow's broken body left unanswered.

All the victim's possessions were found in a trunk in the attic. Another case was solved by the discovery of Carla Winslow and Theodore Matthews bodies buried in the dirt at the far end of the basement. They were apparently his first victims in his murderous spree. As for the surveillance video showing the victims supposedly parking the car and walking to the airport terminal, it was later determined they were two students duped by Winslow. He had given two round-trip tickets to Disney World, as a class project prize. On their return, they were shocked to learn of the professor's death. They never knew the car they drove and left in the lot, belonged to a murder victim.

After her abduction and traumatic rescue, Morgan had trouble sleeping due to nightmares. So, Jonas started staying at her place. With his arms wrapped around her in bed at night, she was able to cope with her kidnapping and feel safe. Only time would help her handle the loss of her twin. That same week, he proposed, and she said yes, but in the distant future. They weren't in a hurry to marry

On Thursday that same week, Caroline's funeral was held with full honors. Numerous townspeople and cops, from in and out of state, attended. Her parents, looking older than the last time Clay had seen them, thanked Jonas and him for finding her killer. The killer was dead, but the closure they needed would never happen. Their daughter would never again come home.

Elizabeth Winslow inherited her brother's estate, plus Father Bortorelli had left a will leaving his brother's home to her. After the TV and newspapers finished splashing photos of the murder house all over the news, the home on Monroe Place didn't have a chance of selling. She sold what could be sold and donated the building on Monroe to the St. Christopher's Church, in Paul's name.

After everything was done, she settled into the little house she and Paul had planned on sharing to raise their child. In her heart, she had married him the first time she had shared his bed. She legally changed her last name to Bortorelli so her son would have his father's name.

Eppie Ortiz and Alfonso Benedict returned to work, and Henry Pope joined AA. Any suspicions against him had been cleared. The man's only guilt was drinking too much after losing the woman he loved. For Jonas' team, each day the loss of Caroline was felt. Time diminishes pain, but never the memory. So their days settled once again into what they knew as normal for a homicide unit, while they worked to solve other murders.

Little did they know that their next case would be a doozy.

# # # #

ABOUT THE AUTHOR

Dreamah H. Lockwood is the pseudonym for Patricia Ross. She loves to read and especially write books with an unusual twist. The name Dreamah H. Lockwood is used as a memorial to her sister who died in 2012.

The romantic suspense, A CIRCLE OF MURDERS, was her first work submitted for e-publishing. Her second romantic suspense is CREATING KATHRYN CROWN.

THE STONE KILLER is her third novel and the first book in the Jonas Black/Morgan Jansen series. It is available now at Amazon.com. It is her first Crime Fiction Thriller with the ghost of Marilyn Heddrix.

THE HANGMAN, the second book in the series, will be available in late 2018.

THE SNATCHER, the third book in the series, is in the planning and writing stages as is THE GARDNER, the fourth book in the series.

Two new romantic suspense novels TO CATCH

A DREAM and ALL FOR THE LOVE OF HANNAH, another love story with a ghost, hopefully, will be completed in 2019.

In the meantime, give her other novels a read.

THE HANGMAN

A Jonas Black Novel

Detective Lieutenant Jonas Black knows there's a never-ending supply of monsters in the world. Another one is loose in his town, per his psychic girlfriend, Morgan Jansen.

She hates the strange abilities her murdered identical twin, Marilyn Heddrix, bestowed upon her when she helped to save her from The Stone Killer.

Now, Morgan receives muddled images and hears things she'd prefers not to know. A violin plays sad music in her mind, followed by the whimpering of a child, mixed with the violent rage from a man wanting his overdue justice. Without knowing vital details, all she can do is warn her lover, Jonas Black, of the evil that is coming.

This time the killer wants his revenge. And he'll dish out his punishment on the people who should have protected him. When a well-known defense attorney is found murdered at his home in the wealthy Broadmoor section of Colorado Springs, Jonas knows the monster has arrived. All he can do is work to locate the killer before another person falls victim to the madman. But too many will die before the killings end. This time, hopefully, Jonas will keep the woman he loves safe from a demented murderer should he discover she possesses special abilities.